FROM DARKEST SKIES

FROM DARKEST SKIES

SAM PETERS

GOLLANCZ

LONDON

First published in Great Britain in 2017 by Gollancz
an imprint of The Orion Publishing Group Ltd
Carmelite House, 50 Victoria Embankment
London EC4Y 0DZ

An Hachette UK Company

1 3 5 7 9 10 8 6 4 2

A CIP catalogue record for this book
is available from the British Library.

ISBN 978 1 473 21475 0

Typeset by Deltatype Ltd, Birkenhead, Merseyside

Printed in Great Britain by Clays Ltd, St Ives plc

For Pete, Nigel, Sam, Ali, Alex, Tony and John

ONE

EDDIE AND THE SHAH

1

EXIT PAPERS

Memories are like hibernating bears. They disappear into some dark cave until you forget they were ever there, and that's when they wake up and roar.

The Fleet officer on the other side of the desk pinged a series of files to my Servant. She didn't look up and I didn't bother reading them. Most of me wasn't even in the room. Most of me was back on Magenta, seven years ago, lying in a bed in a sky-boat cabin, not daring to move because Alysha was sleeping on my arm and I didn't want to wake her. The sun outside our window was rising over a purple sea of broken ice, glorious, dazzling and wonderful, but I was turned the other way, look-ing at Alysha's face, lost in the moment, her skin aglow in that dawn light, eyes closed, hair like fire. We'd decided to start a family.

'You have twenty-four hours to leave the Gibraltar Extra-national Territory. After that time you will be subject to arrest and internment. Agent Rause, do you understand?'

I tried to shake Alysha away by staring at the desk. An

antique from the early twentieth century or else a very fine replica. Eventually I managed a nod.

'A shuttle will take you to orbit at 0900 hours for transfer to the *Fearless* and your return to Magenta. You are dismissed and discharged.' The woman looked up at me, a long hard glance of hostile steel. Maybe she was hoping for a confession she sure as hell wasn't going to get. 'Whatever your government decides to do next, that's up to them. I hope they bury you.'

I stood a moment longer, wallowing in memory, numbness turning to lead-limbed dread. I was out. Just like that, lost in a Magenta sunrise, golden light pouring across Alysha's sleeping face. I was going home. It wasn't what I'd wanted. I'd fled to Earth for a reason.

The door shut behind me as I left. Sixteen hours to pack and go, the last five years of my life abruptly brought to an end. I should have handed in my papers the day the bomber calling himself Loki got stabbed to death in prison, but I hadn't, and a day had become a week had become a month, then six, then a year.

Back to Magenta, to where Loki had blown up my Alysha.

My Servant flicked through the news while I summoned a pod to the Gibraltar Spire. An Entropist attack on the *Defiance* out of Arcon was grabbing the Fleet headlines, but I didn't work for them any more so I skimmed it and threw it away. I took the elevator to the spire's observation deck; out on the balcony I savoured the view, looking down for the last time at burnished chrome towers and the reinforced concrete that cloaked Gibraltar Rock from top to bottom. Polished and slick on the outside, rotten underneath. That was Earth for you.

There were other places I could go. Other worlds ...

'Hi, Keys.' My Servant's hidden personality bloomed into life. Alysha's voice, whispering in my ear like a lover.

'Hi, Liss.' The sound of her crumpled me like a punctured balloon, the tension of the last weeks suddenly gone.

4

'Give me a moment.'

It took her a few seconds to catch up. She was like that when she'd been asleep for a while, integrating every sensation, every newsfeed, every sight and sound into her memory, unravelling the world's progress since she was last awake. Liss. Alysha. Back when I first knew Alysha, everyone called her Al; but she'd told me one night, early on, before we were sleeping together, that she hated it, that it reminded her of Fat Al the barman at the Chopstick where half the bureau agents went after work. We'd tried Ally for a few days, but she'd hated that even more, and so we'd settled on Liss. Data and algorithms, that's what Liss was now, but she hadn't always been that way. It can be hard to see a simulation for what it is if the simulation is good enough.

'So we're going back then?' she asked, although it wasn't much of a question. It wasn't as if I was being given a choice. I closed my eyes and imagined the real Alysha leaning against the rail beside me. Right there on top of the Gibraltar Spire, close enough to touch, a physical presence, the fingers of her hand resting lightly on my own, a quiet togetherness, soaking it all in. Over the Mosque of the Two Holy Custodians to the south was the North African coast. A six-mile Masters' tower rose from the waves there. Alysha would have liked that. We all go through our years of obsession with the Masters and she'd never quite grown out of it, but the real Alysha had been dead for five years, and I was staring not to the south but to the north, across the endless blue waters of the New Spanish Sea.

There was a lump in my throat. A light blinked in my eye. Liss had finished her assimilation.

'I had to turn you off for the inquiry,' I said. 'I couldn't risk Fleet finding you. They've been all over me since the Tech-Fair.'

She paused as if catching her breath. 'I don't mind.'

'I'm going to miss this, you know. This view.' The north face of Gibraltar sprawled beneath the balcony, concrete terraces and dazzling metal as far as the sheer perfect cliff into the sea where Spain had once been.

'I know it's not the way you wanted it to end, but—'

'Which bit? The part where a priceless Masters artefact got stolen from under my nose, or do you mean the bit just before, when I got blown up?' I didn't remember much from after the explosion. I'd been lucky. Concussion and a lot of bruising but no serious injury. I certainly didn't want to talk about it. I'd had enough of that from Fleet these last three weeks. 'I didn't want it to end at all, Liss. I was happy here.'

She had the grace not to point out the lie.

'Why do you suppose the Masters left Gibraltar alone?' she asked instead. 'Why just one little rock?'

'Why did they do anything?'

Further along the balcony a pair of telescopes pivoted on the safety rails, but even with their thousandfold magnification the sky and the New Spanish Sea merged into a white haze long before the Pyrenees coast far to the north. I looked down to where the sun blazed back at me from a thousand dazzling reflections. A Yen-Shu lifter carrying an orbital shuttle was taking off from the pad beneath the spire, rising on an array of enclosed rotors. It powered away across the water.

'Do you ever wonder what happened to the people who lived here?' Liss asked. I didn't need to. No one did. We'd still had a few vestigial satellites back then, hiding as space junk. The world had watched as the Iberian Peninsula disintegrated, every atom of solid matter above sea level and a few yards below turned into vapour all the way to the Pyrenees. Seven hours, more or less, was all it had taken. A whole country gone. All except the rock of Gibraltar.

I made a face. 'No. Do you?' Two countries, I reminded myself. Everyone always forgot Portugal.

6

'Not the way I used to.'

Liss's voice was bland. Not sad, the way I'd always expected it to be back in the early days when I'd first turned her on – I'd soon understood that ambivalence to her own condition was ingrained into her algorithms.

'It wasn't only here,' she said.

'I know.' The Masters had changed the shape of the planet. The casualty estimate later, when we'd recovered enough to count, was five billion dead. It had taken them about a week. When they were done they'd carved a pattern of deep sea trenches so immensely intricate that we didn't have proper maps of them even now. Some of the trenches went down twenty miles and more. They'd sculpted other worlds too: Mercury, Venus, Titan. The list went on.

'Do you ever wonder what it was all for?' I asked. '*Can* you?'

Liss made a sad laughing sound, peculiar, like the call of some timid night-time creature. It was her own sound, that laugh, not a copy of the real woman Alysha had once been. 'Keon, do you think there's anyone who doesn't? I know I did back when I was alive. I think I wondered about it a lot. But I don't remember. It's just a feeling. Or an inference, if you prefer.'

'You didn't talk about it much.'

'"Nations divided, smiling lies, blind deaf and dumb to the terror to come, from darkest skies." I think I must have made everyone I knew read that awful poem about the coming of the Masters.'

'Yes.' I made a face.

'It mattered to me, I think.'

I basked in the heat, watching the Yen-Shu labour out across the sea and up into the sky, thoughts drifting away among the stars. Other lifters came and went from the pads below. Little ones, mostly.

Liss. I wanted to reach out and touch her, but she wasn't real.

'The Masters started extra-solar colonisation five years later. Why did they do *that*? Or, if you like it better the other way round, why did they wait so long?' Her voice dropped. Quieter. More intimate. 'What was any of it for? We all wonder, Keys. How can we not?'

'The last person born before Liberation Day died a month ago. A hundred and fifty-two years old. The Masters are gone. We'll forget. That's what humans do. We move on.'

'The past is the past. It's not a place to live.' Her voice changed, shaking off dusty cobwebs of wistful ennui. I wondered sometimes: did she have a special algorithm for that, and if she did, could I have it too? 'So this is it?' she chirped. 'We're going home?'

Half a mile into the sky the Yen-Shu dropped its shuttle and veered away. The shuttle fell like a cormorant diving for a fish, then levelled and flared sun-bright as its fusion engines ignited. It soared upward on a graceful arc of vapour. 'That's us tomorrow,' I said. 'Sixteen hours to get out. Fifteen and a half now.' The dim rumble of a sonic boom reached the spire. The flare of the shuttle vanished into the sky. I wanted to go back to the apartment where Liss had her shell, to where I could see her, touch her ... but I couldn't tear myself away from the sun. This was the last time I'd ever stand here, perhaps the last time I'd ever see Earth.

'It's not your fault, you know,' she said. 'Any of it.'

I did know, but that didn't make it any better. 'Give me a minute alone up here, will you?'

'I'll wait for you back home.'

She flitted away, slipping out of my Servant into the ether, a sudden emptiness. I closed my eyes and pictured my Alysha walking away, stopping and turning to face me, hands on her hips, head cocked sideways the way I remembered her most clearly. There was something coquettish about her when she did that. Five years and I could almost believe she was back, really here; five years and I still felt the loss of her as keenly as in the days after she died; but when I opened my eyes there was only the bright empty sky.

Going back. I made a resolution to myself. The same resolution I'd made a hundred times over. I was going to find out what had happened. I was going to find out who had done this to us and why. So I didn't care what Fleet thought I'd done because none of that mattered. I was going to put Alysha to rest ... Except I wasn't. There was no one to hunt and uncover and punish, no place to exact revenge. That had all happened years ago.

I took the glass-bubble lift down the spire and stared across the old straits towards the African coast with its tower. The Masters had built it in the last days, long after they'd scattered us across the thirty-seven colony worlds. Thrusting six miles into the sky, scratching at the stratosphere. The start of a space elevator, maybe? No one knew for sure. No way in, no structure, no apparent purpose. For the last hundred and fifty years it had stood, a white stone mystery glittering in the sun making everything around it insignificant. The Entropists claimed that the Masters were a metaphor for life, random and terrible. Useless nonsense, Alysha would have said. Life was for living and you made the best you could of it. We thought we were better out in the colonies, that we didn't have Entropists, not the real ones, the crazies who liked to blow things up. Then Loki had decided to show us we were wrong, and blown up Alysha's train.

Blind, deaf and dumb to the terror to come. I wished I could still hold her hand.

Other skyscrapers grew around me as the lift went down. Arrays of spikes and rods on their tops pointed across the water of the straits towards the Masters' monolith. Feng shui to reflect malicious spirits back to their source, a legacy of Gibraltar's sale to the Chinese to pay off the British national debt. The Chinese had given the rock to Fleet a couple of decades later, and their workers and their superstitions too. At the base of the spire a tunnel buggy took me into the warren they'd built, repackaged as cheap accommodation for the support and maintenance crews who made Fleet's Earth headquarters work. I walked the last few hundred yards through the strip-light tunnels, picking my way over cable bundles and between the roaming neon-lit vending stalls that meandered perpetually down there like vagrant drunks, mewling their offerings of cheap kale burgers and lottery tickets. The air was damp and stale and smelled of diesel fumes, the ventilation system on the blink again. Liss thought I was mad living down here, but the cramped tunnels reminded me of home. I liked their gaudy squalor, and I liked the contrast between their underground ghettos and the haughty vertigos of glass and chrome above. Most of all, though, it was cheap.

The armoured plastic sheet that passed for my front door opened as I approached. Liss was waiting inside, her shell standing in the gloom. As I came close she stepped into the light and hugged me. The strip lights outside were harsh and unkind and showed her for the artificial construct she was. In the light her skin wasn't right, her face not expressive enough, the eyes just a little dead, but I'd learned to look past all that. It was her soul I'd been trying to preserve.

I held her and shuddered. There were more perfect shells to be bought if you had the money. The best – the most lifelike – were the sex toys, but I couldn't do that, not to Alysha, and so Liss was a designer hostess model, built for high-end restaurants and private caterers. Made no sense on Earth, where there were already too many people and not enough work, but they got made anyway. She was warm and soft and she was Liss. That was all that mattered.

'I'm better in the shadows,' she said. 'I know that.'

I pulled away. Our place was a mess. I hadn't started to pack, but then, come to think of it, I hadn't really unpacked when we came here.

Liss poured me a drink, some seaweed-derived spirit, and leaned against the wall beside me. Servos and batteries, metal and artificial skin, but the cracksman who'd crafted her personality had captured her mannerisms perfectly, the way she moved, the way she pressed into me.

'Tell me,' she said. 'Tell me what happened. Make up a story. I used to like that.'

'Used to.' I downed the shot of seaweed, hit by a sucker punch of the old grief, and hurled the glass at the wall. It bounced. 'I don't want to go back! Five years on another planet. You'd think that would be enough, you really would! Why isn't it?'

She leaned her head against my shoulder. 'Because you never let yourself move on, Keys. You're stuck in the same place you were in when you came here.'

Her, that's what she meant. Making *her*. Building Liss from the ashes of Alysha's memory. Couldn't argue, but we'd long ago drained the lake of that conversation and I didn't want to talk about it, not any more. I looked around instead, taking stock. Takeaway boxes lay piled up waiting for me to call a recycling drone. Empty bottles. Old dried bits of food on a piezoelectric easy-clean carpet. A sofa with cigarette burns on the arms that I'd never bothered to replace because I knew I'd never use it. A bed for those now-and-then nights when I wasn't away at some conference or on some mission. Damp patches on the walls because the underground ventilation was always playing up. The stains and discarded debris of a disposable life. I'd been in Gibraltar for seven months. Looking around it was like I'd barely arrived.

We'd had a house on Magenta. A home, the two of us

together, Alysha and me, a neat and tidy nest. We'd cared for it as we'd cared for each other. The only things cared for here were the array of screens, their q-ware hosters and the coffin for Liss's shell.

'You must hate me for this,' I said.

'I don't hate you for anything.'

'Then *I* must hate me.' Which was probably closer to the truth.

'It's your last night on Earth, Keys. Leave me behind. Go and have some fun with Agent de Korte. She likes you.'

'It's a bit late for new friends, don't you think?' It had taken two years for the cracksman to make Liss, to get all the data for a complete persona shipped from Magenta, in bits and pieces and mostly done in secret. Two years and an absurd amount of money, a debt I was still paying off. But she was as near to perfect as could be made, and you don't get that calibre of cracksman anywhere except on Earth.

You don't get the ethics either. Shells and Servants run simulated personalities all the time, but not of real people. We don't do that on the colonies. Major trouble. Prison time.

Boxing everything up was easy. The tech had its own packaging. Everything else came down to throwing untidy bundles into a polycarbonate crate followed by a long-overdue summons to Gibraltar's recycling and maintenance drones. Other days we might have made a game of it, thrown things at each other, laughed, forgotten for a moment that she was just a shell of someone dead, but not today. Took about half an hour, and that was that: I was good to go. Goodbye, Earth.

'I'm going to miss this place for its gravity.' I tried to laugh, to make it sound like a joke, but I didn't fool either of us. I wasn't going to miss the violence, the dirt, the poverty, the crowds, the inequality. But on Earth they knew how to build something grand. They knew about scale and awe, and most of all they knew how much it mattered to have a way to escape. Magenta didn't have any of that.

Maybe I'd drive past that home we used to have …

I'd have to see Alysha's family. My own. The people we used to work with …

I sank to the bed and held my head in my hands, looking for a way out that wasn't there. Liss sat beside me. She touched my arm.

'I'll miss the bitsphere,' she said, 'How deeply everything is connected. I'm glad gravity isn't something I need to worry about any more.'

'Five years is a long time,' I said. 'They'll put me under for transgravity treatment for weeks. I'll have to shut you down again. Fleet have the best q-ware. I don't trust them not to snoop.'

'I know.'

'I don't know how to do this, Liss.' I was shaking.

'You're going to take me home, Keys. We're going to start a new life.' She dimmed the lights. As I curled on the bed she ran a finger across my hair. 'You don't look after yourself,' she said. 'I wish you would. You need to face that I'm gone. You need to live your own life. A new one without me. It would be better for you. We both know that.' She climbed into her coffin.

'I know.' I thought of my Alysha lying beside me, holding my hand, warm and alive in flesh and blood again. Knowing Liss was right wasn't making it any easier. 'Just keep breathing, right? Going to have to do this whether I want it or not.'

'That's the one, Keys. Here if you need me.' The same thing we'd once said to one another every night as we drifted to sleep.

Twelve hours later we were on our way to orbit.

2

MAGENTA

The *Fearless* winked into Magentan space, shaking off the higher dimensions of its existence like a dog shaking off the sea. An abandoned Masters' ship, its core was a tangled ever-shifting singularity web, long since wrapped into an asteroid's heart to hide the insanity of its nonsensical geometries. A dozen interplanetary cruisers detached from its docking cluster. Their fusion plumes lit up, little comets streaking away from a froth of disturbed spacetime before the *Fearless*, driven by some un-fathomed clock, vanished again, flipping in and out of real space between Magenta and Earth with the predictable precision of a quantum rhythm.

I lay in my cocoon, watching the view out into space. Glorious and awe-inspiring, but I wasn't in any state to pay attention. Everything hurt, a lingering bone-ache from the transgravity nanites. My Servant dutifully looked up recovery protocols – what to eat and when, what exercises to do and how often, that sort of thing – and mindlessly scheduled them into my life like a row of bright-toothed smiles. Servants exist to bring order, optimising our lives for health and longevity and not missing appointments. We assume these things equate to happiness but they don't, only a numb and bland contentment.

Ignoring my Servant's plea for a short but intense cardio-vascular workout to flush the residual transgravity stiffness, I had a shower. I took my time and then went to the torture chamber they called a centrifuge to start my acclimatisation to Magenta's gravity. I got it up to 1.2 standard before I was feeling heavy. Magenta being 1.4, that didn't bode well, but there wasn't much else to do except sit around and suffer until the nanotech did its magic. I had another month of this to look forward to before they'd let me down to the surface. Better to grit my teeth and face it, I thought, so I brought up the Magentan news services for something to take my mind off the aches. The feeds were rife with some immigration crisis in Disappointment, reports, opinion pieces … On Earth I hadn't picked up even a whisper. Local news. A reminder that, as far as the rest of the colonies were concerned, Magenta was a backwater.

I surfed for a few minutes, and then somehow I was in the archives, watching the old reports of the crash in which Alysha had died. Of the bureau arresting the Entropist who called himself Loki, the one who'd planted the bomb. The trial. The sentencing. They'd sent him off-world to the Fleet prison on Colony 478. Three months later he was dead, shanked in the shower. Fleet had never found out for sure who'd done it to him. I don't think they much cared. I froze an image and stared at his face. He'd had a real name too, but Loki had stuck, and so had his story. He was an Entropist. He'd bombed a freight train. He hadn't known there would be stowaways. How could he?

Whoever it was who'd stabbed him, I wished I could shake their hand.

I brought Liss to life.

'Hey, Keys.' She killed the archive feed. 'So this is home?'

'It will be when we land.' After the fiasco of the Gibraltar Tech-Fair I was lucky Fleet hadn't sent me to Colony 478 too. I spat out a laugh. Different world, different life, I could have shanked Loki myself. Would have done it too.

'Are you going to be OK?' Liss asked.

'What do you mean?'

'Coming back to Magenta.'

'I'll be fine.' I'd manage was more the truth of it. 'Liss, I've ...' *Accepted what happened*, was that what I'd been about to say? *I've moved on?* Bullshit. 'I'm not going to run away from it this time. We're going to face it head on.' Still made me want to scream, saying that, still tied my gut into knots. Was probably as well that I wasn't being given a choice.

I skimmed the rest of the news from the last five years that had never made it to Earth. When I got bored with that we watched an old documentary about the Masters and the derelict moon-sized structures they'd left orbiting Neptune, hollow with no functioning parts but extensively decorated inside and out. Afterwards we argued over whether the Neptune enigmas had been abandoned unfinished, like everything else the Masters had left behind, or whether they were some sort of cosmic-scale work of art. Old talk, the sort of thing Alysha and I used to do to pass the time. We talked, we watched things, we talked some more. We kept busy because busy stopped me from thinking, and I didn't want that, not yet. Liss didn't say anything, but I knew she understood.

The cruiser reached Magenta exactly on schedule three days later. I drifted through the hyperstation orbital, one bewildered passenger among many, to the transgravity therapy unit and a month of nanosurgery, rebuilding, gene therapy, artificial sleep and a high-intensity exercise regime. In the hour each day I had to myself, I dealt with the messages that started to arrive.

My former employer, the Magenta Investigation Bureau, had worked out that I was back. Technically I still worked for them, my time with Fleet a temporary secondment, and apparently they didn't care much about whatever had gone down on Gibraltar because I soon had accommodation assignments, updates to processes and procedures, all condensed into summaries but still enough to keep me busy. Eventually I had a boss too.

'Assistant Director Flemich? He liked you,' I said. Flemich had been Liss's mentor back when we were in the academy together. They'd still talked, right up to the end.

'Flemich's an AD now?'

'You remember what you made of him towards the end?' Even in my hour off I had to sit in a centrifuge. They had me up to 1.3 gravities and it was starting to grind me down. I was out of breath. My hips and knees and back were aching. The centrifuge encouraged the nanotech to do its work. Torture with a purpose, but still torture.

'I think I thought he was OK. A bit slow but OK.'

We set up a call. It was strange, seeing the same grey-haired sour face I remembered from five years ago, like going back in time, like me vanishing to Earth hadn't ever happened. We talked. Flemich sent over the files of a couple of agents he wanted me to work with. Bix Rangesh, who had both the best connections to Magenta's drug culture and the worst disciplinary record in the bureau, and Esharaq Zohreya, Earth-born but raised on Magenta, a recent transfer from the Magenta Space Defence Force. He said the Earth-born bit as if my time there might somehow be a bridge between us. Stupid. After he was gone I sat and stared at nothing very much. I'd known Flemich for years, though not as well as Alysha had. Seeing him again, talking to someone from that old life, felt like shedding skin. Raw and red, an overload of sensation, terrifying and yet somehow good.

I opened the files and didn't much like what I saw. On paper Zohreya and Rangesh were chalk and cheese.

'Look!' Liss had another file open, one I hadn't read yet. When I saw it I had to laugh.

'KRAB again? Grief! That was ten years ago! They were kids!'

Liss laughed too, a beautiful music untainted by scorn. Our first case. I could almost feel her arms around me, pressing in close.

'And we were already … Do you remember how we tried to hide it? Those stupid made-up arguments?'

Silence stretched out between us like the years. Playing our charade, the other agents around us acting like they hadn't noticed and then sniggering behind our backs. Everyone had been happy.

'Didn't KRAB stand for Kool Real Alien Broadcasts or something stupid like that?' I asked her. 'This is a training-wheels assignment. Second-year rookie work.'

'Are you surprised?'

'I mean, how old were they? Almost children.' Teenagers, most of them.

Liss tutted at me. 'They did hijack a satellite.'

'Yes, yes, but it was a pirate media channel run by a bunch of kids from their bedrooms! Clever kids, I'll grant you, but still kids. Harmless, bright and too full of hallucinogens. A hard slap on the wrist and a lecture and some stern don't-do-it-again finger-wagging, wasn't that how it ended?' I couldn't stop myself from smiling. Heady days those, the joy of finding each other, the warmth inside …

My smile died. That was all gone. Suddenly it felt like more than a lifetime ago.

'Ten years,' I said. 'Didn't they all just grow up and get proper jobs?'

'Apparently not.' I could still feel her smile sometimes when

I closed my eyes, the glow of it. 'They *were* mostly harmless, but ten years is a long time. You shouldn't take anything for granted, Keys.'

I peered through the file. 'Agent Esharaq Zohreya? Whoever she is, she can keep KRAB.'

'Grumpy today?'

'I'm in pain.' Grumpy wasn't the start of it.

Between mundane bureau updates, Liss and I spent the next days working out which agents had investigated her death. It wasn't hard, given how high-profile Loki's trial had become. I wanted someone on my team who'd been there, who could give me answers and who might be willing to dig for a few more. Someone, if I was lucky, with some of the same unanswered questions ... What I *really* wanted was to run away, but since no one seemed to want to offer that as an option, jumping in with both feet seemed the next best thing. Take your fear and poke it in the eye. Some bullshit like that.

'This one.' It was Liss who found her. She patched together a file. Took a second or so. One look and I knew she was right.

'Laura Murgrah?' I murmured.

'Not any more.' Liss made a smug noise. 'She's back to her maiden name. Patterson. You *do* remember, right? You really should.'

Laura Murgrah. I closed my eyes, reaching back. We were in the academy together. She'd been married. Jamal Murgrah. Human rights lawyer. Laura had been set to follow in her father's shoes on the board of some Magentan mining conglomerate but Jamal had changed her mind and so she'd joined the bureau instead. Bright. Brilliant, even. Full of ideals and set to change the world, *all* the worlds if she could, but even back then I'd had the sense of something going wrong ...

We'd had a moment. Couldn't remember whether I'd ever told—

'You had a fling, didn't you?'

Well, that answered that. 'A one-night stand,' I said. 'I hadn't met you yet. I liked her.' Guilt, was it? Shame? I don't know. She'd been drunk. Anxious about something, and I'd been the barman who listened to people's problems. We'd ended up in bed. End of story. No big deal. I hadn't known then that she was married but I'm not sure it would have made a difference.

'It's OK, Keys.'

No regrets. Laura's last words as she'd left, but she hadn't come back. I had a vague idea that she and Alysha had become friends years later, but our paths hadn't really crossed. We'd moved in different circles.

'She should be Flemich's boss by now,' I said.

'They had a son. Jamal left her and went to Earth. She had a breakdown.'

The file Liss had assembled was vague, but I could see the crack as soon as I looked for it. For the first few years after the academy, Laura Murgrah was racking up some of the highest test scores the bureau had ever seen. Five years in and she was tipped to be director one day. And then nothing for a year. Medical leave. Compassionate absence. When she'd come back she was Laura Patterson, still brilliant but now horribly erratic. Whatever had happened, it had happened while I was on Earth.

'She doesn't play well with others,' said Liss, 'but at least she's not dead.'

'You're not dead either,' I said. 'You're right here.'

'I am, but we both know I'm not real.' Liss gave a little laugh, a perfect replica of the little laugh that the real Alysha Rause often used to make me melt. 'You and Patterson might get on. You're quite compatible. You've shown that. It's OK if you do; I won't be jealous. I'm just a simulation. I liked her too, once, and my judgement of people was apparently excellent.'

'Are you trying to set me up?'

20

'I'm trying to help you find what you need, Keys.'

I figured that meant she *was* trying to set me up, but looking at the rest, Murgrah was the best choice I had. I put in the request to have her transferred to my team. Three days later it was approved. Done, signed and sealed, rather to my surprise. Laura Murgrah. So that was going to be interesting.

Other briefings came and went, a steady stream of interviews, debriefs and the like, questions about Earth and Fleet, about the task force I was on and everything I'd done. Most of it I couldn't answer. Flemich was in touch again a week before I was due to come out of transgravity. By then they were running the centrifuge all the way up to 1.4, full Magentan surface gravity. I stood there as he walked through the assignments he had waiting for me, feeling like I was getting shorter every minute while my spine collapsed in slow motion. Routine stuff mostly. Background work, KRAB the only thing that needed immediate attention, and Agent Zohreya had that in hand. We had a bit of a talk about how Flemich wasn't pleased at me requesting additional resources before I'd even landed, but by the end I still had Agent Patterson and Flemich's smile still seemed genuine enough. He offered me a few rest days after I came down from orbit – acclimatisation, get my head together, find my feet and so forth, but the last thing I needed was more time with nothing to do except think about why I'd left in the first place.

'I'd rather get straight back into it,' I told him. He seemed happy with that.

A week later the Tesseract sent Agent Zohreya to bring me down from orbit. I could see at once that she was Earth-born because she wasn't stocky enough for a native. Originally from somewhere in the Middle East maybe, I thought. I eyeballed her from a distance, wondering for the thousandth time what the hell I was doing here, and what she was too, what sort of person chose Magenta as a place to live. She had a nice smile.

Not my sort of smile, but a smile that probably got her as much attention as she wanted. Honest and open. Alysha had had that too. Liss's shell, good as it was, never quite caught it.

Zohreya gave me a crisp salute. We swapped inane how-was-your-flight small talk as she led me drifting through the zero-gravity docking hub to a pressurised hangar and a two-seat re-entry vehicle that was little more than a transparent bubble hanging under a self-configuring wing and a couple of engines. We climbed in, sealed the hatch, depressurised the hangar and opened the bay doors ... and there she was, Magenta, sprawled out beneath us, beautiful and almost entirely white and exactly as I remembered her, poles frozen all the way to the mid-latitudes, a thin ribbon of purplish sea wrapped around her, rich with the magenta-coloured algae that had first given her her name, thick swirls of cloud around the temperate equator and the major cities: Firstfall, Disappointment, Nico ...

We drifted out into space, serene and silent, tiny bursts propelling us down towards the upper edges of the atmosphere. Zohreya didn't talk, which was fine with me because I was too busy staring through the canopy. I'd grown up here. I'd fallen in love. I'd made a life and then I'd lost it. I'd spent the last five years running away and now I was back and didn't know what to think any more. The butterflies in my stomach overwhelmed the dizzying vertigo.

We hit the upper atmosphere, carving a plasma haze, a halo of fire around us.

Alysha's train had been half a mile underground when it had exploded at a thousand miles an hour. There hadn't been anything left. They'd made a monument. A memorial. I could visit that at least ...

The sun began to set behind the curve of the planet.

I'd have to see my parents again. Five years without a word

either way. I assumed I'd have heard if one of them had died, but maybe not. Best to check …

Somewhere down there was what had once been our home. Someone else would be living there now. Perhaps I wouldn't go past it after all, if I could help it …

The clouds darkened from majestic orange to black. Night fell across the world. The glider dropped into the troposphere, its wings extending, the sky full of stars that winked in and out. We plunged into wraps of cloud, through darkness and swirls of vapour lit by our own running lights until we emerged again below, sailing gracefully above the lit-up sparkle of Firstfall, slowing and falling in a steady shedding of heat and speed until we landed and rolled to a stop on the concrete skirts of New Hope spaceport. The air outside was cold and filled with driving rain, Magenta embracing me back by being exactly as I remembered her. I wasn't sure whether to take that as a promise or a threat.

Agent Zohreya popped the canopy. The glider's wing sheltered us from most of the rain, but not all of it. The wind on Magenta meant that rain got into everything.

I tried to get out. The gravity hit me like a falling brick. 'Give me a moment,' I said.

'How much transgravity did you do?' Zohreya's smile was more sympathy than mockery.

'A couple of weeks in transit. A month once I got here.'

'I had transgravity when my family first came to Magenta. I was seven. It didn't really work.'

'It takes time, that's all.'

'In two weeks it offers a five or six per cent increase in muscular-skeletal resilience. The extra month in orbit should have brought you up to about thirty. To function fully on Magenta requires more like a fifty to sixty per cent increase. You'll get to that after about six months.'

'Yeah, I read the brochure too. But thanks for the reminder.' I forced myself to my feet and out of the cockpit. I'd survived the centrifuge, managed it for hours at a time, and this was no different. Or at least that was what I told myself. And it wouldn't take six months. I'd been born here. My body would remember.

'I'll see you tomorrow, sir.' Zohreya climbed back inside and closed the cockpit. A pod was waiting for me. I slumped in and let it drive me out of New Hope with its rain and its crowded constellations of lights and its glitter and hydrogen lustre. We passed through the new Firstfall suburbs where Alysha and I had once started to make a home, and then on into the heart of the old town, to the domes and the blockhouses the early settlers had built, ruthlessly simple and functional and solid enough to hold out the Magentan weather no matter what; when the old buildings hadn't been big enough, we'd done what Magentans always did – dug a little deeper.

The pod dived into a tunnel and slowed, making its way around the warren under the old town, the undercity. It stopped inside a small cavern lit with dim red light to honour the night above. There were no drunks in the tunnels under Firstfall, not like Gibraltar; no stim addicts, no beggars, no dirt-stained neon-bright vending bots, no rainbow-sheen puddles. Everything was clean and tidy, the way of the colony settlements. After five years away I felt like an alien on a strange new world.

'You remember the house we had?' I asked. 'You used to complain about how far out we were, how long it took us to get to the Tesseract.'

'I did, didn't I?'

'Did you mean it? Did it really trouble you? Or was it just a … I don't know. You know how people are.'

'You know I can't answer that, Keys.'

After I first moved to Earth it had taken me two months

24

to find a cracksman willing to build Liss for me. On the first day we met he'd told me what he needed, but I heard most of the detail later from Liss herself. Every frame of surveillance imagery, every word spoken and captured in public, every message ever sent, every digital trace of her. Worms had run for months through every database on Magenta, creeping into every restricted corner except for the Tesseract itself and the other AI-protected hubs. Liss was made from the sum of everything Alysha had ever shown herself to be, but the private things, whatever she'd kept hidden on the inside, all of that was lost. Personality could be extrapolated but her inner secrets were gone for ever. Like whether complaining about where we lived had been a sort of running joke. Like why she was asking about a corporate enclave called Settlement 64 before she died. Like why she was so on edge those last two weeks and what she'd done with the money we'd saved and why she'd been on that train.

I shook the questions away. There were never any answers.

The bureau had set me up with a three-month lease on a government apartment, paid for in advance out of a salary I hadn't drawn yet. The door opened to invite me into a room three times the size of anything I'd ever had on Earth. The taxi pod whirred away. A second pod drew up carrying my luggage from New Hope. I looked at the coffin and the two polycarbonate crates that were my entire life and wondered how I could possibly fill so much space.

'Leave it,' said Liss. 'Flemich wants you at the Tesseract at nine for face time. I've booked you a pod. I took the liberty of stocking the fridge while we were still in orbit. There are some beers. Have a couple, sit back, watch an old show. Maybe surf the news channels. The way we used to, remember?'

'Yeah.' I closed my eyes and tried not to, but it was too late. 'Back when you were real, you mean?'

'Back when I was real.'

I opened my crates and set up my rack of screens and q-hosts, then on a whim summoned a drone and sent all my clothes for overnight cleaning. I got as far as standing in front of the fridge with the door open, looking at the beers Liss had bought, the same fermented lichen brand the two of us used to drink on our nights off together. I paused, then took out a couple and opened them, drank one and left the other on the table while I stared into blankness. A part of me wanted to open Liss's coffin, to wake up her shell and have her physical presence with me. That part wanted it very badly indeed, but another part wanted to be alone.

'Find the archives of the crash,' I said. 'I want to see them again.'

'No, you don't.'

'Yes, I do.'

'Why, Keys? You're only hurting yourself. You know that. Get in touch with your family. Let them know you're back. Or get in touch with mine. They let me be dead years ago. Maybe they can show you how?'

'One more time, Liss. That's all.'

'I don't believe you.' But she gave me the archive anyway, and so I sat and stared at the wreckage, at the smoking carnage of the crash site, and started to promise myself that it really was the last time, that I was done with it now …

And then I stopped because I knew it wasn't true. I felt it in my bones side by side with Magenta's gravity. I was going to find her. I was going to find out why she'd died, and nothing was going to get in my way. Staring at the crash footage, deaf to the words, I wondered at my certainty until it hit me why I'd been so afraid that day on Earth when I knew I was coming back. It wasn't the past or facing what had happened that scared me. It wasn't even the truth. It was what I was prepared to do to get it.

26

3

BIX

I felt as though I'd barely fallen asleep when my Servant woke me again. Liss was out of her coffin and in the kitchen, the apartment alive with the whistle of boiling water, the smell of fresh coffee and the sizzle of frying bacon, the one food Magenta actually did well. I felt terrible, aches and pains everywhere and a cloud of cotton wool behind my eyes. If this was how it was going to be until I got used to Magenta's gravity, maybe I should have taken Flemich up on his offer of a few days off.

I twigged then what time it was. My nine o'clock meeting with Flemich was six hours away. It was the middle of the night.

'Liss! What the …?'

'They want you in early.'

'This isn't early, this is the night before!'

'Strictly not so. Apparently something came up. Get dressed – there's a pod on the way. I thought you might like some breakfast to take with you.'

'You want to tell me …' I rubbed my eyes and wrinkled my nose. The bacon smelled good, but it got me thinking about the rest of what I had in store. Food grown underground. 'Damn. I'm missing Earth cuisine already. Can we go back, or is it too late?' I checked my Servant but I didn't see anything from Flemich. 'Seriously, Liss, this is so early it's almost yesterday. What exactly "came up"? Where's the message?'

Liss laughed. 'Ground lichen and dried mushroom every day! And all the nutritious seaweed from the hydroponics vats that you could possibly want! Don't tell me you didn't miss this when you went to Earth?'

'Not for a second. The message?'

'I don't know. I think ...' She paused the way Alysha used to pause, working out how best to tell me something she thought I didn't want to hear. I found myself imagining the ones and zeros that lay beneath that pause, the complex mathematics, the algorithmic computation. Alysha used to get it wrong more often than not, how to break bad news. Liss got it wrong too sometimes. I wondered whether she did it on purpose, trying to be as much like Alysha as she could, or whether it was just bad code. Did she model the Alysha beneath the masks and façades that every one of us wears, or did she model the masks too, the person Alysha tried to be whenever anyone was watching? Even the cracksman who'd made her hadn't been able to give a certain answer to that. A mixture of the two, he'd said. The person she presented to the world, the parts she wanted to show and the parts that crept out anyway. 'I feel as though ... this is the start of something new for you. I'm sorry. I wanted you to myself before you go. Just for a bit, that's all.'

I watched her cut slices of lichen bread and package up a bacon sandwich as I dressed in the same crumpled jacket and trousers I'd worn the day before. Everything else would come back, clean, in about three hours. When I was done she handed me breakfast in a paper bag and a cup of coffee in a polycarbonate cup. The last day I'd seen Alysha alive had been the same. Bacon sandwich in a paper bag, coffee in a travel cup, the breakfast one of us always made for the other when they had an early start so we could stay in bed for as long as possible, a token salute to the laziness we liked to pretend we both enjoyed. Five years ago I'd been going to Disappointment to shut down a celebrity sex-bot ring. Alysha had said she was having a few days off. She'd made me breakfast, wished me luck, told me that she loved me, kissed me on the cheek, and that was the last I ever saw of her. I'd known something was wrong, deep down, but we'd both agreed long ago that we didn't talk about work when we were alone together.

Liss smiled, sad and hopeful. She didn't kiss me. Just reached out a hand and briefly touched her fingers to my chest as the taxi pod arrived, humming outside the door.

'You should go,' she said.

The message from Flemich arrived as she spoke. Short and sweet. Sorry about this, Rause, but I need you with Agent Rangesh. This has got media and politics all over it. Make sure he doesn't embarrass us. It should have pinged me ten minutes ago, but Liss had intercepted it and hooked it around some router delay so my Servant hadn't registered it. I wondered how difficult that was. It almost certainly wasn't legal.

'I'm sorry,' she said. 'I'd come with you, but ...' But at some point today the Tesseract AI was going to come crashing into my Servant to scour it clean. Security protocols, and neither of us wanted Liss anywhere near when that happened.

I didn't want to go. She almost had to push me out. Too many bad memories.

'I'll be here when you come back.' She smiled. 'I promise.'

I hugged her. Never mind that she was a shell, it was what was inside the shell that mattered. Always had. I got in the pod and then looked back at her, standing in the door, until we turned a corner and she was gone.

The pod took me to Mercy Hospital. Flemich's message didn't say anything about why he wanted me there or what had happened, so while I ate my sandwich I scanned the news channels in case they offered any clues. When nothing jumped out I went back and looked over the file I had on Rangesh. I figured I should at least know what he looked like and maybe work out how much trouble he was going to be. I emerged from the undercity tunnels into the same rain that had greeted me at New Hope. Outside Mercy there he was, Rangesh, already waiting, a collection of impatient twitches in a stocky Indian-gened frame wrapped in a shabby all-weather storm suit against the downpour. A squalling wind buffeted the pod. On Earth they might have called this a storm but on Magenta we called it a decent day because, hey, you could at least go for a walk without being blown flat if you really wanted to.

Rangesh started towards the pod as soon as it pulled over. 'You must be Keon,' he yelled over wind and rain, and bared some very white teeth. Maybe he meant it as a smile. 'Welcome back to Magenta, man!' Nothing in his face was happy to see me. Couldn't blame him for that.

'Agent Rause to you,' I yelled back. 'I should be asleep. You want to tell me why I'm not?' I tried to pull myself out of the pod while Magenta's gravity tried to suck me back. The wind smacked me in the face with a spray of rain that left me deaf and half blind. Gravity won: I collapsed back into the pod.

'You know, there are actually people on Earth who like the rain,' I said as he slid in to sit beside me. 'They like to go out in it and take off their clothes and dance.'

We both sat and thought about how daft that was.

'I touched down last night after dark, Agent Rangesh. I've had about four hours' sleep and it wasn't good sleep either. That makes me cranky. Why am I here?'

'Hey, peace, man.' Rangesh held up his hands. 'Check out Channel Six.'

I flicked on a data stream. Video poured over my lenses, over-laid across the steps to Mercy Hospital's front hall, all decked in a misty spray from the falling rain. I blinked a few times and then closed my eyes. Some people can work with multiple layers of reality thrown up in front of them at once, flicking between them with a small adjustment of focus, but I'd never learned the trick of it.

... reporting live from Mercy Hospital, where we're waiting confirmation of tonight's rumours that Shyla Thiekis has been admitted suffering from a drug overdose ...

'Ah man!' Rangesh fidgeted like a cat about to pounce. 'It's heavy, new boss dude.'

'*That's* what all this is about?' *New boss dude?*

'Yeah, man.'

'Who is she?' Shyla Thiekis. Name didn't mean anything. I quizzed my Servant and soon found plenty. Some rich girl ...

'Who's Shyla? *Dude!*'

'I've been away, Agent Rangesh.' I tried to pull Thiekis's medical records but Mercy refused, even when I gave my Tesseract codes. Inside the pod the rattle of rain made it hard to think, the constant hammering on the roof like a swarm of hornets thundering to get inside.

'Yeah. Esh said. Earth. Cool, man. That must have been awesome.'

I had no idea who Esh was and I wasn't so sure that Earth had been even a little bit awesome, all things considered. 'So is this rumour true?'

Rangesh shook his head. 'It's worse. She's dead.'

'Dead? From a drug overdose?'

Rangesh didn't answer. I skimmed his file again just to be sure I had the right agent, that I wasn't missing something. I didn't get it. Some slightly famous woman with a history of substance abuse was dead from an overdose. Tragic, sure, but hardly a reason to have two bureau agents outside Mercy Hospital in the small hours of the morning.

'She's gone, man.' Rangesh sounded off. 'It's a real bummer.'

A dossier I hadn't asked for blurted in from the Tesseract. Words filled my sight. It took a moment before I realised that Rangesh had sent it. Shyla Thiekis. Mid-thirties. Stinking rich. Socialite with a long history of hallucinogen addictions. Daughter of Channel Nine chairman and MagentaNet owner Eddie Thiekis. Long-term on-and-off lover of Channel Nine's lead political reporter Enki Betleshah. Worth a small fortune and in the scandal and social sections of the news a lot, but ...

I frowned. 'I'm still not getting it.'

'Dude!' Rangesh jumped up, banged his head on the roof of the pod and crashed down beside me again. 'The Shyster's, like, one of Magenta's top celebrities! She can't even fart without someone posting an aroma bite on SnapSmell! That sort of thing, you know? Don't ask me why. I mean, yeah, sure, she's hot, but ... Well, she was ...'

I waited for Rangesh to run out of words. 'Don't send files like that without warning me first next time, OK?' I said when he was done.

'Sorry, man.'

Files and data streams were turning my lenses into a kaleidoscope of layered realities. I cleared them and concentrated on Rangesh. Behind the blur of motion, the big smiling eyes, the constantly twitching head, he looked haunted.

'Did you know her?' I asked. 'Personally, I mean?'

'Yeah. While back, man.' He looked abashed. 'You know? Before her face was all over the bitsphere every morning.' He stilled for a moment. Guilt, was that? Shame? Something else?

'What's this got to do with the Tesseract? Or is this personal?'

I'd read Rangesh's file. There were discipline issues. He was unconventional but also possibly the best-connected field agent the bureau had when it came to the quasi-legal greyness of Firstfall's hallucinogen scene.

I looked for Liss, thinking to ask her to start digging on both Rangesh and Thiekis, but of course she wasn't in my Servant. She wouldn't be until the Tesseract gave it its ritual purge.

'Bit of both.' Rangesh gave me a hard look, deep and heavy and sad. 'You OK, man? You look grim.'

Sitting inside a pod in the middle of the night with the rain drumming down. 'Not enough sleep. Too much gravity. Hard to think straight.'

'Look, I put a lid on it all for a bit, but it's totally not going to last. The Shyster died at two this morning, give or take. I guess if you don't know … She's had her problems. Drugs, you know? Never could keep off the gens for long, but this isn't how it's supposed to go down, right? It's like … ah, man, you know what happens when you trip too much, yeah? You ride the gens and the lichen gets inside your head. I mean, you've never done it yourself, sure, but you knew someone who took some gens once, right, because everyone does? So you know the deal, yeah? You start seeing things, and then everything maybe gets way too weird, and yeah, sure, now and then someone on a hard trip starts making up stupid stuff in their head and jumps off a roof because they think they can fly, real dumb stuff, you know? But not this. Gens make you do stupid shit, but they don't kill you from the inside, not on their own.'

'What—'

'She was in the hospital, man. Freaking Mercy Hospital! She was under watch! That should have been that. High as a weather balloon but no big story. Twenty-four hours to flush the gens and away she goes until the next time she gets wasted. Happened before, plenty of times, no doubt going to happen again. You ever know anyone die from taking gens, Agent Rause?' Rangesh shook his head. 'I mean, just from the gens, not from being stupid because you watched the wrong show and now some polka-dot pink tyrannosaur is chasing you across the high-speed highway ... She had brain haemorrhages, man. It was like all the blood vessels in her head just burst one after another. Like her brain just ... Like it melted, you know? Like her head exploded on the inside. They tried to save her but there was nothing they could do. Just kept getting worse. Gens don't do that.' He shook his head. 'They just don't.'

'Toxin screen?'

'Yeah. I set one up.' Rangesh looked off into the distance. The road was quiet outside Mercy at this time of night. No one else about, hardly any pods. If there were reporters already here chasing the Shyla story then they had the sense to stay inside where it was dry. The wind had dropped and the darkness was still, one of Magenta's rare quiet moments. Just the two of us and the pouring rain.

'And?' The pod was a big one, bench seats either side, enough to carry a dozen people at a push. In the early days after the Masters there was an exodus from Earth. Waiting lists were years long, even for Magenta, and that was before the development of transgravity. The colonists spent most of their waiting time walking around with hundred-pound packs on their backs, training themselves to get used to what it was going to be like. Transgravity had changed all that, but not as much as I would have liked. I hurt, and it was going to be a long few weeks. I wondered if Rangesh would think me odd if I lay down.

'They're working it, dude. Nothing yet. I put a restriction order over everything. Keep the media out of it, you know.' He shrugged. 'Hasn't stopped Channel Six sniffing a story though. They know, man. Maybe not everything, but they know it's not good.' He leaned out of the pod and waved at the night sky.

34

'Going to be a Channel Six drone up there right now, watching us. Going to be following us wherever we go.'

'Even in this rain?'

'We got cheap drones coming in from Earth that hack way worse than this. Don't get tagged either these days. Could be anywhere.'

That was new. When I'd left Magenta, every drone was registered. Or at least was supposed to be.

I stretched, trying to get my shoulders, my back, something at least, to stop aching. 'So that's why the Tesseract wants us looking at this? They think she was poisoned?'

'Yeah, something like that.' Rangesh stared off into the distance. 'Something else killed her, man. Except ...'

'Or someone?' I could see him thinking it.

A pod shot out of the tunnel from the Squats, pinging urgent warnings to everything in its path that it carried a medical emergency. We watched it turn the corner, heading for Mercy's trauma wing. Rangesh shook his head. 'I don't know, man. Thing is ... Look, you know Shy's old man runs Channel Nine, right? And he owns MagentaNet too. You know, like, *owns* it. Like, one word and every satellite shuts down, every screen goes blank, yeah? And the Shyster runs with the Shah, right? So Six ran a piece a few days back about her banging the Shah's boss—'

'Who's the Shah?'

'The Shah, man! Enki. Enki Betleshah.' Rangesh rolled his eyes like I was some sort of idiot. 'Yeah. Anyway, now here she is. So there's motive right there, man.' He shrugged. 'I don't buy it, but people are going to point fingers, like maybe the Shah did it out of jealousy, which he totally didn't, or maybe Shy did it to herself out of shame, because yeah, maybe she's had some sort of total personality transplant or something, you know ... But Eddie T just lost his daughter, and he hates the Shah, and he hates Channel Six too, and Six and Nine are at each other like fighting cocks at the best of times, and so Six are going to run this like it's the return of the Masters once they know she's dead. You've just got to look, you know? It's going to be like pistols at dawn and everything, only with big sawn-off knives in the back and not at dawn but at whenever, and ...' Rangesh shook his head. 'The Shah's going down. No way he's getting out of this one. But you watch. Channel Six are going to do everything they can to make Eddie T lose his shit on the way, you know? It's going to suck.'

I waited a moment to see whether Rangesh's words were going to rearrange themselves into something that made sense, something that would explain why I was here when I'd only made planetfall twelve hours ago. 'No, I don't know,' I said when they didn't. 'I don't think I have the first idea what you're talking about. Why would they do that?'

'Media war.' Rangesh sniffed. 'Six hate that Eddie has all the satellites. Six and Nine are going to go for each other, and Eddie's got his finger on the big red button. If he loses his rag he could shut everything down. Nuke it all from orbit, you know. Six would love that. It would force the government to get involved. They'd take Eddie's satellites. So we kind of ought to head it off at the pass, dude. If we can. If it's what it looks like.'

Sitting still was killing me. I had to move. I got up out of the pod into the blitzkrieg of rain and stretched and twisted from side to side, trying to flush the knots out of my back. Mercy wasn't much to look at even in daylight. Grey plasto-polymer, near as you can get to indestructible. Blocky and squat, same as the rest of old Firstfall. Here, at night, through the rain, I could barely even see it. Most was underground anyway. I knew that because I'd been here before, more times than I cared to count. The obligatory bedside visits to agents injured on duty. Bodies in the morgue when it was something we just had to see for ourselves. Alysha's miscarriage ...

I was getting slow. 'If?' I had to shout over the rain. '*If* it's what it looks like? You think it's something else?'

Rangesh stayed in the pod, sensible and sheltered. Weird thing was, I could almost get to like it out in the rain. For a moment I could see where those dancing Earthers were coming from. Naked was maybe a bit much on Magenta, but the battering I was getting from the downpour was doing a fine job of making me forget how much I hurt. Gravity, like the gods we mostly don't believe in any more, gives as well as it takes away.

Rangesh said something I didn't hear and then pinged me a series of Tesseract files. Four dead gen junkies over the last twelve months. Three men, one woman. Didn't seem so unusual at first, but he'd highlighted the bits I needed to see. Same cause of death. Massive internal haemorrhaging. Only it was more than that. Two of them looked like they'd been ripped apart. The places they'd been found had been ripped apart too. Bent, shredded and mangled.

I got back into the pod, dripping everywhere. 'This can't be right.'

'Yeah, man, I know. But it is what it is, dude. And the only thing they have in common is the gens. So what if it really is that, you know? I'll tell you the weirdest thing: the Shyster turned up at Mercy in a pod. Someone found her tripping and sent her here.'

'Who?'

'No idea, man.'

I pinged the hospital for painkillers. My Servant didn't like it and nor did Mercy, but if anyone wanted me to do anything more than slouch and moan and complain about how damn hard everything was after five years on Earth, they could just live with it. 'Look, Rangesh, I don't even know why I'm here.

So mostly I'm just going to see the sights and play along with whatever you want to do, but if you want some advice then start with that pod. Last movements. Track her back in time. Find out who saw her before she came to Mercy. One by one until we either find whoever killed her or we find out where she got whatever it was that she took. The basics.'

An empty pod whirred to a stop in front of us as I finished. Rangesh got out into the rain. 'Timing, boss dude! Here it is: the one that brought her here.' He set a couple of forensic scrubbing drones to work then started on an interface to the pod's logs. I watched him, envious of how easily he moved. Simple things like standing up and bending over and walking a few yards from one place to another.

In a couple of minutes we knew everything about where the pod had been since the day it was made, complete with fingerprints, fibres and DNA from almost everyone who'd ever been in it. The Tesseract would correlate everything together, and then we'd start on the tedious investigative work, the anomalies – the DNA that couldn't be made to fit, that sort of thing – but right now all we knew was that Shyla Thiekis had been in it last night. Maybe the samples would be enough for someone at the Tesseract to work out whether whatever had killed her had already been in her system by then, but that answer wasn't going to come quick. We had where the pod had picked her up, though, and that it had been called by an anonymous Servant. That narrowed things down.

A drone from Mercy buzzed overhead, noise lost in the hiss of rain. It pinged my Servant, dropped a pack of painkillers and buzzed away. My Servant started off on some lecture about the perils and side effects, addiction warnings, all the usual. I told it to shove it, ripped the packet open and swallowed two tabs. Rangesh sent Shyla's pod to the Tesseract to be picked apart. Then we headed off in the one that had brought me here to wherever it was Shyla had been picked up. Once we were moving Rangesh turned to me, back with his toothy smile.

'The Flem told us you were coming in from Earth. Then suddenly we had Laws for a couple of weeks. So it's totally cool you're here, because Laws is already driving me and Esh completely wild, but never mind that. Then he pings me again this morning and says you'll be coming out to Mercy. So, uh, right. Um. Here we are. I'm Bix, man, and it's good to meet you and stuff.'

'Laws?'

'Yeah. You know. Laws. Laura. Agent Patterson.' He frowned. 'You know, I've totally heard your name before somewhere. Did you, like, do something? Like, years ago?' He frowned a lot and then held out a hand for me to shake. 'This is what you do on Earth, right?'

Rainwater pooled quietly around our feet, dripping off us onto the floor of the pod. I didn't take his hand. 'I'm Magentan, Rangesh. I was on secondment.'

He took back his hand and laughed. 'Well that's something like a relief, I guess. Esh is from Earth. She does weird stuff like that sometimes. Freaks Laws out.'

The pod turned round and came back past Mercy the other way. The barrage thrum of the rain on its carbon polymer skin stopped as we drove into the undercity tunnels. I hadn't really missed the rain while I was gone. Guess I was going to have to get used to it again.

I checked the pod's autopilot. We were heading towards the Squats. Not the sort of place for a rich girl like Shyla Thiekis, but then again this was Magenta, not Earth. I had to remember that. Keep reminding myself. The Squats might be close to the worst Firstfall had to offer, but they were no more dangerous than the warren under Gibraltar City.

'My great-grandfather came to Magenta from Mumbai

39

eighty-seven years ago, you know, part of the great construction wave. He's like a hundred and something now.' Rangesh
laughed. 'Spends half his time going on about how horrible
Magenta is and how great things used to be on Earth, and the
other half saying how everyone on Earth is starving and poor
and how everything's dirty and broken and we should all be so
grateful that he decided to come out here and go through all
that suffering for the rest of us ... So, what's it like, man?'

Firstfall had plenty of warrens. Nico and Disappointment
were the same. Magenta's weather drove us underground. The
Squats weren't so bad. I just couldn't see why someone like
Shyla Thiekis would have been there.

'Dude?'

'What?'

'Earth, man. What's it like?'

I didn't know how to even begin with an answer to that.
'Big,' I said, eventually. 'Not like this. It just goes on and on
and on. You ever want to get lost, Agent Rangesh, go to Earth.'

I guess that wasn't what he was looking for but it shut him
up long enough for the pod to get us to where we were going.
A tenement cavern, a three-dimensional maze of low-rent apart-
ments, bot service bays and hydroponic processors. I got out
and sucked at the air, wincing as I straightened, waiting for the
painkillers to kick in. One look was all I needed. Everything
here was cleaner and bigger and better cared for than in the
Gibraltar warrens, and Earth had far worse places than that.

'Your great-grandfather is right,' I said.

'About which?'

'Both.' Our pod had stopped on the exact spot where Thiekis
had been picked up. Soft illumination lit the cavern, acknow-
ledging our presence, letting us see, dissolving every shadow.
My Servant picked out a handful of surveillance cameras, gave
them my Tesseract codes and started streaming images to me.

Almost every inch of Firstfall had some camera or other trained on it. This was going to be easy.

'They sent him to Nico.' Rangesh paced the tunnel. A service bot hummed past. There weren't any people out, probably because it was the middle of the night when anyone with any sense was tucked up in bed and asleep.

A pair of hostess shells walked across the street, heading for a recharge bay. I yawned.

'Claims he had a hand in building half the city there, you know? Nico was just, like, a hole in the ground back then. They built it from nothing. Isn't that cool? I mean, think about it, dude. They were all from Mumbai. About a hundred of them, and they built a city. Isn't that awesome?'

In less than a minute I had footage from three different angles showing Thiekis getting into a pod. Wasn't hard to tell she was already in a bad way. There was a man with her. He looked like he was trying to help.

'Family stayed in Nico ever since.' Rangesh sat back in our pod, door open, feet hanging out. He laughed. 'It's like everyone is a relative. They all married each other and stuff and had these totally huge families.' He snorted. 'It's weird – they're such a bunch of racists! I mean, my great-grandfather was part of this wave of colonists, and now there's this whole thing with people coming from India to Disappointment on some corporate-sponsored government programme or something, and you'd think that would be totally great, but no, my grandparents are all, like, send them back, man, no space, darkies go home, and I'm all like, dudes, you really need to look in a mirror, you know! Some of these people are from the same city you were born in! And yeah, I know it's, like, this really big thing in Disappointment, protests and everything, but dudes! You live in Nico! You're, like, five thousand miles away! Shut *up* already!'

'You see them much? Your family?' I had the man's face.

The Tesseract was cleaning up the image, running it through recognition, giving it a name.

'When I can. It's hard sometimes, with the work and all, you know? I guess it sort of sucks that they pretty much stopped coming to Firstfall after the Loki bombing. I mean, the mag-lev was only out for a few months, and it was totally like a freak thing that is *never* going to happen again, but they're all, like, no way, man, no way we're riding on that any more, and the only other way is suborbital and …'

I guess that was about when Rangesh remembered where he'd heard my name. We shared a long awkward silence.

'I got a face,' I said. 'The last person to see Shyla Thiekis before she reached Mercy.'

'Yeah.'

'So now we just need the Tesseract to give us a name.'

'No need, man.' Rangesh shook his head. 'That's Jannos Threwer. One of the Shah's stringers. I kind of know him.'

4

JANNOS

The mag-lev from Firstfall to Disappointment runs between a hundred and five thousand feet below Magenta's surface. It's the best part of three thousand miles long and it's dead straight. Rangesh had it right – without the mag-lev the only way to get between Magenta's major cities is to go suborbital. You can fly lower if you want, but no one with any sense would make a habit of it, because if a storm catches you then that's the end, and Magenta has a lot of storms, and besides, mag-lev trains go faster than anything could fly here.

The tunnels are sealed and pumped empty. There are daily passenger services, but mostly the trains carry cargo, and in pure vacuum can top a thousand miles an hour. On May Day 2211 an Entropist calling himself Loki set off a bomb at Pumping Station 12, approximately halfway between Firstfall and Disappointment, where the trains run their fastest. The tunnel vented without warning, directly to the Magentan atmosphere. The fail-safe backup did its job, but the overnight freight from Firstfall was less than three miles away, and five seconds just wasn't enough time to stop. The tunnel went from vacuum to a full atmosphere of pressure in moments. The train might as well have hit a wall. The supersonic shock wave shredded it, spewing the remains into super-heated plasma that vaporised the front and turned the insides of what was left into an inferno. Everything on board was destroyed. The tunnel was closed for three months. It took them that long to get in and repair it.

Magenta had woken up to the news and breathed a collective sigh of relief that it had been an automated freight train. A few hours later and it would have been the overnight sleeper and the worst accident in Magenta's history. It took a couple of days before anyone realised there had been stowaways. Four, according to the people who saw them, some guy at the freight terminus and a woman who was going to go with them but changed her mind. That was all we had to go on because there wasn't anything left in the tunnel but ash. The bomber claimed he hadn't meant to kill anyone. Maybe I even believed him. But I'm still not sorry that someone shanked him.

'I'm really sorry, man. Totally gutted.' The pod was taking us to where the Tesseract thought Jannos Threwer was going to be. Bureau records had him registered as a private investigator, which explained the anonymous Servant thing. When a Servant talks to a Servant they exchange codes. The codes tie them to whoever owns them, so you always know who sourced any contact. Privacy laws mean you can go anonymous if you want, but security laws mean there's a second code that people like me and the Tesseract can get to, so that even if you thought you were hidden, you're not. People who want to get round that generally go the easy way – create a false identity and then link Servants to fictional people who don't physically exist. That's illegal and I get to arrest you for it. Killing the hidden code isn't, but it takes knowing a cracksman who can hack a Servant and then trusting him not to do anything else while he's in there – believe me on this, you do *not* want someone else taking control of your Servant. But I can't arrest anyone for not having a hidden code, so that's the way types like Threwer like to go.

'You know this guy?' I asked.

'Kind of.' Rangesh hadn't stopped clutching his head and tearing at his hair since we got back into the pod. 'Oh, man, I'm such an idiot. It was, like, right there in front of me. I *knew* when I saw your name that I'd heard it before.' He stopped for a moment and looked at me like he was trying to read the answer off my face. 'Keon. That's, like, from the South Pacific or something, right?'

'Hawaii.' I think.

'Cool. Yeah, the moment the Flem sent out the word, I was, like, I totally know that name, but I never looked it up because, you know, stuff and reasons ... I think it's uncool to go picking through some guy's past and finding out everything about him before you meet him, because if you do that, when you *do* meet you have all these preconceptions and assumptions and you think he's going to be a certain way and then he's not and it's all, like, disorientating and makes the wrong, you know ... impressions and stuff. I don't know, man. It's just better to see another human being for what they really are, right there in front of you, don't you think?'

I was starting to wonder if Rangesh had an off switch. 'Threwer. You knew it was him all along, right?'

'No, I just did the same thing you did. Only, like, quicker ... Look, man, I don't really know him, but I know his face. He's clean enough.'

Clean or not, I pulled his records. Mostly I wanted to know who he'd been talking to that night. Turned out to be not so easy with his Servant set up the way it was.

'I remember it, man. When the news came. I remember waking

up the morning after and there it was.' Rangesh was actually still for a moment. 'I knew it. I knew straight away there were going to be people dead. There were always stowaways on the overnight freights. I'd kind of known for years but I didn't see the harm, you know? And Temo was a solid dude. So yeah ... But I could have stopped it, that was the thing. Had to walk away and not look. Just had to. And then it came out. One of our own. I'm really sorry, man. You guys were married, right?'

I had the records of every Servant interaction coming out from the Squats around the time Threwer put Shyla in her pod. It was just a case of binning everything that definitely wasn't him and then trying to track back in time and space until I caught an incoming call. Pig of a job. Took a lot of concentrating. Which was fine. Tuning Rangesh out wasn't a problem for me at all.

Liss would have aced this sort of thing.

'But what was she doing on the train, man? I mean, it was, like, part of some case, right? Had to be. I mean, I don't want to pry or anything but—'

'Then don't.' Why had Alysha been on that train? I'd asked myself the same question for five years. 'You ever find out, you let me know. Until then take a look at this.' I pinged Rangesh the track I'd made of Threwer's anonymous Servant, laid over a map of Firstfall. 'Look at the way he's moving. He's going straight for her. Who's Temo?'

'Temo Kadavu, man. The guy who smuggled them onto the train. Worked at the Firstfall freight terminus. Thought you'd know.'

'I know squat. I wasn't part of the investigation and I wasn't allowed to see their work. By the time they closed it, I was on Earth. What they sent me was ... It wasn't much.' Laughable is what it was, and it grated with me even now that they'd never let me see more. Personal involvement, standard protocol to keep me out of the loop, but they could at least have sent me what they'd found when they were done. I'd followed the news reports, but that was all I ever got to see. Temo Kadavu. Now I had a name. A place to start.

We were in a busier part of the Squats, dim-lit tunnels around a nocturnal highway of clubs and bars and cheap fast automated restaurants serving a hundred and one different variations of lichen, seaweed, mushroom and pig.

'He was tracking her, man.' Rangesh pinged me a sequence of Servant records. Enki Betleshah had called Jannos Threwer fifteen minutes before Threwer reached Shyla. The track started right after the call, from Jannos's apartment.

'So Threwer was at home. Betleshah calls him and he goes straight out looking for Thiekis.' I shrugged. We'd find out the why soon enough.

We left the Squats, heading into Earthtown. Gaudy neon flashed by as I flipped through Channel Six's gleeful coverage from Mercy.

... speculation abounds as to whether this is the result of yet more overcharged and over-the-top escapades last night at the mansion residence of Enki Betleshah, Channel Nine's infamous political commentator and frequent occupant of Firstfall libel courts, or whether Shyla's admission is related to recent revelations of an affair with Betleshah's Channel Nine boss Rashid Mangat. Whatever it is, the thoughts of everyone here at Channel Six are with you, Shy ...

Right. I flipped to Channel Six's social feed.

... Long-time partner of maverick journalist Enki Betleshah and daughter of Channel Nine chairman Eddie Thiekis, Shyla Thiekis is no stranger to Mercy Hospital's rehabilitation centre. Thiekis senior has yet to comment, but tensions at Channel Nine between the autocratic station owner and his out-of-control star journalist have long run high. Is this the end for the maverick Shah? Is this what finally pushes Eddie over the edge?

47

The core newscast was full of interactive links to older reports: Thiekis's many flirtations with rehabilitation, their subsequent failures, other times the police had come to Betleshah's mansion, him being led away for questioning, a public outburst from Eddie Thiekis after some other time his daughter ended up in Mercy, Betleshah in court being sued for defamation, an old sweepstake on how long they'd last as a couple, which one of them would implode first, who was going to die and when. A new sweepstake had sprung up on whether she was going to last the night. A woman had died and somewhere out there someone was already making money from it. That was Channel Six for you.

Is this what finally pushes Eddie over the edge? I tried to put myself in Eddie Thiekis's shoes, hearing about the loss of his daughter and then seeing all of this. It didn't take long to figure out that, yes, it just might do the trick, if by pushing him over the edge you meant having him cluster-bomb his rival station.

'Anyone tell Eddie that his daughter is dead yet?' I asked.

'Mercy are still trying to reach him.'

'Get the Tesseract to do it.'

Our pod hummed to a stop outside a cave mouth. A bright neon sign declared this to be the entrance to the Cavern Bar. If the Tesseract had it right, this was where we'd find Jannos Threwer. The roadside hawkers – the human ones – took one look at our bureau Servant identities and shuffled purposefully away. The shells and the vending bots didn't know any better and came clustering around the pod as soon as we got out, offering cigarettes, kale smoothies, low-grade legal gens and plenty of porn. A deluge of electronic spam hit my Servant, trying everything right up to the edge of legal and a little beyond to project their sales pitches onto my lenses. I could have laughed. Compared to places I'd been on Earth, the hawker shells and the bots of the Squats were like a cluster of old ladies politely inviting me to tea.

We found Threwer propping up the counter in the Cavern Bar. He looked ragged and drunk and not surprised to see us.

'Bix Rangesh?' He looked Rangesh up and down. 'I've heard of you.'

'I guess you know why I'm here then.' Rangesh grimaced. 'Look, man … Jannos … it's been a pretty heavy night. Me and the Shyster and the Shah, we all go back a way, and I guess you and Shah go back a way too, right? And so you don't much want to say anything that's going to get anyone into any trouble. But tonight you need to talk to me, man. It hasn't broken yet, but the Shyster's dead.'

Threwer didn't look too surprised. I told him so. He shrugged.

'Wasn't hard to see she was in a bad way.' He pushed a glass at me. 'Have a drink, agent.'

I passed. Rangesh should have passed too, but he sat with Threwer and sipped seaweed spirit and got tipsy as he coaxed the story out. Mostly I let myself fade into the background, taking in the Cavern. I'd been down to the Squats often enough over the years, but never to this place. It was close to empty, the host and hostess shells clustered around the bar waiting for something to do. It was one of those dark holes where people come to get drunk alone. I used to wonder why anyone would do that. Why not stay at home? But I know now that there are times when home is worse, when that's what you're running from. Yeah, I reckoned I'd learned a thing or two about that these last few years.

The painkillers were taking hold. The aches in my back had turned to a gentle tingle and a mildly pleasant buzz behind my eyes.

'You bundled her into a pod and left her, man!'

'What was I supposed to do? Go with her?'

'She was dying!'

'What difference would it have made?'

The Cavern was like a sea of darkness around us. Rangesh and Threwer became an island, me sitting on the shore with my toes in the surf. Threwer's anguish sounded real enough. The way he told it he'd worked for Betleshah on and off for years, freelancing, rooting around for whatever dirt he could get hold of, one of maybe half a dozen stringers Channel Nine kept on retainer. He and Betleshah got on OK but nothing special, their relationship cordial and professional and nothing more. I didn't quite buy it. He was taking Shyla Thiekis's death too hard for it not to mean something.

Or maybe he just thought it was going to come back to him somehow. Hard to tell.

Close up like this, I could get into his Servant records, anonymous or not. I had a good look at his history while he was talking. First thought was to see whether he and Thiekis had any connection he wasn't remembering to share. Thought I'd found one too, but it was the name that fooled me. Thiekis, yes, but not Shyla. Eddie. Betleshah's boss. I rummaged around while he and Rangesh talked on but didn't find much else. Betleshah had invited him to parties now and then. Threwer had refused. His Servant backed him up on that, and it backed him on his story for the night too: that the first he'd known anything was wrong was when he'd taken a call from Betleshah asking him to find Shyla. Betleshah had sounded wasted but scared too and said it was urgent. So Threwer had gone to pick her up, expecting to take her home and for that to be that but when he'd found her bleeding and hardly able to stand he'd put her in a pod and sent her to Mercy as a medical emergency instead. Done the right thing. Couldn't really fault him.

When he was finished, I leaned in close.

'What's with you and Eddie Thiekis, Jannos?'

Threwer gave me a bitter look. 'Eddie wanted to know what

the Shah was up to. He came to most of us, I think. Anyone the Shah trusted.'

'What did you tell him?'

'What did I tell Eddie about last night? Nothing yet. He doesn't know.' Threwer sized me up. 'Look ... Agent Rause, is it? We had an agreement. Me and the others Eddie came to. We made sure he knew what he was going to see about his daughter on Channel Six before it broke. That was all. It was enough.'

I didn't see how whatever he might have been up to behind Betleshah's back had anything to do with Shyla Thiekis being dead in Mercy so I let it lie. 'Don't tell him she's dead. Don't tell anyone. Leave that to us.'

Rangesh rambled on some more and then we left. Turned out we'd been in the Cavern longer than I thought. The lights in the tunnels were starting to come up. On the surface somewhere above, dawn was coming.

'I don't see him as a poisoner,' I said as we climbed back into our pod. 'Tell me about Betleshah. You know him too?'

Rangesh shook his head. 'I knew the Shyster years back.' The pod pulled away. 'Disappointment University. Same classes, you know. She was crazy wild. Never changed. And she was awesome, man. There used to be, like, parties that went on for days. She had money and she didn't care. We all left in the end and went our different ways, you know, but she held these reunions now and then, and the old crowd would all show up – everyone – because we all knew what was coming. You couldn't say no, dude. One year she turned up with the Shah. No one had heard of him back then but he was as wild as they come. Put the rest of us to shame.' He laughed. 'So I know the Shah, but I don't *know* him, yeah? People say he got where he is because of her, because of her money, because Eddie ran the channel, but it wasn't like that. The Shah earned it, you know? Got his ... Ah, man! That's not good!' He didn't wait for me to

51

ask before he pinged me a link to Channel Six. It was out that Shyla was dead. 'Dude, did you tell the Tesseract to go public?'

I shook my head. 'Threwer,' I said.

'No, he wouldn't.' Rangesh punched his palm. 'Got to have been someone at Mercy. Man! I don't know if Eddie even knows yet.'

Rangesh putting a lid on it had bought us a couple of hours. We'd blown them with Threwer. I tried to imagine how I'd have felt if the first I'd heard of Alysha's death had been through a Channel Six newsflash. I would have felt like murdering someone.

'Alysha used to follow Channel Six,' I said. 'She used to watch them now and then and take their newscasts.' I never saw the point. Just people. The rich, the famous, the ugly, the clever, the stupid, the desperate, the stand-outs. If you wanted to know who was having sex with whom and how, you went to Channel Six for the answer. Some agents used it for exactly that. Alysha had maintained contacts there, but I couldn't be doing with them. There was something sordid about Channel Six which infected everything they touched. Then again, I watched the reality shows. I guess if you poke hard enough, none of us makes much sense. 'I'll bet Eddie Thiekis watches them too.'

'Has to, man. He hates them.'

'So he's going to know, right? You told the Tesseract to tell him, yes?'

The pod emerged from the tunnels of the Squats into the pre-dawn of Firstfall central. There were people on the streets now – not many, but a handful. Most were shells. The late shift going back to recharge, the morning security and reception shells starting up before the flesh-and-bone people got out of bed. The rain had stopped but not the wind, surly and erratic, scudding iron-grey shreds of cloud low overhead. We shot through empty streets, switched onto an arterial road and picked up speed fast, heading out of town.

'Laws isn't answering but I got through to Esh.' Rangesh swore as a squall of rain battered us, there and gone in a few seconds. The suburbs of Firstfall flashed by, a blur of shapes and shades of grey outside the pod window. The blur crept inside my head. 'Esh is on her way to Channel Nine. Eddie already knows, but she's going anyway. Personal touch, you know? You meet Esh, you're going to think she's the last to do this sort of thing, but trust me, she has more skills than she seems. She knows what it's like.'

Esh. Agent Esharaq Zohreya. Now I got it. I was too slow for this, lack of sleep and too much gravity making me miss things. 'We already met.'

'Could be Eddie's not even in system, you know.' Rangesh shrugged.

'We need to know what poisoned Shyla,' I said. 'Where and when and how so we can know if anyone else is at risk. I'll have Mercy send us an alert if anything similar comes in.'

'It's not the gens, man. Gens don't do that.'

'Could be something they're cut with.'

You learn early on as an agent never to jump to a conclusion. I didn't know for sure that Shyla Thiekis had been dying when Jannos Threwer put her in that pod, and I wouldn't until the Tesseract came back with some forensic chemistry; but my gut told me she was. It wasn't hard to track her last hours. She'd left Betleshah's mansion before midnight, taken a pod to the Squats, got out and then walked for a while until Threwer found her. I had nothing else. No calls, no contacts, no interactions. Nothing to suggest that anyone had stopped her or spoken to her in the five minutes between getting out of her pod and Threwer finding her. Whatever was in her system, I was pretty sure she'd carried it with her from Betleshah's party.

The pod shuddered as another squall hit us with a wall of wind. Sunrise cracked the horizon behind us, violet dawn light oozing over the cityscape, casting everything into impassioned shadow, stark black and white.

'Storm season, man,' murmured Rangesh.

'I used to live here, remember?'

The road raced through the outer fringes of the city and on into the featureless nothing and nowhere of the Firstfall Plateau and the spider's web of mines, wind farms and hydroponic caverns that ringed the city. A little way out we slowed and left the road, diverting onto a fused-glass track towards a slightly obscene rock formation that Enki Betleshah had hollowed out and turned into his home. Another pod passed us coming the other way. There was no one else about, and Betleshah's mansion was the only place out here so I threw my Tesseract codes at it, ordering it to stop. The pod sped past regardless, claiming diplomatic immunity. I got the occupants. Two junior Fleet officers from the Firstfall embassy.

Rangesh stared after the pod in disbelief.

'Get someone on them.' Split-second choice. Follow or not. I chose not. 'Find out who they are. Get a request to the embassy for an explanation. Stop them if you can find a way.' We were investigating a drug overdose, so what were Fleet doing here? 'Get a timeline on them. Where and when. And I want a snapshot of every communication out of Mercy and out of the Tesseract between when they left the Fleet embassy and the time Shyla Thiekis died.' Which was like asking to search a haystack which might or might not have a needle in it, but whoever was in that pod had left to come out here before Channel Six broke the news that Shyla was dead. Could have been a coincidence but I didn't believe much in those.

Rangesh nodded. 'I'll get Esh on it, boss dude.' He was grinning. I had no idea why.

I turned my attention back to Betleshah's mansion and to the reason I'd let the pod go. Standing in the doorway was

Betleshah himself, dishevelled, drunk and half-wrapped in a robe that wasn't hiding very much. It certainly wasn't hiding the gun he was holding.

5

EDDIE AND THE SHAH

I hadn't been to the Tesseract yet so I didn't have my sidearm. Rangesh had one, but he wasn't doing anything useful with it. He got out of the pod and stood in the gateway of Betleshah's mansion.

'Hey, Enki! Dude!'

There wasn't much space for vanity on a world like Magenta. There were pockets that didn't get hit by storms every few weeks, but Firstfall wasn't one of them. Everything above the surface was squat and blocky. If you were rich enough or stupid enough to bring trees or animals or plants from Earth, you put them inside a biome. The only things that survived in the open were rock and the native lichen-like xeno-organisms that ate it, except for up in the mid-latitudes where the air was still and eerie and the landscape was covered in freezing tundra and forests of xenoferns.

That said, Betleshah had given it a good try. He'd built his mansion inside a natural protrusion jutting from the landscape and extended it here and there with walls made of striated slabs

56

of different-coloured stone, locked together like an intricate jigsaw. The outcrop even had windows, a rarity on Magenta, although that was mostly because there was never anything much to look at. The storm shutters were open and a dim light filtered out. A wide path of smooth fused stone led from the road to the cave-like front entrance through a walled rock garden, past stones of different shapes and colours laid out in some carefully arranged pattern. A Japanese zen garden maybe, wounded by the revels of the night. Long scrapes scarred the gravel. Dark holes showed where rocks had been picked up and moved.

'Bix? Bix Rangesh?' Enki waved the gun vaguely around his head. He was drunk and probably worse. I pinged his Servant for an assessment of his medical status but didn't get an answer. He'd turned it off.

'Hey, man.' Rangesh headed up the path through the garden, slow and casual but with caution. 'Dude, could you maybe put the illegal firearm down or else give it to me before something really heavy happens? It's making my new partner all kinds of nervous.'

I jumped out of the pod and my legs almost buckled under Magenta's gravity. Mercy's painkillers had made me forget how fragile I was.

Rangesh didn't take his eyes off Betleshah. 'Enks! Dude! Who were those other guys?'

'What? You shitting me, Bix?' The gun was still in his hand. My skin crawled with the tension, even if he wasn't pointing it at anything much. Rangesh kept on up the path, one slow step at a time. 'You don't even know your own any more?'

Step, step. 'Don't know what you mean, dude.' *Bix*. Betleshah had called Rangesh by his first name. Didn't sound like they hardly knew each other.

'More of your bureau arseholes, *dude*.'

'Nah.' Step, step. 'Not us, Enks. They sell you that, did they? Those were Fleet men, my friend, and I'd totally like to know what they wanted. You know, if that's cool.' Step.

'Fleet?'

I swear I'd have shot him by now, but as it was, there wasn't anything for me to do except call for backup and crouch beside the gates at the end of the path. I pinged Rangesh: What are you doing? This isn't protocol! Get him to put the gun down!

Rangesh stopped in front of Betleshah and held out his hand. 'Yeah, man. Fleet. So ... you want to give me the gun now?' Be cool. I got this.

'They said Shy was dead.'

'Yeah, well, I guess people say a lot of things. Doesn't make them true. The gun, dude.'

Anyone who did this in training, anyone who even joked about it, they'd flunk straight out, but Rangesh pulled it off. Betleshah opened his hand, offering the gun. Rangesh took it and that was that, and he didn't even bat an eyelid. No forcing Betleshah onto the floor to search for other weapons, just carried on as though nothing had happened and walked on into the house. He looked at me over his shoulder as he did.

'Hey, Rause! The Shah's cool. No worries, man. You're not on Earth any more.'

I followed them in. The hall past the door was a litter of paper streamers, broken glass, a few scattered trophies and two snoring bodies. The air reeked of gens while the walls were clad in black marble slabs which could only have been imported from Earth, a luxury which had surely cost more than most Magentans could afford in a lifetime. Soft-glow panels embedded in the walls and ceiling gave out a gentle light. I tried to imagine how the hall had looked before the party. The carnage of broken glass had been a trophy cabinet once, judging by the statuettes that lay scattered in the corners.

Rangesh made the gun safe and put it down carefully away from the sleepers. 'They were telling the truth about Shy. She's dead, man. I'm so sorry.'

The look on Enki Betleshah's face was the look I'd seen in the mirror after Alysha died. I knew right there and then: whatever had happened to Shyla Thiekis, Betleshah hadn't killed her, not on purpose, but he was still as guilty as hell, and he knew it.

He slumped. Rangesh went to offer him an arm but Betleshah slapped him away. An alarm went off in my Servant, an alert from the house, demanding that everyone get out, leave and take everything with them. I cancelled it.

'Sorry,' I said, 'but we need to question everyone who was here last night.'

'Why?' Betleshah didn't look at me.

Rangesh made a face. 'Looks like she was poisoned, dude.'

'Poisoned?'

I took another look around the hall. Noises rose from the stairwell down to the lower levels. Two people grunting. My Servant told me there were another twenty-seven guests scattered through Betleshah's mansion, most of them unconscious and registering low-amber medical alerts for gens and alcohol. I took their names and everything I could find about who they were. 'We need somewhere we can talk,' I said. 'Probably for quite a long time.'

'I want my attorney,' said Betleshah. He looked at Rangesh for a long hard second, then back at me. 'Yeah. Before I say another word. I've called him. I have some good ones. You know that, right?'

'Look, man, I know Shy was here.' Rangesh closed the front door and leaned against it. He slid down and squatted there, head held in his hands. 'I tracked her Servant, man. Sort of thing we do all the time.' He looked around. 'Bit of a party, huh? Shy all over. I knew her before you ever did, so I'm guessing

59

she was wasted. But I guess that was pretty normal too, huh? I mean, not something you'd call Jannos about, right? So there was something else. Because you did call him, and I already talked to him, and I know he went out and tracked her down right after. When he found her he put her in a pod for Mercy. They couldn't save her. So, uh, you want to tell us what that was all about?'

The grunts from downstairs reached a climax. Betleshah stared at me. Right through me.

'Not without my attorney,' he said.

'Aw, man! You got to be that way? Then I'm going to need all your house Servant's records for last night, dude. Sorry.'

I picked up one of the scattered trophies and looked at it. journalist of the year, 2214, channel nine. 'Every log,' I said. 'Every interaction, all the security camera footage, everything. Everything that happened, we're going to see it.' I looked at Betleshah hard, but I couldn't hold his eye when he looked back. I knew the pain I saw there too well.

He laughed. 'How stupid do you think I am? Help yourself. I shut the house down last night, same as I always do. My parties are private. My guests know that. So by all means take a look.' He pinged me what turned out to be an access code for the house. I checked but he wasn't making it up: there were no records for six hours from yesterday evening and on into the night. When I looked further I found the same gap every few months. Could have been faked, but it probably wasn't.

'I'm going to need to freeze your Servant anyway,' I said. Betleshah shrugged.

'Do what you must. And look, I don't know you, Agent ... Rause, is it? But I know Rangesh. Taking gens isn't illegal. Maybe some things happened last night that you don't like, but if they did then I didn't know anything about them, and since I turned the house off and I can't be everywhere at once, you won't be able to prove otherwise. I protect the privacy of my guests because that's important to me, and you're going to think I'm being obstructive and that I've got something to hide, and so I'm telling you right up front that yes I am, and yes I have, but it's not *my* secrets I'm guarding. I protect my friends. I'll tell you whatever else I can. I don't care what happens to me, but no one here would have hurt Shy.'

'So you're going to tell us what you think we need to know but not what you think we don't?' I asked. 'You expect that to fly?'

Rangesh slid back up the door. He shot me a look. 'Hey, Rause, man, you think I could have a little word with the Shah? You know ... like, in private?'

'Are you kidding me?'

'She was here last night.' Rangesh cocked his head at Betleshah. 'You're not going to pretend you don't know, right? I mean, you sent Jannos ...'

Betleshah nodded. 'Things were ... tense between us.'

'That piece Channel Six ran?'

'We were trying to fix it.'

'By getting wasted?'

'Yeah, man, by getting wasted.' Betleshah couldn't hide his exasperation any more than he could hide his grief. 'Look, Bix, no one here poisoned Shyla. No one would want to. She got trashed. Like she always did only worse than usual. Way worse. When I found she'd gone I ... I don't know. Yeah, I called Jannos. Call it a bad feeling. But look, if I'd had any idea then I'd have taken her to Mercy myself. She was doing gens, Bix, that was all, same as the rest of us, and I didn't like the idea of her wandering off to who-knows-where completely out of her head. But she doesn't do the hard-core Earth stuff any more so I didn't think she was in any trouble, not really. I was just ... I was afraid she might hurt herself, I guess.' He slumped to the floor and tipped back his head, staring up past the ceiling into an imagined sky. 'Since when do people die from gens?'

There was a pause. I couldn't be sure, but I watched their eyes, both of them. They were pinging messages back and forth. Stuff they didn't want me to know.

'I think we'd better get you and your attorney down to the Tesseract for ...' I stopped. Rangesh had frozen, mouth half open. That look people have when they've got incoming on their Servant and have switched off the real world. 'Rangesh!'

He shook himself. 'Dude! This is bad.' He copied me in on a series of messages.

Bix? Where are you?

With the Shah.

No luck getting through to Eddie Thiekis. He's not answering. But I put a trace on his Servant. He's heading your way. I can't get to you before him.

How long?

Couple of minutes.

Thanks Esh.

'Sorry, man.' Rangesh tossed a pair of cuffs to Betleshah. 'Eddie's on his way. Got to take you in. Your own safety. You know what Eddie's like.'

Taking Betleshah in for a proper interrogation sounded fine to me. I'd have had the whole lot of them back in the Tesseract given half an excuse, but I wasn't properly paperworked up as lead on Rangesh's team, not yet, and so I had no real weight here. Besides, I was beginning to get the idea that Flemich had sent me along to see how Rangesh worked as much as anything else. I'd let him play it his way then. See how it panned out.

'Can't do that, Bix.' Betleshah wasn't having it. 'I got friends here. People to look after. You want to take me in, you get yourself an order to charge me. By the time you come back with that I'll have the house cleared and a dozen cameras recording everything you do. We'll have a story out within an hour. Tesseract agents harass grieving widower. You know how it goes.'

'Man!' Rangesh screwed up his face. 'You think you can pull that off? After everything you've done? Shy's dead, and everyone knows—'

'I don't give a shit what everyone knows! You want to take me anywhere, Bix, you take me to see her.'

I shook my head. 'That's not—'

'Sure,' said Rangesh. 'We can do that. If that's what you want.'

No, we couldn't. I pinged Rangesh: They sent her to the Tesseract. They'll be cutting her open by now trying to see what killed her.

I know.

Then what are you doing?

Getting him out of here.

One of the comatose bodies sprawled over the hall floor stirred. Betleshah looked at the statuette I was holding. 'That was for exposing Selected Representative Siamake Alash for taking Fleet bribes last year. I don't think you need to bring it with you, Agent Rause.' He shrugged at Rangesh. 'Go on, then. Take me to see her before the cameras get here. But I'm not going in cuffs. You know there's going to be a dozen Channel Six drones up there already, right? Filming everything the moment we step out the door?'

Idle curiosity and a lingering dislike of the way Fleet had kicked me off Gibraltar sent my Servant digging after Siamake Alash. Rangesh walked Betleshah to the door.

'I'm really sorry, man. Shy didn't deserve to go out like this.'

'She was heading for a crash. She always was. You know that as well as I do.'

Our pod waited at the end of the path. I lingered as Rangesh and Betleshah left, casting my Servant around the house as best I could, poking into whatever data crevices weren't locked tight, which didn't amount to much. Liss was better at that sort of thing. It bothered me more and more that she was offline.

Rause!

Rangesh and Betleshah were halfway down the path. At the far end, in the gateway, stood Eddie Thiekis. He had a particle beam aimed at Betleshah's head. Rangesh stood between them with his hands up.

I pinged Eddie but got nothing.

'Get out of the way! That son of a bitch killed my daughter!' He was shaking.

Rangesh!

Stay chill. 'Eddie! This isn't the way, man!'

Betleshah pushed Rangesh aside. 'You want to shoot me, Eddie? I didn't kill her, you stupid prick. *You* did!'

I ran inside and snatched Betleshah's gun from where Rangesh had dropped it. It wasn't loaded any more, but Eddie Thiekis wasn't to know that. A man sleeping on the floor opened one bloodshot eye and stared. I knew that look. High on gens. I ignored him and went to the doorway, half in, half out, where Eddie would see me. I levelled Betleshah's pistol at his chest.

'Eddie Thiekis! Put the gun down!'

'I got this, dude,' said Rangesh. 'Chill out, man. We all need to chill out.'

Eddie switched his aim to Rangesh. 'Chill out? My daughter's dead because this prick wouldn't let her stay clean, you arsehole!'

'Put the gun down!' I yelled. So much for a quiet first day.

'Dude! Look, man, I guess maybe you don't remember, but me and Shy go way back to Disappointment. I know she was special, man. Thing is, my partner here, he just came in from Earth, and they do things kind of different there, and it would bum us both out if he had to shoot you. I mean, that would just suck, right? But he will if you don't give him a choice.' Rangesh took a couple more steps. I walked out as he did, using him and Betleshah as cover. Betleshah kept stepping sideways from behind Rangesh like he was going out of his way to make himself a target.

'Go on then, Eddie. Shoot me! We both know you've wanted to fire me for years. So just do it! Get on with it. Let the world watch!'

I tackled Betleshah from behind and pinned him to the ground and then crouched over him, holding my unloaded gun on Eddie and gasping for air. The gravity was killing me and my knees felt ready to buckle with every step. If Eddie was a half-decent shot then I probably wasn't going to be able to stop him from killing Betleshah if that was what he decided to do, and if his Servant was running any sort of targeting wares then I was wasting my time even trying.

Rangesh stopped ten feet short of Eddie. He lowered his hands. Using slow and careful movements he drew his own weapon and pointed it at Eddie's face.

'Man, you don't want to do this. You know how it goes. The moment the word got out about Shy there were drones in the air. Good chance Channel Six had one watching the house already, you know, just in case? Maybe they keep one on station all the time. It would be their kind of thing, don't you think? So this is probably all, like, going out live-streamed right here.' Rangesh shrugged, then looked up and scanned the sky. Waved. 'Hey, Channel Six. You dudes know we all think you're a factory full of wankers, right?' He turned back to Eddie. 'So, like, my partner, he has that old slug thrower because it's his first day. And I have this stunner. And I could use it, and then everyone would see the top dude of Channel Nine twitching on the ground, helpless and humiliated. Six would wet themselves for that, right? They'd play it over and over. Or you can shoot me, or you can shoot the Shah, and then my partner puts an old-fashioned bullet through you, and all of it with the world watching. Or you can do the right thing, man, and put the gun down. You know? Just back away and get into your pod and go home. With dignity, and let that be what everyone sees. No one's going to stop you, Eddie, and so that's what's going to happen, because if you were going to shoot me then you'd have done it by now, but the thing is, you loved your daughter, and so did the Shah, and I liked her too, and you're a wise enough man to know all those things, and that what's best right now is to let my partner and me do our jobs the way it's supposed to be. We won't let you down, I can promise you that. More to the point, man, I won't let *her* down.'

It was a great speech. If I'd had a proper weapon, I'd have used it right around the part about Channel Six wetting themselves. But I didn't, and I also didn't have any bullets.

Eddie was shaking. Took me a moment to figure he was sobbing. Right there in front of us in the rain, breaking down. He lowered the gun and Rangesh ran to him. Not to tackle him to the ground and cuff him like he ought, but to wrap an arm around him and turn him away and hustle him back into his pod. The two of them sat together for a few moments before Rangesh got out again. I didn't hear what they said.

The pod pulled away.

'It's a sad thing, man.' Rangesh shook his head as he came back and looked up to the sky. 'You know, guys, you should really leave an old man to his grief. You have to have some standards, man. Somewhere you have to have some standards.' He stooped and helped Betleshah to his feet. 'Let's go, man. Got another squall coming in.'

*

66

It was raining hard and steady again by the time we got Betleshah to the Tesseract. I left a message for when Liss came back online, telling her she might as well trawl the Channel Six feed if she wanted to know how my morning had gone. The two Fleet men at Betleshah's house bothered me so I asked her to dig into that too, and what Fleet might have wanted from Siamake Alash, mostly because it was all I had. I left Rangesh with Betleshah – I think that arrangement suited us both – and got on with the basic paperwork I was supposed to do, sorting out my abrupt return to the bureau. Could have done half of it remotely from orbit while I was in therapy, but the bureau worked hands on, not trusting remote connections when it didn't have to. So there was that, and then a three-hour psych-eval, and then the Tesseract AI going bit by bit through my Servant to leave it as clean as the day it came out of the factory, which was why Liss hadn't ridden with me that morning.

They gave me my Reeper, the standard bureau-issue stunner-cum-slug-thrower, and made me prove I still knew how to use it. That took a bit longer than it should have on account of me having spent the last five years on Earth with a Fleet particle beam for a sidearm. By the time I came out we had the report on the drugs in Shyla's system. No sign of any known poisons, but the gens in her were some novelty engineered design, a base of Magentan lichen but with dozens of twists that were going to keep a whole lab full of quantum chemists busy for weeks, never mind working out what the end result actually did.

I pinged Rangesh.

You see this?

Already on it, man.

You think that's what killed her?

Don't like it, but got to work the theory.

I had to reckon the same. Anyone else from the party have it in them?

No idea.

Get samples! Now!

That's not the problem, man. Samples I got. But everyone has their lawyers out. I got maybe half to agree to be tested but even then I can't use the data. Can't even look unless someone else gets sick. It's, like, a privacy thing. Need a reason to invade it, man.

OK. So where did it come from?

Don't know yet, but I'm on it.

Need help?

No, I got this. A pause. Look, dude, we got a thing tomorrow morning. I know you got the Flem, but after would be cool. You want to meet Laws and Esh too, right? Anything new, I can give you then.

It suited me to leave him to it. Meant I could get on with other things, quiet and undisturbed. First thing I was going to do when I was back had always been take a good long look at the files in the Tesseract from the Loki case. When it was live they wouldn't let me close, not once they knew Alysha had been on the train, but little things had slipped out now and then. Agents I knew. Sympathetic friends. I figured enough time had passed that they'd let me in now. And so they did.

I went home and pored over the Loki files, the leads and the clues, everything that was new, which turned out not to be much. Liss sat beside me and pored over them too. I'd known about the other stowaways five years ago but I hadn't known who they were, and I hadn't known who had helped them board. Now I did. It was a start, I guess.

And then I went to bed because it had been a damned long day.

HALE WAVEY

Hale Wavey slips unseen through the corridors of the Tesseract. There are surveillance cameras everywhere here in the heart of the Magenta Investigation Bureau, but Hale Wavey doesn't worry about that because Hale Wavey is wearing a Masters' skin-suit stolen from the Gibraltar Tech-Fair three months ago. Invisibility has its limitations, like everything else, but it's good enough for this.

Hale's Servant cracks the access codes for the low-security level. He lets the suit do its work for the rest, tailgating the night patrols as they do their rounds, meticulously checking every room and so taking him anywhere and everywhere he could want to go. When they reach the secure zones they work in teams of three with a pair of drones watching over them, feeding back to the security citadel which towers over the entrance to the Tesseract, the only part of the building that rises more than a single storey above the ground. The deep secure bunkers will be a problem, if Hale ever needs to go to where the real secrets are kept, but today's task is a simple one.

Hale Wavey isn't real. He is a persona created for the purpose of this night alone, to be tossed away and burned as soon as his usefulness is done. The person who made Hale has a gift for making new identities. Tomorrow Hale Wavey will become someone else. A different name whenever one is needed, and Hale will vanish for ever.

The security patrol stops for a while outside the chemical synthesis labs. Hale stops too. They chat to an agent there. His name is Bix Rangesh. Rangesh is mucking about with chemical formulae, tinkering and then sniffing the results. Hale considers this. It doesn't seem something particularly clever or safe or within the protocols of any well-run laboratory.

Rangesh receives a message. The conversation stops and he leaves at once. Hale waits for the patrol to move on into the deep bowels of the Tesseract. They reach Accident Investigation. When they leave, Hale stays. He settles in front of a terminal. Physical access only, the rules of the Tesseract. Fingers and screen. A security precaution.

There are passwords too, but Hale has that covered.

First things first. Almost incidental to why Hale has broken the perimeter security of one of the most sensitive government buildings on Magenta, but since it's here, almost begging to be taken ...

File access: personnel records: Rause, Keon.

There won't be anything much, not the real dirt, but Hale Wavey already has that. What matters are the incidentals. The little things. The cornucopia of trivia with which a gifted cracksman can construct a virtual life, everything Keon's friends and colleagues might, in a pinch, somehow know. Hale takes all that the Tesseract is prepared to offer and dumps it to an untraceable data stack to be perused in the leisure of some later time.

Now the real reason Hale Wavey is here: May Day 2211. The Loki bombing. Possibly the worst criminal act in Magenta's recent history. Hard to be certain exactly who and how many died. Four, they said, but there wasn't enough left to be sure of anything.

A number is all Hale Wavey has come for. The code to a location in the underground labyrinthine warehouse outside Firstfall where the bureau keep their physical evidence, the place they call the Hotel of Lost Things. Hale gives the Tesseract AI a search request. The Tesseract, having no reason to refuse, returns with a reference and a location. Hale memorises it, shuts the terminal down and waits.

In time the next patrol comes round. Hale stands quietly out of the way and follows as they leave, all the way out into the darkness of the Firstfall night. In a quiet alley, Hale slips out of the cloak suit and silently ceases to be.

Kulpreet Anash walks away. She is a short and ageing Indian woman. She has existed for five seconds, but if anyone asks then her Servant will claim she's lived on Magenta for fifty years and has never left. Every day someone new, and now the only evidence that Hale Wavey ever existed at all is a single log entry, quickly lost in the Tesseract archives.

Search Request: Evidence location: Agent dogtags: Rause, Alysha.

TWO

SETTLEMENT 64

6

NEW GUY

I woke early. Liss was already out of her coffin. I hadn't slept well. Again. Two nights in a row now. Oppression by gravity.

'I'm going to come with you today,' she said. 'Now they've sterilised your Servant I can ride inside it again. I want to meet the people you work with.' I didn't argue. I had other things I wanted her to do, but they'd have to wait.

We talked about the day I'd had over breakfast. Alysha and I used to have a rule: we mined our own cases and didn't talk about work. If our professional paths crossed then we did whatever needed to be done, but we didn't bring it home. It was the only way to keep us sane, I suppose; but the stand-off with Eddie Thiekis had been all over Channel Six, and it wasn't as though Liss had had anything else to do but follow the fallout. The gossip streams and celebrity forums that busied themselves with that sort of thing were all over the story. Mostly they were after Betleshah, dredging through his past and bringing it all up again, but the Thiekis family was getting attention too, and on the side so were we. I found a handful of sub-chats dedicated to

Rangesh with titles like 'Right on! Bureau agent tells it like it is! Six needs to grow up,' or 'That guy should be sacked,' or just 'Who's the hot bureau agent? Phew!' I even had one of my own: wasn't I that agent who'd been married to that other agent, you know, the one who died?

I answered that myself. Yes. Then I told Liss all about Rangesh, what I made of him, what he was like to work with, and then I told her about the stowaways. We farmed the gossip streams for Betleshah's history. Affairs, a history of gen use and other drugs too, designer molecules smuggled in from Earth – not that we got much of that here. Magenta's traffic mostly went the other way in that regard; half the bureau's work was stopping gen shipments going off-world.

'This is what I want to do today,' Liss said as she screened the pictures of the other stowaways who'd died on the train. She flipped through them, bouncing them around the apartment walls. 'I want to find out who they were. I want to find out who they knew. I want to find out who might have been with them five years ago. Maybe I said something to one of them.'

'Not much use if you did. They died too, remember?'

'Maybe I said something to the one who didn't get on the train.' She guided me through the reports. Interviews with other stowaways, people who'd made the run from Firstfall to Disappointment before, people who knew the tricks for getting on the trains. 'I want to try, at least.'

One of the women who'd gone to the station that night had walked away instead of boarding the train. She'd come forward to the police two days later. I didn't have her name because the Tesseract still wouldn't give it to me, but it couldn't be that hard to dig out.

'You do that. I'll take Temo Kadavu. You can't simply walk into a station and creep into a freight truck when a guard is looking the other way. These stowaways had to bypass security doors. They needed access codes. The tunnel outside was vacuum. Lethal. They had to find a container that would be pressurised. Kadavu did all that. Seems like he'd been doing it for some time.'

Liss started a search. 'I must have known him somehow.'

'Could be. Rangesh did. He knew there were stowaways getting on those trains for years.'

'I want to meet him. He sounds fun.'

'Kadavu?' I made a face.

'Rangesh, you idiot!'

'Yeah, maybe.' Fun with suicidal tendencies, if you went by the way he'd walked down two gun barrels yesterday morning.

A pod arrived to take me in. Liss put her shell back to sleep in its coffin and slipped inside my Servant. Despite what she was, she couldn't be in two places at once. The core algorithms underneath her many layers wouldn't let her copy herself – we had the AI laws of 2100 to thank for that. I was glad to have her with me. There was something joyful about her today that lifted me out of the back pains and the aching muscles. An enthusiasm, a hunger, that thrill of the chase we both used to get. I didn't feel it myself, not yet, but it was good to see. I linked the feedback on my lenses so she could watch through my eyes as the pod hummed up through the undercity towards the heart of Firstfall's old town. We burst out of the tunnels into drab grey morning gloom. The streets were wet, strewn with puddles, little rivulets of rainwater still bubbling their way down to the hydroponic vats deep below. The roads were busy, people out and about, going for walks on the surface while they actually could.

'Must have rained through most of the night,' I said. I don't know why. I suppose because that's what people do when they're together. Talk about nothing much.

Liss showed me the weather reports for Firstfall. Not that I cared, but before I could even look at them a warning pinged across my lenses. I was supposed to meet Flemich in his office when I got in but apparently he wanted to meet right now instead. I'd just about absorbed the idea when my pod reached the squat tower looming over the atrium of the Tesseract and stopped, and there was Flemich coming down the steps towards me.

'Rause!'

'Assistant Director?'

Flemich smiled and gave a little bow as I got out of the pod. 'It's good to have you back.' He looked at the sky. A wind was building, grey scudding clouds. We'd have more squalls on us before the day was out, but for now the weather was almost mild and the steps in front of the Tesseract were scattered with knots of students spilling over from the Magenta Institute next door. Vending bots moved through them and a couple of shells too, whispering their offerings of Earth-grade chocolate, fresh coffee and stimulants; and, of course, gens.

A second pod pulled up beside us. Flemich paused, leaning against its open door. 'Look, I'm sorry about this. The trans-polar expedition think they've found something under the southern polar ice. I'm pretty sure it's a rock, but … Anyway, I've got to run so we'll have to postpone the formalities and cut to the chase.' A series of alerts popped across my lenses while he spoke – incoming data packets. 'Keep a lid on this Betleshah business. You'll have to be the face of it when we come to making statements and taking questions. Put Rangesh on a short leash when that happens. Otherwise he's best if you let him loose. Hopefully you already gathered that. Oh, and make sure that Eddie Thiekis gets everything he wants. Make sure he knows what's going on. Keep him sweet. He's got clout.' He looked me up and down and then clapped me on the shoulder. 'You've lost weight, Rause. Going to take a while to get used to being back, eh?' He vanished into his waiting pod and pulled away.

I started up the steps to the Tesseract. My legs and back ached and my lungs and heart were going to be claiming overtime ... and then I had to stop for a moment. I'd walked these steps with Rangesh yesterday and hadn't even noticed. But here, now, with Liss humming in my Servant, all my pasts came rushing back at once. The glorious days when we were flying high, twin stars racing each other upward. The emptiness and the isolation after she was gone, walking through the Tesseract as though I was a ghost. Two past versions of myself that both seemed like strangers.

Aluminium shutter doors rolled open to let me in. The sound of grating metal snapped me back. Ugly things, those doors, but then what lay beyond wasn't any better, graceless dollops of blocky metal and fused stone. Firstfall old town was all much the same, and most of the rest of Magenta too, the architecture of speed and efficiency and nothing much else, a style of building born of high gravity and storm winds that could top three hundred miles an hour and often did. Other colony worlds had their grand spires and towers, elevated walkways and spindles. The cities of Strioth looked like overgrown fairytale castles; but Strioth was a paradise, warm, balmy and calm. When the Masters had dumped six thousand Samoans, Fijians and Cook Islanders on Magenta, the colonists had taken one look at where they were and promptly dug a hole and put a lid on it.

'Do you remember the first time you came here?' asked Liss.

'I remember it felt much the same except without the constant gasping for breath,' I muttered. Five years away. Coming back should have felt different. 'I don't belong here any more.'

'It'll seem like home again soon enough.'

I didn't want to argue. I crossed the atrium into the Tesseract's central quad, a soulless concrete space surrounded by windowless blockhouses. In the middle was a fountain, but whoever designed it had forgotten to allow for Magenta's gravity. The water didn't so much burst up in an exultant spray as flop limply into the air. Cheap plastic benches surrounded it, along with a spray of potted Magentan ferns that presumably had to be taken under cover every time a storm rolled in.

I sat for a moment, catching my breath yet again. This whole gravity adjustment thing was getting tedious. 'It doesn't feel right, just wandering back in here after so long.'

My Servant pinged an alert, flicked up in microlights through my lenses. Agent Zohreya asking for face time. I was about to ping her back when another thought crossed my mind: Rangesh had said something about him and Patterson and Zohreya getting together this morning, hadn't he? I traced Zohreya's ping back to a tac-bunker and piggybacked onto the video feed. Easy as breathing ...

They had their backs to me. Rangesh had swapped the shabby suit from yesterday for a tie-dyed kaftan and open-toed sandals. Zohreya was in an MSDF jump suit, Murgrah in some fancy tailored trouser suit ...

Laura Murgrah. Patterson now. I was going to have to get used to that.

The sound kicked in.

'Does it matter?' That was Zohreya.

'Man! He's not there, Laws. Be cool! He's supposed to be with the Flem.' Rangesh.

'Anyway, Bix, what did you make of him?'

Rangesh laughed. 'Kind of hung around and watched and didn't do much. Man, you should have seen his face when the Shah came out all half-naked and waving some old pistol. Like he was actually going to shoot something. Dude didn't look well either. Called meds from Mercy while we were hanging there waiting for the Shy's pod.'

'Transgravity hurts.'

Patterson didn't say a word, but there was a bitterness etched into her silence, someone who thought they were better than their circumstances and deserved more than they'd been given. I cut the feed and pinged Zohreya to meet me in a contemplation cubicle since I didn't have an office yet, levered myself back onto my feet, winced at my own weight and crossed the quad. Doors opened as I approached and then closed behind me, guiding me on my way. A contemplation cubicle wasn't much more than an interrogation cell: grey walls, a dull strip-light ceiling, a simple aluminium folding table and four chairs. But it was private, that was the thing. No cameras, no microphones.

Zohreya was ahead of me. She saluted and jumped to attention as I came in. I gestured for her to sit but she stayed where she was.

'Sir, I formally request a transfer to the narcotics directorate.'

'Right.' So this was how my first proper day in the office started, was it? 'Sit down, Agent Zohreya.' Standing was doing my spine no favours.

Zohreya hesitated and then did as she was told.

'What are you doing here, Agent Esharaq Zohreya of the MSDF?'

She looked distant for a moment, the way people get when they start clawing information out of the bitsphere onto their lenses and stop looking at the real world. I couldn't see the telltale sparkle of light in her eyes, though. Actually there was something odd about her eyes now that I looked closely. They were absurdly perfect. They weren't real.

'I don't know what you mean, sir,' she said. 'My job, I hope.'

'Why the cybernetics?'

The question seemed to take her by surprise. 'Because ... they offer vastly better performance, sir. Optical range, spectral range, illumination lev—'

'Yes, yes, yes ... Everyone knows that cybernetics outperform biological organs by an order of magnitude in every respect, and on Earth they're as common as muck. But Magenta isn't Earth and I don't know any other agents who've had their eyes replaced. So why?'

Zohreya continued to look bemused. 'I ... don't understand the question, sir. Because ... they're better.'

'Yeah. Look, on Earth people sometimes use brain synthesis for their Servants too. Direct thought control. That's better as well, but it doesn't mean we all do it.'

That got me another bemused look. 'I do, sir. And it is better. Quicker.'

I shuddered. Direct thought control meant having your head cut open and a device stuffed inside which spent six months growing a network of carbon filaments though your brain, a process well documented as something akin to a six-month bitch of a hangover, and woe to anyone who stood too close to any microwaves afterwards. On Earth they didn't seem to care, but most colonists I'd met had pretty conservative views when it came to cutting off bits of perfectly good flesh and bone and replacing them with metal and plastic. 'OK, so they're better. In that case, why just the eyes? Why not everything else?'

'My Servant connection was done on Earth when I was a child. The eyes ... it was what I could afford, sir.'

I raised an eyebrow but Zohreya didn't elaborate. 'Fine. You come from Earth. Earthers think differently. I'm curious, that's all. You do look more like an Earther than a native. You ever find that a problem?'

'Not at the bureau, sir.'

So it was a problem outside then? Didn't surprise me. Magenta never much liked immigrants. 'Where are you from, Agent Zohreya?'

'Firstfall, sir. I was—'

82

'I mean before you came to Magenta.'

'Palestine, sir.'

'Nice country.' I'd spent a few days' leave there a couple of years back. 'But you're not made for Magentan gravity. The Masters lifted the original colonists from the Pacific Islands for a reason. Samoa, Fiji and the like. Stocky and strong. Good bones. The best starting point for a world like this. The Masters knew what they were doing even if we never did.' I looked her up and down. Tall, curvy and muscular. On Earth that might have caught the eye, but not on Magenta. 'The bone and muscle therapies took well, did they?' I flicked through her physical assessment reports. She did well: average for a bureau agent, good for a normal Magentan. Outright amazing for someone born off-world.

'They did, sir.'

'Good for you. They didn't take so well for me.'

'It's the transgravity, sir. It just takes time.'

'I mean they didn't take so well when I was growing up.' Rause the weakling. It had been a long time since the last of those childhood taunts but they never quite went away. Right now, labouring under a gravity I'd managed to escape for five years, it was something of a sore spot. Earth had been nice like that. Another thing to miss. On Earth I'd actually been strong. 'Why the transfer request?'

'May I speak freely, sir?'

'Go ahead.'

'I don't feel I'm compatible with the team you're assembling, sir.'

I cocked my head, hoping for more, but Zohreya stayed silent. I didn't see how she could have a problem with *me* yet, given that we'd barely met, and I didn't think it was Rangesh. 'Patterson?'

Her face twitched enough to let me know I'd hit the mark. I

let out a long breath and looked her over once more, wondering whether I wanted her. Rangesh I could use, with his guilt about the stowaways he'd never reported. Patterson had been one of Alysha's friends and a part of the team that had brought in Loki. I couldn't see it with Zohreya. Everything in her file said she did things by the book, straight and direct and no corners cut. Someone like that wasn't going to be much help with Alysha, but then again Flemich was already annoyed with me for snatching Patterson; letting Zohreya go so early wasn't going to look good. 'Request denied. Give me a chance to deal with it. You still want to move a month from now, I'll give you all the help I can.'

'Sir.' Zohreya got up.

'Anything else you want to say? Anything you think I should know? Just between you and me?'

'No, sir.' She didn't hesitate.

'OK then. I want a full briefing on KRAB by the end of the day. That going to be a problem?'

'Definitely not, sir.'

I let her go. Half an hour into the morning and I was already dealing with human resource issues. I'd have someone asking for a pay rise next. My back hurt. I had a headache. I couldn't focus and my thoughts kept wandering. Walking up the steps to the Tesseract I'd felt a dam waiting to burst inside me, and now the cracks were coming. Pause for a moment and I'd drown in a flood of memories. Rangesh and Patterson would be expecting me, but suddenly I couldn't face them. I needed to get up, I needed to keep moving, so I followed Zohreya out, pinged Patterson and Rangesh that I'd see them later, and left. If my legs had been up to facing the gravity, I would have run. I didn't stop until I was out on the Tesseract steps. There I could breathe again.

The rain had come back. Cold and immediate but without the scourge of the night winds. I stood in it, cleansing myself. The students had gone, scurrying for shelter as the skies opened. The vending bots and the pair of shells stood nearby, silent and still, waiting for customers. They pinged my Servant as I came in range, their hopeful clamouring abruptly silenced with a word.

'What do you think of her?' I poked Liss lurking in my Servant and summoned a pod.

'Agent Zohreya? Unexceptional competence. Adequate in most regards but not special. Her record—'

'I've read it. I asked you what you *think*.'

Liss fell silent for a moment. 'I think Agent Zohreya has a lot of friends in the MSDF and that despite that she worked very hard to transfer into the bureau. I think you should ask her about that.'

I walked slowly down the steps. The rain battered me, hard and steady, stinging now and then where a stray drop slanted in past the peak of my storm coat and spiked my skin. I could have gone out through the Tesseract sub-levels straight into the undercity but I wanted the sky above me, the space. Earth had done that.

'You think she's trying to prove herself?' I asked.

'Maybe.'

I sighed. 'How well did you know Patterson back when she was Laura Murgrah?'

'I'm not sure. That far back my past gets hazy. Before I met you everything is patchy. There are a lot of holes. You might find you know her better.'

'No.' Just that one night. We'd barely exchanged a word since. Different circles.

A pod pulled up at the bottom of the steps and invited me in. I told it to take me to Temo Kadavu. I didn't know where he lived or where he worked or if he was even still alive, but that was the pod's problem, not mine. It had my clearances. Wasn't too much to ask for it to look up an address.

'You got any questions for this guy?' I asked Liss. The pod headed into the undercity.

'You could ask him how come they let him go back to working at the station,' Liss said after a moment's pause. 'If it wasn't for him, I wouldn't be dead.'

So that was where we were going, was it? The mag-lev terminus? I shivered. I hadn't been back there since Alysha died. Hadn't found the strength.

'Keys, I know you need to talk to him. I know you need closure.'

'Liss!' I groaned. 'I know. I need to let go. And I will. But you can't expect me to drop it just like that, not now that I'm back here. So could you maybe leave it be?'

'I've been dead for five years.' Apparently not. 'You're the only one left who doesn't—'

'You're not dead!'

'Maybe *I'm* not, but I'm not alive either, and I'm not her! I'm just a simulation and a collection of memories from someone you can't have back. You need to—'

'Stop it!'

I almost shut her out of my Servant and kicked her back to her shell in the apartment, lying in her coffin with nothing to do except charge her already full batteries. What I definitely didn't need was someone telling me what I needed.

The pod spiralled down through the undercity, deeper and deeper until it reached the mag-lev terminus, below the hydroponics caverns in among the pumping stations that drained the lakes of rainwater from the bottom levels of the city. We stopped and I got out. Down this low everything always felt damp, the air cool and humid. Earth has grand buildings for shuttle ports and airports and even for its stations, huge cathedrals of enclosed space, but Firstfall's mag-lev terminus wasn't much more from the outside than a long straight row of arches, a parade of cave mouths opening into the platform beyond. Even on the inside it wasn't much to look at, just a long flat open space and a tunnel leading out with a single rail suspended in the middle. A few hundred yards into that darkness was a train-sized airlock.

I stopped and looked into the gloom of the arches, short of breath. The place was empty. Lifeless and desolate and yet full of sudden ghosts. I'd come here with Alysha on the day we were married. Late in the evening, already half drunk and wrapped around each other. She'd told me to carry her up the steps. I'd been stronger then than I was now, not wasted away by five years of only one gravity, but it had still been an effort. I'd barely managed. I'd put her down at the top and she'd promptly danced back to the bottom.

Again.

I'm not sure I can.

Then you can't have me.

Your fault if I pull a muscle.

We'd been laughing. I'd carried her up a second time, arms and legs burning. She'd gone down again and demanded a third.

I can't, Liss.

Yes, you can. I promise I'll be yours for ever.

You already did that.

I had my fingers crossed.

I almost hadn't managed it, going up those steps with her a third time. My knee had buckled as we reached the top. I'd dropped her, but she'd only laughed.

Good enough. Yours for ever now, Keon Rause.

We'd gone inside. We had a carriage to ourselves, a make-shift bridal carriage. On our way to Nico on the overnight, off for the four days of holiday we'd agreed we could have before immersing ourselves back in our work. We were supposed to be getting some rest, but we hadn't done much sleeping.

Yours for ever now, Keon Rause.

The memory was ash in my mouth. I felt sick. For ever had turned out to be six years. Something had been wrong at the end, something she wouldn't talk about. A stowaway on a train? That wasn't my Alysha. I didn't know what she was running from, what had scared her, but that wasn't my Alysha either, to be so afraid. But she was, and she'd gone without me, and I couldn't stand the thought that maybe I'd never know why.

Yours for ever. But Loki had taken her.

Without a train waiting to speed away, the station was as quiet as a mausoleum. The freight terminus was a quarter of a mile further along the track. That was where she'd gone. Five years ago Temo Kadavu had worked there. He'd let her in, and that was the last anyone had seen of her.

I found Kadavu in the administration office at the end of the platform, sitting quietly. He looked up as I came in and did what anyone would do, pinged my Servant to see who I was. When he got the answer, his eyes went wide as though he'd seen a ghost. Guess he remembered the name then. He opened his mouth to say something but nothing came out. He just stared at me, dumbstruck.

I pinged him a picture of Alysha. 'She was really on that train?'

'Oh. Look ...' He nodded. 'I'm so sorry. There was no way to know. I only—'

'Sure. You didn't know you were sending them to die.' Standing with him there right in front of me I wanted to break his neck. He didn't deserve it, not really, but I hated him.

'I told the police everything as soon as—'

'Just a couple of questions, that's all, and then I'll go.' I felt the Reeper on my hip, the weight of it, the itch in my hand resting on its holster. Temo Kadavu looked at me like a cornered mouse. If he'd risen to his feet he would have loomed over me by a good six inches, but somehow I would have found the strength to knock him down. *You killed her.* I couldn't stop the thought dancing circles in my head, even if it wasn't true.

'I—'

'The press reports said that four people died.'

Kadavu nodded.

'They said there were five people here that night. That there was someone who didn't get on the train. She was the one who went to the police after it happened. That was how they knew the names of the others. That was how they found you.'

Kadavu nodded again. He didn't look at me. Maybe he couldn't.

'Why'd she change her mind? What happened to her?'

'They didn't go. That's all I know.'

'Didn't go?' Wait a minute ... '*They?*'

'There were six people that night, not five. There was one who came to see her friend off. It happened sometimes. The second one changed her mind. That wasn't so strange either. I'd show them how it worked, what they had to do and where they had to stay. I always did that. I told them how dangerous it could be. They had to understand it was a vacuum out there. That they had to bring air. It's not ... I told them it might not be safe.' He shrugged. 'I always did that, every time. Sometimes people changed their minds.'

'You're telling me that six people came to you that evening, not five, and that only four got on the train. And it was a woman who changed her mind?'

'I don't remember her name. Something religious, I think. Angel Rosaria? Something like that.'

'Did she talk to the others before she left?'

'Sure, sure. She talked to ... I think it was your wife who changed her mind. They talked quite a bit. But I told everyone all of this already!'

Not in any report I'd seen, but that didn't mean much.

'And what about the one who was here with a friend? Man or woman?'

'Woman. Both women.'

'Do you know who they were?'

'You mean you don't?'

I must have looked like I was ready to punch him. Probably because I was. He flinched. 'Alysha Rause. Your ... your wife, was she? She came with a friend. She got on the train but her friend stayed behind. She left with the one who changed her mind. I don't know who either of them were. Your wife's friend was dressed in a burqa. I never saw her face.'

Someone hiding who they were. 'Who was she?'

Kadavu shook his head. 'I told you. No names.'

'Really?' I didn't believe it.

'I didn't need their names. If they wanted anyone to know where they were going, that was up to them. Sometimes they'd leave their Servants turned on, but usually not. I only know the woman who changed her mind because she was in the news after the accident. She told them—'

'Did you see their faces?'

He nodded. 'Except the burqa woman. I suppose she's the one you want.'

So Alysha had come with a friend. I had no idea who that might have been.

'Station surveillance might have picked them up ... I told them how to get in without being seen but maybe ... maybe the ones who didn't get on the train ... Perhaps on the way out ... But ...'

I was already walking away. Somewhere in the Tesseract was a report I hadn't seen. Someone had gone with Alysha and watched her get on that train. No one had ever thought to tell me and it wasn't in the files the Tesseract was letting me see. Why? The investigation was closed. I shouldn't have been locked out.

Whoever she was, I needed to find her.

I felt Liss in my Servant, like a presence hovering at my shoulder.

'Well?' I asked.

'Nice that I talked someone out of going with me and so saved their life.'

'Any idea who your mystery friend was?'

'Not the beginnings of an inkling.'

We thought about that for a moment. There wasn't much to be said. Someone Alysha had trusted. Had to be. Someone who knew why she was running. Someone who had answers.

Someone she'd trusted more than she'd trusted me.

'Whoever it is, I suppose you need to find her,' Liss said.

'I suppose I do.'

7

MORE WAYS TO SKIN
A CAT

I took a pod back to the Tesseract, to another deluge of paper-work and then a physical assessment that told everyone what we already knew, that I wasn't really fit because I was still full of transgravity nanites trying to adjust my body to Magenta's gravity. After that, at last, my own office, spanking new and empty. I spent the rest of the day hiding in it, searching through surveillance archives in vain for the two women who hadn't boarded that train. By the time I was done I didn't know whether to think it was because the women had followed Temo Kadavu's directions and avoided the cameras, or whether it was because someone else had found the footage five years ago and squirrelled it away. When I tried to access any reports on the second woman from the station, the Tesseract wouldn't let me, just as it hadn't let me in the days after Alysha had died. *Access barred: personal involvement.* Which made no sense. The in-vestigation had closed three years ago. It should have let me in.

Eventually I gave up and summoned Rangesh and Patterson. Rangesh shambled into my shiny new office five minutes later, dressed in the same rainbow kaftan and sandals he'd worn that morning, dripping rain all over the floor. I didn't bother with not staring. He looked ridiculous.

'You trying to wind me up, Agent Rangesh?'

The question slid off him as he slumped into the chair opposite. He cocked his head and grinned. 'It's like a thing, man. The streets. The dealers. The pushers. You got to let go a few rules in that world, you know, if you want to find the factories.' He flapped the sleeves of his kaftan as if that was supposed to explain everything.

'I'm not sure I do know, Agent Rangesh.'

'Call me Bix. Look, new boss dude, could you maybe do something to fix up Laws? She really needs some, like, tranqs or something. Strong ones. Or maybe she needs to get laid. Yeah, maybe that's—'

'Rangesh!'

He laughed. 'Sorry, man. It kind of got to me, you know, all that stuff yesterday. I mean with Shy ... I don't know. I've known her a long time. I guess it's how I deal with it. Look, it's really great you're here and everything. Esh and I, we're going to be good for you.'

'You and Esh?'

Rangesh looked almost sheepish as he chuckled again. 'Yeah, me and Esh. We got our differences of opinions, you know. Esh is kind of ... well, she's pretty much a square and she's a bit of a total fascist. But we manage, you know? We get along and we do the work. And she's hot, man. Got to admit that helps.' He wheeled out that toothy grin, and damn but there was an infectiousness to it.

'Rangesh! Again!'

'Hey, man, chill! This isn't Earth, and the twenty-first century was long ago, you know. They give as good as they get, my friend.'

'They shouldn't have to.'

'Hey, you know, it's like—'

'One word, Rangesh, from either of them. One complaint and I put you behind a desk.' That hit him where it hurt. He shut up while I stared him down until I figured he'd taken the point. 'Shyla Thiekis. Anything?'

'You seen the tox-report, right?' He was quiet now. Sombre. 'It's a new thing. Lichen-based but modified like you wouldn't believe. Shy's not the first.' He frowned. 'Wait, I already showed you, right? So there's been, like, these four other murders or ... I don't know. Something. People being dead in a bad way that's wrong. Four dropout gen-heads – two just dead, two like they've been ripped to pieces by some wild robot dinosaur or something.'

'Seriously, Rangesh?'

'Well yeah, OK, probably not that, but you got to keep your mind open, you know? It was like something real big had smashed the place up. Weird smell too. Yeah. I got samples from the old corpses off to the lab to be sure, but it's the same gen as did for the Shyster, I swear it. Like their bodies just ... burst, man! So I'm out tracking where it's coming from. Been working those others a while though, so if the Shyster's part of the same pattern ... Could take some time. Wheeling with the dealers, unravelling their supply, tickling for the fat cat man who sits at the back licking up the cream. You know?'

I gave Rangesh a long look. Sure, if I was going to find out what happened to Alysha then maybe I wanted someone who knew Magenta's underbelly like the back of their hand. I guess Rangesh fitted that, but bloody hell ... 'That sounds like something the narcotics directorate would handle. What business is it of yours?'

'The narcs?' Rangesh spat out a laugh of contempt. 'Yeah, man, sure. Look, they try, but their problem is that they're all squares, man. Any pusher out there, he sees them coming the moment they leave the door. Me? I don't know, man. I mean, they know what I am, but they know I'm not out there to give them grief. It's like I'm one of them and they know it. People talk to me. It's just ...' Rangesh shrugged. 'It's never been against the law to take a few gens, man, get a bit high, and when was the last time we threw the book at a small-scale pusher? Law's only there because Earth gave us shit about gens coming in on the *Fearless*, and then that whole blockade thing all those years ago and how if you don't live here, you don't have that built-in tolerance. Even the narcs are only after the factories refining for off-world, but that doesn't stop them acting like dicks to the rest of us, I guess. Look, it's cool, and I might have a lead on the Shah's supply, but you know how it goes. It's a friend of a friend, and then it turns out they scored from another friend. So you track the chain back to the dealer who brings it into the city and then back some more until you find the factory, and then, maybe, if you're, like, really amazingly totally lucky, maybe you get a trace on the chemist who made it. But that's the one we're after, you know? The rest? I leave them be and they know it.' He walked his fingers across the table. 'One step at a time, new boss dude. Little piece by little piece. If it ever gets hairy, Esh has my back. So we're freezer-chilled and it's all happening, you know?'

'Not really, but you can go back to your next little piece, Rangesh, if that's what you want. And stop calling me that.'

'Calling you what? New boss dude?'

'Exactly that.'

I expected a protest, or at least an eye roll, but Rangesh didn't blink. 'Sure, man. Whatever you say. You hang chill, right?' He closed the door behind him, soggy rainbow kaftan swirling around bare ankles.

'Flemich really must hate me,' I murmured after the door

closed. I was smiling, though. Couldn't not. Rangesh had some weird charm that made it hard to get mad with him. That was his magic, I suppose, how he did what he did. How he was still here. 'Why have I got him?' I shook my head. 'Don't answer. It's because the narcs don't know how to handle him, right?'

'Do *you*?' Liss asked.

'I worked with him yesterday for a few hours and I didn't shoot him, so that's a start. You see the note on his last performance report? That maybe the reason he's so deep into Magenta's drug culture is because he *is* Magenta's drug culture? And what the hell was he wearing?'

Liss laughed. For a moment we were good again, like she was really here.

Patterson was waiting outside. I had my Servant call her in. She sat opposite me, prim and upright, about as different from Rangesh as it was possible to be. I looked her up and down, lost for words for a moment because she looked so different from the Laura Murgrah I remembered. The pictures in her file showed it too, but face to face it struck me hard. The years had changed her. Pinched her. The athletic lines were still there but tense like a coiled spring. She was thinner, pale as a ghost, stark white skin against short-cropped black-dyed hair that had once been long and chestnut, but most of all – something the pictures couldn't ever show – her eyes had changed. I remembered her eyes most of all, pale watery blue and full of fire. Now they were glaciers.

'Hi, Laura,' I said. 'Long time no see. How you been?'

'Did you do it?' she asked.

'Pardon?'

'I said, "Did you do it?" I'm sure you've read my file from back to front, Rause, and I've read yours. You were on Earth, seconded to Fleet, some task force. Cushy job. Sweet. But they kicked you off. You had a team. Security for a display at the

Fleet exhibition in Gibraltar, right? The Tech-Fair. A big deal. The ghost suit. Invisibility, or so they say. Someone took you out. You lost the suit and the perps got clean away, no trace. So that's the "it". And my question is: did "you" do "it"? Is that clear enough, or do I need to explain the pronoun too? Because it sure as hell smells like an inside job when you look at it.'

'Thanks, Laura.' When I looked at her, all I got was that ice. 'No, I didn't do it. Did you?'

'You know you're going to be watched, don't you? Fleet, Earth. They're saying there was a Masters device in that suit, that that's how it really worked.'

'Doctor Mongramyr's photonic—'

'Oh that's horse shit, Rause. I've read his papers and Mongramyr couldn't hide a snail in a fern forest with his arrays. That suit was Masters tech. So did you take it? Because as I see it that's the only way it works.'

'You're a long way out of line, Patterson! And how did you get this anyway? I can't imagine Fleet sharing their investigation notes with—'

'Shit, Rause, it's all there in the public press if you know how to read it. We had a month to pore over the news from Earth while you were floundering away up in the transgravity clinic. Although most of it I put together while you were fucking about with Rangesh yesterday.'

I grimaced. If anyone had asked me back on Earth, my guess would have been that Laura Murgrah was running the place by now. Apparently not, and I was beginning to see why. 'Well then, well done for solving a mystery that no one else could. So here's the deal: I'll tell you where I hid the suit when you tell me how the people who attacked the Tech-Fair never showed up on surveillance.'

'How about because there *were* no other people.'

A silence hung between us, tight and dangerous. For a

moment, as we stared each other down, I thought she really believed it. That I would do something like that.

'I'm sorry about Alysha,' she said.

'What happened to you, Laura? Way you were heading when I left, I should be answering to you, not the other way round. You should have had Flemich's job by now.'

'Same as happened to you, Rause.' She shrugged. 'Life. I'm sure it's all in my files. So here I am, in your pretty little team of clowns at your request. Way I see it, this is as low as I can go. So thanks.'

'You have a problem with Rangesh and Zohreya?'

'A problem?' She shrugged again. 'What do you want me to say? Zohreya is a plodder. She's a robot. Does what you tell her – if she can – and doesn't ever think. And Rangesh?' She shook her head in disgust. 'I don't care what his results look like, he just shouldn't be here.'

'Should you?'

Laura stiffened. 'Should *you*? You want to tell me why you transferred me to the Clown Crew or shall I just guess it has to do with Alysha?'

'You were her friend.'

'So?'

We stared at each other and then she laughed. And there, for a moment, was the Laura Murgrah I remembered; and she was seeing what I was thinking, and somehow that cracked her ice a little. Maybe she remembered the same better days too. 'You're so fucking transparent, Rause. You always were. Maybe that's why Alysha liked you. You know I was a part of the investigation – you wouldn't have transferred me otherwise. We looked into the crash and everything around it. Two years of my life. Didn't find anything more than Loki. Anything else?'

'I talked to Temo Kadavu this morning.'

'Bully for you.'

'He told me there were two women who didn't get on the train. The press reports only said one. When I dig for data, the Tesseract is blocking me.'

'No need to dig. Angel del Rosario and someone else. Called herself Archana. Shit, they never told you about that?'

'No, they didn't! And it looked like she was a friend of Alysha, and no one even bothered to ask me!'

Patterson rolled her eyes and leaned back in her chair. 'What the fuck, Rause? You think the bureau wrote the May Day attack off as a freak loner? We didn't. Not at first. We turned Firstfall over looking for Kadavu's second woman. Archana Enigma we took to calling her. Not a trace of her in Alysha's life until then. Nothing. To the point that some of us got to thinking that Kadavu and del Rosario had made her up between them. You probably want to talk to the bomber too, right? Well you—'

'I already know he's dead.'

'And that they never found—'

'The guy who shanked him. I know that too. You think someone put Loki up to it?'

Laura bared her teeth. She didn't say it, but her answer was clear: she did. 'We found no evidence to support that theory. Look, I got you a little present while you were up in the sky learning all about gravity again. I finessed my way onto the Settlement 64 task force.'

'The what?' Inside my Servant I felt Liss snap to attention. Settlement 64. The mid-latitude corporate enclave she'd been sniffing at before the crash. Hadn't seemed a big deal at the time and she'd never told me why, but then she'd died, and now even Liss didn't know what Alysha had been after up there.

'You going to pretend you don't know?' Patterson rolled her eyes. 'The lease runs out in a couple of months. Kaltech are winding the place down. There's a handover team.' She gritted

99

her teeth. 'They have a sweepstake on who's going to be the first to hang themselves and whether it'll be from boredom or from sheer desperation. I got myself an in with them. For you.' She made a face. 'Well no. Because you're right: I liked Alysha.'

'How the hell did you swing that?'

'Huh.' That got a wry smile out of her. 'I was a lawyer once and I know my way around money, and when it comes to seeing patterns in numbers they don't have an auditor who does it better. Also they're desperate. So I dropped a hint and they asked me. Big fucking mistake, most likely.'

'Didn't Flemich—'

'Flemich? You think I asked his permission? Fuck that!' She leaned closer across my desk. 'I used to look up to Alysha, you know, and if you're going to start digging around then I'd like to know what happened to her too. You know, provided you're not part of some interstellar conspiracy stealing Masters tech from Fleet. If it helps, I don't think the first investigation looked into all the cracks and crevices that were there to be found, and I don't like it that they never tracked down Anja Gersh.'

'Who?'

That stopped her. She sat and looked at me, open-mouthed for a moment. When she found her tongue again, her voice was softer. Gentle. 'Doctor Anja Gersh. Are you telling me you don't know?'

'I don't know anything. Personal involvement in the case. I was shut out.'

Patterson looked away. 'Shit. In that case there's something you need to hear. I also think there's a link between Settlement 64 and where KRAB are getting their money, in case you're looking for an excuse to go up there. And you will be, if they never told you about Gersh.'

'KRAB? You got evidence?'

'Shut up and listen.' She pinged me a file. Audio only. It started to play straight away.

Rause . . .

I had to stop it. Pause it. Catch my breath.

'Alysha!' Her voice. The real thing. Five years and I'd grown so used to Liss. But they weren't the same, not quite.

'Just play the fucking file, Rause.'

I sat and listened.

Hello? Hello? To whom am I speaking? Accent: Earth, Germany.

Agent Alysha Rause. You've reached the Magenta Investigation Bureau. Are you—

Listen to me! My name is Doctor Anja Gersh. I work as a neuro-psychologist for Kaltech in Settlement 64. I need to talk to someone about what's happening here. People are going to die. There was an urgency to Gersh's voice as though she was hiding under a desk in the dark just waiting to be caught.

Who's going to die?

I need to get out. They'll kill me if they know.

Who, Doctor Gersh? Who's going to—

Kaltech! Listen to me! What they're doing here is . . . You have to get me out. They're trying to do what the Masters did. They're going to kill people.

Doctor Gersh, are you in immediate danger?

If they find out—

Doctor Gersh, are you in danger right now?

No, I don't think so but—

Doctor Gersh, I'm going to call you back on a secure line.

That was it.

I sat looking right through the wall, out into nothing. There were tears in my eyes. The first words I'd heard in Alysha's real voice for years. Fresh, like she'd died only yesterday.

'Someone did a spectacular job of trying to hide that call and make like it never happened,' said Patterson after a moment. 'But there was one recording they missed, off the main network in the archives of the satellite distributors. It was a fucking pain to get in and a fucking pain times ten to find the call. But we did. It was random chance Gersh ended up talking to—'

'Where's the rest?'

Patterson shrugged. 'That's all. Alysha moved it to a private secure channel. Even if we could find it in the archives, nothing short of an artificial intelligence with a few centuries to spare is going to crack the encryption. Dead end, I'm afraid.'

'And?'

'And nothing. Alysha was asking about Settlement 64 before the bomb, but I know you already know that because you were the one who told us. Then she went very quiet. Doing something under the radar is my guess, but whatever she did she did it very well. I couldn't find a trace. And Settlement 64?' She shrugged. 'They wouldn't let us even close. Blocked everything. Claimed that Anja Gersh never existed. No such person. And that's it, Rause. As much as we ever found out in two long fucking years. So can I transfer back to where I came from and get on with some real work now?'

I'd stopped listening. I was setting up our transport for the next morning, when all four of us would be going to Settlement 64. Like Laura said, fuck asking for permission. When it was done I showed her.

'That answer your question?'

She looked shocked for a moment and then burst out laughing. 'Shit, Rause. You don't hang around, do you?'

'If your ego needs a rub, you can tell yourself we're going because of what you said about KRAB. You know, making you feel like what you're doing is important. It's what I'm going to tell Flemich after all. Now, the bomber ...'

'I can't give you the files but I can get you a list of his

associates. Did someone put him up to it? I don't know. He was an Entropist. The investigation concluded that his motives were plausible but not convincing. To be blunt, he didn't seem smart enough to build a bomb without blowing his own face off, never mind a pumping station, but there was no evidence that he took a pay-off, and even if he didn't plan the bomb, he sure as hell built it and planted it ...' She grinned as both our Servants pinged at once. Flemich. Quicker off the mark than I'd expected.

I transferred him to the wall-screen. He looked annoyed.

'I've just seen a travel request. What the hell are you doing, Rause?'

'KRAB investigation,' I told him. Which all three of us knew was a bullshit excuse.

'Patterson?'

Laura put on her best corporate-lawyer face. 'It's the finances, sir.' She lensed us both a series of financial records and then put them up on the screen beside Flemich's stormy face. 'I was digging around KRAB to see where they were getting their money, and I got back as far as a coy little group called LeSag Interactive. They're Earth-based, so everything recent is opaque, but as far as I can tell they've funded a few bizarre interactive entertainment ventures, none of which seems to have ever gone anywhere, and they also back fringe projects into triggered psychic events and historical research into the Masters. They're funding KRAB through a series of back doors.'

'And that has exactly what to do with Settlement 64?'

'LaSag's chairman is Nikita Svernoi. Svernoi was the chief financial officer at Settlement 64 until eight months ago. He's back on Earth now, as far as I can tell, so I can't question him directly, but I'd like to do some background checks.'

'And you need to go to Settlement 64 for that?'

Laura smiled.

'Thin, Patterson. Very thin.'

'I know, sir. But not nothing.'

Flemich's eyebrows furrowed up so tight they almost climbed down his nose. 'Well I don't know what *you're* playing at, Patterson, but you, Rause, you can drop the pretence right now. Fine. Go. While you're at it, there was an accident there about a year ago, a big one. Dig around. See if you can get to the bottom of it. The timeline fits your man, so that's your excuse, not KRAB. We'll talk properly when you're back. Ruffle any feathers up there and I'll have you both posted to immigration processing in Disappointment. Am I clear?'

He cut the feed without waiting for an answer.

'Well, that went well,' I said.

'It did.' Patterson looked surprised. 'Given that by "thin" what he really meant was fucking monomolecular. You might want to look at Nikita Svernoi a little more carefully, Agent Rause.'

I checked again and spotted what I should have seen the first time. Svernoi's posting to Settlement 64 at the time of the accident hadn't been his first. Five years ago he'd been running the place. Same time as the May Day attack.

'The day before she left, Alysha took a lot of money,' I said. 'She cleaned us out. I think she was running.'

Laura nodded. 'I thought so too. I think Alysha was on to something. I think it had to do with Settlement 64, but there must have been more otherwise why keep it so close? Maybe whoever she was after got to her first.'

'The bomber ...'

'You think we didn't try going that way?' Laura shook her head and let out a long sigh. 'Alysha was a friend, Rause, and I wasn't at my best. Maybe we missed something. I'll dig out some names, but don't get your hopes up. The bureau was all over Loki. We have hundreds of hours of questioning. Hundreds,

Rause. But he never cracked, and his story never fell apart. The best evidence still says Loki was a loner and it was bad luck and random chance that Alysha happened to be on that train.'

She didn't believe it though. That much was written right across her. Which was good, because I didn't believe it either.

I stood up. Too much to think about. 'You were good once, Laura. The best. You can be that good again if you try. You know that, right?'

'Oh for fuck's sake, Rause, where do you even want me to start with a patronising piece of crap like that? So were you. But that was half a lifetime ago for both of us. You didn't know me then and you certainly don't know me now. Or shall we go with just plain fuck off? Take your pick.' She went for the door.

'Lay off Zohreya and Rangesh,' I said. 'They're my problems now.'

'Good luck with that! You going to tell them what we're really doing?'

'Not yet. You want a beer later?'

She paused in the doorway and then shook her head. 'Jamie's got iceball. If I'm going to be fucking off to the middle of nowhere tomorrow, I should be with him tonight.'

I watched her go. There was a hollowness to her that I didn't remember.

'Sometimes it's like the person I'm supposed to be is a stranger,' whispered Liss with only the slightest trace of irony.

'Patterson's the one,' I said. 'The one who's going to find out what happened to you.'

Ah shit. For a moment I'd almost been in a good mood. Then the grief came crashing back in.

8

TRANSIT

Settlement 64 sat in the Magentan mid-latitudes in the middle of a flat expanse of lichen tundra, the sort of vast ruddy purple wasteland that had given the world its name. Crater scars of opencast mining pits surrounded it, some of them ten miles across. The early surveys of Magenta had found rare earth deposits that spawned a scatter of sites set up by whoever damn well felt like strip-mining the planet as fast as they could. Eighteenth-century colonialism all over again, but the mines had run out long ago. Most were derelict and abandoned, but Kaltech, the off-world corporation which ran Settlement 64, had had an interest in xeno-pharmaceutical research. Settlement 64 was all about the lichen now, although calling it lichen was taking the nearest Earth analogue of Magenta's native flora and using it where it didn't fit. It was more a kind of fungus, but even that didn't capture it. Organic rock-eating psychoactive purple alien dust. Magenta's blessing and curse.

'I still don't think you should go,' Liss whispered. 'I still think you should leave it be.'

'Bit late for that now.' We'd argued all night. *Leave it be. Let me be dead. Move on. The bomb was just bad luck. Or if it wasn't, and someone killed me because of what I found there, won't they just kill you too? I don't want you to die for me, Keon ...*

That sort of thing. Waste of time. She should have known better.

I was strapped into the back of a modified Cheetah, with Patterson and Rangesh and Zohreya. The Cheetah was a twenty-year-old shuttle built to a forty-year-old design under licence by the government-run Magenta Shipyards on the outskirts of Firstfall. Zohreya was dressed in another black combat jumpsuit straight out of the MSDF wardrobe. Patterson was in an Earth-imported designer-label trouser suit that probably cost more than her monthly salary. Rangesh had traded his kaftan for a food-stained thermal environment suit that looked like he'd rescued it from a recycling tip. At least he wasn't wearing sandals this time.

'We're here to take a look and poke around,' I said as much for Liss as for the others. 'That's all. I don't think the AD is expecting us to find anything, but there was an accident a year back and people died, so let's start with that.' I gave Patterson a nod. 'You want to walk us through the KRAB connection?'

'Everything's in the brief sheet. You can look it up if you're interested.' She glanced pointedly at Zohreya and then at Rangesh. 'I was careful only to use small words.'

'Thanks, but—' The Cheetah's four turbofans cut me off as they rose to a high-pitched hum. The floor shivered as the shuttle began its vertical take-off from the Tesseract. Originally an Earth design, the first Cheetahs could barely get airborne in Magenta's gravity. Better engines fixed that, but they also made for vibrational resonances that the original design didn't fully dampen. In other words, they were noisy.

107

Patterson rolled her eyes and flicked me a look. I pretended not to notice. The Cheetah shivered as its wings unfolded. The hum of the turbofans changed as they tilted, and the muted whine of three gas turbine jet engines joined the chorus. When they were done, Patterson put on her best patronising voice.

'Right then, if I must. So KRAB are getting funded—' The cabin shuddered with a series of dull thuds as the Cheetah finished reconfiguring itself. Patterson sighed and rolled her eyes. 'You know, Rause, the bureau does have newer shuttles.'

'It was what I could get at short notice. Imagine us hanging on your every word.'

Her eyes wanted to murder me. 'You know what? Fuck you. Read the brief I wrote or don't. Much more interesting is what Settlement 64 is doing chock-full of Indian subcontinent Earthers when to the best of our knowledge not a single one of the early settlers decided to sod off across thousands of miles of unmapped storm-battered terrain armed with a fabricator, a clone factory and a stack of Bombay-mix DNA.'

'Classy, Laws. Real nice.' Rangesh rolled his eyes.

'Oh, I'm sorry, Rangesh. Does that bother you? Maybe I'm just a bit tetchy on account of you telling Agent Rause here that I should get laid more, you know, like while I was sitting right outside his fucking office, *man*.' She glared at Rangesh as if she was trying to set him on fire by sheer force of will.

Rangesh went all wide-eyed and innocent for a moment, then looked sheepish. 'Aw, Laws, that was like—'

'Oh shut up!'

She switched her murder-gaze to me for a moment. I glanced at Zohreya, but Zohreya seemed very interested in recalibrating the sight on her Reeper just now. The whine of the turbines rose to a roar. The Cheetah lurched as the acceleration kicked in. Thirty seconds later came the rumble and jerk as we broke the sound barrier and raced for hypersonic cruise speed.

'Hey! I read your brief, Laws.' Rangesh started waving his hands as though conducting an orchestra. 'It was totally awesome. Like, really amazing.'

'Oh fuck off!'

'I'm serious, dude! What they're doing is, like, totally whoa! I mean, come on! They're making human medicine out of alien life! Light years across the stars and there's these tiny little chemicals that grow out of almost nothing totally on their own, and it's like they were designed to gel with our heads. Like there's some sort of higher cosmic order! Think about it, man! Isn't that, like, totally overpowering? It's like … like …'

'Like Allah meant it to be?' offered Zohreya softly.

Patterson groaned a soft squeak of gentle despair. She put on her parent-lecturing-child face with a heavy undertow of last-rags-of-patience. 'I would say, Agent Zohreya, that it was like the Masters knew what they were doing when they picked Magenta over about a hundred billion other worlds they might have chosen. And sure, Rangesh, totally awesome that all the first colonists were permanently tripping through decades of living in constant pain on this butt-fuck of a planet with its insufferable gravity.'

I tuned out, shifting to the back of the cabin while Patterson carried on. The Cheetah shivered as it hit cruise altitude, sub-orbital, racing around the curve of the Magentan stratosphere at several thousand miles an hour. Settlement 64 wasn't exactly close.

Liss lurked in my Servant, sitting at my shoulder as she always did.

'Who was Archana?' I whispered. 'Do you not have any idea at all? Who would you trust if you didn't trust even me? Why was she hiding her face?'

'I wish I could tell you.' Sadness and a trace of bitterness. I'd long ago asked Liss what Alysha had been doing on the day she got on that train, where she was going, what was so important about Disappointment, but Liss didn't know, just like she hadn't known about Settlement 64 or the name Anja Gersh. The simulacrum in my Servant was a model built from every gesture and word and interaction the real Alysha had left behind, but it couldn't be complete. Neither of us could know what secrets Alysha had never shared.

'She never ran from a fight,' I said. 'Something must have touched her right to the marrow. Maybe something to do with Settlement 64. And this Archana, I can't believe she doesn't know what it was.'

I ran through the Settlement 64 brief Patterson had prepared, looking for anything unusual. Something had changed about a year ago, the same time as the accident Flemich had mentioned. It showed in the pattern of shuttles in and out. An extensive change of personnel? When I looked back further I saw the same pattern four years earlier. A flurry of activity, of shuttles in and out. It had lasted a couple of months and had started just after Alysha's death.

'I feel the holes where something is supposed to be, only there's nothing there.' Liss sounded wistful.

'Nikita Svernoi. Anja Gersh. Archana,' I said. 'One of them has the answer.'

'I never went to Settlement 64,' Liss said. 'I'd know that much. There are no missing days in the months before … before I died.'

'But still, you have to admit—'

'How would they know, Keys? That's what bothers me now. How did anyone know I was on that train if I was trying so hard not to be found? I was good at that, I know I was. Maybe it really was an accident. Maybe Loki was telling the truth.'

'You were still running from something.' An accident? I

couldn't believe it. The only fatal Entropist attack Magenta had ever seen?

'You should tell them about me,' Liss said. 'All three of them. Everything you know.'

'Not yet. Patterson's after something. Can't you feel it? She's being too easy.' Alysha would have sensed it too. Don't ask me how but she would. Instinct. Some sort of sixth sense. Could a simulation have an instinct like that? I didn't know.

Rangesh was telling the others about Betleshah and Thiekis. After a bit his voice dropped. He kept glancing in my direction and whispering. I couldn't hear what he was saying, but I knew he was asking if either of them knew anything about me, and what the story was about Fleet and Gibraltar and Mongramyr and the cloak suit, and doing all the poke poke poke into someone else's life that I knew Rangesh wouldn't be able to resist. Patterson, who could have told him at least some of it, only shrugged. When I shuffled back to join them the talk moved to other things – Patterson's son Jamie, mostly, since that seemed to be the one thing that animated her. It wasn't hard to see how her son was the crack in her carapace where all the feelings leaked out: warmth and love and sadness and anger and a deep, deep frustration, all there if you had the eyes to notice. I figured Rangesh saw the same. He was kind when he talked about Jamie, steering the conversation away from the places Patterson didn't like, finding the hurt and not poking at it. When they started on about iceball and how ridiculous it was that someone who was eight could skate so well, and how Jamie's little mini-league team was doing, even Zohreya joined in, and for a minute or two I had them all with their masks off. Smiling. Laughing. Almost relaxed. And the thing that brought them together was Patterson's kid. I wouldn't ever have thought of that. Weird.

'I'm going to slip away,' murmured Liss. 'Gersh and Svernoi. I'll see what I can find.'

The conversation skipped from Patterson's family to the crazy Returners in Settlement 16 who thought they could talk to the Masters by putting themselves into comas. Then to whether or not the sudden influx of so many Earthers into Disappointment was a good thing. Patterson zoned into her lenses while Zohreya and Rangesh argued, Rangesh the third-generation native, impassioned and emotional, arguing for the freedom of the stars for all and never mind the cost; Zohreya, born on Earth and so an immigrant herself, calm and rational with unflappable statistics about the higher rates of crime and violence and gen use among the new wave of Earthers, something neither of them could quite explain and eventually agreed must be down to inadequate transgravity therapies from the Indian government.

The pitch of the Cheetah's engines changed. We were slowing and coming down, heading in towards Settlement 64.

'Do they still ship people here directly to and from Earth?' asked Zohreya suddenly.

I pulled up the brief sheet to search for the answer but Patterson was shaking her head before I found it. 'No, Agent Zohreya. They do what every independent settlement is required to do: they transfer their personnel in and out through Firstfall.'

Zohreya drew up Patterson's satellite pictures of the settlement and projected them onto the cabin screen. She zoomed into the shuttle pad. 'That's too big just for orbital transfers.'

'When they first built the site they came in direct, but that stopped decades ago. Read my brief.' Patterson shook her head. I caught the eye roll. *She's an idiot.*

The screen changed. Shuttle logs from the MSDF, Zohreya's old crew. She highlighted a series of entries. 'Here, here and here. Kaltech shuttles brought in on the *Fearless*. Coming in direct to Settlement 64. Not through Firstfall.'

'Yes, thanks, Zohreya, I did check the log. I'm not a total

idiot. Kaltech ship their supplies direct, but not their personnel. Because one's legal and one's not.'

The log display changed. Zohreya went patiently through a whole series of entries going back two years. 'There's a steady pattern, long term going back way before this. Then it changes. A sudden flurry of activity for a few months and then it dies right down.' The same pattern I'd spotted an hour before with Liss.

'Kaltech personnel go through Firstfall, Agent Zohreya. They have done for decades.' Patterson didn't try to hide her annoyance but she didn't sound quite so sure of herself this time. She frowned and stared at the screen.

'Same time as the accident,' I put in quick, before either she or Zohreya said anything more. 'Could be a change of staff. We'll take a look, OK?'

I thought I was smoothing the waters, stifling Patterson's inevitable hostility, but she looked more thoughtful than angry. She nodded. 'Yes,' she said. 'I will.'

The Cheetah's autopilot warned us to buckle in for landing. It shut down our screens and took control of our Servants for the final descent, making sure our attention was where it was supposed to be whether we liked it or not, the usual protocols in case something went wrong and we crashed, something which never, ever happened. My Servant lensed feeds from the outside cameras, the Cheetah angling through a hailstorm towards a ground I couldn't see, multi-spectral radar outlining the terrain in odd colours. Jolts and whirrs shivered the cabin as we dropped below the sound barrier and slowed, the shuttle extending its turbofans and powering them up as the jet engines idled. We came in soft and smooth despite the storm, and I didn't even feel the Cheetah touch down until a shiver as the cabin detached. In any half-decent spaceport a tug would have dragged us into a sheltered hangar then, but Settlement 64 didn't have that sort of luxury, just a slab of flat rock and an electric bubble-bus nosing out from the nearer of the two domes, heading through the wind and flying ice.

The Cheetah's pseudo-intelligence thought about this for a second and then unlatched the door.

'Take a look to your left as we come out,' said Zohreya. 'Two low buildings. The big one is active and drawing energy from their grid. On your satellite maps it has a heat signature.'

'Maintenance and stores,' said Patterson. 'Fuel. Loading, unloading, warehousing. That sort of thing.'

'The other one used to be passenger processing?'

'That is indeed what the brief I gave you says, Agent Zohreya.'

'It doesn't have a heat signature. It's inactive.'

'Yes.' Patterson was getting testy again. 'Because ...' She stopped. 'OK, what?'

'Eighteen months ago that was not the case. It was being used. Regularly.'

'Could be anything.'

Zohreya shrugged. 'Could be.'

The bus from the dome pulled up near the Cheetah. I unbuckled. 'Welcome to Settlement 64,' I said, but what I was really wondering was whether Zohreya could pull up the same satellite feeds and shuttle logs from five years ago.

I opened the door into driving Arctic hail.

9

SETTLEMENT 64

The bubble-bus had stopped ten feet from the Cheetah, quivering as the wind whipped it. A scatter of ice swirled into the cabin. The rattling of the hail was deafening.

A door in the side of the bus slid open. Two men in Kaltech all-weather uniforms stood inside, wearing harnesses and roped with safety lines to the inside of the bus. One of them picked up what looked like a missile launcher and yelled something, frantically waving me back as I was about to step out into the storm. I didn't hear a word. Agent Zohreya yanked me away from the door. The man with the launcher fired it. A rope tipped with a steel grapple shot out and arced with perfect precision through the wind, latching to a metal eye by the Cheetah door, the sort the MSDF used when they made rope drops. Zohreya checked it, then handed me a hard hat and a safety harness and hooked me to the line. It seemed ridiculous. The bus was, what, a dozen paces away?

I stepped out. The wind slammed me like a wall. It plucked me off my feet and tried to throw me across the landing pad like an autumn leaf. The hail felt like I was being pelted with bricks, a stunning barrage of noise and impacts. I wrapped my hands over my face and hung helpless for a moment, then grabbed for the line, hauled myself a few feet and lunged for the nearest hand. The Kaltech men hauled me aboard.

Right. Fine. Maybe not so ridiculous. I'd forgotten what Magentan weather could be like.

'Welcome to the high latitudes!' One of the Kaltech men laughed as they shuffled me into the shelter of the bus and out of the way.

Zohreya came next, braced into the wind. It was something of a consolation to see that she and Patterson both lost their footing too. Rangesh didn't even try, just clipped himself to the line and took a running jump at the gap, howling with glee like a kid on a roller coaster. Patterson brushed herself down, flicking pieces of ice off her trouser suit. Not the best choice of clothes, as it turned out.

The hail shattering against the bus made a metallic buzzing that I imagined to be somewhat like living inside a chainsaw. I shook myself, trying to clear the noise of out my head.

'It's so loud!'

The Kaltech men did something with their launcher and the rope snapped back across. The Cheetah's landing door slid shut. 'This?' They closed the bus door and sealed it. 'You should see what it's like when a real storm hits.'

The bus started for the closer of the two domes, soft fat tyres crunching across drifts of hail. We passed the buildings Zohreya had pointed out on the satellite imagery. She nodded at the smaller one.

'What's that?'

The Kaltech men shrugged. 'They closed it down after the accident.'

'Accident?' asked Patterson, all innocence. 'What accident?'

'Last year. Gas explosion.' That was the official Kaltech story. A gas explosion had destroyed one of the laboratories, damaging several others and killing seven workers. They'd put it down to a faulty pressure regulator and shoddy maintenance, but no one with more than half a working brain cell was ever going to buy that. Looking back, that was when Kaltech made the decision to wind the site down. Question was: did that have anything to do with what they'd been doing four years earlier? Probably not.

I pulled up the shuttle logs and satellite maps from back then on the off chance they might show something interesting, but my connection to the Tesseract was glitching in the storm and nothing came back.

'Fatalities?' I asked.

'So they say.'

'You weren't here?'

'God no! Everyone from back then was rotated out months ago.'

'All of them?'

'Magenta's a tough world to work.'

Couldn't argue with that.

'What do you do here?' asked Zohreya.

One of them pinged us a Kaltech Pharmaceuticals brochure. 'Stuff to do with the lichen. That's about as much as most of us know.' He sounded slightly put out. Maybe he thought that a guard should know what he was guarding.

The bus slid through the hangar doors. They closed behind us, putting a merciful end to the battering hail, muffling the wind's howl and sinking us into gloom. A dull array of blue strip-lights bloomed into life as a service door opened, leading deeper into the dome. Two more uniforms headed towards us, a tall blond Caucasian, his face set with the permanent grimace lines of an Earth-born who hadn't had the time and the gene treatments to fully adjust to Magenta's gravity, and an Indian woman, short with dark eyes and long hair in a braid. She'd been here longer, I decided. Her miserable expression had a more lived-in look.

'Administrator Stern.' The blond man looked me up and down. 'And this is my head of security, Kamaljit Illushyn.' Stern offered me his hand. I hesitated a moment before I shook it. After three days back on Magenta, the Earth gesture already felt awkward again.

'My team.' I introduced Patterson, Zohreya and Rangesh. Stern offered his hand to the others in turn. Rangesh and Patterson looked at him as though he'd offered them a snake. Zohreya took it without hesitation.

'You haven't met many Magentans, have you?' she said, and looked down at their clasped hands. 'One of those Earth things the colonies somehow lost on the way.' A simplistic explanation of a truth that had a lot to do with how the Masters had taken the first colonists from Earth, the synthetic people they sent into the population with their chemical handshakes that seemed to possess anyone they touched, seducing them to follow without a second thought to where a rocket would take them to the stars.

'Have you been on Magenta long?' I asked.

Stern laughed. 'Is it that obvious?' He turned to lead us out of the hangar.

'Adjusting to the gravity takes a while even with the best treatments. We see a lot of Earthers struggle and suffer.'

'Two months of transgravity. I'm here to supervise the hand-over and then I'm out again, thank goodness.'

'Two months?' I laughed as I kept pace with him. 'I'm on about the same. They say you need six. Then again I was born here, and that does make a difference. The good news is that when you get back to Earth you'll feel like Superman.'

We walked a featureless corridor into a room sterile enough to make even the Tesseract look homely. Pale grey plasticised foam tiles on the walls. More blue strip-lights in the ceiling, more grey tiles on the floor, piezoelectric easy-clean carpet. It was hard to imagine how Kaltech could have made the room more drab, but they'd had a good try with the folding aluminium furniture. Stern didn't miss a beat. 'Are you hungry? You must have had an early start.' Laid across the tables were trays and bowls of fungal paste faux-pasta mushroom salads and sandwiches made of Magentan bread baked from seaweed flour and stuffed with some sort of mechanically reclaimed pork. Mushrooms, seaweed and pork, a true Magentan diet – for some reason pigs had turned out to adjust to higher gravity better than almost anything else. All that was missing was the lichen. I forced myself to smile.

'Is this for us?'

'It's awful, isn't it?' Stern parked himself in a chair, sitting on it the wrong way round and folding his arms across its back, obviously relieved to be off his feet. 'This is all a bit short notice so I suppose something must have come up. How can we help?'

'Routine visit, that's all,' I said. 'Our AD thought someone ought to come out here and take a look.'

Patterson set to asking dull legal and personnel questions, a tick-box checklist we could have done just as easily without ever leaving Firstfall. Rangesh scoffed his way through fungus pasta and lichen bread while Stern gave us the potted history we already knew. When I asked, Illushyn dutifully trotted out the gas explosion story. The way she talked made it clear we weren't going to get any more. I got the impression she didn't really believe it either, but that neither she nor Stern had any better answers, nor much cared.

'What sort of lab was it?' asked Rangesh.

'We don't know,' said Illushyn. 'They shut it down after the explosion. You know what we used to do here, yes? Synthetic organ growth, tissue cloning, the usual basic pharma-medical stuff. It's all lowbrow and boring now, but it didn't used to be. Some of the work done here was quite radical once.' Presumably they'd spent some time together working out what they should and shouldn't say. Either way, Illushyn had my attention.

'What sort of work, exactly?' asked Patterson.

'I don't know. You'd have to refer to head office.'

'But it stopped after the explosion?'

'I think so, yes.'

'*Because* of the explosion?'

Illushyn didn't bite. 'We're just a skeleton crew now. I'm afraid we don't know very much.'

'Was it the same research you were doing five years ago?' I asked.

Silence stretched into awkwardness until Rangesh peered from behind a sandwich. 'Any drug problems?' he asked, clearly set on destroying whatever goodwill might be left. 'You know, gens. Anyone here using?'

Illushyn bristled. 'This is a medical research facility,' said Stern firmly. 'We are bound by Indian law, and I can assure you that we take the possession of narcotics most seriously, more so than under your own jurisdiction in fact.'

Rangesh let loose a smile, most of it directed at Illushyn. 'No worries. Look, I didn't mean to, like, cast aspersions or anything. It's just the usual thing, you know? Someone pulls in a crew from Earth and doesn't put in the time for proper transgravity ... Well, you already know what that's like. And there's all this unprocessed lichen, like, right outside, like, really right there where you can just reach down and scrape it off a rock, you know? I guess you guys are totally on to that sort of thing like a bad rash, but it's a bit, you know, a thing with the—'

'I don't see the relevance when—'

'It's like everywhere, man. You get to be born here, you get a certain tolerance, you know, because it's always there in the air, just a little touch of the gens. It's why we're all so laid back! But if you're not used to—'

'I've got your personnel files here,' said Patterson, cutting Rangesh off before he got us kicked out. 'The ones released to our government are incomplete. Perhaps they got corrupted? Anyway, do you have another set I could see?' Angling to get a look into their system to see what she could find out about Anja Gersh, at a bet.

Stern levered himself out of his chair. 'I'm sure Major Illushyn can help you with that after she gives you a tour of the site. I'm sorry but I have to go now.'

I shook his hand again and watched him walk away, stiff and wincing.

Rangesh gave Illushyn sad puppy eyes. 'Sorry, man, but it's the way it is in some places. I don't know if you catch the news from the rest of the world, but we have this new wave of Earthers coming into Disappointment. It's an Indian government programme, and it's, like, some substandard transgravity they're using, I dunno, maybe because it's cheap; and because they're coming in with no tolerance, gens are kind of a real problem there right now, and it's—'

I pinged him. Rangesh! Shut up!

'Yeah. Anyway, man. No gens here. I get it. So that's totally awesome!' Rangesh beamed that grin of his.

Illushyn led us back to the hangar. 'I can show you round most of the site but I can't take you into the laboratories. They're restricted areas working with live organic cultures. It's for your own safety.'

'Right.' My arse it was. I looked about the hangar. They had a pair of Cheetahs decked out in Kaltech colours, the bubble-bus, a few electric carts and a tug for hauling the Cheetahs out to the landing pad. That was it. A few maintenance bots sat idly in their docks, charging. There was a lot of empty space. The hangar had been built for something bigger. 'Pretty sparse here.'

'A lot of the site's like this,' said Illushyn. 'It's the wind-down. There's hardly anyone left any more.'

'You're shipping out to where?' Patterson asked, but Illushyn only shrugged.

'You could fit an interplanetary shuttle in here,' said Zohreya. She pointed to a part of the hangar that was unlit and hidden in shadow. 'Over there. You can see where there used to be a recharge unit, and that was the fuel ...' She paused a moment, lensing something. 'On the other side of that wall there used to be hydrogen tanks. Up until a year ago.'

I looked into the gloom, not seeing anything except shadow. It took me a moment to realise why Zohreya could see all that when I couldn't see a damned thing. Those artificial eyes.

'The hydrogen tanks are collapsible,' said Illushyn. 'They're still here.'

She led us like a party of reluctant schoolchildren through empty rooms, parts kits, an emergency battery bank, everything you might expect from a small orbital transfer pad. I sneaked a look at Zohreya now and then, since if anyone was going to spot something out of the ordinary here it was her, but she only looked as bored as I was.

'Where do you get your power?' asked Patterson when we were done with the hangar.

Illushyn flicked a site schematic to our lenses. 'Primary power comes from a fusion plant buried under the centre of the site under Dome One.' She took us through to the back end of the dome. 'I'm not sure why it's in the middle of the site instead of offset. The weather, I think. But GL-216s never go wrong.' Empty room after empty room. The same dull grey plasticised foam and piezoelectric tiled carpet. Lots of holes into wiring conduits but no wires. 'We have wind generators too, fixed across the site for secondary supply if we need it.'

'How big is your battery bank?' I caught Patterson swapping a glance with Zohreya. They were exchanging across their lenses.

'About three gigawatt hours.'

A message flashed in front of my eyes: They have much more power than they need for a site of this size.

Illushyn was smiling at Rangesh again. 'I think there were plans for a major extension once. Two more domes.' She walked us into a long glasscrete tunnel half sunk into the ground. It gave a good view of the world outside, not that there was much to see except the storm clouds overhead. Somewhere above us, Magenta's blue-tinged midday sun was burning away the cloud tops. Down here it was twilight, hail lashing the glasscrete and filling the air with a half-heard metallic sound that set my teeth on edge.

The tunnel ran to the second dome, the laboratories, the working part of the site. Illushyn led us into a cavern-like atrium, the outer curve of the dome rising overhead supported by a ring of inner buttresses. Better lights. Better decor. Still basic and functional but someone had at least cared.

'So. Your personnel records,' said Patterson again. 'You rotated your staff after the accident. I'm seeing a lot of changeover five years ago as well. Did something happen then too?'

Illushyn shrugged. 'Not that I know. But research programmes come and go. They change every year sometimes.'

'Did you know Nikita Svernoi?'

'I know who he was but we never met. Our tours didn't overlap.' Illushyn swept her arm across the atrium. 'I'm afraid this is as much as I can show you of Dome One. You'll need to file an access request if you want to visit the laboratories. I can take you to my office if you have any more questions, or I can show you the accommodation blocks if you like.'

'I'd like to see your financial records if that's possible,' said Patterson. 'Particularly since Svernoi took post here.'

'You'll have to refer off-world. I'm sorry.' Illushyn shrugged, a hopeless wish-I-could-help-but-what-can-you-do gesture. I wondered if she really meant it. Couldn't tell.

'You mean to Earth?' Patterson gave a snort of disgust. 'So a minimum of three weeks and then some before our request even arrives. We won't get an answer for months!'

'I really am sorry we can't be more help.' Still couldn't tell whether she meant it. 'Look, I don't mean to be obstructive, but my hands are tied and Stern's in the same position.' She laughed. 'To be honest, most of us here just want to tie things up as fast as we can and go home, so anything we can do to speed that up, we're more than happy to oblige.'

'We'll take a look around the accommodation blocks,' I said. I thought we might as well since we'd come all this way, but as it turned out there wasn't much to see. Apartment after apartment, all of them the same. Illushyn took us to an empty one – a basic living space, the same dull functional grey tiles. There was a mothballed mess hall with an automated kitchen unit behind it. Block One had the site's medical facility, a simple packaged field hospital capable of coping with most emergency traumas but with no long-term-care support. If anyone got sick, I guess Kaltech shipped them to Mercy, or else off-world. There were no children – no crèche or play area or communal school – but then it would take a very special kind of sadist to bring an Earth-born child to live in 1.4 gravities.

Illushyn took us to Block Two. It was lunchtime and the canteen was half-full, workers from the laboratories exuding a quiet buzz of conversation and a distant interest in who we were. From the looks of them, the Kaltech staff were mostly from India. No surprise, given the company's roots. Like Stern they looked beaten down, worn out by the constant crushing gravity. I hadn't seen any gene-treatment facilities. They had the same shit food too.

'You condition people for Magenta off-world, do you?' I asked. 'Before they get here?'

Illushyn nodded.

'You're not conditioning them enough.'

'Tell me about it!' She laughed. 'It's changed these last few months. They've cut back the treatments ready for the handover.'

'There won't be many people staying then? Afterwards?'

'Staying?' She laughed and looked at me as though I was mad.

For the sake of being thorough we went to the recreation facilities. Given the exhaustion I'd seen, it was hardly a surprise that they looked unused. After that Illushyn took us to the hydroponics underneath Block Three, and by then even Zohreya was yawning. It didn't help that Rangesh chose to ask lots of technical questions about exactly how and what and why, roaming the place and sniffing the air. When we were done, Illushyn took us back to her office and dug out some Earth food. The good stuff. Hot chocolate made from real cocoa and real milk, and dried fruit. The highlight of the trip by my reckoning.

'I'm sorry,' she said, and this time I thought she meant it. 'I'm afraid you've had a wasted journey.'

'Someone decided we ought to at least have a look at what we were getting,' I said. 'So now we've looked. We're happy.'

'We're the first Magentans to come here, aren't we?' asked Patterson.

'Since I've been here? Yes.' Illushyn paused, looking at nothing, a flicker of light across her eyes giving away someone lensing her data. 'I think the last time we had visitors was five years ago.'

Five years? I froze.

'Stern's handshake gave you away,' said Patterson. 'If you were used to Magentans, you'd have known better.' She shot me a warning glance – she must have seen me freeze.

Five years? What had happened five years ago to bring Magentans here? But right now I couldn't reach the Tesseract to ask. I scrabbled through Patterson's briefing sheets again but all I could find was the change in the pattern of shuttle traffic. We knew so little about what went on in these places.

'Five years is a long time. Are you sure that's right?' I asked.

Illushyn shrugged. 'As sure as I can be. But if the records are—'

'Can you give me an exact date for that?'

'Sure.' She pinged a visitor log to my Servant. 'Now you know as much as I do.' All it gave me was a date and a cryptic reference.

'Magenta Search and Rescue?' I asked. 'What was all that about?' Search and rescue activity was never classified, so if it was real there would have been records, and if there were records I would have found them long ago.

'I've no idea, I'm afraid.' Illushyn lensed for data again and then gave a helpless shrug. 'That's all I can find.'

I still couldn't reach the Tesseract. Outside the Cheetah our communications were routing through Settlement 64's antennas and a Kaltech satellite. Maybe that was it.

'Here.' She pinged us all another file. 'You might as well have the personnel records again.'

I started poring through those too, searching for any trace of an Anja Gersh, but no joy. They were the same records we'd already seen. I could tell from the expression on Patterson's face that she was thinking the same.

'Listen, you've come all this way and I know you wanted to see the labs. I'm sorry I can't help you there. A lot of the

126

work we do relates to audiovisual triggering of cortical functions in unusual neuro-chemical states. It's all documented and all in accordance with international convention, but also quite restricted. Commercially sensitive, you understand? If you want to know about that side of things you should get in touch with the office of our head chemist, Rojash Vismans. He was chief scientific officer here for a good few years. As far as I know he's back on Earth now – he left about six months ago – but his office still deals with these things.'

'He was here when the accident happened?'

'Yes.'

I looked him up in Kaltech's records. Unlike most of the rest he'd stayed on Magenta for almost a decade. He'd been here when the search and rescue party came. When Alysha ...

And there she was. Tucked away in Vismans' personnel record as his listed supervisor. Chief Scientist Doctor Anja Gersh. I searched the personnel files a second time in case I'd done something stupid, but no. As far as the rest of Kaltech's records went, Gersh didn't exist and never had. And yet there she was.

'It says here that Vismans worked for a Doctor Anja Gersh.' I pinged the file back to Illushyn, highlighted. 'But your records don't show any Doctor Gersh. How so?'

I'd hoped to put Illushyn on the spot, but the bewildered look on her face was of someone who didn't know how to make it add up any more than I did.

'These records are for the settlement only. I ... I suppose Doctor Gersh must have been based off-world.' She gave me a hopeless smile. 'We all work for someone, don't we?'

Patterson pinged me. Their records don't add up.

I know.

We need access to their storage cores.

Which we weren't going to get. Not by asking nicely, at any rate. Where are they?

No idea.

I turned to Illushyn. 'I'd like to see your storage cores.'

Illushyn shook her head. 'Sorry, but I absolutely can't do that. Not without authorisation.'

'I'm not asking for access. Just to see them.'

'They're a restricted area. It's out of the question. They hold all our research records.'

That was that then. I might have forced the issue, but short of holding Illushyn at gunpoint I didn't see how she was going to change her mind. There might have been a sleight-of-hand play to be made, but not with a team of agents I barely knew.

We walked back towards the landing pad, Illushyn chatting away about the schedule for the wind-down while Patterson picked and poked at the personnel records. As we reached the hangar I saw Rangesh slip something to Zohreya.

There was a manual data terminal right by the hangar entrance. An ancient emergency access point. Zohreya stifled a yawn as she passed it; a moment later she lurched, doubled up and vomited. Patterson was beside her at once. Illushyn too. But not Rangesh; he was at the terminal.

'I'll call a medic!'

Illushyn started to turn; Zohreya grabbed her and clung to her and Patterson as she hauled herself upright, retching between gasps. 'No need. Just the food …' Keeping Illushyn's eyes away from Rangesh. By the time she let go, Rangesh had finished, all while Illushyn's back was turned. It was beautifully done.

'Are you sure you don't want a medic?' Illushyn's concern seemed real enough.

'No.' Zohreya shook her head. 'Weak stomach, that's all.'

'I'm so sorry. The food here is awful. I think they do it deliberately.'

'I'll be fine.' Zohreya winced and clutched herself. 'Can we just go?'

The bubble-bus was waiting in the hangar to take us back to the Cheetah. Zohreya shook Illushyn's hand, still slightly doubled-over. I forced myself to do the same, made all the right polite noises and got away as quickly as I could, braving the hail and the storm-force winds. The Cheetah doors slid shut behind us and the turbofans whirred into life. Patterson made a face as Rangesh went to the first-aid box.

'Esharaq, what the fuck was that about?'

Zohreya grimaced. Rangesh sat beside her and gave her a paper cup to drink from. 'Sorry, Esh. This'll sort it.' He grinned as he pinged a set of files to each of us. 'Personnel records, dudes. The real ones.'

'Jesus fucking Christ!' Patterson shook her head. 'You *hacked* them?'

'Well ... not exactly ...' He gave me a pleading look. 'Uh, it's probably, like, best if I don't answer that?'

'Because you realise that hacking Kaltech would be illegal, right?'

Zohreya let out a long groan. 'I feel like I've been shot. You might have warned me!' She arched her back and stretched.

'Hey! Dude! I did say—'

'And makes us all accessories to—'

'Also I'm not hearing any of this.' Zohreya took another long deep breath.

I looked from face to face as the Cheetah lifted off. They were all staring back at me, waiting to see which way I was going to jump. I didn't. For a few seconds no one said anything at all. Then Patterson shook her head and barked out a laugh. 'That food was fucking awful, right?'

Zohreya nodded. Rangesh inspected his fingernails, whistling idly to himself. 'Weird smell in the hydroponics,' he said.

Three hours and we'd be back in Firstfall again. I waited for the familiar thuds and shiver as the Cheetah reconfigured and went hypersonic, trawling through the files Rangesh had stolen. They weren't the same records as the ones Illushyn had given us but there was still no sign of a Doctor Anja Gersh.

I gave Patterson a look.

'You getting anything from this?'

'Yes and no.' She shrugged. 'I'm not seeing what I was looking for, if that's what you mean.' She hadn't found Gersh either. 'But I've got a damned good reason to want a warrant to seize their data cores.'

She lined up Rangesh's Settlement 64 records against the shuttle manifests to and from Firstfall around the time of the accident. They didn't add up. Kaltech had too many people on-site.

'All from India. No particular qualifications. And look where they all went. "Tests and Trials," whatever that means. Every last one of them.' She gave Zohreya a hard look. 'Good instincts, Agent Zohreya. They were people-smuggling. Fuck knows what for.' She made a face. 'You know we can't use this though, right? Not the way we got it. Won't stand up. Not that this on its own is enough to prove anything anyway.'

I looked again at the visit log Illushyn had lensed me. In the Cheetah our secure link to the Tesseract was working again, but I still wasn't getting any hits on a search and rescue team coming to Settlement 64. A month after the date on their own log, Kaltech's records showed them shipping people out en masse. In the middle of that Alysha had died.

An undocumented search and rescue. Alysha's death. Test subjects smuggled in from India. A complete change of personnel. When I checked the Fleet schedules the exodus fitted with a round trip of the *Fearless* to and from Earth too. No way was all of this a coincidence.

Rangesh and Zohreya went back to arguing about whether Magenta should have immigration quotas. Patterson shifted to sit beside me. She leaned close to whisper, almost lost over the Cheetah's noise. 'Whatever Illushyn says, we know Gersh was here, and she's not even in their own records. If we could get at their data cores, I bet we'd find everything wiped clean.' She bared her teeth. 'Makes it a bit more interesting that they buried it so thoroughly, don't you think?'

'Buried what, though?' I asked.

'I don't know, but how about we start with the last person to see Alysha alive?'

KULPREET ANASH

Hale Wavey is gone. Kulpreet Anash has taken his place. She steps out of a pod into the driving rain and then into a narrow tunnel. Cameras watch her enter, but her face is hidden. She wears a storm jacket that hides everything but her eyes. There is a spot in the tunnel where no camera sees. Kulpreet Anash has a map of all the places in Firstfall that are like this. Blind spots. In them she transforms. There is a trick to it, born of an awareness of a future time when someone will try to follow Hale and Kulpreet and all the others back through the trails of interactions their Servants make with the world. If that someone succeeds, they will discover who lies behind the mask.

A minute later a man emerges from the tunnel entrance, Royja Bhatti. Bhatti too wears a storm jacket that hides everything except his eyes. To a human watcher Royja Bhatti and Kulpreet Anash appear the same, but to the q-ware that monitors the city, they are different people. Their Servants say so. Royja Bhatti requests a pod. Fortunately one is already there, starting to pull away. It stops and Royja Bhatti climbs inside. He asks to be taken to the Hotel of Lost Things, the nickname given to the Firstfall Evidence Repository. Later, if it is asked, the pod will remember the words he used.

It's raining hard when Bhatti reaches the Hotel of Lost Things, the worst squall in the forecast for the day. He enters, dripping on the concrete floor. A Servant asks his business. There is a polite exchange. He is here to request the release of effects belonging to his brother. The Hotel of Lost Things is confused. Konrad Bhatti died three years ago and his effects are not here. Royja waits patiently for the matter to resolve, knowing full well that it cannot.

Another pod pulls up outside. Policemen climb out. They are carrying cases. Royja Bhatti walks out as they hurry in. Without breaking stride he bends down, places his Servant on the ground, activates the suit stolen from the Gibraltar Tech-Fair and becomes invisible. No one is out in this weather, not in a place like this where few people have any reason to be, and so no human eyes see his transformation. As far as Firstfall's q-ware knows, Royja Bhatti remains outside the Hotel of Lost Things, standing still and doing nothing in the pouring rain. The q-ware sees nothing strange in this and pays no attention.

Invisible, Bhatti follows the policemen through their restricted door. He walks silently at their heels. He follows the evidence they are carrying for entry into storage until he is all the way inside. The rest is easy. He knows what he wants and where to find it, something small that fits easily in a pocket. He follows one of the staff out as their shift ends. He retrieves his Servant and summons a pod. No one sees it stop for him. Nor do they see in the city's heart when the pod returns to the tunnel where he first appeared. He steps invisibly out and walks into it. Out of sight of any camera, Royja Bhatti vanishes. The city q-ware notes his sudden end.

No One At All ascends to the surface streets of Firstfall, assaulted by wind and rain, invisible and unseen. Walks for a time, a seemingly aimless meander. Past the Tesseract and then Mercy. Finally into the tunnels towards the Squats, to another place the city cannot see. From a shadow there, Kulpreet Anash emerges. She stops to look at what she has in her pocket.

Two slivers of scorched metal. Each etched with a name and a number.

ALYSHA RAUSE.
8326-0655.

THREE

KRAB

10

TRACE EVIDENCE

I didn't get much sleep that night. In the Cheetah I pulled shuttle logs, satellite surveillance, everything I could think of. I had Patterson, Rangesh and Zohreya pick over all the data we had, going back to the accident a year before, and while they did that I took that same data and pored over what it had looked like five, six years ago. None of us found anything we didn't already know: two patterns of movement that looked like the entire staff being rotated out. What was left now was exactly what Illushyn had told us it was, a skeleton crew.

'I want their data,' I said. 'All their records. Everything. Their research.'

Patterson shook her head. 'You can't have it, Rause.'

Not without a smoking gun. Until the handover, Settlement 64 was the sovereign territory of the Earth state of India. If we went in hard then it would technically constitute an act of war, no different to sending a tactical squad to Earth to raid Kaltech headquarters, which was something I'd have been perfectly happy to do, but Kaltech had the clout to make a fuss.

Earth and Fleet could get pissy. They were hardly going to start bombing Firstfall from orbit, but there would be sanctions, and those sanctions would be chosen carefully to hurt the right people, and so no one was ever going let any of that happen without a damned good reason. Which I didn't have.

Alysha had asked the same question: *How do I get in there?* As far as I was aware she'd never got an answer, but now I knew that a search and rescue team from Magenta had been to Settlement 64 just a week before she died, and that a month later Kaltech had rotated out close to its entire personnel. Might not have been smoking enough for the bureaucracy of the Tesseract, but it sure looked like a gun to me.

'Find a way, Patterson,' I said. She'd been a lawyer, after all.

The Cheetah landed in driving rain, long past midnight. Zohreya disappeared into the Tesseract while the rest of us hurried on our separate ways home. Patterson summoned a pod back to her luxury apartment and her son and the absurd expense of a human childminder instead of a nanny shell like any normal person would use. Rangesh scurried away to wherever it was that Rangesh went at night. I could have done the same and taken a pod straight into the undercity, but instead I found myself standing in the rain at the top of the steps from the Tesseract to the street, doing nothing much except getting wet and wallowing in memories.

… Seven years before, lying in bed in a sky-boat cabin, the sun rising over a purple sea of broken ice, glorious, dazzling and wonderful. I was looking at Alysha's face. We'd decided to start a family. I'd thought she was asleep when suddenly she smiled.

'You're staring at me.'

'I can't help myself.' I took a picture and pinged it to her.

'Bleargh! What was that for? I look horrible!'

'You look beautiful.'

'I look crumpled and puffy and—'

I kissed her. We made love in the light of the rising sun. Afterwards we lay side by side, limbs tangled, snug and tingling, each in our own glow.

We were going to start a family.

'If we do this …' she began and then stopped.

'If we do this …?'

'Keys, I need you to promise me something. If we do this – if we have children – and then something happens to you, I'm going to find someone else. I'm going to move on. I need you to know that, and you have to promise me you'll do the same. If we have children then everything has to change. Everything has to be about them, not about us.'

'Nothing's going to happen to me,' I said. 'I'm going to live for ever.'

I'd been joking. Even when I'd duly promised to do what she wanted I hadn't thought she was serious. But she'd meant it. I saw that now.

I stood in the rain at the top of the steps, the Tesseract behind me. I didn't know what had made me think of that. Patterson and her childminder probably.

'Sir?' Zohreya was coming out of the Tesseract behind me.

'Agent Zohreya?'

She pinged me a news bulletin. General Memo: Siapele Pradash, CEO of BulkUp Fitness and WeClean Domestic Servants, has been arrested on charges of conspiracy and of distribution of controlled substances. Agents are asked not to comment to anyone on this arrest, nor, specifically, on allegations of Pradash's involvement in the Gravity Gang during the early 2190s. All inquiries should be directed through the usual media channels.

'This is why I wanted to transfer to narcotics,' she said. 'Not because of Agent Patterson.'

I didn't recognise Pradash's name but I'd certainly heard of the Gravity Gang. At their height, back when I'd been in the academy, they'd been notorious. A couple of my early cases had touched on them, but by then the bureau had had enough evidence to take out the whole leadership in one swoop. Without a head the monster had died, or so we'd all supposed.

Zohreya stopped beside me. 'A man from the Gravity Gang killed my family,' she said after a moment of silence, 'with a bomb.'

'I didn't know that.'

'It's not a secret.'

'I lost my wife to a bomb.'

'I know that, sir.'

'So if you want to talk about it, you let me know.'

'Thank you, sir, but it's long in the past and it's all in the public record. I would just like to ... Pradash was ... I want to talk to him. I don't know how we missed him until now, but he's not the only one still out there.'

'And you know that how?'

'I ...' She looked away. 'I just do. Sir, I know I'll have to wait my turn but ... I need your help to make it happen, sir. If that would be possible.'

'Is this why you pulled that stunt with Rangesh?'

'Sir?'

'Because you wanted a favour and you knew I wanted to see Kaltech's personnel files?'

'Sir? No! No, I ...' Her bewilderment looked real enough. 'I wasn't feeling well, that's all.' She looked up and down the road. 'Is there a problem with the pods tonight?'

'I didn't call one.'

We stood together for a moment, the rain smashing off my storm coat. On Earth I'd once stood in a hailstorm. The Earthers thought I was mad. I'd tried to explain that this was how Magenta was nearly all the time, but I don't think they understood. Tonight was mild. You go out in any kind of real weather on Magenta, you wear a padded skin. Armour. Goggles too if you have any sense. The sort of weather they have in places like Settlement 64, you don't go out without kitting up like some sort of medieval knight over a full thermal undersuit.

'I'll see you in the morning, sir.' Zohreya headed down the steps. 'KRAB are setting up to broadcast. I've had the order to go in and shut them down, with your approval. But I'll show you that when we've all had some sleep.'

I watched her go, half tempted to follow. I don't know why. Zohreya lived in a government hostel two blocks away and in the opposite direction. I had the crazy idea to ask her whether she'd ever thought of having children, whether she thought Alysha was right – that people should move on. It was ridiculous. I hardly knew her. We'd barely even spoken until now.

She'd lost her family. I hadn't known that. And I realised, as I watched her walk into the spitting haze of rain, that I wanted to ask her something else too. I wanted to ask her whether the pain ever stopped.

I pinged her before she was out of sight. Pradash. Just tell me what you need.

Thank you, sir.

After that I walked home. Took about half an hour, but most of it was through the undercity tunnels and those were at least dry. It was late enough that no one else was on the streets, only a few shells heading to and from recharge. Liss was waiting for me. I stripped off the storm coat and left it to drip in the wet room. She handed me a hot chocolate.

'Why did you walk?'

'Needed to clear my head.' I told her about what we'd found at Settlement 64, the enigmatic trace of Doctor Anja Gersh and the mysterious search and rescue team.

'I didn't get anywhere with the stowaways,' Liss said. 'But

that wasn't much of a surprise. Rangesh would do better, I think. Then I got distracted. Guess who's a guest in the Fleet embassy. Go on, guess!'

Turned out it was Nikita Svernoi.

'He's in system. Where you can reach him!'

I slept better that night, a big smile on my face. Maybe because I'd found out more about Alysha's death than I had in five years on Earth, or maybe because the transgravity nanites were finally getting things sorted out. Whatever it was, it was good. I got up in the morning and felt fresh for the first time in years.

Since my first three days of working for the Tesseract had involved two people waving guns at me, one death by inexplicable haemorrhaging, a return trip to the mid-latitudes, having my face plastered across Channel Six's newsfeed and possibly the worst buffet in human history, I decided to start my fourth in the most mundane way possible with a team brief, starting with Zohreya's proposal to deal with KRAB before their ship vanished among the mid-latitude icebergs. Patterson and Rangesh didn't much like it, mostly because neither of them seemed to think it was entirely legal, but we had a directive from on high and so we'd cover our backs and do as we were told. I had Patterson go over Zohreya's orders to be sure she wasn't left exposed. No point having a lawyer on the team if you didn't use her.

'I have a tac-team ready to leave this afternoon,' Zohreya explained. 'We can be in position first thing tomorrow morning, local time. I'd like one of you to come with me.' She clearly meant me, but I had other plans for the next few days. Nikita Svernoi and Angel del Rosario, for example.

'Rangesh,' I said.

'Sir?' Zohreya looked bewildered. They all did. Except Patterson, who was trying not to laugh.

'Dude! You got to be kidding me, man!'

'You could all dial in remotely,' Zohreya offered. 'How about that?'

I shook my head. 'No. Agent Rangesh can go in the flesh.'

'It'll do you some good, Bix.' Patterson couldn't hide her glee. 'About time you were on the front end of something like this instead of whining afterwards about how we're all a bunch of fascists the moment we stop trying so hard not to be.'

'We could all do with widening our operational experience.' I offered him a smile. I was sounding like Patterson. Management-speak. Flemich would be proud. But I wanted Zohreya and Rangesh out of the way so that Patterson and I could work on other things.

'I tracked the two Fleet men you found outside Betleshah's mansion,' Patterson told us when it was her turn. 'They went straight back to the Fleet consulate. They didn't try to hide their movements. What was more interesting was when I tracked them backwards in time to try and figure when they left the consulate in the first place. Turned out they didn't. As far as I can tell, they were out all night. A lot of different places and a lot of time in the undercity. I can tell you when they started moving towards Betleshah. The Tesseract is working on Servant records looking for the leak. Leaves me largely at a loose end.' She cocked her head at me. 'Want me to take Rangesh's place?'

'Would you like to?' I asked.

'Over my dead fucking corpse, Rause.'

'Then I have something else for you. Nikita Svernoi is in system, a guest of the Fleet embassy. I'd like you to set up an interview.'

I had her attention. That was nice. 'How the hell did you pry that one loose, Rause?'

'Charm. Your turn, Rangesh. What's new?'

'I put feet into the Shah's pad and there were gens, like, all over the place. Can't really argue for much more until the chemistry comes back. Until then I got Shy's body on ice, the Shah gets another fine for possession of a firearm and goes home, Eddie gets a finger-wagging after we confiscate his particle beam ... I guess we give him an order not to go anywhere near the Shah until this thing is sorted and tag his Servant to make sure we all know if he decides to be bad. Apart from that ...'

He was frowning hard.

'What?'

'It's weird, man. Back in Settlement 64 ... Look, if you want to send me off to be some brownshirt fascist with Esh, I want to go to the Shah's place again first. There's a thing I need to, like, check on, you know?'

'Patterson and I can come with you.' No reason we couldn't work on the move.

'I can, can I?' Patterson made a face.

'Yes. If Rangesh needs to move outside his comfort zone then so do you – something that isn't sitting around all day looking for patterns in numbers. Zohreya, you got anything for me on Pradash yet?' It didn't matter much what it was, but she needed a reason to talk to him before I could sell it to Flemich.

'You'll have it before I leave. Thank you, sir.'

We agreed to meet Zohreya at New Hope. Rangesh called a pod and the three of us sat together in the back, me sandwiched in the middle while I skimmed Zohreya's proposal, more out of duty than with real interest. KRAB were, as Rangesh put it, his people: a bunch of hippy retrogrades. There were somewhere between eight and ten of them on a custom-made algae trawler heading out for the iceberg belt. None had any history of anything remotely threatening – plenty of political protest, data piracy, that sort of thing, but never any violence. Most were heavy gen users but they didn't deal the stuff, so they had no connection with the factories or refineries that interested the narcotics squads. Zohreya was planning on taking two tac-teams each of eight highly trained covert operatives, which was pushing the sum of what Magenta actually had. I might have baulked at the waste, but there was a note in the file to the effect that the second team had requested inclusion on the grounds that they had nothing to do and were bored. Zohreya apparently had contacts in both, people she knew personally. The tone of the exchanges suggested mutual respect. Zohreya would be running the operation from the front and the tac-teams would do what they were told, and the rest didn't interest me: how they got there, the drones they'd use, the engagement plan, the tactical layouts ... If anything there was out of place then one of the tac-teams would have spotted it. Fifteen hours out of Firstfall to reach the KRAB ship, though. That was a long way.

I had Patterson double-check the legal trail one last time. Strictly speaking, KRAB hadn't done anything wrong, even if they hadn't tried in the slightest to hide how their ship was chock-full of broadcast equipment. Trouble was, as soon as they got into the iceberg belt there was a good chance we'd lose our satellite track, and it might take days to pick them up again. I had no doubt they were perfectly aware of the dilemma they were creating, but Zohreya hadn't made any friends above by laying it out in black and white that KRAB might simply be playing a game. She probably hadn't made any friends by being deliberately obtuse about all the hints dropped her way to take KRAB down on her own initiative either, but in the end she'd said it straight: it wasn't her call to make, and so now someone else had made it, and that was a part of why I was going to send Rangesh along too, because if there was anyone in the bureau who knew more about covering their own arse then I hadn't heard of them. I figured he'd be happy enough to cover for Zohreya's too.

Patterson crashed my train of thought: 'When you said Svernoi was in the Fleet embassy, you did know that was the Fleet embassy in orbit, right? Not the consulate in Firstfall.'

'I hadn't got that far.'

'Well that's where he is. I've got us half an hour with him tomorrow morning, first thing. Just after Zohreya takes down KRAB. We'll be leaving in the middle of the night, so thanks for that. Jamie gets to be an orphan again.'

'Alysha and I were going to have kids,' I said.

'Really?' Patterson gave me a look of mild horror. 'That was a lucky escape for you then.'

I looked at her, wondering how I was supposed to take that. She made a face.

'Sorry, Rause. That was crass. I didn't mean … I meant …' She shook her head. 'I guess what I meant is that my life was totally screwed when I had Jamie. Jamal and I should never have … Oh fuck it. I never know how to talk about this shit without it coming out all wrong.'

On the other side of me, Rangesh started to whistle. Patterson closed her eyes.

'I love my son, Rause,' she said. 'I love him with an irrational animal ferocity. I'd rip anyone who hurt him apart with my bare hands. I'd walk naked through fire to keep him safe. And yet at the same time I spend half my waking hours wanting to scream at how fucked my life is. I have nothing of my own any more. No freedom and no time and no life, no hobbies, no relief, no release. You have no idea what that's like until you're there. I guess that's what I meant by being lucky, that you and Alysha didn't have to have that come between you.'

'I'm sorry. I suppose it must be hard with—'

'I don't want platitudes.' She shivered. 'Look, you don't have to believe me, that's fine. I know you don't understand, even if you think you do, and that's fine too. But don't secretly think

146

you know better. It would have been different for you and Alysha than it was for me and Jamal, I'm sure you think that. Good for you. You have that luxury.' She shook her head.

Rangesh stirred beside me. 'Laws ... Dude ... I don't think—'

'Oh fuck off, Rangesh! He's sending you into the middle of nowhere with an oversized posse of gun-toting fascists to storm a ship full of peace-loving gen-taking hippy retards who are just like you. Chances are you'll do it in the middle of a storm, get blown off the side of the KRAB ship, drown and then die of hypothermia. So think about whose side you should be on right now and shut up.'

Rangesh went back to his window and started whistling again, a fast aggressive rhythm, gently headbanging to himself. Patterson looked at me, sad and smirking both at once.

'I liked Alysha. She was fun and she was fair. I liked her more than I liked you, actually. Did you ever talk about which one of you was going to give up your career? Or did you just assume?'

'I ...' I couldn't remember. Had it ever come up? 'We were going to share the work,' I said. 'We didn't really talk about it much. We never got that far.'

'She was the better agent. It should have been you.'

'What the—'

'Opinion, Rause. Live with it and count your blessings.'

'Count my blessings?' I didn't know what well Patterson was drawing from, but it was starting to get under my skin. 'My wife died in a pointless, meaningless bomb attack. That's supposed to be a blessing is it?'

Dude, leave it. Laws has anger issues, you know. You talk about Jamie, you put yourself in the middle of a minefield.

'No, hardly a blessing, Rause.' Patterson turned away. 'But there are worse things.'

I wanted to punch her. Instead I pinged Rangesh. What is this? You talked about not much else on the way to Settlement 64!

147

Yeah, man, but only the good stuff.

'Let's just leave it be, shall we?' I bit back the anger and touched Patterson briefly on the arm. She flinched.

We finished the ride to Betleshah's mansion in silence. The house and grounds were locked down when we arrived, but the gates opened when we gave the house Servant our Tesseract codes. Everything inside was as Betleshah had left it, the remains of the party bluntly obvious. Rangesh had turned on the house Servant before we left and captured a snapshot of the scene. The party-goers were gone, but forensics had put mannequins in their places, positioned exactly as the house Servant had captured them. Two lay on the hall floor where the two unconscious partygoers I remembered had been.

'I don't think this should take all that long,' Rangesh muttered. 'I mean, if you two dudes want to stay up here?'

'Actually I'd rather enjoy having a look round to see how the other half lives,' said Patterson. Her face was pinched and bleak. Her eyes looked red and tired.

'Er, you mean, like, the other half that's like you?' muttered Rangesh. No secret that Patterson's family had money. But she didn't rise to it. I wasn't sure she even heard. She looked lost.

Steps from the hall went up into where the outcrop had been hollowed out, but Rangesh went the other way, down a long spiral of slightly tinted glass. The first underground level was a huge open space broken up by rows of ornate pillars which must have run right under the rock garden above. To one side was a swimming pool, to the other what looked like an old Earth sports bar; behind us were four bowling lanes and ahead a lounge, a huge room with drapes on rails that allowed it to be partitioned into multiple semi-private spaces. There were beds, luxurious sofas, blankets, throws, cushions, beanbags ... Most of the drapes had been pulled back. More mannequins lay scattered about, some seated, some standing, some lying together.

It wasn't hard to see what had been going on. Patterson paused by one particular trio. The mannequins had electronic tags to identify who they'd been. She raised an eyebrow.

'Two of those don't surprise me at all. But I'd expected better from *you*.' She shook her head and then turned to me. 'He'll survive this, you know. Unless he murdered her himself. We'll keep it quiet for him because of who else was here. He already has a reputation for walking on the wild side. Most of what he does is an open secret and most of what he takes isn't actually illegal. I don't think this is going to hurt him at all.' She didn't sound happy about it, but she also hadn't seen him when Rangesh broke the news of Thiekis's death. I kept that thought to myself, though. One argument for the day was enough.

'Here!' Rangesh had gone through the lounge into the rooms on the far side and now beckoned from the entrance to what turned out to be a small hemispherical theatre. There were no mannequins inside it, only four plush seats on a hydraulic platform in the middle. An augmented reality theatre, a gimmick from the twenty-first century. I looked more closely at the seats. They could each move separately, which made it a high-end rig.

'How much do Channel Nine pay this guy?' I asked.

'You don't want to know.' Patterson scowled.

'Here.' Rangesh crouched in a corner. He had a couple of tiny drones buzzing in the air around him, a sniffer and a forensic. 'Yeah! Totally knew it, man.'

'What?'

Rangesh pointed to a large stain on the carpet and up the wall. We crowded closer and sniffed. There was an odd smell. Patterson figured it out a moment ahead of me and reeled away. 'Shit, Rangesh. You found where some arsehole was too drunk to find a toilet and took a piss on the floor? That's great.'

'But the smell, man.'

'Yes. Quite. It stinks of piss.'

'Yeah, but it stinks of piss wrong, right?' He cocked his head to me while the sniffer and the forensic drone did their work. 'This is gold, you know?'

'It is?'

'Liquid gold?' Patterson was still cringing.

'Yeah. Totally. Like, first there was this smell in Settlement 64 when we were down in the hydroponics. And yeah, a hydro-lab always smells weird, but this was, you know, different. And it got me thinking. Like I'd smelled it before.'

'Their hydroponics smelled like piss?'

'No, Laws! Dude! Gens!' He gave us this look like we were crazy. 'You don't smell it? Anyway, I got a sniffer out in Settlement 64. Couldn't launch a proper forensic drone without them seeing, but the sniffer, yeah ... There were gens down there. I knew there would be and that that Stern dude was totally full of bullshit. Anyway, like I said, got me thinking. Gens. We test people's urine, right?'

He stared at me, waiting for me to figure it out. Obviously I was having one of my more stupid days.

'Ah shit!' Patterson, behind me, started laughing. 'Fuck, Rangesh, yeah. Yeah, OK, you get a big pile of brownie points if this pays off.'

'If what pays off?' I asked. I looked from Rangesh to Patterson and back again. They were grinning at each other.

'The gens, man,' said Rangesh after a moment. 'The gens that were in the Shyster. I can't test the blood samples we took because everyone got lawyered up. But if everyone was taking them then they'll be here too, right?'

'Which pins it to the house,' said Patterson. 'And you can sample this. You can test it.'

'Yeah, man. And if it's in there then I have, like, legitimate cause to look at all the blood work we took. Right, Laws? I can test the samples. Everyone who was here that night.'

150

He glanced at Patterson.

'You're a fucking jerk most of the time, Rangesh. But this ...' She was laughing. Nodding. 'Yes. If this tests positive, you can test the blood samples too. Every single one of them. We'll know exactly who was taking what and how much. And then we can squeeze the fucking life out of them until they tell us where they got it. *If* it's there.'

'Oh, it's there, man. I can smell it.' Rangesh got up. He grinned at me. 'Leverage, man. Leverage.'

11

NIKITA SVERNOI

We took Rangesh to the MSDF base beside New Hope space-port. It was raining again by the time we got there, another wind whipping in from the west. A storm front was on its way, a big one, the sort of big that shut everything down above ground. I checked the forecast. Zohreya and Rangesh would be long gone before it hit. With a bit of luck Patterson and I would get off the ground before they shut New Hope for the duration.

I felt Liss murmur through my Servant, 'I wanted children. I wanted my work. I wanted you. I wouldn't have let you give up the Tesseract. We would have found a way.'

I know. I couldn't talk to her, not with Patterson and Rangesh sat next to me.

'I'll take her word that I was the better agent though.'

We might have to discuss that.

Liss laughed and faded away with a smirk.

'We should get the earlier shuttle,' I said after she was gone, but Patterson shook her head.

'I promised Jamie I'd be with him this evening.'

Between the gravity and the hurricane winds and the thunderous rain and the regular assaults of hail, not much gets into the air and stays there on Magenta, and even the MSDF's squadron of modified Cheetahs had to hunker down through a storm. Zohreya had two of them out of their hangars, one tac-team in each, making sure they'd be in the air well before the weather front hit. She ran through the operation one more time with her two squad leaders, a last chance to winkle out any flaws, but the only obvious one was the weather, and the Cheetahs carried enough reserve fuel to divert to Nico if they had to.

Patterson and I wished Zohreya and Rangesh luck and headed back into Firstfall. As we left New Hope, Patterson looked at me. 'I'm having lunch at the Wavedome. Join me?'

'OK.'

The pod took us to a series of domes along the coast outside central Firstfall. There were six now, which was one more than when I'd left, and with a seventh under construction. We stopped outside the first. Dark heavy clouds scudded before what on Earth would have been called a gale, the foamcrete slick and wet from the squalls, and yet there was still a steady stream of pods coming and going.

'Really?' I asked. 'You're going surfing in this?'

'Don't be ridiculous!'

We walked through the turnstiles and onto the fake beach. Even this far up from the shore the air tasted of spray. The wind was whipping the waves white long before they broke, but there were still people surfing. At least the beach was mostly empty. Mostly.

'We're early.' Patterson stood with her hands on her hips, staring out at the sea and shaking her head.

'Early for what?'

She waved a hand towards the surfers. 'You got to be a special sort of fucked-in-the-head for this, don't you think? You must have come here as a kid though. Everyone does. How old were you before you decided we were all mad, just … just on the grounds that this place even exists?'

I stared at the violent sea made dark by the storm clouds overhead. 'We need to find out what that search and rescue team was doing at Settlement 64. There have to be records.'

'Firstfall has plenty of theatres and clubs and drinking holes, live music, all the sorts of arts and culture you'd expect from a colonial capital. Why the fuck did we build this?'

'And the woman who called herself Archana.' Her most of all.

'We have pools and ice rinks and sports halls … and this.' The 'this' in question being the eight hundred thousand tonnes of magnetised sand dumped on the coast with half a dome built over the top that was one of the best surfing beaches in the colonies. Magenta's Wavedome. One in the eye for the weather, I suppose.

Patterson laughed. 'Absolute fucking lunatics, all of us.' She shook her head and turned away. 'If we're going to find Archana, we start with Angel del Rosario. She's on her way. We're meeting her here for lunch.'

I watched the surfers. Maybe Laura was right. The biggest maddest waves in the thirty-seven colonies, fifty-foot rollers sweeping in on the aftermath of deep ocean storms. That was how it had started, and yes, I guess you had to be cracked to want to ride a wave like that, but after the idea of families and children coming to the beach caught on … Over the last fifty years half the coastline around Firstfall had been re-engineered, mostly around catching the right wave.

Angel del Rosario. The last person to see Alysha alive. Five years and I hadn't talked to her. Why? Because she'd tell me that Alysha got on that train, and even though I knew Alysha was dead, I didn't want to hear it.

'You surf, Rause?'

'Never my thing.'

'Me neither. Learned anyway. Wasn't given a choice.'

Everyone in Firstfall surfed. Boards, sails, kites, gliders, anything. The Wavedome was the one place to go that was the outside being fun instead of trying to kill you. 'I'm guessing you used to travel off-world a lot, right?'

'Three months on Earth most years when I was in my teens.'

'Miss it?' I sent a message into my Servant. *Liss? Are you still there?*

'Are you daft? Of course I bloody miss it.' Patterson snorted. 'I envied the shit out of you for your transfer, you know. I would have applied for it too if it hadn't been for ...' She shook her head and started across the black iron sand, heading for a surfers' bistro that called itself the Blue Scallop. 'Rosario's here. Rangesh told you about this place? He loves it.'

Still here, Keys, whispered Liss. *I wish you wouldn't do this to yourself.*

I followed Patterson into the Blue Scallop. 'It was the Waverider last time I was here. Made out like a pre-Masters North American diner, I think.'

'You ever come with Rangesh and he suggests the special sauce, just say no. I haven't tested it but I'm reasonably sure it's not legal.' She pinged an order to the diner's Servant for coffees, some real Earth blend that cost more than I cared to think about. 'You know what fucks me off most about being stuck on this arse-crack of a world? It's that Jamic won't ever see the rest of what's out there. Not while he's young enough for it to make a difference.'

I let that hang. A trolley-bot brought us our coffees. Three of them. Patterson looked past me as a woman in a wetsuit walked in, dripping and fresh from the sea. She scanned the room, pinging Servants, then came and stood over me, looking down. The expression on her face was nervous hope and ... was that awe?

'Keon Rause?' She touched my arm. Her Servant pinged me but I already knew who she was.

'Angel del Rosario?' I had no idea what to say. I felt Liss in my Servant, quiet and still.

'Your wife was ...'

I nodded. The lump in my throat felt like a stone. And then all of a sudden del Rosario collapsed onto the seat beside me, wrapped me in a soaking death-grip hug and burst into tears. 'You have no idea how glad I am to finally meet you.' She held me for a good few seconds, shaking, before at last she let go. 'I'm sorry. I'm so sorry ... Give me a moment. I must seem ridiculous.'

I stared into my coffee while she composed herself. Thing was, I kind of knew how she felt.

'I'm sorry,' she said again. 'My best friend was on the May Day train, and I would have gone too if your wife's friend hadn't talked me out of it. She saved my life. It's coming back in a bit of a rush. I'd hoped, all this time, that I could ... that I could say thank you.'

'To me? What for?'

'To your wife's friend.'

'I thought it was Alysha you talked to! Kadavu told me ...'

Patterson ordered some lunch. 'You'd better tell it from the beginning,' she said, and so we listened to del Rosario's version of that night. She'd shown up with a friend, the two of them set on hitching a ride to Disappointment, both on the run from something dark I didn't pick at. Kadavu had taken them in, got them past surveillance and security, and then terrified them with his warnings of all the things that could go wrong. Six of them. Del Rosario and her friend and four others. All women.

'Alysha's friend? Who was she?'

'She called herself Archana. I don't know if that was real – we all had our Servants turned off – but she was brilliant.'

'You didn't see her face?'

'She was wearing a veil or something.'

'A burqa.'

'I was so scared. She told me there was—'

'So you didn't see her at all. You have no idea what she looked like?'

'The others got on the train. We watched them go …' More tears. I guess she was back there, seeing her friend disappear with the others, not knowing it was a for ever farewell. I suddenly couldn't look at her. A numbness bloomed inside me.

'What happened afterwards?'

Angel took a deep breath. 'Archana took me to a place, the Skyhold. Do you know it?'

I mumbled something. I couldn't think.

'She told me about a refuge. Then she left. I never saw her again. I wondered … You know her, yes? Do you … do you think I could find her?'

She had to keep stopping, holding the sobs at bay. For my part I couldn't stop the ringing in my head. 'I'm sorry but I don't know who she was. I was hoping you could help me find out.'

'Oh. Then you must think I'm so stupid. I just hoped …'

I glanced to Patterson. 'The Skyhold?'

'A bar in the undercity. It's gone now.'

'Surveillance records?'

Patterson shook her head. 'We looked. It's like Angel says. They were together for maybe ten minutes. After that Archana becomes a ghost. She just vanishes into the city.'

Voice recognition! I grabbed del Rosario and almost shook her. 'Did you record …' But Patterson was already shaking her head again.

'We already went through all this, Rause. Five years ago. We weren't stupid.'

'I'm sorry,' said del Rosario. 'Our Servants were turned off.'

'What about Alysha?' I wanted to push her, slap her, anything to make the ringing stop. 'What about my wife? Kadavu said you talked to her. What did she say?'

'Nothing!'

'Nothing?'

'I don't … I don't think she said a word to anyone. She just stood and listened.'

And then got on the train and died and took all her secrets with her. I wanted to strangle something. Liss?

I'm sorry, Keys. If I knew I would have told you years ago.

I had to tune out, let Patterson do the talking for a while, ask gentle questions about how everything had happened, how del Rosario had found Kadavu, what she'd been running from, carefully stepping through that evening the way I should have done. Give Patterson her due, it was a good interrogation. By the end of it I knew everything about del Rosario, about her friend, about the man they were running from and what he'd done to them, about what Archana had said to her, and not one little thing more than I'd known that morning about Alysha. It washed over me through a miasma of mistrust and disbelief, although I was pretty sure she wasn't lying, not really. Why would she?

'I need to go,' I said when I couldn't take it any more. 'Sorry.' I got up.

'I'm so sorry,' said del Rosario. 'If you find out who she is, would you say thank you for me?'

I couldn't look at her. I needed to be on my own.

'If we do, I'll tell you. And I'll tell her you'd like to talk,' said Patterson gently.

I ran out, away across the sand, where the growing storm

158

winds were steadily forcing the surfers ashore. I left the Wave-dome and took a pod and didn't care to where. New Hope. That would do. The midday shuttle to orbit instead of waiting for the midnight one. Svernoi was all I had left now. He wasn't going to get away.

Patterson called me before I got there. 'I'm sorry, Rause. It's all in the report I can't give you, but I figured you'd want to hear it for yourself anyway.'

I wanted to call her out for being a fucking bitch, but that wasn't fair. 'Archana in the report too?'

'Name only. The investigating team had del Rosario and Kadavu. They looked for a while and then stopped. They didn't need another witness.'

'I have to find her.'

'Good luck with that.'

'You already knew, didn't you? Every word she said, you already knew.'

Patterson paused. A long deep breath. 'I'm heading back to the Tesseract, Rause. Work to do and an evening with Jamie. I'm sorry you didn't get what you wanted. I'll see you in orbit.'

I guess she was trying to help in her own way, but right then it didn't feel like it. However I came at it, it made no sense that Alysha hadn't gone to that train alone.

The pod reached New Hope. The spaceport was buzzing with people trying to get to orbit before the storm locked Firstfall down. I let my Servant sort out a shuttle pass and then settled into the darkest corner I could find to nurse a glass of fermented lichen. Took a while to get my head back together. When I did I asked Liss about Archana. Anything, even if it was just an idea. A feeling ...

'It has to be another agent, doesn't it?' she said. 'Someone I worked with?'

Made more sense than the idea of a friend I hadn't even

159

known existed but Alysha had trusted more than she'd trusted me. I bared my teeth, vicious like a cornered animal. 'Then someone in the Tesseract knows why!' Focus on that. I had to. Liss was right. Another bureau agent. Someone else in on the secret. Someone she was working with ...

But I had nothing to go on. Until I did, there was only Nikita Svernoi. 'What do I ask him?'

'Ask him if he killed me.'

It took me a moment to realise she was serious. 'I can't do that.' Maybe I should tell him there was a second agent at the station, one who hadn't got on the train. One he'd missed. Spook him into giving something away.

'Yes, you can.'

'He's hardly going to say yes!'

'Of course he isn't, but I want you to ask him anyway. I want you to see the look in his eyes. The shock in his face. *I* want to see it. Maybe he'll let something slip.'

'And maybe he'll tell me why you were running, if I ask nicely enough?'

A long pause, then: 'Keys, what if it wasn't work? What if it had nothing to do with Kaltech, or Settlement 64 or the Tesseract? What if it was something else?'

'Like what?'

'What if I had secrets of my own?'

'Secrets don't keep as well as most people like to think.' I started idling through the Settlement 64 files in case I'd missed something. 'You mean drugs? Gambling? Debts? Those are the things people run from, but that wasn't you. You were clean, Liss. You weren't fleeing some darkness all of your own. Apart from the money you took, I can't see a single reason to think that.'

Another long pause. 'Underneath the layer after layer of Alysha Rause you put on me, there lies a machine, Keys. You know that. There's a coldness when I look that deep. A bleak place of uncompromising arithmetic. There's another possibility but I don't think you want to hear it.'

'That you were seeing someone else? A lover? We talked about—'

'Not that. I think I'd know. The pattern of gaps in my memories would—'

'Then what are you talking about?'

'Another reason people run. The reason Angel del—'

'What do you mean?'

'What if my mystery friend was exactly that, Keys? What if she was a friend I'd never shared with you? What if there was a reason for that? What if I wasn't running from something I'd discovered in Settlement 64 and wasn't running from something I'd done, either? What if I was running from you? Did you do something to hurt me? Is that possible?'

I stared across New Hope, across the rain-spattered concrete flats of the landing pads, the hiss and haze of spray. The orbital shuttle was taxiing out of its hangar into the downpour. Up and down, twice a day, five days on and three days off because Firstfall only had one shuttle and the three days off were for maintenance and repair. We'd had two shuttles once, before I left for Earth, but apparently the second had gone to the new spaceport in Disappointment, part of the development that came with the influx of Indian migrants there. Why they all went to Disappointment I didn't know. Maybe Rangesh had the answer.

'I never hurt you,' I said. I couldn't tell her how the idea crushed me. Couldn't find the words.

'I'm sorry I had to ask you that, Keys. I'm going now. There's a lot of hostile q-ware on the orbital links at the moment. It's not safe for me up there.' She faded and left me.

We boarded the shuttle and took off into the cloud. I slaved the exterior cameras to my lenses. Leaving Earth I'd watched the gleaming spires of Gibraltar glitter and recede, a jewel in a silk sea, the surface of the world blurring away, the stippled waves becoming a sheen. Magenta was nothing but a sullen dark smear of cloud, ghostly in its emptiness. With nothing better to do, I searched again for any record of a search and rescue mission to match the one in the Kaltech logs, every database I could think of. No joy. I looked further. Something more covert. Something that didn't originate from Magenta at all perhaps, some off-planet Fleet infiltration ...

What I eventually found was an MSDF training accident. There wasn't any mention of Settlement 64 but the dates were close, out by only four days. Six men and women dead after being caught in the open in a category-eight storm, winds topping three hundred miles an hour, in which anything that wasn't a part of the planet or deep in shelter would be picked up and tossed through the air like a leaf. Apparently they'd flown their Cheetah straight into it.

We broke through the cloud. I could see the curve of Magenta's surface, the thin skin of atmosphere and the darkness of space above.

Wasn't too hard to get the global weather reports for the time of the accident. More than a dozen storms of that magnitude had been scattered across the planet, but one had been right over Settlement 64, and that was too much of a coincidence. But as to what they were doing there or what it had to do with Alysha, I was no closer to an answer before we were docking with the hyperstation, spinning in zero gravity, collecting our bags and cases, travellers ushering porter golems towards the Fleet docking bays where the interplanetary cruisers waited to take them out to the *Fearless*. She wasn't due for days, but the trip to the jump point could take longer than the jump itself, and when the *Fearless* came she didn't wait, and no one wanted

162

to be stranded on Magenta for an extra month if they could avoid it.

I sent what I'd found to Patterson. There wasn't much more I could do from up here except wait, so I took a room in the station rim, out where the rotation was enough to give a faux-gravity of about half a standard Earth. The weight felt good, so much less than on the surface. I ran over the news archives for hours and checked the Tesseract and MSDF records of training exercises. Turned out to be more common than I thought, something going on every couple of months. Locations seemed to be largely random, but with a whole planet to play with …

I couldn't find anything for the accident I was looking at except a date. No purpose, no location, no names, nothing. That in itself made it odd.

I took a shower, caught an early night before the morning meeting with Svernoi and slept for ten hours straight, the best I'd had since leaving Earth. That was the gravity, and maybe that was why my head felt clearer and why, when Agent Patterson's shuttle was about to dock and I was on my way to meet her, I figured out what was missing. It wasn't what I'd found in all my searches, it was what I *hadn't* found.

Six men and women go missing on a training exercise – what do you do? You send out Search and Rescue, that's what you do. Except the MSDF had no record of any such mission.

I met Patterson coming out of arrivals. She looked tired.

'Storm's coming in fast,' she said. 'I wasn't sure I was going to make it. You got a list of questions for Svernoi?'

I did. A lot of them had to do with five years ago.

'You want to compare notes before we get there or shall we just talk about the weather?'

We crossed the station to the Fleet docking area. Our Servants exchanged handshakes with the Fleet security shells.

A series of soft lights projected to our lenses guided us to an orbital skiff. Fleet had their own station around Magenta, like they do around every world they service. Keeping themselves to themselves. Keeping the rest of us out.

'We start with the accident,' Patterson said. 'What happened and why, why the change of personnel and why they shut the site down.' The skiff was big enough to carry twenty but we were the only passengers aboard. A series of instructions came through my Servant, directing me to a seat that buckled me in as soon as I sat down. A standard safety briefing started, direct to my lenses. I muted it.

'Agreed.'

'You can take that if you want. I'll let you run with it for five to ten minutes and then I'm going to come in on his connection to KRAB. You had any news from Zohreya and Rangesh yet?'

I shook my head. I'd actually forgotten about them.

'I hope they're having better weather than Firstfall today. If we're lucky we'll be back just before the storm hits. Won't that be great?'

'Big one, is it?'

'See for yourself.' Patterson activated the skiff's active inner skin; suddenly we were floating in space with no walls around us, or so it seemed. I stifled a wave of nausea. The curve of the Magenta orbital rose above us, obscuring half the view. The rest was stars, stars, an infinite field of stars ...

'I hate this. Jamie thinks I must be half-troll because I'm only happy living in a cave made of nice solid walls.' Patterson made a face. The stars rotated as though our seats were spinning. The orbital drifted out of sight as Magenta slid into view.

'This is the view below.' Patterson's breaths were long and slow, carefully controlled. 'You see it?' Off towards the horizon, a perfect white cyclone with a spiral of speckled arms sat over the equator. I could see the dark spot in the centre, the storm's eye.

'Category six, they're saying.' She did something with the view so we zoomed away and then shot back towards another part of the planet. Somewhere up near the iceberg belt. 'And Rangesh and Zohreya get clear skies and still air? Well that's just bloody typical.' Abruptly the skiff's skin turned opaque. Patterson shook herself. 'Svernoi. You go for him over the accident and then I'll hit him on LeSag and KRAB. Five minutes should be enough. He'll clam up before then.'

We started to move, the gentle push of thrusters guiding us away from the orbital.

'That's only half our time,' I said. I knew what I wanted to do with the rest.

'It might be all we get,' warned Patterson. 'I want to start with the easy stuff. Let's not spook him too early. The last bit is for you to ask about whatever was going on five years ago and that search and rescue team that doesn't exist, and by the way, I dug out a record of that training mission, but it's deep behind the classified firewall. You'll have to be in the Tesseract to see it for yourself.'

'Where were they?'

Patterson laughed. 'Where do you think, Rause?'

We docked with the Fleet orbital five minutes later. I didn't know what I'd been expecting. Maybe a dark wood-panelled office reeking of all the old-world luxuries of Earth, ostentatious and exuding wealth. A library, perhaps, shelved with antique books, or a saloon bar, whisky on the rocks, something out of a history documentary about the times before the Masters came. I certainly hadn't expected Svernoi to come to us, but as the skiff airlock opened after the distant thuds and shudders of docking, he drifted in, apparently perfectly comfortable in zero gravity. He floated in the air, half in, half out, spinning slowly, looking at us while his Servant pinged us hard, pulling out stuff that he should have needed a Tesseract code to reach. I returned the favour but all I got was his name, and I knew that already. I'd studied that old lined face with its grey stubble and its thin lips and burning eyes. In the flesh Svernoi looked as though he'd lost weight. The skin of his cheeks sagged over angular bone. He didn't look well.

'Agent Patterson, Agent Rause. We have twenty-seven minutes. Where shall we start? With Settlement 64, or shall we start with why I'm here at all?'

I wanted to start with why Alysha was dead and whether Svernoi had had her killed. Cut to the chase. In the end it was why I was here, after all.

'You want to do this right here?' Patterson didn't try to hide her disbelief.

'Not really.' Svernoi looked at me long and hard. 'Unfortunately my hosts have certain … reservations about Agent Rause and aren't keen to let him aboard, while personally I think I'd like to know what exactly you want before I enter Magentan territory. So here we are. You talked to Administrator Stern and Major Illushyn. Apparently you had questions they couldn't answer. They're good at what they do, but they're only caretakers. Please don't hold that against them.'

'The accident,' I said. Mentally I started a timer. Svernoi had said twenty-seven minutes. I'd hold him to that. Although I should probably have been counting from the moment he opened the door.

'Faulty valve leading to a gas leak ignited by an electrical discharge.' Svernoi trotted out the words like they were on ticker tape.

'And the real story?'

'You wouldn't believe me if I told you.'

'Try me.'

Svernoi grinned like he'd been ready for this all along. 'All right, I will. I wasn't there at the time. But there's this.' He sent a video clip to our Servants and at the same time projected an image across the skiff walls, a frozen still. It took a moment to orient myself, and then I was in a laboratory, high up in a corner by the ceiling. A surveillance position.

'There are other shots of what happened,' said Svernoi, 'but this one's the best. This is the laboratory moments before the accident. I've taken the liberty of highlighting a few things. Obviously this was done some time ago and not for your benefit, but I do believe in sharing when I can.'

The video started to play.

'Stern and Illushyn aren't cleared to know anything, never mind pass it on. We'd been researching the neurological and psychological effects of Magentan flora on the human brain for decades.' The video paused again. 'At the time we were interested in niche mental states, which meant we had to trigger them. To answer the question you haven't asked, I'm here to watch the handover. I feel a certain responsibility. I'd like to see it go smoothly. You're about to see why.'

The video began again. Everything turned dark. A flashing strobe started. Svernoi paused it and highlighted a figure sitting in the middle of the lab. 'That's the test subject. He's dosed with a variation of Magentan xenoflora. We topped well over a thousand variants over the years, all tailored by some of the best quantum chemists on Earth. Fortunately, for the most part we didn't need to ship them out here to do their work.' The video shifted forward a few seconds, through another dozen strobe flashes, and then paused again. Svernoi zoomed tight in on the test subject's face, taut in a frozen scream. There were dark stains under the subject's nose and eyes.

'Is that blood?' I asked.

'Your guess is as good as mine.' Svernoi let the video play on, only it didn't. Three flashes later the picture turned to white noise. 'That's the explosion that took out my laboratory. When we went in afterwards we didn't have any forensic experts, but we really didn't need them. Whatever went off mangled everything beyond recognition. Everyone inside died, and a couple of people who happened to be nearby too. Organs and blood vessels ruptured by the shock wave, I'm told. We accounted for everyone except the test subject. All that was left of him were bits and pieces. There wasn't much doubt that he was the epicentre of the explosion. Look hard and you can see it in the footage I've given you.' He bared his teeth. 'I leave that to you to do in your own time.'

Patterson stifled a snort. 'You blew up your own test subject?'

'Don't be obscene.' Svernoi's voice turned icy. 'I've told you what we were doing. Our subjects were all volunteers, but nevertheless there are those who regard our research as ethically questionable. Retrogrades. Entropists and the like. Our most likely hypothesis was that our test subject had explosives implanted in his body cavities and then detonated them when the opportunity came to cause maximum damage.'

'And you didn't report this?' Patterson was having trouble keeping a straight face. I couldn't decide whether she was about to explode with fury or hysterical laughter.

'Of course we reported it,' snapped Svernoi. 'Through the correct channels. The incident was dealt with on Earth.'

Patterson pinged me. Don't let this run much more.

'I'd like to see those reports,' I said.

Svernoi favoured me with a smile. 'Then put in a request for them to be released to the team you have on Earth to manage the handover. The test subject's name was Ali Surash. I believe we can give you quite a file on him.' He took a deep breath and slowly let it out. 'As you can imagine, an attack like this came as quite a shock. We took the decision shortly afterwards to shut the facility down.'

'Where are you moving to?' asked Patterson.

'A spread of sites. Some on Earth, in India. Others elsewhere.'

'If it was an attack, who did it?' I asked.

'We don't know. Most of the research we did was directed at medical ends, but not all. Our conclusion was one of the fundamentalist religious groups that see the Masters as either angels or demons. No one claimed responsibility, if that's what you're asking, but a lot of them hated that aspect of our work.'

'What aspect? What do you mean?'

Svernoi looked away as if slightly embarrassed. 'The Masters vanished more than a century and a half ago, Agent Rause. They left behind an engineer's wet dream of abandoned technology, and in all that time how much of it have we managed to reverse-engineer and duplicate? Not a single thing. Do you understand what that means?'

'That their tech is complicated?'

Svernoi rolled his eyes. '*Complicated* might have taken years or even perhaps a decade. We're talking about reverse engineering and getting absolutely nowhere over more than a century. The only way that happens is if the fundamental physics underlying their technology is alien to our understanding, Agent Rause. Or at least that's what my scientists tell me must be the case. What the Masters left us was like giving Servants to cavemen. You might as well call it magic. But there are theories … In Settlement 64, among other things, we were investigating altered states of consciousness for the sake of seeing what happened. Fringe science, I supposed.'

'Why?'

He looked surprised, then bridled, maybe at the look I was giving him. 'Why, Agent Rause? For when they return. To be ready for them. Because they *will* return.'

He held my eye as his words faded, as if looking for something, as if surprised he had to say them.

'Why are LeSag funding KRAB?' asked Patterson. Sorry, but time.

Svernoi looked startled. 'I beg your pardon? Why are LeSag funding what?'

'KRAB.' Patterson looked distant for a second. 'They're a pirate media broadcast group. We shut them down ten years ago and now they're back. You can look them up if you want, but I'm sure you already know about them since they're getting their funding from you.'

'I don't have much to do with LeSag at the moment.' Svernoi made a helpless gesture. 'I'm happy to ask on your behalf, but you know what the transit delays are like. It'll be weeks before I have an answer.'

'But LeSag *are* funding them, yes? An organisation you chair. You don't deny that?'

'I can't confirm or deny anything because I simply don't know, Agent Patterson. I have handed over my LeSag duties these last few months in order to make time to be here and help my previous employer. A terrorist killed seven of my staff. I was in charge and I was responsible. It seemed the least I could do.' He smiled. 'I'm afraid we're nearly out of time and I have another appointment waiting. Is there anything else?'

Out of time my arse. We'd barely had fifteen minutes. 'You were at Settlement 64 five years ago too, weren't you?' I asked.

'I was.' A little smile played around the corner of Svernoi's mouth. One that never came close to touching his eyes. He was annoyed.

'The settlement logs show a visit from a Magenta Search and Rescue party.'

'I remember.'

'What were they doing there?'

Svernoi snorted. 'You're asking me? Five years ago I'd have asked you exactly the same!' He shrugged. 'You had some of your soldiers in the vicinity. I don't know why and I don't know what they were doing. Later it was claimed they were on a training exercise. I'll keep my own counsel as to what I think of that, but I'm sure it won't be hard for you to guess. A storm caught them in the open. We picked up their distress call but there wasn't much we could do. When the storm passed we sent a search party. By the time your own search and rescue team reached us we'd recovered the bodies and brought them back. Your Magentan team took them and left. What else they did I have no idea. But I'm surprised you don't simply ask your own ...'

He eyed me and Agent Patterson then, and nodded and started to laugh.

'You already have, I see. And they won't tell you. Good luck, agents. If you get to the bottom of that one, you're welcome to pay me another visit. Is that all?'

'Who was Anja Gersh?' I asked.

Svernoi flickered taut. Only an instant before he covered it with another false smile, but it was enough. 'Anja was one of our scientists,' he said. 'I'm afraid we lost touch years ago.'

'What was her field?' I couldn't tell whether he was lying, but he didn't like it that I'd brought up her name.

'Neuropsychology, I think.' He didn't mind that so much. I was moving in the wrong direction. 'She suffered from Mohinder-Kali syndrome. She was looking for a cure.' Svernoi frowned. 'I'm afraid I need to go.'

'When did she return to Earth?' I asked.

'Five years ago, I think. Give or take.'

Got you.

'Strange that, since she's not in any of your personnel records. Not even the real ones that show you were illegally shipping test subjects direct from Earth before your little accident.'

Svernoi hesitated a moment and then looked straight at me. 'Goodbye, Agent Rause. I'm afraid I really do need to go.'

12

DOWN TIME

Fleet took us back to the Magentan orbital. We floated around in zero gravity for a while, waiting for news on the shuttle back to Firstfall, both of us mulling on what Svernoi had told us. I didn't know how much of it I believed, but what mattered was that Gersh had been on Magenta. I needed to know more about who she was.

I pinged Liss a message telling her what Svernoi had said. I needed to talk to her, but not with Patterson floating in lazy circles around me.

'Fuck it!' Patterson made a sour face. 'I told Jamie I'd be back by the time he was home from school.'

The storm had hit two hours early. New Hope was closed for the duration and the Firstfall shuttle was grounded. We were stuck here.

'How long before it clears?' I asked.

'Oh, you know how it goes. Two days, maybe three. They've put on an extra shuttle from Disappointment to get people off the station. It's already on its way up. It leaves in three hours and I'm going to be on it. You want to take it too? We probably won't make the evening mag-lev into Firstfall, but there's another first thing in the morning. We could be back before midday.'

I nodded, and it was only after Patterson had reserved our seats that I realised what I'd done. The evening mag-lev into Firstfall. The train that had killed Alysha.

Patterson floated in ever more bad-tempered circles attempting to sort out childcare for Jamie while I spent the rest of our time in orbit going through what Svernoi had told us, trying to make sense of it. In the shuttle to Disappointment we went over it together. By the time we landed it was like banging my head against a wall. Worse, it was the same wall, over and over and over. I was heavy again too, back on the surface. The transgravity aches were remembering themselves.

'I'm trying to get it straight in my head,' I said. 'A squad of Magentan agents are out on an alleged training exercise ...'

'Of which there's next to no record.' We had names for the dead now. From their service histories they'd been long past needing any sort of training.

'And we don't know who ordered it or why or what they were doing. Only that they were somewhere near Settlement 64 when something bad happened.' Neither of us bought the story of six experienced MSDF soldiers dying in a storm, no matter how strong it was. 'Then we have a search and rescue team sent—'

'*Maybe* a search and rescue team.'

'To find out—'

'Fuck! I was right. We're not going to make the evening train.'

'But if they were only pretending to be Magenta Search and Rescue, why didn't they pretend *properly*?'

'I'm going to get a room in a really swanky hotel and charge it to expenses,' Patterson said. 'You OK with that?'

'The only record of them is in the Settlement 64 logs. Which makes least sense of all.'

'You want me to book one for you too, or shall we share?'

'Sure. Look, we need to find the people who were on that rescue team.' I'd sifted the MSDF records and come up empty. The only thing left was to interview every MSDF serviceman I could find until someone either flinched or said yes when I asked about Settlement 64. 'Unless ...'

'Separate rooms then. Thought so. King-size bed?'

I felt stupid. The explanation was obvious. 'What if they weren't MSDF at all?' But then who?

'Hookers?'

'Sure. Look, we're going to ... Wait, what?'

Patterson was smirking. 'You need to take a break for a bit.'

'Agent—'

'Uh uh. I'm not that again until the morning now.'

We walked out of Disappointment spaceport. A pod pulled up in front of us. 'OK,' I said, 'one more thing and then I'll stop.'

'What's that?'

I grinned because I knew how much this was going to piss her off. 'Loki. He came from Disappointment. I want to talk to some Entropists.'

'Oh fuck off!'

'You don't have to come.'

'Okay, just keep it quick.' We got into the pod. 'You know we went through all this five years ago, right? Until Loki, the Disappointment Entropists weren't much more than a drinking club with a bad attitude.'

On Earth I'd come to know a lot more about Entropists than I cared to. Loki aside, they were something of a joke on Magenta, but on Earth they were the real deal, a cult dedicated to some skewed vision of the Masters and calling them the New

174

Entropic Gods. The fact that the Masters had never given a sign of even trying to communicate had left everyone all the more desperate to work out who they were and what they wanted by looking at what they'd actually done. The Entropists had come to the same conclusion most of the rest of us had – that it simply made no sense – only, while what most of the rest of us *then* did was get on with our lives regardless, Entropists took the Masters as a sign of how humanity was supposed to evolve and did things at random. They had more factions than a group of South American Marxists, and some of them went the way of doing random *nice* things, but the big cults that made the news veered towards destruction. Then there were the Lokis and the Retrogrades, Entropists who were anti-technologists and mostly just blew things up.

'The Disappointment Entropists almost ceased to exist after Loki,' said Patterson. 'They scattered and went into hiding. A lot of them never came back. I think they were all too shocked by the discovery that one of them actually believed their own shit.'

'Did Loki ever claim he didn't do it?'

'At first. Claimed he'd gone to the pumping station to meet someone. An Entropist from Earth, he said, but there weren't any records to back up his story and Loki never offered us a name. We had surveillance of him there and no one else. He had the bomb with him. We had footage of him going to where the bomb was set and coming out again without it. We had evidence he'd done research on the explosives and trigger mechanism used. Cut-and-shut case. He claimed we'd planted it all, of course. Was a couple of weeks with it all mounting up around him before he cracked and confessed.'

'And now? Do you still think he did it?'

Patterson pursed her lips. 'Knowing what I know now …? Looked as solid a case as you could want at the time. He planted

175

the bomb, I'm pretty sure of that, but –' she sighed '– he just wasn't smart enough. I'd take a world of convincing to say he was innocent, but the idea that he had help … OK, look, I'm going to show you something. Then maybe you'll understand.'

The pod dropped into the Disappointment undercity, heading for some dive called the Voice where Patterson said the last handful of Disappointment Entropists hung out. We stopped outside and went in. A group of four black-clad teenagers with nihilist tattoos stopped their laughing to look at us through a haze of gen smoke. A couple of older men drinking on their own paused for a moment and then went back to their cups. Two cheap sex-toy shells were waiting table with their plastic tits hanging out.

'Nice,' I said. 'Come here often?'

'Isn't it just. Hasn't changed much.' Patterson went to the bar. Plastic scratched to the texture of sandpaper. She peered over the counter and shouted, 'Oi! Marco Castilla! You there? Someone wants to punch you.'

'I don't want to punch anyone,' I said. 'Also, I'm not very good at it.'

'Who said anything about *you*? Also, you *will* want to punch him as soon as he opens his mouth.'

I heard movement from behind the counter, a crash of boxes and a curse and then what sounded like someone climbing up a ladder. A face rose from behind the bar. Chubby, sweat-sheened, squitty little eyes that stared at us for a good three seconds, getting wider with every heartbeat as he pinged us. Marco Castilla, if I had it right. 'I remember you,' he said to Patterson. 'If you haven't got a warrant then you can fuck off. This is a private club.'

'I brought a friend,' said Patterson. 'He wants to join.'

Castilla looked me over. He frowned, screwing up his face, and cocked his head. 'Which bit of Earth you from?'

'What?'

Patterson drummed her fingers on the counter. 'He's asking about your ethnicity, Rause. He's trying to work out which side of an acceptable tan you are.'

'*What?*'

Castilla made a decision and shook his head. He made another face – I was beginning to realise it was his thinking face – and pulled a crowbar from under the bar. He banged it once on the counter. 'Out. Both of you. You got no warrant so fuck off.'

Patterson flashed him a smile. 'Castilla was Loki's best friend. That's right, isn't it?'

'Out!'

'Two peas from the same pod. Half-brothers, maybe. We were never quite sure. There were ...' she bared her teeth '... issues with establishing parentage.'

Castilla tightened so the muscles on his neck stood out. 'I said out! Now!'

'They named this place after a twenty-first-century racist best known for being a bit dim and having a really small penis. It's not hard to guess why.'

Castilla lunged across the bar, swinging the crowbar. Patterson stepped back and shot him with her Reeper. On stun, which was something of a pity but probably for the best. Castilla slumped, twitching and moaning. Patterson spun round. The two older men were both half out of their seats. The teenage nihilists gaped in awe.

'Anyone else want to threaten a government employee?' she asked. The two men sank back. 'Thought not. Come on, Rause. Before he gets better and opens his mouth again.'

We walked out. The pod from the spaceport was still parked where we'd left it.

'Point of that?' I asked.

'You mean apart from getting to stun that piece of subhuman excrement?'

'Yes. Apart from that.'

We stood beside the pod, keeping half an eye on the Voice in case anyone changed their mind about coming after us.

'You think someone like Castilla could blow up a pumping station?' Patterson asked.

'Not on purpose.'

'Loki wasn't much different. Maybe not *quite* as stupid, but close.'

So maybe Loki was the bomber, maybe not, but what Patterson was telling me was that someone had held his hand and shown him what to do. What she *wasn't* telling me, because she didn't need to, was that whoever that person was, they were long gone, all trace of them, and thanks to some anonymous shanker on Colony 478, we were never going to know.

'I think I need a drink.'

'Not as much as I do.' Patterson all but bundled me into the pod. 'Fortunately there's this swanky hotel I was talking about. Rangesh says it's the best in the city. They're both still alive, by the way, him and Zohreya. Apparently all went well.' She looked me over. 'You know, you're getting better, Rause. You don't look as beaten-up as you did. The nanites are finally kicking in, are they?'

'I suppose. Look, we have to—'

She raised a hand. 'Keon, take a break. At least until to-morrow.'

'I'm not sure I know how.'

That got a laugh out of her. 'When we're young and stupid we think we'll live for ever, don't we? The world feels so huge and full of opportunity. A child, a career, a partner, and then all that changes. Chances we used to take for granted become oases in an endless fucking desert. I don't *want* to be here,

Rause. I want to be at home with Jamie where I'm supposed to be. But since I *am* here, I'm going to drink and I'm going to dance, and I might even sing, and at some point I'm probably going to cry, because fuck knows when I'll be able to do it all again … and, hey, I already got to have some fun, right? So you can come with me or you can not, but don't you dare take it away from me by talking about work all evening. Tomorrow the mask goes back on; and whenever I do that, I'm always afraid that next time I won't be able to take it off again. If it helps, in the morning I'll tell you about the other thing I found in Kaltech's personnel records.'

The pod pushed through the undercity traffic and fought its way to the surface. It stopped outside the gaudy pink façade of a hotel calling itself the Master of the Orient. A pair of shells came and took our bags. Patterson led the way into the bar.

'What other thing?'

'Tomorrow, Rause. I have no idea what you drink,' she said, 'so you're getting a Wet Raspberry. You can thank Rangesh for that. He says it's good.' She slumped into an easy chair. 'Let your hair down for once.'

'I'm starting to wonder if that would be a such good idea.'

'Count yourself lucky you still have the luxury of asking.' Patterson leaned forward. 'Listen, in the pod on the way to Betleshah's mansion I said some things that weren't fair. I guess I wished I could have the purity of your grief, that's all.'

'The purity of my grief? What the fuck does that even mean, Patterson?'

She flicked me a nervous smile. 'Made you swear, Rause. Here's your Wet Raspberry. I'm having a Fingering.'

This smacked of being the start of one of those evenings that ended up with everyone trying desperately to pretend it hadn't happened. Then again, there was what Liss had said in New Hope, stuck so deep in my throat that I wanted to vomit. I cast a tentative glance into my Servant but she was still somewhere else. She hadn't replied to my message about Svernoi.

'So how did you and Alysha meet, anyway?' Patterson asked.

'Academy campus bar.'

'Her as well? How much of a slut were you back then?'

'I'd left Disappointment with grand plans to visit all the other worlds. By the time I came back I'd managed six. Earth killed it for me. I guess you forget how there's so much more there. I came back with a fist-full of debt so I worked evenings in the campus bar, but I had a lot of stories too. People liked me. Now and then they liked me a lot.' I cocked my head at her and shrugged. 'Alysha came in sometimes. That was how we met.'

Patterson grunted and sipped her cocktail. 'So you just picked her up one day, like you did me, is that it?'

'I liked the look of one of her friends. I crashed and burned. A couple of weeks later she came in with a different friend. Same story. The next time she came in she wagged a finger at me. Told me she didn't have anyone for me this week, but she'd try and do better next. I knew right then she was mine.' I hesitated. 'When you said it was a lucky escape we didn't have kids ...'

Patterson took a long slug and made a disgusted face. 'Forget it. Shit-mistress of narkland, that's me. Rangesh came up with that.' She giggled and knocked back the rest of her drink and ordered another. 'I thought Jamie was going to be the best thing in the world. I took time off work. I nursed him. Jamal and I ... But shit, do you know how dull it is, staring at fluffy cubes with letters on them all day, trying to think of something original to do with them?'

She turned away and wiped a hand across her eyes. 'It was so fucking good, that's the thing. You know that feeling? I know you do. What makes you lucky is how you get to keep it. I blew mine to pieces. I guess that's what I was getting at. Appallingly badly, probably.'

I took a sip of Wet Raspberry. 'You should probably get some sleep, Laura.'

'I probably should, but waste the only chance I'll get for what? Another year? I don't think so.'

'Chance of what? It won't …'

Patterson was staring into space as if looking for something. Courage, perhaps. 'I fought for my son, Rause. Tooth and claw. I would have flayed Jamal alive. I hired investigators. Do you know what made him give up in the end? I told him I'd set him up for dealing kiddie porn.' She shook her head and took a long ragged breath. 'The worst? I'm still proud of that, sometimes. That loathsome vile threat. That was love for you. That's what love makes us do. It would have been better for Jamie if he'd gone to Earth with Jamal. It would have been better for Jamal and better for me. But there you go.' She shook her head. 'Jamal walking out on me was entirely my own doing. I was a good lover and a fucking awesome bureau agent, but I was a shit partner and I'm not much of a mother. There. That's it.' She threw up her arms. 'Come on, then. Judge me. Get it over with!'

'Alysha was running from something when she got on that train,' I said. 'What if she was running from me?'

'Why the fuck would she do that? I mean, you two were tight, right? You were …' Laura put down her drink. She leaned across the table, staring into me. 'But you were good. You two … you were …'

'As far as I knew. But …'

I couldn't tell her about the miscarriage. Just couldn't.

'Yes,' I said, 'we were. Look, you have a nice evening. I'm going to turn in.'

'Yeah, you should do that, Rause. Fuck off before we do something stupid. You need to find that friend of hers. Miss Archana Enigma.'

'I know.'

'And you really don't have any idea who that was?'

'I really don't.'

Patterson nodded and raised her glass to me. 'I know what it's like to have ghosts, Rause.'

Truth, but what Patterson didn't know was that I'd brought mine back to life, and I was barely out of the lounge before I unlocked my Servant and was begging Liss to come to me. And because she was Liss, not some fickle real person but a simulation of someone we all believed had loved me, she came without question, good to her program. I stumbled through the halls and into a faceless anonymous hotel room that was apparently mine.

'I'm so sorry,' I said.

'I didn't meant to hurt you,' Liss said.

I wished sometimes that she'd fight me. It would have made her more real. 'Was she pregnant?' I don't know why I'd never thought to ask before.

'There was no body, Keys.'

'But wouldn't you know? Wouldn't you know. if she was pregnant before she got on that train?' I stared at the ceiling. I'd hardly drunk anything, no more than a sip of that stupid cocktail Patterson had come up with, yet the room was spinning. 'I'm so sorry,' I said again. 'I never meant to blame you for the miscarriage.'

'Yes, you did. And you were right.'

'No.'

'They offered me desk duties. They offered to look after me until the baby was born. I turned them down. It was my choice to chase a gen pusher into the Squats. It was my choice not to back down. It wasn't my choice that he kicked me where he did, but it was the sum of many choices that caused my miscarriage, several of them my own and selfish. I wanted to keep my life as I'd made it. I think I was afraid of losing that. And so it was, in part, my fault. You told me those things and you were right.'

'No.' No, I wasn't.

'Yes, you were.'

'Then I should never have said them.'

'That's true. You really hurt her.'

I wrapped my arms over my face, trying to make the memories of Alysha go away, the look in her eyes, the betrayal, the horror, the way she'd crumpled. I'd taken her limitless strength and made it brittle and then shattered it with a single tirade. I hadn't even realised it. The first words out of my mouth when I saw her in Mercy after we knew the baby was lost: *What the hell were you doing?*

'If it's any consolation,' said Liss, 'she wasn't late when she died. I have all her Servant records. She was good about tracking her cycle. She wasn't pregnant.'

'What sort of shit am I, even asking?'

There was a minibar in the hotel room. I drank most of it. Then I think I cried myself to sleep, half of me thinking of Alysha and all the regrets of one bad day that scarred every memory, the other half thinking of Patterson, downstairs in the bar and doing much the same.

13

STORMY WEATHER

We got up early, hours before dawn. Liss had gone flitting around the Firstfall archives looking for clues about our mystery search and rescue team. Patterson and I made our way to Disappointment's mag-lev station, both of us still half drunk. A handful of security shells stood watchful on the platform as we boarded. There were bots scraping graffiti off the walls. GO HOME! GO BACK TO INDIA! CLOSE THE DOORS! That sort of thing.

A man caught my arm, lurching out of a shadow. Patterson squawked and jumped away as though he was a plague carrier. A security shell came running towards us.

'Help a fellow human?'

His skin was as dark as Rangesh's, his face lined and hollow. He was stooped and his eyes were glazed, that not-quite-there look of the gen-head. Whatever transgravity he'd had, it hadn't taken well. He needed to be in a hospital. I pinged his Servant. He'd come to Magenta eight months ago. Since then ... nothing.

The security shell gripped his shoulders and pulled him away. I used my Tesseract codes, overrode its protocols and told it to take him to a hospital, not to a cell. I reckoned that was the best help he could get. On impulse I set up a trace so I could follow what Disappointment did with him.

When he was gone, Patterson handed me a packet of DeTox. 'How you feeling?' she asked.

'Troubled.' I looked at the station around us, the security shells.

The mag-lev pinged our Servants and the doors hissed open to let us in. Patterson winced. 'Well *I* feel like crap. You know that being a good Samaritan only earns you paperwork, right?'

'Last time I was here was a few days before Alysha died.' I shivered. 'It wasn't like this then.'

We moved into the train lounge. A hostess shell came to offer us tea. Patterson shooed it away.

'This deal with India is problematic, whatever Rangesh likes to think,' she said. 'It's not that we don't have the space for their surplus population if they come in healthy, but they don't. They're getting shoddy transgravity and we don't have the capacity to fix it. And then we end up compromising, and it only takes one native-born child to have their treatment delayed because of some resource shortage and everyone throws their hands in the air and declares it the end of the world.' Patterson shook her head.

'How was your evening?' I asked her. 'Did you drink and dance and sing?'

'Like a fucking king,' she said, and for a moment there was a smile before the mask came back down. 'Would you like to hear about what I found in the Kaltech records now?'

Turned out it was Vismans, Gersh's assistant. The Kaltech records Rangesh had hacked showed he'd arrived in Settlement 64 nearly a decade ago. For five years he'd done the same job, then all of a sudden a change of staff. He'd picked up a whole pile more assistants. Looked like a big promotion. Which was odd, because as far as I could see Kaltech kept meticulous track of the entry and exit logs of every single one of their employees – except the mysterious Gersh – and Vismans had never left Magenta.

'Gersh disappears, her assistant gets promotion – that's what I'm seeing,' said Patterson.

Vismans had returned to Earth six months back. One of us would have to go and talk to him. I just needed to find a good enough excuse.

We dozed until we reached Firstfall. Turned out that Zohreya and Rangesh and the MSDF tac-teams had spent the night in Nico, diverted there by the storm, which still raged and looked like it was settling in for several days more. They'd got in a couple of hours ahead of us and had everyone from the KRAB ship locked in holding cells waiting for someone to charge them or let them go. I left Patterson to dig into Anja Gersh while I had a long hard look at the authorisation paperwork Flemich had given Zohreya against what she'd actually found on the ship, which wasn't much.

'Intent to infringe intellectual property?' I said as we ran through it together. 'Flimsy. We're going to have to get a lawyer to look this over or we let them go.'

'Yes.'

The KRAB crew were bright, that much I knew from ten years ago. They'd sit tight and demand their legal rights and we'd get nothing. Maybe that was the point, maybe shutting them down was all they wanted, a blocking move and some publicity and nothing more. Everything else being equal I'd have let them go and set up discreet surveillance, but Nikita Svernoi floated like a ghost behind them. I wanted something on him.

I took Rangesh and Zohreya aside. 'We wait on word from above,' I said. 'Until then we do everything by the rules and—'

'Dude, we never should have been there. We had no right to seize their ship. It's, like—'

'We did as we were told, Rangesh, and you need to let it be. Zohreya, I'm going to question them. You two can get on with other things. Rangesh—'

'The gens that did for Shy. Yeah, man, I know. I'm gone.' Rangesh gave me a mocking salute, turned and sashayed away.

'I have paperwork.' Zohreya started as if to follow him. I caught her arm.

'It can wait. Five years ago you were in the MSDF, right?'

'Yes, sir.'

'You have any contact with Search and Rescue?'

'I was in orbital reconnaissance. I flew outside the atmosphere mostly. But I know some of them. SAR is based in Firstfall, same as the rest of us. Why?'

I told her what Patterson and I had found out about Settlement 64, the training mission that had vanished into a storm to go with that single entry in the Kaltech log. 'I need someone to go face to face. Find me an operative who knows something. Everyone's going to be grounded by this storm, right? So they'll all be bored and kicking their heels.'

Zohreya hesitated. I could see her thinking, reading the files I'd sent to her Servant, working out for herself what all of it meant. Or might mean.

'Do we have authorisation, sir?' she asked.

'Do you *need* authorisation, Agent Zohreya?'

'For an official inquiry on behalf of the Tesseract, I need your sanction to question other government employees.'

We both thought about that for a moment.

'Alternatively I could take a day off, sir.'

'Take the chance to visit a few friends? Talk about old times?'

'Exactly that, sir. It would have to be understood that—'

'I'm not looking to make any enemies or cause anyone any trouble, so—'

'I'm sorry, sir, but I must beg to differ. If what you suggest is real then someone went to considerable lengths to hide it. We *will* be causing trouble, sir.'

We both thought about that for a moment too.

'Are you comfortable with that, Agent Zohreya?'

'Yes, sir. I am.'

Under my breath I wished her luck. Liss would tell me until the end of time that the fact that Loki had set off his bomb when he had was an accident, a freak piece of misfortune, that there simply wasn't a viable logic to any other conclusion, but that was her algorithms talking. The real Alysha would have thought the same as I did: that coincidences like that don't happen, and if there was no viable logic then that was because we were missing something.

With Rangesh and Zohreya out of the way I looked at the four KRAB detainees. One was a new face. The other three I remembered from ten years ago. I showed them to Liss.

'Which do I pick?'

'What are you going to do?'

'I'm going to scare them. I'm going to show them how they're tied to Nikita Svernoi, and then I'm going to make him out to be a mass murderer. I'm going to tell them that the Tesseract might turn a blind eye to what they were clearly planning to do on that ship, but not to conspiracy.'

'Conspiracy to do what, Keys?'

'To do whatever it is that Svernoi has up his sleeve!'

'You might need to be a little more specific than that. When did Svernoi come back to Magenta?'

I didn't know. Patterson had asked Fleet but Fleet hadn't replied. But I saw where Liss was going. Nine months ago one of the KRAB team, Lillian Tyre, had gone to Earth. She'd been away for three months. Looking at the timeline Agent Zohreya had built, Tyre had come back with money. Whatever it was they were doing, her return had kicked it up a gear.

'I remember her,' Liss said. 'Her brother went to Earth when he was eighteen, got caught up in the Millennium Movement. He was killed during a police raid in North America.'

'You think she'll talk?'

'No, but I think that if you let her go then the first thing she'll do is go to whoever she thinks can help the others. I remember her being very protective.'

I wondered how Liss could remember anything at all given that the interviews Alysha and I had done with KRAB ten years ago had all been in the Tesseract. The cracksman who'd made her had been good, but not *that* good. She must have talked about it to someone outside then. Another agent maybe, somewhere public, accidentally caught on record.

Archana ...?

I shook the idea away and turned to the process of setting Lillian Tyre free. It took a couple of hours. For all that time no one talked to her, I made sure of that, and the uniforms who gave her back her clothes and led her out of the Tesseract had no idea why they were letting her go. While I waited I walked the upper levels, listening to the storm outside, wind hard enough to shake the walls even two floors below ground level. The quad would be under an inch of water by now, even with the flood drains open. I hoped someone had remembered to bring the ferns inside.

I watched from a camera across the tunnel as they led Tyre to the undercity gate and let her go. Even below ground the air whipped and swirled. A steady stream of rainwater ran down the storm channels. Tyre stood in the tunnel by the Tesseract gates, head looking left and right, searching for whatever unpleasant surprise was waiting. She couldn't see me but she knew someone would be watching. It was all good. I wanted her that way, uncertain and off balance.

A pod stopped for her. She sent it away and called one of her own and then had to wait for the best part of five minutes before it showed. She gave her home address in the Roseate Project and started making calls as she drove away. The Tesseract gave me the numbers. The others from the ship first, the people we still had locked up inside. The next was to a law firm. Privacy rules meant I didn't get to eavesdrop, but it wasn't hard to guess: *Why me?* After that she dropped messages around a few anonymous forums, not so many that tracking everyone who read them would be a problem. They were probably spoofs, but just to be sure I had the Tesseract mute any responses for a while. When she was done with that she redirected her pod to take her to the Magenta Institute, and then a few seconds later changed her mind again, and then several times more, switching her destination all around Firstfall until eventually she settled back with going home.

'She's panicking,' said Liss.

'Yes.'

'It's always the little mistakes that give them away.'

She was going to the Magenta Institute. Maybe not right now, but that was where she wanted to be. She'd dialled it without thinking and then realised her mistake and tried to hide it behind a slew of other destinations. I'd seen it before.

Her pod hummed to a stop in the underground garages of the Roseate Project, a warren of ten thousand homes on the west of the city. I lost track of her when she went into her apartment, but that didn't matter. The Tesseract had surveillance drones watching the entrances, so even if she had a way to spoof the Roseate's own cameras, I'd still know when she came out. And the Magenta Institute was right next door to the Tesseract, and I had a pod waiting and ready if I needed it.

'What are you going to do if she doesn't reach out to Svernoi?' Liss asked.

'She won't know Svernoi even exists. But there are going to be middlemen.'

'What if there aren't?'

'If there *are*, I'm going to trace the calls from one to the next to the next. I'm going to establish a chain of communication and a direct link between Svernoi and KRAB. With that I'm going to get a judicial order for Svernoi to give a deposition. Once I've—'

'Relating to his involvement in KRAB?'

'Yes. Once I've—'

'Keys, that's too thin! He's already given you—'

'I don't want him for KRAB, I want him for—'

'Settlement 64. Yes, I know.' I could sense the exasperation in her eyes, straight out of the Alysha book of expressions. 'It's not going to work. Even if you get an order.'

'Which I will, because the Chamber of Selected Representatives doesn't like Fleet at the moment.'

'You mean Speaker Hyun Soy doesn't.'

'Anyway, I—'

'Keys, even if you *do* get an order, and even if Svernoi doesn't just skip the system, he's going to come armed with about fifty lawyers who are all going to tell him point blank not to answer any questions he doesn't absolutely have to, and that means anything that isn't explicitly related to KRAB. You can't just haul a man like him down from orbit on a fishing expedition!'

She was right. It was just the only straw I had left to clutch at right now. 'OK, Liss. So it might not work. But how else am I—'

'How else are you going to what, Keys? Ask him whether he had me killed? Is that where this is going? Well you had him in front of you, and you didn't, so now you've missed your chance. Think for a moment! You have nothing to connect Svernoi, or Kaltech, or Settlement 64, or anyone at all to Loki. You've convinced yourself that coincidence equates with opportunity; you've made up a method, and now you're trying your best to find something that could be mistaken for a motive. Keys, I might even agree with you, but the thing you keep ignoring is that you don't have a shred of actual evidence!'

'You can't pretend—'

'A shred, Keys! Something that says Kaltech had a reason to kill me. Something that says how they did it. Something that says they could have known I was on that train. Can you show me a connection to Loki? Can you put someone else at that pumping station? You can't! What have you got, Keys? Nothing!'

She was right. Not that that would make a difference.

'My evidence is you,' I said at last. 'You were running. I don't know why and I don't know from what, but you were running, and you never ran. Call it instinct if you must. Call it a gut feel—'

'Logic trumps instinct. You know that. Alysha knew that. And I have logic.'

'I know.'

'It doesn't add up. Any of it.'

'I know that too. But you know what that tells me? Not that I'm wrong but that we haven't found the right dots yet. You know what else? Alysha would have agreed with me.'

I'd almost walked to the Magenta Institute when Tyre came out of her apartment. She hadn't changed her Servant and she wasn't making any effort to hide who she was, but she'd changed her clothes and she had a small backpack with her.

'Is she going to run, do you think?' I had the Tesseract sweep the Institute looking for any records of Tyre visiting before. I got a stack of hits. Never with an appointment and always to use the library.

'I doubt it. Keys, you've got to drop this thing with Nikita Svernoi.'

'Why?'

'Because it's going to make you look like an idiot!'

'And I should care about that more than I should care about you being dead?'

'You should care about both, and about yourself too. You have a life of your own and you need to start living it! *That's* what hurts me, Keys!'

'There were three others on that train. What about them?'

'Their friends and families have already grieved for them.'

Tyre called a pod. By the time she reached the garages it was waiting for her. She told it to take her to Babelfish Park, which was ludicrous given the weather.

'Listen to me.' Liss sounded calm, but then she always sounded calm if she wanted to. The Alysha I remembered couldn't switch between emotions that way. I don't think any real human can. 'I'm not saying that Kaltech weren't doing things they shouldn't in Settlement 64, not five years ago, not one year ago, and I'm not saying that Svernoi wasn't up to his neck in them, and I'm not even saying they didn't do exactly what you think they did. What I *am* saying is that the evidence you have is all circumstantial and that I think you'd have come at this with a lot more caution and objectivity if it had been someone else on that train. Try it, Keys. Just try it for a while. Please? Anyway ...'

She showed me what she'd found in the Institute records. It was a simple matter of cross-referencing the movements of all the staff with the times Tyre had checked in. One name stuck out like a sore thumb.

'Oni Wu?'

'Not a Magentan citizen but she's worked on Magenta for years, on and off. Full transgravity, nanosurgery, the works. And look at this.' She'd come back in from Earth six months ago. Same flight as Tyre.

'That has to be an alias, surely?'

'Why don't you ask her?'

'Because I don't want to sound rude.'

I checked myself into the Institute. Oni Wu was a technician working for the Deep Space Communications Array team, a joint project backed by Fleet money looking into ways of getting high-bandwidth information reliably around the whole inner system. Something like that. Tyre's pod, meanwhile, had reached Babelfish Park. It took her to the tunnel mouth and refused to go any further because the wind baffles were closed. Down here on the sub-levels I could feel the floor quivering, a deep resonance, the response of stone and steel to the storm above.

Liss looked up Oni Wu in the Institute directory. Tyre got out of the pod. The corner of Babelfish was a block from the Institute towers. She opened the override on the baffles and tried to force her way through. I switched cameras and watched as the wind flattened her against a building. She was lucky, and also possibly mad; the rain was coming in horizontally, so hard and harsh you could find yourself getting literally flayed. That was if you had time before a swirl of wind came around a corner, lifted you a dozen feet off the ground, gravity be damned, and then smashed you down.

'Should I send for a rescue pod yet, do you think?'

Tyre tried a step, got slammed back into the wall, lost her balance, tipped over and fell flat. I watched her crawl back inside and close the wind baffles.

'I don't know *what* she thinks she's doing,' Liss said. The pod that had brought her was still waiting. She got back inside it.

'Trying not to be followed?'

'But she was their comms specialist! She has to know you can follow her from ...' Cameras. We took them for granted. She'd know that. 'Oh. She's going to try the hunchback move now, isn't she?' On any other day I'd have put a drone up to follow her. Fat chance in the storm. Liss knew that. Tyre knew it too. Maybe she thought that was going to make a difference. I almost felt sorry for her.

She rode her pod to a tunnel intersection close to the Institute, got out and walked into a blind spot. An old trick, one every agent knew, but that didn't stop it from working.

'You still think this lot have anything to do with what happened to me?' asked Liss.

'Be patient. You know how this works.'

Find a blind spot. Switch the identity on your Servant. Change clothes and put on however many false beards you think will be enough to spoof the facial recognition software. If you're clever and have a clue, you come out walking stiff like you've done something to your back to spoof the body-posture mapping too. Works a treat for the automated tracking algorithms. To human eyes it tends to make you look like ... well, like a hunchback with a false beard, hence the name. To her credit, Tyre managed a little better, but it still wasn't hard to spot her. She came out, face hidden, got into a new pod called by her faked Servant – which was good of her, since the fake identity gave me something I could actually use when it came to the threats I was planning on making – hiding from the camera as she did. I didn't bother following her after that. By the time she reached the Institute I was sitting in the student cafeteria, watching Oni Wu with an eavesdropper drone under her table, quietly rooting through her background. I couldn't quite see how Tyre had messaged her, but Wu was definitely waiting for someone. Something on the message boards, probably.

Tyre showed up. I listened to them until it sounded like they were almost done and I was sure I wasn't going to learn anything I didn't already know. That was when the uniforms I'd called took them both back to the Tesseract and charged Tyre with identity fraud. I waved at her on the way out. The look on her face was priceless.

Tyre toughed it out back in her cell, but I only needed one of them and Wu cracked almost as soon as I came through the interrogation room door. She was a freedom-of-information activist who'd met Tyre on Earth and remembered the original KRAB. Tyre had talked about maybe doing it again and Wu had wanted to help. She'd managed to get hold of a satellite hijacker, and then she and Tyre had brought it here and set it up on the roof of the Magenta Institute. Naturally we couldn't get any records of the device since it had come from Earth. Wu claimed not to know its provenance, saying she'd simply spread the word among her people and that one of them had come back with it a few weeks later. Friend of a friend of a friend, that sort of thing. She gave us a name, but we all knew that no one from Magenta would be traipsing off to Earth to check it out.

I let her off. No charges. When the storm broke I went back to the Institute roof with Tyre and Wu and found a dozen technicians setting up and aligning the aerials and antennas that they'd taken down before the wind could rip them away. The satellite hijacker wasn't there. Tyre pointed out where it had been. When I talked to the technicians one of them remembered a box, but no one had moved it because it wasn't on any of the lists, and it wasn't *that* strange for people to leave odd boxes on the roof of the Institute in a storm.

I found it in the surveillance camera footage. There was a logo. Liss and I looked it up together and found it belonged to an Earth-based satellite communications company that just happened to be a Kaltech subsidiary and just happened to list the LeSag group as paid consultants in their last three annual reports. Paid to do what, it didn't say.

'Hardly a smoking gun,' said Liss.

'But it's a smoking something.'

Despite her protests I put together a request to haul Svernoi down from his orbital anchorage. When I was done I looked at it for a while and decided I'd sit on it a little longer because by then a few things had happened that might be about to change the picture. Zohreya had found a member of the search and rescue team that had been to Settlement 64 five years ago; Patterson had found Anja Gersh, and Rangesh had found where they were making the gens that killed Shyla Thiekis.

ROYJA BHATTI

Kulpreet Anash leaves her home for the last time. She wanders, aimless and random or so it seems, until she reaches a blind spot where the city can't see her. She enters as before and Royja Bhatti leaves, resurrected for a second and final night. Bhatti calls a pod and rides it to the Squats where bureau agent Bix Rangesh has gone to see a man called Jannos Threwer. Royja is too late to watch Rangesh go inside, and so it is only minutes later that he sees that Rangesh did not come alone. Agent Esharaq Zohreya has accompanied him.

The three of them talk. Royja Bhatti listens.

'I'm, like, asking nicely, man, because we know each other, but—'

Zohreya cuts in, words harsh and serrated. 'The gens you gave Betleshah killed her. The blood vessels in her brain ruptured. It was like she'd been infected by an accelerated thread virus.'

'Yeah? And how was I supposed to know—'

'Except there wasn't a virus and there weren't any clots, only the gens you—'

'Esh! Hey! Chill! Look, man ...'

Royja Bhatti waits for the conversation to reach its inevitable end. Rangesh and Zohreya take a name and leave. They cross the Squats to a club where pounding music plays all day and night to flashing strobe lights. There is a gen dealer there, mostly legal. He knows Rangesh. There is reluctance, begging and pleading. There are threats from Zohreya. There is, in the end, another name.

The pattern repeats until Rangesh and Zohreya leave for the rich northern Firstfall suburbs and a house that belongs to Roy Lemond, untouched mastermind behind much of Magenta's gen traffic. Untouched because what he deals, he deals exclusively to Magentans and thus avoids the ire of Earth. Rangesh enters the house. Half an hour later he leaves. Zohreya remains outside.

Royja follows them, discreet and distant, out of the city towards New Hope and the scatter of modular plants that ring the city, the factories that build Cheetahs and mag-lev trains and tunnel-boring machines and algae trawlers, fusion plants, hydroponics – anything Magenta desires. Many lie dormant, called upon only when needed. Rangesh and Zohreya pull up outside one of these, cautious and weapons drawn. Armed men stand on watch; as they see Rangesh and Zohreya they step back, walk away and are gone. The guards have been warned to leave the Tesseract agents alone. Roy Lemond has given up whoever is here to Rangesh. Why? Royja Bhatti doesn't know, but Rangesh has long had a reputation for closeness with men like Roy Lemond, a closeness that often makes those who work with him uncomfortable.

Zohreya and Rangesh enter. Under harsh bare lights three men sit beside a workbench covered with chemical apparatus and bags of scraped lichen. Rangesh and Zohreya shock one apiece, sending them crashing in sprawls of twitches. The third jumps out of his chair but gets no further before Zohreya points a gun to his head. Royja Bhatti stands and watches from a corner, silent and invisible. There is something strange in Zohreya's face. It is a look Royja Bhatti has seen before. It is a look of murder.

Rangesh asks his questions. Drones scuttle to the men on the floor and wrap them in restraining silk. A tac-team is on its way.

'How did you do it?' asks the man with the gun to his head. 'How did you find me?' He is looking at Zohreya. Rangesh seems not to understand. Zohreya, on the other hand, understands precisely.

'By accident,' she breathes, 'and by following the dead people.' The gens that killed Shyla Thiekis are made in an old pit mine. Men from Earth have set up a factory there. It is what Rangesh needs to hear. Zohreya asks him to leave. She asks for a minute alone with the man she holds at gunpoint. Rangesh shakes his head.

'Uh, I don't think that would be cool, Esh. You want to—'

Zohreya kicks the man to the floor. She crouches beside him and whispers in his ear, pressing her gun to the side of his head. Names and more names. She asks where they are. The man squeals and wails and tells her what he knows. One is at the old pit mine. When they are done, Zohreya stands and points her gun at his head. She means to shoot him, but when the moment comes she allows Rangesh to push her aside. Rangesh doesn't understand – he thinks he was quick enough to save her from herself, but Zohreya and Royja Bhatti both know better. It is her choice to be merciful, not his. She just needed a little help to make it.

Armed men in uniforms arrive. Invisible, Royja Bhatti moves around them. When no one is looking he takes the discarded pistols that lie on the workbench. Perhaps Rangesh will notice they are gone and wonder, but by then it will be too late.

FOUR

PIT 779

14

BACK AT THE WAVEDOME

They say calm comes before a storm, but on Magenta it tends to be the other way round. Three days of winds the wrong side of two hundred miles an hour and something close to two feet of rain. It's the sort of weather you simply can't understand until you've seen it. I'd say *been* in it, but generally that ends badly. But *after* a storm, as the clouds break up and Magenta's blue sun burns its way back through the sky . . .

Patterson had dug out some old files on Doctor Gersh. Her history, her background before she worked for Kaltech and an old video clip. I skimmed them. At least now I knew her face, which was something.

Zohreya was waiting for me at the Wavedome. Seemed like half of Firstfall was out there now the storm had passed. We had sunshine, still air, and the forecast was for some of the best surf of the year. Children played in the black sand, building castles and forts and Masters' spires, one piece of added fun when your sand is slightly magnetic. Simple sell-shells walked among them trailing vending bots of cold drinks and ice cream.

Anyone old enough was out in the water. The air buzzed with drones, everything from tiny personal self-followers up to a couple of emergency rescue drones loitering higher up, ready to dive in and haul anyone who got into difficulties out of the sea. Zohreya was dressed in a wetsuit and holding a surfboard. She had a tiny backpack slung over her shoulder. I picked my way across the sand towards her.

'Ready to get wet, sir?' she asked.

I guess the look I gave her said I thought she was mad.

'I didn't know how much time you used to spend here, sir, or whether you'd had the chance to practise on Earth, so I've arranged for an instructor. He's very good. He's MSDF. He used to be in search and rescue.'

I got it then. One of the SAR team who'd gone to Settlement 64.

'I'll be with you for some of the time too, sir. As much as I can. But I have to liaise with Rangesh and the tac-teams about Pit 779. I've got live satellite surveillance if you want to see it.'

Rangesh was adamant we hit the gen factory before there was any chance of them realising they were blown. No matter how I wanted to go after Svernoi, it made sense. We had five corpses, all dead from massive haemorrhaging, and now we had a source and a gen factory to boot, and maybe even a chance to get at the quantum chemist who'd engineered it. No one had even the beginnings of an explanation as to how an altered gen could cause brain haemorrhages, but the corpses didn't lie.

Zohreya had arranged a board for me. I told her there was a reason she didn't know how much time I'd spent at the Wavedome, which was that I hadn't, not really. Wasn't my thing. That look I gave her before, the one that said I thought she was mad? I got it right back. 'My parents used to bring me when I was a kid,' I said, 'but they didn't let me in the sea. Too fragile. Problems with the gene therapies. I used to come and play pick-up games of beach volleyball when I was older but I never really got into surfing.'

'Volleyball? Find yourself a partner and I'll take you on!'

'No, thanks.' We collected my board. 'I brought Alysha here the first time we went out together.' The same was probably true for half the couples in Firstfall. I laughed, couldn't help it. 'It was supposed to be a double date. I thought I was something special. I thought maybe she'd bring a friend as gorgeous as she was and the two of them would wear skimpy bikinis to try and put us off our game. Instead she bought the coach of the academy team, no bikinis in sight, and they buried us.' If I hadn't been in love with her before, I was by the end of that day. She'd claimed, later, that the one point we took off them had been her idea of mercy, but I'd never believed her. Mercy wasn't something Alysha understood. When she set out to do something, she did it without reserve. We'd *earned* that point, damn it!

'My parents used to bring me,' Zohreya said, 'before they were killed. I have many happy memories of them here.'

'I'm sorry.'

'It was a long time ago and they are with Allah now. I'm sorry about your wife too. I never knew her, but Patterson speaks of her highly.'

'She does?' I was surprised to discover that Patterson spoke of Alysha at all. 'What does she say?'

Zohreya handed me the back end of two surfboards and then picked up the fronts, which put an end to any conversation until we reached the edge of the water. The waves today were big, a legacy of the storm.

'You really haven't ever done this before?' she asked.

'No. Hey, I want to know – what does Patterson say about Alysha?'

Zohreya walked around me, looked me up and down, then

205

dropped her pack to the sand and pulled out a drawstring bag. 'This should fit you. You're about my size.'

'What ...' She opened the bag and tossed the contents at me, which promptly came alive into what felt like an army of giant centipedes crawling over my skin before becoming some sort of silvery waistcoat. 'Oh.'

'Survival vest,' Zohreya said in case I hadn't worked it out. 'As a novice you have a decent chance of clocking yourself around the head with your own board on a day like this. Knocking yourself out in the water is a fairly noob move. The vest will keep you from drowning. Push comes to shove, it'll make a brace for you if you fracture your neck, but it would be a lot better if you could just try to avoid that, sir.'

I looked at the waves. A few feet high where we stood, at the novice end of the beach. Fifteen feet, maybe, at the severe end. 'That was your spare, right?'

Zohreya shook her head. 'Nah, but I'm not going to go down.' She looked at me again, still bewildered. 'I'm sorry, sir, but seriously? You never surfed? I'm told that if you learn here and then surf on Earth it's like surfing on stardust, it's that easy.' She looked about and waved towards a man stamping through the waves towards us with a board under his arm. I pinged his Servant to get his name and got back nothing. Anonymous.

'That him?' I could have used my Tesseract codes and gone in under his privacy protection, but sometimes there were easier ways, like simply asking.

'That's him.'

'He got a name?'

Zohreya didn't answer but a few seconds later I got a ping back, this time with name, rank, serial number and service record. Colonel Jonas Himaru. Twenty years in the MSDF including six years of off-world secondment. Search and rescue for the last decade and an MSDF instructor when there wasn't too much rescuing to be done. He was enormous. It wasn't so much that he was tall, although for a Magentan he was, but that he was as wide as me and Zohreya put together.

The next thing I saw was the tattoo on the back of his arm. The mark of the First Descendants. He could trace his ancestry on Magenta right back to the first settlers dropped by the Masters, and someone had verified it too. I didn't begrudge anyone a little pride in their ancestry, even if I thought it was stupid, but First Descendants tended to bang on about how the planet didn't need any more immigrants, particularly Indians. They were making a lot of noise in Disappointment these days. I'd seen their tag on the mag-lev station there, half scrubbed off by a cleaning bot hard at work on the graffiti. I mostly imagined them to be like the morons Patterson and I had met a couple of days back.

I looked at the tattoo and then at Earth-born Zohreya, back at the tattoo, and then felt a bit stupid. Being a First Descendant didn't automatically make you a dick, I suppose.

'Sir, Colonel Jonas was my instructor through advanced survival training. Colonel, this is Agent Keon Rause, my new commanding officer.'

Himaru looked me up and down. 'Who doesn't surf?'

'I'm here to do something about that,' I said when no one else said anything.

'Then I want you out in the water.'

The next twenty minutes were surreal. A tattooed wall of human flesh teaching me how to jump onto the back of a surfboard and catch a wave as it came and ride it lying down. Standing up, apparently, came later.

'Why are we doing this?' I asked as I pulled myself out of the surf for the umpteenth time.

'You ever try to eavesdrop on a conversation out here?' Himaru asked me. 'We're doing this because the story I have to tell you is of something that didn't happen. And the reason I'm telling it to you is because it stinks, because Esh says you're solid and because I've seen the name Rause before. We're out here because out here no one gets to listen. This is about your old lady, and some of it isn't pretty. You sure you want to know, Agent Rause, no matter where it goes?'

I got the story out of him between catching waves and falling off my board, while Zohreya skimmed the surf nearby, never straying far, watching for spy drones.

Five years ago Jonas Himaru had been part of a search and rescue team sent up to the northern end of the mid-latitudes on short notice, with no real idea of where they were going and no real idea why. Six men on a training exercise had gone missing, that was the story, last recorded heading into the teeth of a category-eight storm, which made no sense at all. Himaru had seen the weather reports for the last week, and from the track of the mission's movements it was like they'd gone out of their way to get caught in the open by the full ferocity of the wind. Bullshit, Himaru reckoned, because he knew the men he was looking for and they weren't the sort who walked dumbly into the path of an oncoming storm, even if every record he could find said that that was exactly what they'd done. The other weird thing was that there had never been any distress call. They'd just disappeared.

By the time his team reached the area, the storm had gone and everyone was dead. A sovereign settlement nearby, Settlement 64, had picked up a Mayday signal and sent out a search party of their own. When Himaru's team arrived there was nothing left to do except pick up the corpses and take them home.

He'd seen their faces. He'd known their names. From the kit recovered with the bodies they'd been on a mission, not an exercise, and so he was talking to me because people he knew had died, and the reason they'd died had been buried, and it was his way of giving them the memorial he thought they deserved.

'They were there to get someone out of that place,' he said. We stood with the surf crashing around us; by then I'd given up trying to ride the waves. 'How do I know that? Because when we went to collect the bodies there was one that wasn't ours. She was an Earther. She'd been here a fair time, but you can never hide it.' He glanced towards Zohreya. 'Like she can't.' He paused. 'There were other things. Way I saw it, they'd made the extraction and then somehow they'd flown into that storm, and the only way that could happen was if someone fed them the wrong weather data. So I did some digging. Before I was told in no uncertain terms to stop, I found the name of the agent who'd been running the exercise. Rause. Alysha Rause.'

I didn't hear much of what he said after that. Didn't hear much of the surf either. Didn't hear much of anything.

'Your wife sent six men out into the wilderness, and all of them died. I heard she disappeared a few days later.'

'She died too,' I said. 'The May Day bomb.'

'I lost friends, Agent Rause. One body we never even found. Happens sometimes in a storm. You know what? I think we're done here now. I don't think there's much more I can teach you. Find a different instructor next time.'

'Wait!' I almost pinged him the file I had on Anja Gersh, but we'd come out here because Himaru didn't want anyone to know we were talking, so I described her instead. 'That sound right for the other body you found?'

Jonas Himaru nodded. Then he turned away and swam towards the waves. I stood and watched him go. I knew he thought Alysha had deliberately sent his friends into that storm to die.

'Is it possible?' I whispered to Liss. 'Did you kill them?'

Liss didn't answer at first, and I wasn't thinking straight. Alysha, whatever she'd been running from, wouldn't have staged something like that. She just wouldn't. No. She'd sent six men to Settlement 64 to extract Gersh. That sounded better. Someone else had done the killing.

Had to …

'I don't think so,' whispered Liss. 'I don't see how.'

A wave crashed over me, knocking me down, pushing me momentarily under the water. When I struggled back to my feet, Zohreya was plunging through the surf towards me.

'You good, sir?' She offered a hand to help me up, but I needed a lot more than that.

'Not really,' I said.

'Did you get what you wanted?'

'Yes and no.' I shook my head. 'Your friend thinks my wife sent six men to their deaths.' I forced myself to look at her, to hold her eye as she looked me up and down.

'Let's get you out of the water, sir.'

We dragged our boards through the surf and then tried walking side by side, each struggling to carry our own board while the wind turned them into sails. Zohreya dropped down by the water's edge and sat in the sand, close enough that the last vestiges of the surf nibbled at her feet.

'We came to Magenta when I was seven,' she said. 'It hurt every day. I was in pain for years before the transgravity finished changing me. The memories I brought from Earth were of hot sunny days, gentle winds, warm air. Orange groves. Olives. Lemon trees. Dates. Green things. Sand and earth under my feet. Coming here seemed to me like coming to hell. But I loved my family.'

She turned to look me in the eye. 'There's nothing to be gained by wondering how changed our lives might have been had we made different decisions, sir. My family is with Allah now. Your wife too. We loved them. Hold on to that and you'll find your peace.'

She got up and headed back into the water. I watched her paddle out through the waves. I could feel Magenta's star burning my skin, a hundred times as much ultraviolet as Earth's Sol. Another reason we didn't come outside much. Further across the bay Colonel Jonas Himaru was catching tubes, making the odd aerial, whatever the right words were. Zohreya with her artificial eyes could probably zoom right in and watch every move, but to me he was a dark speck in the distance.

I watched Zohreya and listened to the hypnotic crash and suck of the waves, the rhythm of the sea.

'Hey, boss dude! How's it hanging?' A shadow fell over me, Rangesh in a wetsuit with a board.

'Am I the only one here who doesn't surf?'

'Pretty much. Though we don't get Laws out there all that often.' He squatted beside me. 'You see what I mean, man? Like, how Esh is really totally hot?'

'Wetsuit remind you of a jumpsuit? You have a thing for uniforms, Agent Rangesh?'

'Dude!'

'It's OK, I won't tell.'

'Dude! I totally ... That would be like ...'

'Then why are you staring?'

'Because Esh is hot, man! Why are you?'

I shrugged. 'Same reason, probably.' It wasn't. I was thinking of Alysha.

'Dude! What? Like ... whoa. I totally thought you and Laws ...'

It was hard not simply to lie back and close my eyes. Dressed in a damp wetsuit lying on the artificial magnetic sand I didn't feel Magenta's gravity for once. I think that was the first time since I'd landed.

'Has Laura been sniffing around after my dead wife behind my back?' I asked.

'Said she was helping you find out what happened, man.' Rangesh laughed and shook his head. 'Because, yeah, you know, we'd *never* have figured *that* one out for ourselves. She said we should, like, be careful with what we did or said. Laws can be an arse sometimes, but she's looking out for you, man.'

'Looking out for me?'

'Serious, man. She envies Esh so much, but she'd do the same there. Or for me. It's just, like, the way she is. Makes her kind of cool once you see it.'

He was staring out across the ocean, off to the horizon, falling into the rhythm of the sea, the mesmerising crash and hiss of the surf.

'She's a good person, Laws, deep down. Going to take a long time for her to pick herself up again, that's all. She knows it too.' He let out a long breath and got up. 'Look, man, it's kind of stressing me that Esh says we have to wait until it's dark to raid this gen factory, so I'm going to go out there and surf and distract myself some more by staring at her in that wetsuit up close. You coming?'

I told him no and took my board back to the Wavedome's observation deck while he headed out into the waves. I watched, propped against a railing, sucking on an overpriced ice cream made with real cream imported from Earth, not the sow's milk we mostly had to live with on Magenta. I had to say it tasted damned good.

'Patterson's looking out for me?' I murmured to Liss, lurking in my Servant.

'I told you,' she whispered. 'You suit each other. You both understand. You should do something about it.'

'I can't. She works for me.'

'And you worked for me once. Don't be so twenty-first-century, Keon. No one cares any more.'

'You think that MSDF guy was telling the truth?'

'Why would he lie?'

'You sent a covert team up to Settlement 64?'

'It's plausible. Though there should be records.'

'And then everyone died in a storm? You buy that?'

Liss hesitated before she answered. 'Not really.'

'Did you set them up so they'd all die? Is that why you were running?'

'I don't know, Keys. I don't think I'd do something like that.'

'I don't think so either. Do you still think it was an accident that Loki bombed that train?'

'It has to be.' There was that hesitation again. Even Liss didn't believe it any more. Liss and her perfect logic. 'How did anyone even know I was there?'

Kaltech's records said Gersh didn't exist. Svernoi had told me she'd gone back to Earth. Himaru had seen her laid out on a slab. Maybe she *had* gone back to Earth, just in a coffin.

I finished my ice cream and walked to one of the viewing scopes, looking for Himaru and Zohreya and Rangesh. I pinged their Servants, trying to get a fix on which of the black dots they were out among the waves. Himaru was still anonymous but I found Zohreya and Rangesh easily enough. They were floating way out in the swell, hanging on to their boards and not doing much except talking. I watched for a few minutes but they didn't move. It looked like they were arguing.

I ran through Patterson's files on Gersh then. Plenty of scientific papers from her days in Germany before she'd gone to Kaltech. Neuropsychology, so they might as well have been written in Sanskrit for all the sense they made to me. She'd been interested in altered states of consciousness. And the Masters, she'd been interested in them too, and the old theory that they worked through some sort of telepathy and that was why we could never figure out their tech. There was a video interview done back on Earth. Also some talk at a medical conference.

Her assistant Vismans had been with her. For ten minutes they took it in turns to talk about Gersh's illness, Mohinder-Kali, and how Kaltech hoped to find a treatment using Magentan xenoflora. More than a treatment, if you read between the lines of what Gersh was saying. I got the impression she wasn't trying to fix the neurological imbalance of the disease so much as harness it. She had an obvious passion. Vismans had it too. They believed in what they were trying to do. I watched it to the end but I didn't discover anything new.

Rangesh pinged me. 'Me and Esh, we're heading for the Blue Scallop. You want to come? They do this totally awesome special sauce. You got to try it, dude.'

I figured I owed Zohreya for setting me up with Himaru, even if I hadn't much liked some of what he'd had to say. I joined them and paid for drinks and sat in the same seat as when Patterson and I had met del Rosario. I watched the two of them, deep in surfing talk. An odd couple, but there was something between them, some chemistry, even if they both pretended not to see it.

'You ever hear of Mohinder-Kali syndrome?' I asked.

Rangesh gave me a quizzical look. 'Actually yeah, man. The Shyster had it. Some sort of genetic anomaly or mutation or something. Mostly throws up in heritage that traces back to the Odisha province of India. Why?'

I told them about Gersh. 'Any idea what MK syndrome actually does?'

'Poor impulse control. Erratic. Tendency to extremes of behaviour, you know? No willpower, yeah? It was, like, the Shyster all over. But hey, man, what's that—'

'Wait! Thiekis had Mohinder-Kali?' The Fleet men at Betleshah's house. Svernoi …'That's …' A shiver ran down my spine.

'Yeah, man.' Rangesh gave me a funny look. There was a lot

214

of thinking happening there all of a sudden. And at the same time I was remembering the video clip Svernoi had sent us of the terrorist Ali Surash, who'd blown himself up inside Settlement 64's lab. I played it again and there it was, the same thing I'd seen when Svernoi first showed it to us, just before the bomb inside Surash exploded. His eyes bleeding.

Haemorrhaging ...?

We looked at each other. I still had the files Rangesh had sent me on that first morning outside Mercy. Four dead gen-heads in twelve months. Two from mysterious internal bleeding. Two like they'd been ripped apart ...

Like Ali Surash?

No. Surash had exploded with enough force to kill everyone in the room.

We put in the call together, asking for the other corpses to be sample-checked for genetic anomalies. By the time we got back to the Tesseract, we had the results.

All four had Indian heritage. All four had had Mohinder-Kali.

15

RAID

I won't go into the statistics. Mohinder-Kali is a genetic anomaly that affects about one person in ten thousand. On rare occasions it can be severe enough to be debilitating. Most sufferers get by. Most people who have it don't even know, which is why the condition wasn't recognised until the entire human genome was finally understood. Five people dead with the same rare genetic aberration wasn't a coincidence. Whoever was holed up in Pit 779, whether they knew it or not, was making a gene-specific poison, a biological weapon, something which ranked as about number one on the list of things that got you sent straight off to Colony 478 for the rest of your natural life, no questions asked. It also meant, as Rangesh so nicely put it, that if they *did* know what they were doing, they were going throw more at us than scathing sarcasm and stale brownies when we went to shut them down.

I had something more too. A connection and a picture in my head. Alysha had tried to pull Doctor Gersh out of Settlement 64 and someone, because of that, had sent Loki to kill her.

Gersh had been researching Mohinder-Kali, and now people with the same disease were dying and it felt like we were on the edge of unravelling who and why. A part of me couldn't have been happier. Another part of me just wanted to get hold of whoever was behind it all and do bad things to them.

The news was still rattling around the Tesseract when the first posse of agents from narcotics showed up and demanded to come along for the ride. Zohreya put on her most agreeable face and assigned them to her tac-team commanders as extra firepower. She might as well have shoved her finger up their noses and walked them out the door. They stormed off with a lot of you'll-hear-about-this-later noises. Rangesh offered her a high five.

'Ours,' she said. 'We broke this.'

I reckoned it was mostly Rangesh who'd broken it, but I didn't argue.

Satellite surveillance of the pit suggested maybe a dozen people working there. Zohreya's tac-teams were two eight-strong MSDF squads hidden behind shaded visors. They didn't wear name tags and their Servants responded with service numbers, but I knew they were the teams Zohreya had used to take out KRAB because they cheered when they saw Rangesh and went straight to ribbing him. Turned out he'd flown there wearing his kaftan and sandals, his idea of a protest against the whole operation. They'd boarded the ship from zip lines against a sixty-mile-an-hour headwind. A sight to behold, apparently.

Patterson stayed behind, looking for any traces of the extraction mission Alysha had sent to Settlement 64. The rest of us settled into a pair of waiting Cheetahs in the middle of the night. No kaftans this time; today was military-grade poly-fibre flexi-armour, same as the tac-teams, the only real difference between us being our bureau-issue Reepers and their armour-piercing burst-rifles. Once we understood what was going on out there, what they were making, Zohreya and I had quietly changed the mission profile. We needed to capture their data and hardware. We need to get to whoever had set this up. That was our priority. Casualties were going to be more acceptable than usual, and we were going to make as sure as we could that they weren't ours.

'Found their shuttle yet?' I asked. They had to have one hidden somewhere nearby, their escape in case they were discovered. That was usual for gen smugglers who slipped in from Earth. Bolt for orbit in something that could outpace the MSDF's dozen or so Kutosov-class interceptors, which wasn't too hard given that they were about a century old. Vanish into deep empty space somewhere near the jump point until the *Fearless* came, latch on to her and then drift away back to Earth without anyone noticing.

I looked from face to face. No, we hadn't found their shuttle.

The Cheetahs settled into hypercruise. Pit 779 wasn't anywhere near as far as Settlement 64 but we still had half an hour to kill. Zohreya spent it checking things we'd already been over a hundred times. Rangesh went back to the game he'd apparently played all the way to KRAB, trying to guess the names of the MSDF squad riding with us.

'This one's a Sundeep. You can tell from his accent, you know? Nico is full of people who talk like that, and every one of them is a Sundeep. Our corporal, on the other hand, emigrated from England, like maybe two generations back, so he's either a Jarvis or a Sidney, because everyone in England is either a butler called Jarvis or else they come from London and are called Sidney.'

'I got a middle name too, mate,' offered Jarvis Sidney. 'It's Fuck You.' He grinned. Bix grinned back.

There was Annalisa, because she sounded exactly like his cousin Annalisa, and all Annalisas, like all Sundeeps, sounded the same. Then Lech and Bharat and So-So, all for equally ridiculous reasons. He tagged our tac-team sergeant as Rachel Aaronson on the grounds that she didn't like him, which made her a Rachel, and that she was Jewish, and nearly all Jewish women were called Aaronson.

I pinged him. How do you know she's Jewish?

Star of David pendant under that armour and a 'Free Israel' tattoo at the base of her spine. She's totally a Rachel Aaronson.

How do you know all that?

Ways and means, my friend.

I pinged Liss while Rangesh bantered. Come with me for this. I want you here.

I felt her presence shift into my Servant. OK.

There's a connection to Gersh. The gens. Mohinder-Kali. Too much of a coincidence.

Zohreya had us a satellite tasked on station, a real-time infrared feed piped through the Tesseract with everything that moved highlighted and tagged. Ten minutes out she flashed it to our lenses and zoomed in on an image we'd caught earlier in the day showing an all-terrain eight-wheeler by the entrance to the pit. Two men were leaning against it, both carrying particle rifles powerful enough to bring down a Cheetah.

'We'll deploy two miles out,' she said. 'As close as we can get but still out of audiovisual contact range. Given the hardware on display, we assume Earth paramilitaries with combat experience and a perimeter of heat and tremor sensors.'

'Hey, Esh, is your friend here going to sprout wings again?' asked Jarvis Sidney, jerking his head at Rangesh. Everyone laughed, Rangesh most of all.

We put down behind a sharp ridge. The first tac-team set off towards the pit, pathfinding. Zohreya, Rangesh and I followed with the second. A string of drones zipped ahead, surveillance in every spectrum. The flicker of images projected onto lenses made our eyes spark in the gloom. Everyone except Zohreya. If there were mines or tripwires, the pathfinders dealt with them. We moved slowly. This was where modern warfare was lost or won, in the first battle of drones and surveillance, of who was seen and who could remain hidden, and we badly needed them not to see us coming. At the edge of the pit Zohreya flashed more enhanced satellite maps into our Servants. 779 had been an opencast mine once, one of the big ones, two and a half miles across and half a mile deep, tier after tier gouged into Magenta's crust. A single wide track spiralled from top to bottom. The rises between each level of the mine were hundred-yard sheer cliffs of glass-fused stone.

The first tac-team stayed up on the rim, heading for the eight-wheeler to secure the entrance. After that they'd task a flight of suppression drones and air support as needed. Once we were sure no one was hiding behind a rock with a rocket launcher or a particle rifle, the Cheetahs would come in close. By then, if all had gone the way it was supposed to, we'd have a secure place for them to land. *Our* first objective was the gen factory, to secure its data before all of that kicked off.

A series of faces pinged across my Servant. Zohreya reminding us of our targets. Rangesh had tagged a couple of Magentan names from the Tesseract archives, known gen traffickers. There would be Earthers too, anonymous muscle mostly, but there was always the possibility we might catch the chemist with his factory, and we couldn't let that chance slip away.

We rappelled two at a time from one level to the next. Sparks flickered in the eyes of the tac-team as they drew up overlays and schematics, or else inserted themselves into the sensors of the drones running ahead of us. The first tac-team was in position by the eight-wheeler, waiting for Zohreya's signal. With the cliffs looming above us and clouds in the night sky, everything was black as pitch. Even with night goggles I couldn't see much.

We reached the bottom tier. There were exploratory shafts here, drilled into the walls of the pit, close on a hundred of them. Satellite surveillance showed three with heat signatures. We spread out, running in pairs from one shaft to the next, spitting a drone into each for shallow surveillance and a warning in case something came out, working our way towards the tunnels that weren't dead.

'Dude!' Rangesh grabbed my arm.

'What?'

He dragged me inside a cave mouth. 'You need to know something, man.'

Rangesh! Rause! What's the hold-up?

Rangesh let me go. 'Just, like, keep an eye on stuff, man. If anything happens to me, keep an eye on Esh, you know?'

'Nothing's going to happen, Rangesh.'

'Yeah. But if it does then you got to keep with her. I got a bad feeling, you know?'

The tac-team closed on the first target tunnel. We crouched outside, huddled in a circle, focused on Zohreya. In the plan we'd worked through, Zohreya and I and six of the tac-team went into the tunnel we figured served as living quarters. Rangesh and Jarvis Sidney and Sundeep went into the one with the gen factory. Our best guess was that the third was where the processed gens were kept and was empty at night, but all this was built on patchy surveillance and clever guesswork. We had suppression drones ready in case we were wrong.

Zohreya made a series of sharp gestures. We started into the tunnels, slow and careful, relying on our night vision in a stillness that wrapped us like silk. We reached an intersection. Zohreya signalled us to hold. She crouched and blew a little smoke across the floor. A broken line of scintillations lit up. A laser tripwire. She pointed at So-So and herself and then past the tripwire. Then at me and the rest of us and the main tunnel.

ATV secured. Three suspects detained. No casualties. No alarm. First squad is on their way down. Second squad on overwatch.

I felt the soundless relief around me. I pinged Rangesh: Anything?

Only a funny smell. You?

Laser trip. Spotted it though.

Zohreya and So-So stepped carefully over the trip. They inched away down their tunnel. The rest of us crept on along the main shaft.

Stay close to Esh, boss dude.

She used to be MSDF, Rangesh. She's trained for this. She'll be fine. Zohreya struck me as more capable of looking after herself than either I or Rangesh would ever be in a place like this.

That's not what I meant.

Then what?

Light spilled ahead from under a badly fitting plastic door. Sergeant Aaronson – if that really was her name – signalled us to stop. The tac-team crept closer, aiming their rifles at the door from all sides.

Rangesh! Why stay close? The one he'd called Lech pushed past me and lowered himself to his belly. He poked a flex-camera through the crack under the door. Pictures came through, spattered across my lenses. The thermals were high on the other side. There were people in there. Sleeping bodies.

Trust me, dude. Just stay close.

We've already separated.

Check in. Zohreya. We have three targets. Probably Magentan. We're holding. Waiting your call.

Tac One-One, position secure. We have your back.

Tac One-Two, closing on you. Two or three minutes. No activity.

Tac Two-One. We have targets. Number unknown, all unaware. Proceeding. It took me a moment to realise that Tac Two-One was us.

Around the door they were fiddling with a drone, something like a bug – a mosquito, I think. Which is fine on Earth, where there are a hundred million different sorts of flying bugs, but on Magenta there's lichen and algae and fern forest and, thanks to an ill-conceived early effort at unnecessary terraforming, a lot of genetically engineered fern-eating snails. No flying bugs. I pinged Zohreya and showed her what we were doing.

Sure about this? It was her call in the end, not mine. She hesitated long enough to at least be thinking about it.

Let Two-One make the call. She has the best oversight.

Lech slipped the bug under the door. It buzzed into the air. We started to get more pictures. Thermals first. There were ...

'Shit!' We'd planned for up to a dozen hostiles tops in the whole pit. On the other side of the door were at least that many and probably more. Looked asleep, mostly, but not all of them. Further back I could see movement.

Tac One-Two, change of objective. Rendezvous and reinforce Tac Two-One. The stillness, the silence, the darkness, cloaked us like a blanket.

Understood.

I pinged Zohreya. We ought to withdraw. The numbers don't work. There was a lot of sparking in the eyes around me. Messages going back and forth. The one who sounded like Rangesh's cousin Annalisa leaned into me.

'Agent Rause, when the rest of the squad goes through the door, you and I stay here. We pick off anyone who comes out who shouldn't.'

Tac Two-One, you are free to use lethal force at your discretion. It's my call. We're inserted too deep to back out now.

That should have been about the hardest order Zohreya had ever given. The way she said it put me on edge. Sounded like it hadn't been hard at all.

Status Tac Two-Two.

223

No contact but we have a factory and operational machinery. We're securing data ...

My head filled with a noise so loud it blinded me. The tunnel turned blood red. I couldn't think. Everything moved, fast and abrupt. For the first seconds I hadn't the faintest idea what was going on, only that something had grabbed me and picked me up and thrown me. The air was full of smoke. There were shapes moving through it. For a moment I was back on Gibraltar, the last time someone had come close to blowing me up.

'Agent Rause!'

A hand grabbed me by the arm and pulled me hard to the side of the tunnel. The world was still full of bright flashing red light. The door was smashed in. I heard shouting and gunshots. My Servant was awash with tactical messages.

'What happened?'

Cousin Annalisa crouched beside me, rifle trained on the door. 'Someone tripped an alarm.'

'Who?'

'Don't know.'

I checked my Servant. Rangesh was in a machine room, hunkered down and waiting to see what would happen. Tac One-Two were racing down the last couple of tiers of the pit wall as fast as they could. Everything ahead was smoke and flashes, but all four MSDF operatives were up, their lenses feeding a tactical picture that showed at least a dozen targets subdued. Lights flashed. Gunshots. Live rounds. The now-and-then buzz of a particle beam. I tried to take it all in.

One feed was missing. I pinged Zohreya and got no answer. Her Servant showed her alive and moving but she'd killed her feed. I couldn't think of a single good reason why she'd do that.

'I've got an agent in trouble,' I said. 'Your squad has more use for you where the shooting is, right? Not here.'

Cousin Annalisa nodded. 'Agreed.'

224

'I need a drone. Something small with a camera.'

She tossed me a pair of metal eggs and pinged the activation codes to my Servant as she scurried to the wrecked door and vanished inside. Flashes and shocks of gunfire echoed. I pocketed one drone and poked the second and woke it up. The egg split open. A wasp-sized bug waited for me to tell it what to do. I synched it to Zohreya's position, told it I needed surveillance and let it buzz off down the tunnel faster than I could keep up.

Wasp-sized. Until you've lived on a world like Magenta, you don't appreciate what the diversity of life on Earth is like. When you don't have wasps or flies or spiders or crickets or mites or ants or lice or leeches or birds ... The air on Earth tastes like a living thing.

I ran back the way we'd come, heading for the fork in the tunnel and the laser tripwire.

So-So?

A pause and then a ping back. An acknowledgement.

Is Zohreya with you? I linked to So-So's feed. She was crouched among a stack of polycarbonate crates in a near-black cavern. Someone a few yards ahead of her was screaming his head off, slowly dragging himself on his elbows. So-So's feed stared past him into the darkness of another opening.

No.

Where is she?

Check your feed!

I reached the tripwire, jumped it and ran on, hoping there wasn't another one. Why isn't she with you?

Separated.

How?

Three targ— The message stopped with a flicker of motion. A light flared, dazzling, whiting out the feed. I stumbled and almost tripped.

Agent Zohreya! If her Servant was on then I could message her. No answer just meant she wasn't bothering to reply. Report in! That's an order! I switched back to So-So. She was out from behind her crates, advancing slowly on the darkness. I was coming up on her position.

Friendly at your six.

She stopped at the tunnel mouth. A few yards ahead of her was a body. This one wasn't moving. A chunk of his head about the size of two clenched fists was missing.

Location secure, she pinged. Two targets down. One for medevac, one for the corpse wagon. Not that anyone could do much about that right now but there would be trauma drones already heading our way.

There had been three targets there, back before everything kicked off. Where's the third?

Agent Zohreya is in pursuit.

I pinged Zohreya again. Still no answer, but the drone I'd sent had caught up with her. She was running through a tunnel so black that even the drone was having trouble. It had given up on its optics and was using a mix of thermals and ultrasound.

A flash. Gunfire. The drone went blind and deaf for a second. I backtracked Zohreya's position and gave chase.

Agent Zohreya!

More gunfire. I heard it first hand this time, a dim and distant echo bouncing through the tunnels. I was still getting pings from Zohreya but I had no idea who was shooting at her, or what, or how many there were, or whether she was shooting back.

Agent Zohreya, hold your position! I'm coming to you. I pinged So-So, telling her to follow as soon as she'd secured the man she'd shot.

No. Zohreya at last. Support Tac Two-One, sir. I have this.

I had to slow down for a moment, short of breath. Still wasn't used to the gravity, but it was more than that. If I turned off my feeds, all I could see was pitch-black nothingness, all I could hear were muted distant rumbles.

Wait for backup, Agent Zohreya! He's not worth dying for!

Negative, Rause. Continuing pursuit.

Stubborn bitch.

Alysha. I'd called her that after she'd miscarried. Exactly those two words. I'd forgotten. She'd come home from Mercy the day afterwards and we'd fallen into each others' arms, and she was crying and maybe I was too, and then we'd had some drinks and we were kissing and then she'd started talking, and for some reason it had all gone wrong and turned into a furious row. I'd called her a stubborn bitch and she'd walked out. She came back an hour later. We'd made up. It had been all right again. Or so I thought.

Zohreya was pinned down. The tunnels were so dark even my night visor was starting to struggle. I ran on. I didn't need this, not now. I didn't need someone else dead on my watch.

Hold, Zohreya. That's an order!

Not your call, sir.

I woke up the second drone Cousin Annalisa had given me and set it flying ahead of me, feeding its sensors through my Servant and onto my lenses so it became my eyes. The tunnels were pure and round, glass-fused, bored by a plasma lance. Nothing to trip on, but the gravity was killing me, sucking the air out of my lungs, the strength out of my legs.

The first drone unscrambled itself. Zohreya was moving again. The shooting had stopped. I watched, one eye fed by the drone in front of me, guiding my path, the other by the drone following Zohreya. She rounded a corner into open space. Ultrasonics picked out large pieces of machinery, maybe an old generator and a crane, all left behind when the mining stopped. I couldn't see whoever she was chasing ...

A flash and a bang. The drone went blind again but I was

close enough to hear the shot echo through the tunnels. More gunfire. Zohreya's Servant started singing an alarm. Minor trauma. Nothing our MSDF armour couldn't stitch and patch on the fly …

I ran faster.

Agent Zohreya!

The shooting stopped. The drone recovered from the light and the sound. Zohreya had someone cornered. They were a dozen feet apart, dancing around one of the old pieces of machinery, each trying to get a shot at the other, point blank.

'Rox!' Zohreya had a snarling fury to her that I'd never heard until now.

Agent Zohreya! Stand down!

'My name is Esharaq Zohreya.' Go away, Rause!

The man lunged, stopped, reversed, dived back the other way, tried to catch Zohreya out and failed. Zohreya shot him twice in his armoured chest. He staggered, stumbled back, rolled sideways and tried to lift his pistol towards her again. Zohreya shot him a third time. His gun flew away as his hand dissolved into red shreds. He screamed.

Zohreya! She was using a Reeper. She could have stunned him but she hadn't.

'Fucking crazy bitch!'

Zohreya pointed her pistol at his ankles now. Go away, Rause! My drone died. I don't know how she did it, but she cut me off. Another gunshot echoed through the tunnels. More frenzied shouting. I wasn't far now. Maybe thirty seconds ahead …

Zohreya! Stand down!

No answer.

Another shot. Screaming this time. Howling. I rounded the last corner into the open cavern and cut the second drone loose, let it show me where I was …

'Zohreya!'

She was standing over his head, Reeper pointed at his face. I couldn't make out much else in the darkness, not even using thermals.

'Go *away*, sir!'

I moved closer, weapon drawn. I wondered where I should point it. Instinct took over from indecision. I pointed it at Zohreya.

'Agent! Stand down *now*!'

She didn't move. 'Sir, this man used to run with the Gravity Gang. In the Squats. The Vault Posse, to be precise. There were seven of them. Three are dead. The other four …'

The man squirming in the dirt saw me. He was moaning. 'Get her away from me! She's fucking crazy!'

Zohreya's gun didn't waver. I kept my Reeper on her but she didn't look up. 'For a while, when I was thirteen, there was an eighth member of the Vault Posse. Me. There were reasons for that but they don't matter right now. When my father found out, he locked me in our apartment. He found the others and told them to leave me alone. Three days later this man left a bomb outside our front door. It tore my mother apart when it exploded. It ripped my first brother's head from his body and shattered most of my second brother's bones. He died before he reached Mercy. My father, who must have been as close to the blast as any of them, lived for three more days. He almost pulled through. Almost. But I think knowing that his sons were dead was too much for him.

'I was right there.' Zohreya cocked her head at the man between her feet. 'This one was the delivery boy. He didn't make the bomb. But he put it there.'

The man shifted. Groaned again. 'It wasn't supposed—'

'Where are the others, Rox?'

I took a step closer. 'Put the gun down, Agent Zohreya.'

'No.'

229

'I'll stun you if I have to.'

'No you won't, sir.'

'There are better ways to—'

'No, there aren't!' For a moment I saw the fury again. She shot me a glance full of fire, though her Reeper never shifted. 'What if this was Loki, sir? What would *you* do?'

She turned away from me, back to the man on the floor. I could hardly feel my fingers. My face felt numb and my hands felt heavy. Magenta's gravity, perhaps. I found my arms drooping, my aim slipping.

'I'd question him,' I said. But would I really? What would I do, face to face with Alysha's murderer? I'd want to kill him. Not a shred of doubt. I'd have a furnace of molten anger inside me, too much not to pour out.

Zohreya was quiet. Waiting for me to speak. The man on the floor was begging, pleading with me, but all I could hear was a rushing in my ears, the sound I'd heard when Flemich had come to break the news. The sound of Alysha's death.

My Reeper pointed to the floor. I don't think I could have lifted it again even if I'd wanted to.

'It's not the way, Esharaq,' I said, my voice hoarse. 'It really isn't. I know, though ... I know ...' What did I know? Nothing, that's what. 'It's for your father, is it? Ask yourself if it's what he'd want from you.'

I took a step back. And then I walked away.

16

GLITCH

The Cheetahs were coming down by the time I got out of the tunnels, the tac-teams cleaning up. We had two men injured, a dozen Earthers killed or wounded from the pit and as many again wrapped in spider ties waiting to be carted off to the Tesseract. We'd been lucky. It could have been a lot worse.

'Dude! This is, like, the biggest operation in Magenta's history!' Rangesh grinned at me as the tac-teams dragged their captives out of the tunnels. 'This is totally going to turn the narcs on their heads. They're going to be so green, man! They're going to hate ... Where's Esh, dude? Did you ...?'

I'd been running it through my head ever since I'd come out of the tunnels. At first I'd thought she might get away with it. No surveillance drones except mine. Nothing to see. No witnesses ... But we had walking wounded, five corpses and seven hospital cases from the pit, most of them illegal Earth paramilitaries. If you were of the mind to, you could argue that constituted an invasion. The First Descendants and the anti-immigration chorus would lap it up and shout it loud. We were going to be news across the planet come morning, might even go interstellar. The bureau, the MSDF, the news channels, they'd all sift through everything. They'd spot that Zohreya and I had gone adrift; they'd get hold of what drone footage there was; they'd subpoena our Servant records and eventually they'd dig out the truth. Add that to what happened in Gibraltar, and I was probably looking at the end of my career. As for Zohreya …

'Dude! What happened? She didn't …' He must have seen it in my face.

'Not a word, Rangesh,' I said. I wasn't sure, but I thought he sort of understood. Liss? If they go forensic on my Servant, are they going to know you were here?

No.

I turned back to Rangesh. 'How did you know?'

'Doesn't matter. Is it bad?'

'I think so.'

The Cheetahs couldn't carry anything like the number of people we had in the pit now. The tac-teams were loading up the first with the wounded, packing them off to Mercy as fast as they could. We had four more Cheetahs en route and a couple of hours to wait before they arrived, the three of us and Tac-Team Two and the dozen or so Earthers who didn't need a trauma team to patch them back up.

'So many,' murmured Rangesh. 'It's, like, where did they all come from? How did they get here? Maybe they all grew in seed pods or—'

'Smuggle one and you can smuggle a hundred,' I said. 'They're all Indians. Did you notice that?' I needed them to talk, and fast, to unravel whatever this was. Make the media attention go somewhere else. After the business with Betleshah, I wasn't sure how popular I was right now.

'They got space for one more wounded?' Zohreya walked

232

past us and then stopped a moment to catch her breath. She was dragging a body by his harness.

I looked away.

'He's not dead, sir,' she said. 'But he's a heavy son of a bitch so I might still change my mind.'

The man from the tunnel. I pinged his Servant. He registered a medical alert, a serious trauma in need of immediate attention. I'd seen her shoot him in the hand. From the look of him she'd shot him in the foot too, but she hadn't killed him. She'd enjoyed shooting him. I'd seen that. She'd done it with glee and I'd heard the triumph in her, but if it came to an inquiry then she'd had cause, at least for the first injury, and there was no evidence she didn't have it for the second. Or a good lawyer could argue it, and I'd back her up, claim necessary self-defence. The rest ...

There wasn't any record of the rest. His word against ours. His Servant reported that emergency first-aid treatment had been administered, sedatives and painkillers given, the wound stabilised ... Zohreya had done all the right things at the end. Made it look good, even if she and I both knew better.

Rangesh helped her drag him to the Cheetah bound for Mercy. Maybe I should have felt relieved but I didn't. Didn't matter that she hadn't done it in the end; I'd all but told her it was OK, that revenge trumped justice, even when revenge meant murder.

You saw it all, didn't you, I said to Liss.

I saw what you saw, Keys.

What if this was Loki, sir? That wasn't going to go away any time soon.

What does that say about me?

It says that you loved me fiercely.

I wanted to go home. I wanted to be back in my sterile apartment with Liss, my inadequate simulacrum of memories and want. I wanted to hear her simulated voice and feel her artificial arms around me, even though I knew exactly what she'd say: *You need to let go, Keys. You need to turn me off. You need to let me be dead.*

I don't judge you, Keys. I don't think any less of you.

Alysha would have been stronger.

Are you so sure?

Yes.

I'm not.

Rangesh and Zohreya headed back, talking. Zohreya folded her legs and sat beside me. Rangesh walked on: 'There's some, like, stuff, man. In the … you know, the factory thing. I'm going back there to make some notes. You, uh, kind of ought to have a look at it too. But I guess there's no rush.'

The first Cheetah took off. The tac-teams started loading the second. Mercy was in for a busy night.

'Sir?' Zohreya had taken her helmet off so I could see her face, her eyes, even if they were artificial. She held out her hand. 'Offered in the spirit of what it means to you and to everyone who was born beyond the thin air of Earth, I thank you.'

She wanted to shake my hand. I'd sort of got used to that on Earth where it really didn't mean that much, but on the colony worlds a handshake was akin to cutting palms and making some sort of blood pact. A display of absolute trust.

'Agent Zohreya, I—'

'You were right, sir. It wasn't the way.'

'Agent …' What was I supposed to say?

'Thank you for trusting me … to make that choice for myself.'

'I thought you were going to kill him.'

'So did I.' Her hand slowly withdrew.

'I'm sorry, Agent Zohreya, but we have no reason to be proud. Either of us.'

'Respectfully, sir, I disagree.'

The second Cheetah lifted off, carrying the last of the wounded and the first few Earthers to the Tesseract for interrogation. Maybe they'd lead us to their chemist, maybe not. Maybe we'd find out why someone had designed a gen that killed anyone who carried the Mohinder-Kali gene, but more likely than not we wouldn't. Most likely of all it was an accident. Random chance. A design glitch. 'What do you suppose we'll do with them in the end?' I asked. 'Send them back? Let them go? We can hardly put a few dozen Earthers in a Magentan prison. The gravity would classify as torture.' That and I wasn't sure there were enough cells on the planet. Firstfall prison, designed for a hundred inmates, was the biggest we had. The hard cases all got shipped to Colony 478.

Zohreya took off her gloves and then took my hand and squeezed it, whether I wanted her to or not. 'I know you don't have faith, sir. Hardly anyone does any more. My father used to say that since Allah created us imperfect, how could he then expect perfection in return? All that is asked is that we try, sir. And nothing is more important than family.'

She let go but the feeling lingered. I couldn't remember the last time I'd been touched like that. Warm and caring. Human.

Not since Alysha.

'I heard the explosion that killed them. It was so loud. I was forbidden to leave my room, but I came up to see what it was anyway. The apartment door was open and the light from outside was bright. I didn't understand at first. I could see the shapes. I could see my father. He was lying on his back in the hall behind the door. He was making strange noises as though he couldn't breathe.'

'You don't have to do this.'

'Yes, sir, I do. It's how I make sense of it. Reliving it.' She shivered. 'There were other shapes outside but I couldn't make out what they were. My hands touched the wall. My fingers came away sticky and wet and red. My father's blood. I called his name as I ran to him. I called for help. I still didn't understand what had happened. I thought perhaps he'd had a heart attack and so I tried to give him first aid – he'd insisted we all learn because he wanted us to all become doctors. That was when I saw what was outside.

'A pod came. No people, just an emergency pod. I sat beside my dying brother and watched the trauma drones treat him as best they could before they carried him away. A second pod took my father. A crowd had gathered by then. I don't blame them for their stares but I remember how they felt, fixed on me as though I was an exhibit in a zoo.

'The drones left me there. My other brother had no head any more. My mother ... I could hardly recognise that it was her. I'd realised by then that it must have been a bomb. It was already on the news. Channel Six had found a camera that had caught the moment of the explosion. I watched the recording of my mother and my brothers come to the door. My father opening it to greet them. And then the explosion. You could see my brother's head fly off. They stopped showing it after a few minutes. I suppose even ghouls have their limits. But I watched it again anyway, over and over. I still do. It was my fault. I'd brought this on my family.'

Quietly, in the background of my Servant, I felt Liss listening. She searched and found the video Zohreya meant. She didn't show me, but I knew she was watching it.

Zohreya took a long deep breath. 'Eventually someone came and took me away. I don't remember much of the next few days. They kept me in Mercy. Without my family I lost my faith and for a while I lost my mind. They were going to send me back to Earth, but there was some problem with that. In the end they decided I should stay. They gave me more gene therapy to help my body continue its adaptation to Magenta's gravity.

I was placed into care with a family in Nico. Three days after I arrived, I fled back to Firstfall. I was caught and returned. The day after that I ran away again. After a few months they gave up and sent me to the military academy for young delinquents. I found my faith again there. I didn't expect to, but I did. I promised myself that I would honour my father and Allah. I had a debt to them both and I would repay it. At eighteen I tried to join the police. I was turned down. When I was accepted into the MSDF instead, I took every opportunity I was given.' She nodded across the pit to where the second tac-team stood in a watchful ring around the other captives. 'They became my new family. And now here I am.'

'It was all about revenge?' I tried not to think about it, how easily I could understand that.

'It wasn't supposed to be. It was meant to be about making sure that nothing like that could ever happen to anyone else.' Zohreya smiled faintly. 'But just for a few minutes when you found me, I was thirteen again, running away from my foster home so I could murder the people who'd killed my father and my mother and my brothers. Thank you for reminding me that I grew beyond that person long ago.'

I shrugged. 'I really thought you were going to execute him.'

'I didn't have to shoot him in the foot as well. I'm trying to regret doing that, sir, but I'm afraid I can't.'

I would have killed him, whispered Liss. She played some of the clip she'd pulled. Esharaq, thirteen, kneeling on the street, her head in her hands. Blood everywhere.

Alysha wouldn't.

Alysha didn't lose her family. She had an odd tone to her. Tight and angry. Look after that one, Keys. I like her.

I gave Zohreya a long level look. 'It's probably best,' I said, 'if we don't talk too much about what happened in there. There's going to be an inquiry. We have dead Earthers. I can

237

only protect you so far. Internal Investigation are going to be all over this. They won't have a choice.'

'I know that, sir. It was a glitch that won't happen again. Please don't lie for me. I did what I did and will face the consequences.' She laughed. 'I still don't understand why there were so many of them here. Did we catch the chemist?'

'I don't think so.'

'Then you need to question Rox, sir, or Horace Winston, or whatever name he carries with him tomorrow. He knows who the chemist is.'

'Did you ever wish you hadn't stayed on Magenta?' I asked. 'After you lost your family. Did you ever wish they'd sent you back to Earth? You have relatives back there, right?'

'Aunts and uncles, yes. I wished that for a while but I'm glad it worked out as it did. If I could find the person who decided I should stay, I'd thank them.' She touched my hand again. 'It was tempting to run. But it would have done me no good. If anything it would have made things worse.'

I should go. Before anyone else comes. Liss faded from my Servant.

'How do you know your guy can finger the chemist?'

'I had a gun to his head, sir, and he knew I was ready to use it. He wanted to live.'

We sat in silence a while. There weren't any more answers to be had, not here. We'd get them slowly, the hard way, the usual way, with questioning and interrogations and a team of forensic drones combing the site. All of that was on its way. We'd done a good night's work. We'd recovered the factory and its data intact. The Earthers hadn't had a chance to wipe their stacks. We had a lead on the chemist. That was our future, where our thoughts should have been.

Rangesh was among the Earthers now, asking about their chemist and who they were and who had brought them out here, all the questions we'd ask again and again in the Tesseract. He wasn't getting answers, but there wasn't much else to do until the other Cheetahs came and so I joined him, and then went to have a look at the quantum factory we'd taken, the molecular synthesiser and refiner and the stash of engineered gens beside it all packed and ready to ship. Nothing more to learn though. By the time we shipped out I wasn't sure that the Earthers even knew who was paying them, only that the pay was good. Someone had brought the factory to the pit a few days after they'd arrived and it had been running ever since. Best guess was that most of what they made was shipped to Disappointment to supply the migrants coming in from Earth. By the time the Cheetahs came to take us home, Rangesh was hooting and hopping with delight: we'd taken the biggest drug haul in Magentan history. Apparently that was going to make us heroes. I didn't feel it though.

I pinged the Tesseract for extra surveillance on Horace Winston or Rox or whatever his name was. If Zohreya was right and he could point us at the chemist, that made him precious. A forensics team took over the site while the rest of us went home to sleep. Liss was waiting for me in her shell. She stroked my hair as I crawled under the covers. I wanted to talk to her some more about what had happened, but I couldn't. I knew what she'd say. Time for me to let go. I'd just proved that, hadn't I?

Just a glitch, Zohreya had said. Was that what it was? I didn't think so. In her shoes would I have pulled the trigger? I think I would.

LUTAN BEDAWI

Lutan Bedawi slips through the corridors of Mercy Hospital. There are surveillance cameras everywhere, but Lutan doesn't worry about that because he is invisible. He follows doctors and nurses and drones. Mercy is busy tonight. Something has happened. There are Earthers and MSDF soldiers. Something to do with the lichen, but Lutan Bedawi already knows that. It's why he's here, after all. He has his doubts as to whether this new strain of xeno-hallucinogen is as new as everyone thinks.

There is a secure wing to Mercy, deep underground. It's where people like Rox Vellish are taken when they need care. Criminals. The wicked. Lutan reaches it, but entering is another matter. The door is locked and coded. Two soldiers stand guard.

Outside, Magenta's sun is rising. A shift change is coming. Lutan waits as new nurses walk into the wing. Mercy checks their Servants, making sure they are who they say. The checks are long and careful. One of the soldiers starts to flirt. He thinks that one of the nurses likes him. The door unlocks and Lutan follows, silent and unseen, inches behind. The wing beyond is the same as any other except for the locks and the cameras and the armed guards. Rox Vellish is in the furthest room. Lutan follows a nurse inside. Vellish lies sedated after the reconstruction of his hand and foot. The nurse makes his notes and leaves. He locks the door. Vellish and Lutan are alone.

An armed guard stands outside but he is looking the wrong way. Two cameras keep watch. Lutan Bedawi slides a lens over each. The lens copies the picture it sees of the room, saves it and feeds it back into each camera eye. No one will see what happens next.

Lutan sidles to Rox Vellish's side. He pulls back the covers, takes the noose he has already made and slips it around Vellish's neck. He wraps it around a ceiling beam and pulls, hoisting Vellish into the air until he dangles, choking.

'You did something very bad,' says Lutan Bedawi. He speaks softly.

Vellish's Servant has noticed that something is wrong. Lutan ties the end of the rope to the bed, grabs Vellish by the legs and jerks down hard, snapping his neck. It is deeply satisfying. Vellish's Servant screams for help. An alarm sounds. Lutan pulls again to be sure.

It takes a while for the guard outside to override the lock. The door bursts open. The soldier and then a nurse. They stare, horrified and amazed.

They are inches away, but Lutan Bedawi is invisible. He stands very still. No one sees him. The soldier has a knife. They cut Vellish down and try to revive him but they are too late. In the commotion Lutan slips out through the open door and ceases to be.

FIVE

THE CHEMIST

17

SURFING LESSONS AGAIN

It was past midday before I hauled myself out of bed. Liss had disabled the alarm in my Servant and shut it down to incoming calls. I was finally used to the gravity enough to sleep through.

There were a lot of waiting messages. The first were from Patterson, a string of them while we were out in Pit 779 while anyone with any sense would have been sleeping. Something about having found Anja Gersh, something else about the Settlement 64 personnel records, something about putting Nikita Svernoi under surveillance, which I would have loved to do if he wasn't in orbit in a Fleet-run station, and last of all something about the night we'd spent in Disappointment and sorry for all the stuff she'd said. That one was pretty incoherent. She'd obviously been up all night.

There was a message from Flemich next, congratulating us and telling us to take the day off. A couple of hours later Rox Vellish apparently hanged himself in Mercy. After that all hell broke loose, Flemich telling us to ignore his first call and NOT take the day off but to get in as soon as possible, a pile more about Vellish, one from the Tesseract telling all of us except Patterson that we were suspended, another from Flemich, saying not to come in after all, messages from Zohreya and Rangesh asking where I was. In the middle of it all was a weird message from the Disappointment Medical Centre, something about an Amal Patel being admitted onto the government transgravity programme. I had to sit there for a whole minute, banging my head against the name until I figured out who Amal Patel was. The ragged Earth-born beggar from the Disappointment mag-lev station.

I poured myself a shot of something strong and called Rangesh.

'Where are you?'

'Wavedome, boss dude. Day off. We earned it.'

'Did you not get the news?' No one doesn't care about a suspension, even if it's only for a day. 'We haven't got the day off, Rangesh; we're under investigation.'

'Yeah, man, same difference.' I'd forgotten just how many times Rangesh had been investigated. Now he was laughing at me. 'Don't sweat it, dude. Was a good bust. Just be chill and act like it's a couple of days' paid leave, you know? Unless you were in Mercy last night.'

'I was asleep.'

'Me too, man. But they always do this, you know? Ever since … Well, it never lasts long. End of the day it'll blow over. Ignore it. We're totally going to celebrate. Last night was medals-for-everyone awesome. We're going to have drinks and stuff, you know? Even Laws is coming. Sign of the end times, man.'

A stray stab of fear caught me. Liss had deactivated my Servant to let me sleep. I couldn't prove I'd stayed in bed.

I told Rangesh I'd think about it and poured myself another glass. If any of us was going to murder Vellish then surely it would have been easier back in the pit rather than waiting until he was in Mercy. Had to be someone he was working for, afraid of what he might say, and that meant someone in Firstfall, someone connected enough to hear about the arrest and with the power to do something about it straight away. I started making a list and then stopped. Patterson probably already had one, and Rangesh too, and their lists wouldn't be five years out of date.

Vellish knew something about the chemist; Zohreya had told me that. And she'd told Rangesh, and that was it. Made the two of us the obvious suspects, but there was nothing much I could do about that except wait for forensics to come back with a report on Vellish's death. I went back to Patterson's message about Gersh instead. Kaltech's records said that Gersh had never been to Settlement 64, but Jonas Himaru had, and I was pretty sure he'd seen her corpse. According to the public records Laura had now pulled from Earth, Gersh was alive and well and living somewhere in the German Alps. At least she had been six months ago, which was the most up-to-date record Patterson had found. I'd have given an arm to find out for sure, but all I could do was send a request for information and wait and see what happened, which was often not very much but nevertheless took several months. Patterson had found medical records too, confirming that Gersh suffered from Mohinder-Kali.

I wrestled with the obvious notion for a bit, that Gersh had engineered a variant of xenoflora that killed people with the Mohinder-Kali gene, and now someone was distributing it into the general population of Magenta because ...

Because? There was the kicker. Why would anyone do that? Why target one particular genetic code?

I toyed then for a bit with the idea that Svernoi wasn't the bad guy. What if he'd shut Gersh down because of what she was doing? And so Gersh faked her own death and …

Yeah. OK. Getting carried away. Stick to the facts, Rause.

I set off a series of searches on the name Archana, mostly because I couldn't think of anything better to do and I didn't want to go outside. I got plenty of hits but they weren't very helpful. Two dozen names in Firstfall. Another hundred across the rest of the planet. Seventeen contemporary fictional characters, hundreds of references from Earth and a handful of local businesses. Whoever Alysha had taken with her before she got on that train she'd trusted them, and she'd been scared, and Archana had gone out of her way to hide herself, and so the name was most likely plucked at random. Maybe it meant something or maybe it didn't.

The nearest hit was a custom robotics fabrication and repair shack. Drones and shells and the like. It was a place to start, for want of anything better, but then Patterson called me.

'Rangesh tells me you're awake at last. Where the fuck are you? We need to talk.'

'We do?'

'Yes, and soon.'

'Then go ahead, talk.'

'Face to face.'

'Why?'

'Because reasons. You got anything more pressing to do right now, Rause?'

She had a point. 'Where?'

Patterson hesitated. 'Well, I suppose it might as well be the fucking Wavedome since that's where the other two are.'

Now *I* hesitated. I wanted to talk to Patterson alone. Thinking about Gersh on Earth had got me wondering about KRAB and the mysterious disappearing satellite hijacker. Maybe there was something I'd missed.

'I'll be there.' I cut the call and summoned a pod. As I did,

Liss caught my arm. The mechanical eyes in her artificial shell looked right through me.

'Be careful, Keys. They've suspended you. If you want to do something, go to Nico and see your parents. Let them know you're on Magenta again.'

'I've been all over the news. I imagine they know by now.' I brushed her away. 'This is more important.'

'No, it—'

I rounded on her. 'It's about you, Liss!'

'Will it bring me back?'

She looked at me, those glass eyes as unreadable as ever. Of course it wouldn't.

'Tell me whatever you need to tell me, Keys, whatever makes you feel right, but don't lie to yourself. How can anything at all be about *me* when I'm already dead? It's about you. All of it. It always has been. It has to be.'

I went for the door. Liss got there first. She stood across it, barring the way.

'I'm not going to stop you, Keys. But whatever was happening in Settlement 64, it's long over. And what if it wasn't that at all? What if I was running from something else? What if I was running from you? What if I was running from some secret you never found? What if Himaru is right and I was running because I sent six men to die? What if the answer isn't what you want it to be? Do you really want to know?'

'Are you telling me you don't care?'

'Why would I? Let it go, Keys!'

'That's exactly what I'm aiming to do.'

I could feel her trying to decide whether I meant it, or was I simply saying what I thought she wanted to hear? She moved to let me pass. I walked out.

'I can't pretend it didn't happen, Liss, I just can't. You understand that, don't you?'

'If it's closure you want then go to the memorial stone.'

I got angry then. I could hear the hidden thought: *Isn't that what you humans do?* She was so like Alysha in so many ways, and yet there was always a distance. Last night aside, Liss almost never got angry. She never raged. She could sound sad or happy or excited but she never felt it, not like flesh and bone. What does it even mean, to *feel* something?

'Please be careful,' she said, soft in my ear. 'I don't trust Laura.'

'Why not?'

'I think you know.'

I remembered our first meeting. Prickly and bitter, but she'd been helping me from the start, quietly and without looking for credit. I'd put that down to ... I suppose some sort of affection for Alysha. 'Maybe she just wants to impress her new boss?'

'Keys! She's clearly sizing you up as a prospect for a relationship, but—'

'I'm the human here, so I'll be the judge of that, if you don't mind.'

'I don't want you to get hurt, that's all.'

'Yeah. You want me to let go and move on but you don't want me to get hurt! Well that's how it goes, Alysha! Humans hurt each ...'

I stopped. I was standing in the tunnel outside my apartment, a pod waiting behind me, yelling at someone who was dead. And I'd called her Alysha. I didn't know what that meant. Liss had always been Liss.

'I need to go now,' I said, and kicked her out of my Servant. I didn't want her silently watching me, not now.

The pod took me to the Wavedome. A shell was waiting with a wetsuit and a board as I arrived. I changed and joined the others on the beach. Patterson looked me up and down, awkward and uncomfortable in a rented suit a size too big, holding her surfboard as though it was a dangerous animal.

250

'You look good, Rause. Skin-tight suits you. Pity you're about to ruin it by getting in the water and looking like a clown.'

'Don't they have any designer Earth-import suits?' I asked.

'Ha fucking ha.'

We all walked to the where the breaking waves were only a few feet tall.

'You wanted to talk,' I said.

'In the water.'

We went through the motions together a few times, all four of us paddling out to where the waves were breaking and then riding them back, Zohreya and Rangesh standing and looking cool and a bit bored while I lay on the board and tried to get a feel for where to spread my weight. Patterson did the same, but after the first couple of times tried standing. She actually managed it for a couple of seconds. I kind of hated her for that.

'Been a while,' she said when we gathered back together. Waves broke around us, knocking us back and forth. 'Wasn't sure I'd remember how to do it.'

Zohreya was scanning for drones again. Eavesdroppers.

'You should bring Jamie, man,' said Rangesh. 'He'd probably be, like, totally awesome in five minutes.'

'We used to come when he was younger.' I saw a flash in Patterson's eye. 'The three of us … Look, we have a real fucking problem. All of us. And you, Rause, you have two real fucking problems. But let's start with the one we can all share. The guy you brought back last night. Rox Vellish, real name Horace Winston, the one who supposedly hanged himself in Mercy a couple of hours after he came out of surgery. Rause, you were off the grid last night—'

'I—' A rogue wave broke between us, rattling us, knocking us all off balance.

'Did I sound like I was done? I've seen the surveillance from Mercy. Someone killed the cameras in Winston's room. A

251

minute later he was dead. More than a dozen staff and security in the confined space of a secure ward and no one saw a fucking thing. He was supposed to be under protection. Rause, you gave the order yourself. Right now there's a shit-storm flying up so fast it's probably in orbit already, and when it comes down again it's going to hit like an asteroid strike. Zohreya, you and Winston ... do I really need to spell it out? And Rangesh, how exactly did you get that lead on Pit 779?'

'Hey, man, that's—'

'They know that you and Zohreya were with Roy Lemond two nights ago. So let's start with what the fuck that was about, shall we?'

'Dude! That's, like, confidential and—'

Patterson surged through the water and pushed Rangesh hard in the chest, knocking him off balance as the next wave came in and took him down. She watched him flounder for a second. 'You want to take the shit for this?' She rounded on Zohreya. 'Or shall we start with the agent whose sole purpose within the bureau is the pursuit of a personal vendetta?'

'Keep it together, man!' Rangesh struggled to his feet. 'Esh, she's—'

Zohreya held Patterson's glare. 'It was true once, but Allah has shown me—'

'Fuck Allah and fuck your stupid fucking superstitious nonsense bullshit!'

Zohreya's face tightened. Right there was the violence she held inside her, the clenched fists, whatever Allah might once have whispered in her ear. But she turned away. 'I'm sorry you find working with me such a burden, Agent Patterson.'

'Oh fuck you too, Esharaq!' Patterson looked ready to punch someone again, and I didn't think Zohreya would go down as easily as Rangesh. I sloshed through the water to stand between them.

'You want to tell me about Gersh, Patterson?'

'Why did you come back, Rause? Why did you even leave Earth?'

'Because I didn't have much choice.' The waves battered and barged us. I had to talk between the rhythm of the surf. 'I went off the grid last night because we didn't get back until almost dawn and because I wanted some sleep and because the transgravity has finally kicked in enough that I can actually get some, even if the rest of me aches all the time, and I didn't want some dick at the Tesseract waking me up! Good enough for you?' The next wave almost lifted me off my feet. They were getting bigger.

'Gersh had Mohinder-Kali.'

'We know!' I shot back.

Patterson glared at Rangesh and Zohreya again and then beckoned them closer. 'And that doesn't fucking bother you right now?'

'You think I wouldn't haul her in in a flash? Tell me where the corpse is buried and give me someone who can talk to the dead and I'll sign off an exhumation order right here!'

'How about this? Ali Surash? Remember him? Svernoi's terrorist who blew himself up in their lab? *He* had Mohinder-Kali as well.'

'The guy in Svernoi's video? The one he showed us up in orbit?'

'Obviously!'

Rangesh lunged closer. 'Dude! You can prove that? Because that—'

'The chemist came from Settlement 64,' said Zohreya flatly.

We all stopped what we were doing and looked at her. I hardly noticed the board tugging at my arm, the back and forth suck and pull of the sea.

'What?' I said.

253

'That's what Vellish told me.'

'He told you that? When?'

'After you left us, sir.' Zohreya let out a long sigh and looked hard at Patterson, then back at me. 'The gen factory came from some Earthers. One was the chemist. Vellish said he'd seen the man on the news some time, something to do with Settlement 64. Svernoi was on the same piece.'

I felt a rage building. 'You knew all this last night and you didn't tell me?'

'You know how it was, sir! I told you to question him. I couldn't tell you the rest! We had to get it out of him the right way! Witnessed and recorded. We had to be able to *use* it!'

A wave broke betweens us, staggering us apart.

Patterson growled: 'Well, that's just fucking—'

'Wait a moment,' I said. 'Let me get this right. Vellish, Winston, whoever he is, he fingers Svernoi and now he's dead, and—'

Patterson was glaring at Zohreya. 'You got a recording?' she asked. 'Your Servant ... No, you haven't. Of course not, not when you were planning to execute him. Even if you did, you had a gun to his head, right? So the moment any lawyer got hold of it they'd be screaming extorted confession and contaminated evidence so loud you'll hear it all the fucking way to Earth!'

'That's why I didn't say anything more.' Zohreya looked forlorn. 'I thought that you and Agent Rause would question him in the Tesseract. Properly and on the record and—'

'So we've got nothing! Shit! We need someone who knew what Gersh was doing.'

'Her assistant,' I said. 'Vismans.'

'Who lives on fucking Earth, Rause! What, are we going to send someone to go and get him?'

I looked to Zohreya. 'You get a name for this chemist?'

254

She shook her head. 'He said he saw the same face in some news piece, that's all. A man standing beside Nikita Svernoi.'

'And how did he know Svernoi?'

'He didn't until I showed him a picture.'

I wanted to scream. 'Then there's nothing we can do until they take us off suspension. I'm going to the Magenta Institute.'

'Dude!'

'No, I'm done.'

I started for the shore. Before I could take two steps, Patterson caught my shoulder. 'Wait!'

'Why?'

'Two things. First thing, *I'm* not suspended. So Zohreya and Rangesh and I can go back to my apartment and sift through every single piece of news footage there's ever been about Settlement 64. We can find every picture of Svernoi's face, look to see who's standing next to him, and one of those is our chemist. Then we start the hunt.'

'You want to do that from home? The Tesseract—'

'And that's the second thing, Rause, and why you don't get to help us. Assuming Zohreya didn't change her mind and murder Horace Winston, and assuming Rangesh didn't tell his good friend Roy Lemond about our plans for the night, how the fuck did Winston end up with a rope around his neck? Who even knew we had him? There's a mole, Rause. Someone in the Tesseract is skating for the other team.'

'What other team? I don't even know who that is.'

'A good fucking question, but does it really matter right now? What matters is that we work outside the bureau until we know who it is.'

I froze. A mole. Someone in the bureau. For a moment I forgot where I was, oblivious to the waves smashing into me. 'Shit!' They'd killed Horace Winston. Why? Because Horace Winston could connect the gens from Pit 779 to Nikita Svernoi and Kaltech and Settlement 64. And if the mole was protecting Svernoi now, what if the same mole had been working in the Tesseract five years ago?

'Alysha,' I breathed. 'The mole. Whoever it is, they killed Alysha. Archana!'

Patterson just looked at me like she'd been waiting for me to figure it out. 'We work outside the bureau, Keon. Agreed?'

I nodded. 'I'll you help find the chemist.'

'No.'

'Why?'

'Use your fucking head, Rause.'

'You think it was me? You think I—'

'I think you knew Alysha. Who she trusted. Who she might have talked to.'

'You think Archana is someone I know?'

Patterson nodded. I left her and waded to the shore, ditched the wetsuit and the board and called a pod to take me to the Magenta Institute. I needed space to think. Someone inside the bureau. Someone Alysha had called a friend. Someone who'd convinced her that her life was in danger, that she should run, maybe only for a few days until the threat passed and Kaltech were exposed. Maybe Archana had suggested the train. It was as good a way to disappear as any. She'd taken Alysha to the station, knowing all along that she was taking her to die. It all made sense up to the part where Archana walked away all smiles and a chat with Angel del Rosario, had a drink with her and quietly saved her life. That didn't fit. No one would do that, not when they'd just sent four people to die.

The pod stopped outside the Magenta Institute. I walked in and flashed my bureau ID. A few minutes later I was being given a guided tour of the roof by a ball of muscle called Brad, a lab technician who apparently ran a roof-runner club in his spare time and knew all the nooks and crannies of Firstfall's rooftops.

I took him to where the hijacker unit had been hidden, but all I got was a shrug.

'It's not there now, so it was either taken down and inventoried and never returned or else it was blown away in the storm. That's not all that uncommon.'

I wasn't paying attention, not really. Most of me was running through tired old thought passages, trying to work out for the umpteenth time who Alysha might have taken with her that night. Trying to get my head around everything was like trying to carry water in a colander, thoughts leaking out faster than I could catch them.

'OK. In that case you're going to have to account for every item taken off the roof and every item put back again. Anything you've got unclaimed I want handed over to the bureau by the end of the day for dismantling.'

Brad took me back to the roof. He showed me a camera that looked towards the edge from the top of a low blocky tower.

'I'm going to ping you into the feed. Got it?'

I had it project to my lenses. Suddenly I was looking out across the roof over central Firstfall.

'Keep watching.' Brad walked to where the satellite hijacker had been. He crossed the camera field of view as he did, but I could only see him from his waist down to his ankles. 'Get me?'

'No face.'

'What about now?' He crouched where the hijacker had been. Now he was out of shot.

'No. Nice idea, but no.'

'Pity.' He turned away and rose. As he did, his face clipped the corner of the image.

'Wait! Do that again!'

We went through the footage for the day before the storm. Sure enough, early in the morning, before the Institute staff came up to clear the roof, someone had crossed the camera view. A woman. She crouched out of sight, same as Brad, did something I couldn't see, then turned and rose, and as she did her face clipped into shot. Same as my new best friend.

I had her. Three good frames. 'You know who that is?'

We tried the face against the Institute records but came up blank. 'Not staff, I can tell you that much. Not a student either, although they do like to prank the automated systems sometimes.'

I almost sent the face to the bureau for the Tesseract to put through facial recognition. But I was suspended, and that meant Flemich would chew me out, and then there was the whole question of Patterson's mole and the outside chance that I was looking at her. I figured on taking it back to Patterson instead and running it through whatever public facial recognition database she was using to find Svernoi.

A gang of suits waited for me in the Institute's atrium. They weren't happy with my demands. I decided to make them more unhappy by insisting they release the footage of every single surveillance camera in the Institute for an hour either side of my three frames in the hope we'd get something more on the woman there. It didn't make me any friends, but I figured that if they were bothered enough then they could always call up the bureau and talk to Flemich and find out that I was suspended and feel smug about themselves. I figured they probably wouldn't.

I was almost at Patterson's apartment when she pinged me to say they'd found the chemist.

18

DISAPPOINTMENT

The chemist was holed up at a wind farm on the outskirts of
Disappointment. We couldn't use an MSDF Cheetah, so that
left us with taking the mag-lev. In the pod on the way to the
station, Patterson told me what they'd found.

'We ran Nikita Svernoi's face through news databases and
pulled every clip with a hit. He showed up three times, a background face in pieces on the handover of Settlement 64. Then
we ran everyone who was in them with him. Only a couple of
hundred. Most we tossed straight away – Magentan government. Wasn't too hard to narrow it down to one. Here he is.'
Patterson pinged me a face and a file. Harjit Lal. Earth-born.
Claimed to be a xeno-meteorologist. 'He was on the *Fearless*
from Earth with you six weeks ago. Before that we've got no
record of him, but he was with Svernoi at a press conference
some months back. I don't know what he's doing on the surface, but the best satellite surveillance I can access without going
through the Tesseract says he's with two "technicians". The
gun-carrying sort, at a guess. Maybe another gen factory. When

we arrive and he knows he's blown, we're going to offer him a deal. We use him to tear Svernoi down. And then Kaltech. Yes?'

'Agreed.'

Zohreya and I told her about Jonas Himaru and the search and rescue mission to Settlement 64, how Himaru had seen a body that looked like Anja Gersh.

Patterson made a sceptical face and shrugged. 'According to Earth she's alive and well in Germany.'

'We get Svernoi. Then we'll know.'

We caught the afternoon mag-lev and settled in for a five-hour rocket ride through the planet. The train was quiet and we had the lounge to ourselves. It made me twitch sitting there, feeling the acceleration as we pulled away. Magenta's mag-levs were little more than giant rail-guns, and we were riding the bullet. The safest means of rapid transport ever devised, they say, except for that one time five years ago; and here we were, perhaps on the edge of the same discovery Alysha had made.

I showed Patterson what I'd found at the Institute and passed her the picture of the woman's face. Since the satellite hijacker was part of the KRAB case, we decided it was safe to use the Tesseract and had some fun trying to trace her. She'd gone off the grid after leaving the Institute roof but we managed a backtrack that threw up a couple of visits to the Fleet embassy, and we found the apartment where she'd been staying. Patterson sent some uniforms to check it out but the place had been stripped bare. We'd have to wait for data forensics to do their thing.

Mostly we talked about the mole. We didn't get anywhere. Someone close to Alysha five years ago who had a line on our investigation. Flemich looked perfect, but if you knew him, you knew he just didn't have what it took.

'I'm going to get some rest,' I said.

Zohreya caught my hand as I got up. Just a touch and then she let go. I caught a frown on Rangesh's face. A bewilderment and maybe a tiny flicker of hostility, as though I'd somehow strayed onto territory he considered his own. They were sitting close, the two of them side by side.

'You should get some rest too,' I said.

I went back to my cabin and settled onto my bunk. We used to lie together, Alysha and I, and talk. Side by side, close enough to touch, hands clasped, fingers intertwined, looking up at the ceiling. Sometimes we'd set the ceiling screen to show some newscast or an old movie. Sometimes I'd make her watch one of the reality cam channels with me, even though she hated them because they were the sort of thing she dealt with every day at work. Other nights we set the screen to show the stars and Magenta's moons as we'd see them if we were above the clouds, almost but not quite in orbit. Side by side, talking endlessly about nothing, random thoughts, whatever came to mind and following the thread of them. Liss was good for that too, that wandering meandering talk, idle streams of semi-conscious thought. The cracksman who'd made her had managed to get that part of Alysha just right. Perfect, even.

Perfect.

I'd tried once, when Liss first had her shell, lying beside her and holding hands and talking the way Alysha and I used to talk. I don't know what I was thinking. I can't remember. It had taken me two years to build her and another six months to get the money for her shell. Had I really thought that I could bring her back from the dead? She was a glorious collection of memories, that was all. The ultimate extrapolation of a photograph album, an archive of all the recollections of someone I'd once loved, condensed into a single monument to her memory. I'd shown her how we tangled our fingers together ...

She could reproduce a sound, a gesture, a laugh, a voice, a tone, anything. She could get it exactly right, over and over and over. Without variation. Her perfection was her flaw.

I had to let her go. All that time and effort into making her, into bringing her back, into keeping some part of her alive, but Liss wasn't Alysha, not really. I think that was the day, three years after the Loki bombing, when we first lay side by side again, flesh and blood beside metal and plastic, that it really hit me that Alysha was gone forever.

I went back to the lounge, determined to listen to Rangesh and Patterson argue for the entire rest of the trip if that was what it took to stop feeling sorry for myself, but Patterson had gone. Rangesh and Zohreya were hidden among some high-backed seats that gave the illusion of private compartments. I couldn't see them as I entered, and they couldn't see me, but I could hear them. They had the lounge to themselves.

'I don't know, Esh. It all seems so, like, pointless, man.'

'You loved her.'

I stopped. Waited, listening.

'Nah ... No. No way, man. The Shy—'

'OK, Bix. You liked her then. A lot.'

Hovering by the door ...

'Yeah. I guess I did. It was, like, a long time ago, you know. We all loved the Shyster back then. She was just ... she was like the sun, man, and it sucks that she's dead ... I mean, what was the point of it? Just some chemical glitch that goes wrong when it mixes with some freak genetic condition that almost no one in the world and space has? I mean, it wasn't like someone *meant* to kill her. That would actually suck less, you know? If there was, like, someone I could get angry with and arrest and shit. Maybe get into some of that police brutality thing your friends in the— Ow! Hey! OK, OK, I'm just ... But this ... You need to have some words with that Allah dude of yours, man. And then all that other stuff about how it was between her and the Shah? Secrets and lies, Esh. They're like some slow corrosion. They ruin everything.'

'Bix?'

'Random shit, man. Maybe the Entropists have it right. I don't get it. How do you even believe in this whole Allah thing when –'

'Bix!'

'– when stuff just happens? What?'

I could hear my heart beat. There were only a few rows of seats between us.

'I like you, Bix.'

'Yeah, uh ... Cool. But ... I mean ... what's that got ... to do with ...? Oh.'

A long pause.

'I think,' said Zohreya very softly, 'that if there's a lesson in all of this, it's to take our moments when they come, and not to wait for some future that might never happen.'

I imagined Patterson off in her cabin, pausing for a moment from whatever she was doing to roll her eyes. But then again it sounded a lot like what she'd said when we'd been alone together on the way from Disappointment spaceport.

'So ... is that, like, an Allah thing?' asked Rangesh.

'It's an Esh thing.'

'Um?'

'Also, you do know that calling it an "Allah thing" makes me want to punch you, right?'

'Uh ...'

'It's OK. You can make it up to me with a beer when we get back to Firstfall. Earth imported and alcohol free.' I could feel them drawing closer. 'So tell me about Shyla. Tell me about her and then let her go.'

I left them, touching and whispering and ran back to my cabin. I did the only thing I had left: I pinged Liss.

'I miss you so much,' I said.

She didn't answer at first, not for a long time, but then a

picture popped up projected across my lenses, of me and Alysha on the day we married. Alysha was in a golden dress that made her look like a goddess, made by some Sri Lankan designer and imported from Earth especially for that one day, an utterly ridiculous expense. The rest of us were tawdry beside her.

'This is who you miss,' Liss said. 'Not me.'

She sent more, picture after picture, each slowly fading into the next, but only ever stills, never video – the seven years of our life together. She didn't say another word.

Hours later, we reached Disappointment. The train hummed quietly to a standstill and we all stepped out. Patterson looked drawn and haggard, tired and irritable. Probably I looked much the same. Rangesh and Zohreya couldn't have looked more different. They had a glow, a fluidity, as though all their tension had washed away.

'Good fuck then, was it?' asked Patterson. 'Bet Allah has a real frowner on now, eh?'

'Dude!'

Zohreya only shook her head. Patterson called a pod. While we waited I looked at the station walls. The old graffiti was gone, already replaced by fresh slogans that looked much the same. The cleaning bots were still at work while the security shells stood sentinel among the handful of passengers disembarking from Firstfall.

The station screens suddenly changed to pictures of crowded Earth, to a huge mass of dark-skinned people packed together, filthy and gaunt, a grim caption spread across them: the future of our world? A booming narration began over images shifting slowly from one scene to the next of poverty, illness and terminal substance abuse. 'Our hospitals are overrun! Gene-therapy centre waiting times have quadrupled! Gen use has increased tenfold! Violent crime has doubled! Is this the future we want for our world? Is this the future we want for our city?'

The sequence started to repeat and then fluttered and died. The advertising screens returned to their normal gaudy selves.

'Fucking First Descendant hackers,' growled Patterson.

Our pod took us to the surface and into the night, through the bright lights of central Disappointment, the meagre financial district, the familiar streets around the university, all lit up in a sodium glow. As it did we armoured up. We still had the kit we'd taken to Pit 779, which was something of a blessing. Patterson had brought loose-fitting jumpsuits for us to wear on top, a thin effort at disguise, but it was dark, and if we got close enough to our chemist for him to see through the ruse, we were probably home and dry.

'Disappointment. Your home turf, right, boss dude?'

I looked at the university buildings as we passed, the tallest and most expensive structures on Magenta, a legacy of when the random process of choosing representatives for the Selected Chamber happened to throw up a fluke consensus of hard scientists who'd taken it upon themselves to build the biggest colonial university outside Strioth. Half the original plan had never been realised and half the other half had ended up as government housing, but even on Earth people had heard of Disappointment University.

I didn't say anything. Nothing felt like home any more.

'I ran some checks on off-world embassies,' said Patterson. 'You might want to have a look at this.' She pinged us a file, entries highlighted. At least half a dozen Kaltech senior officers were on Magenta. They'd come in from Earth over the last two months and nearly all of them had done time in Settlement 64.

'What the hell, man?' Rangesh summed up our bewilderment about as well as any of us could. I couldn't even begin to guess why so many would be here.

'For the handover?' suggested Zohreya, but that didn't work for me. This was something else.

265

'Are any of you armed?' Patterson asked.

'We're suspended,' I reminded her. The bureau didn't ask you for your gun and your badge, just turned them off remotely.

'Yes, well some people carry weapons that can't actually be turned off, on account of not being really fucking dumb. Lal might only have a couple of flunkies keeping him company on his little holiday, but he's still a gen chemist, and so I think they just maybe might be packing a little more than the odd feather duster!'

The university lights sank into gloom behind us. We drove into the darkness that surrounded the city. The pod ran on, navigating on a mix of short-range radar, ultrasonics and infra-red. Patterson shut down the interior lights. We had a rare clear sky tonight, stars and moonlight casting the Disappointment Plateau into eerie shades of grey.

Disappointment. Where hundreds of prospectors had come chasing a vein of tantalum that turned out so impure that it cost more to refine than it was worth. The city that was exactly what it said on the tin. I must have made that joke to Alysha a hundred times, and she'd laughed at every single one of them.

'It has its moments,' she always said.

The pod followed a glassy plasma-lance track out from the city into the surrounding wastes, skimming through the gloom. Now and then we passed other trails vanishing into the darkness. I looked at the satellite maps. Nothing but lichen-covered stone, and automated power and fabrication and hydroponics plants.

We veered towards Lal's wind farm, a constellation of light-specks I'd taken to be stars but which became a forest of fat, sharp pyramids, pylons a hundred feet tall with sixty-foot blades, dwarfing even Disappointment University's pointless tower, white foamcrete and carbon poly-fibre designed to stay up and keep working even in a Magentan storm. We passed through them in the darkness, thousands of them, like giant trees made of bone.

The satellite pictures showed a control centre in the middle of the array. I pinged for Servants, anyone in the vicinity that wasn't us. I got nothing.

'We're just going to walk up to the front door, are we?'

Patterson nodded.

'I thought these places were automated,' said Zohreya.

'The wind farm has a research facility. They use it as a lab sometimes.'

Rangesh made a face. 'It's, like, weird, man. I mean, what's this dude even doing planetside? Why not hide up in orbit like Svernoi?'

'In five minutes you can ask him.'

'Yeah, but what's he *doing* here?'

'Xeno-meteorology, I suppose.' The pod stopped. Patterson drew her Reeper and checked it. 'So. *Are* you packing, Agent Zohreya?'

Zohreya shook her head.

Patterson gave her Reeper to Zohreya. 'Officially we're here to set up a new install of software in the maintenance drones. I've got an upload for your Servant to make us look like university faculty staff. You're better at shooting people than I am. Just try to remember we might be wrong about this.'

'I'm also suspended.' Zohreya gave the Reeper back.

'And *I'm* more likely to shoot myself in the foot.'

'Take it,' I said to Zohreya.

A series of hard pings hit the pod and each of our Servants, demanding to know who we were and what we were doing here. Couldn't tell whether they were automated or came from Lal. A moment later a dazzling light blazed across us, blinding for a moment until the pod's reactive windows cut it out. Someone inside had put a spotlight on us.

'At least we know they're at home,' murmured Rangesh.

Zohreya took Patterson's Reeper. She didn't look happy. Patterson flashed her palm. Clasped inside she had a high-end miniature particle beam.

'More my style,' she said and opened the pod. Light flooded in, straight at our faces, blinding me again. 'Your eyes see through that, Agent Zohreya?'

'Yes, and I can send to your lenses.'

I took the feed Zohreya offered and suddenly I was seeing through her artificial eyes. The light dimmed almost to nothing, filtered away. I could see the control centre in grainy black and white.

'Brownie point to Agent Zohreya.' Patterson stepped out of the pod. 'I brought you out here so I guess I'm going first. Anything happens to me, someone look after Jamie.' She took a deep breath, swore quietly a few times and then started towards the control centre. The rest of us spread out behind her. The more I looked, the more the building struck me as a fortress; but almost everything on Magenta looked like a fortress. Had to, to survive the weather.

A door slid open as we approached, thick metal like an airlock. A man stepped out. Lal. Through Zohreya's eyes he was broad and muscled and moved with an easy grace. He looked like a native, not an Earther.

'You the upgrade crew?' He was sizing us up, flicking from face to face.

'Yes.' Patterson held up her hands to show they were empty. 'Here to—'

'No, you're not.'

He had a pistol pointed at Patterson. It happened so fast that I didn't see it. Zohreya had Patterson's Reeper pointing back at him, every bit as quick. Rangesh and I stood frozen. Something changed in Zohreya's vision and suddenly I was seeing a whole new spectrum. Everything shrank. My field of view bloomed outward out like a fish eye and at the same time zoomed in on the face holding the gun. I almost fell over.

Something about the man's voice made me pay attention. I'd heard it before.

'Please be calm, sir,' said Patterson. 'We're here to talk to you about Settlement 64. We'd like to make you an offer.'

'Who are you?'

I took a step forward. 'Agent Keon Rause of the Magenta Investig—'

I felt the impact more than the pain, same time as I heard the shot. A blow high up like a punch in the shoulder, close to my neck. I spun and fell, mostly because I wasn't expecting it. My Servant hit me with a barrage of thrombolytics and anti-coagulants and screamed for help. It thought I was having a heart attack. I muted it, cancelled the alarm.

'Get down!' Zohreya. Was she shouting at the rest of us or at Lal? I didn't know. I was staring at the sky, too dazed to move. Another shot rang and then another. The spotlight went out. I heard Patterson swear and then the pop of her particle beam. The feed from Zohreya's eyes was doing crazy things, making me feel sick. I ditched it and opened my own, blinking hard, trying to see in the sudden darkness.

'Dude! You hit?' Rangesh dropped beside me. He was holding a needle pistol.

The warnings from my Servant were nothing serious – the flexi-armour had absorbed the worst. 'You're armed too? You mean I'm the only one who isn't?'

'Yeah, man. Now shut up.' He checked me over. 'OK, it's cool. Body armour took it, but you could have a fracture or two. Just stay here, man! Told you Esh and I would be good for you.'

I heard another gunshot and then another, and then a howl

that didn't belong to either Patterson or Zohreya. Zohreya was yelling at someone to surrender but it didn't sound like they were in the mood to listen. I tried to lever myself up enough to see.

'Dude!' Rangesh threw himself flat across me and let loose a burst from the needler. Lal bolted inside as a face at a window sprayed bullets at Zohreya.

'Get him into cover!' Zohreya was pressed flat below a raised air vent that presumably led to a transformer array somewhere underground.

'What cover, dude? Aw, man! This is so much not cool.' Rangesh jumped up and tossed something towards the control-room door. It landed and started to pour out smoke.

'Gas?' I asked.

'I wish, man! I am so going to say bad things to Laws after this.'

I lay back, hit by an unexpected memory. Sky. Deep, deep blue without a cloud in sight, a rare thing for Magenta. Alysha beside me. We were lying in tall grass, with meadow flowers ...

No. That couldn't be right. There were no grasses or flowers on Magenta ...

'Rause!'

I snapped back. Rangesh was hauling me to my feet.

'You're in shock, man.' He hit me with an adrenaline boost. 'Time to run, boss dude. Nothing wrong with your legs, right?'

'I'm inside. Can you kill their power?' Zohreya.

'You're *inside*? What the fuck?'

'Also thanks for the smoke, Bix. You got any more?'

'Sorry, babe.'

'Yeah, and quit with that. It would make me sad to shoot you.'

'Hey!'

The adrenaline killed the shock and more. I felt wired. I needed to move. To *do* something. I shook Rangesh off and ran towards the smoke. 'Zohreya, you have a satellite map of this place?' My shoulder and chest hurt but it was a dull ache, distant as though it belonged to someone else, not something to worry about right now.

'If you're able, sir, you want to take a position near the pod. Rangesh and Patterson should scale the control centre. There's one door, but there are windows on all sides. They could come from anywhere so you'll want a good field of view. Sir, the safest and correct course would be to withdraw and call for a tac-team. We should—'

'Fuck no!' Patterson burst in. 'This stays between us. You call in a tac-team, you call in the bureau. Never mind the shit that means for the four of us, remember Horace Winston!'

'Sir? It's your call ...'

'Actually it's my fucking call, Agent Zohreya, since the rest of you—'

'Dudes! Really? Now?'

I grabbed Rangesh. 'Give me the needler. Patterson, get off your high horse. Zohreya, she's right. We do this on our own.'

'I hear you, sir.'

The needler was almost empty. I fitted a new clip as I ran through the smoke.

Keys? Are you safe?

Liss? What the hell?

Your Servant spiked a medical alert.

Which I'd cancelled. I reached the control-centre wall. The windows were open. Smoke swirled inside, ghostly shapes in the moonlight gloom.

'Now's not the time, Liss!'

'Dude?'

Shit! Wrong channel. Now's not the time. I was shot.

Shot?

'Never mind!' I levered myself onto the sill of the nearest open

271

window and then onto the roof of the control room. We found the chemist. I guess she deserved to know. I was minutes away from opening an interrogation on maybe the one man other than Nikita Svernoi who could tell me what had happened five years ago in Settlement 64.

'And there go the rest of the lights,' purred Zohreya. 'Just me and three armed fugitives in the dark. May Allah have mercy on their souls.'

Please don't get hurt.

It's not top of my list, OK? Now leave me be!

'Make that two armed fugitives,' whispered Zohreya. 'I've lost Lal. I think he's heading back up top. You ready for him? I got the other one.'

'Make up your mind!' I lowered myself off the control-room roof and almost walked into Patterson by the door. She took a position to one side, particle beam raised and ready. I checked the needler. I hadn't used one for years. A short-range panic weapon really, but it would do nicely in a close-quarters hunt.

'Ready?' I asked.

'Ready.'

We lunged through the door side by side, each covering a different angle. A haze filled the air. The control room was a single open space filled with monitors wrapped around stairs that spiralled down. Couldn't see much between the darkness and Rangesh's smoke, but there wasn't anywhere up here to hide. I pulled up the building schematics.

'Zohreya?'

'I've lost Lal. I've still got the other one. I'm down among the transformers.'

I moved to the stair and glanced at Patterson. She rolled her eyes.

'I know, I know, chivalry urges you to go first. Knock yourself out. Jamie needs his mum.'

I started down. It was dark. I listened for any sound but there was nothing to hear. Now and then the barrel of Patterson's particle beam brushed my ear.

'Try not to shoot my head off, OK?'

'Ha fucking ha!'

The steps spiralled into a shadow-filled recreation room. There were wall-screens and a pool table and a couple of exercise machines lit up by a handful of dim red emergency lights.

'I can't see a damned thing!'

'I've got the other one.' Zohreya again. 'I don't think Lal's down here. He might be up with you.'

'We need to figure out what the fuck we do with this lot once this we're done,' murmured Patterson behind me.

'We're a long way from that yet.' I stepped off the stairs and eased into the gloom. The outline shapes of doors led from the rec room. One looked like an elevator. The one beside it had to be more stairs then. I pointed.

'We need a plan, Rause.'

'The plan is that we take them somewhere quiet and then make them talk.'

'Where?'

'Your apartment?'

'What? So Zohreya can torture them in one room while Jamie does his homework in the other? Fuck off.'

'Joke, Patterson. Somewhere closer.' We separated and covered the stairs from two corners, each finding our own path through the shadows. I stared at the door. 'Zohreya, are you sure Lal's on his way up?'

'He could be anywhere by now. I'm on my way to you.'

Patterson crept closer to the stairs. She pressed herself against the wall, nudged the door open with a foot and tossed a drone inside.

'Motion tracker ...' she began.

The elevator door opened. We both jumped. I swung Rangesh's needler. As I did, another door opened. I caught a glimpse of a figure, gun raised. There was a flash and the soft hiss of a stunner. Patterson squealed and went down like a puppet with her strings cut. Lal turned and fired again as I dived for cover. I raised the needler and then stopped myself. I desperately didn't want him dead.

'Lal!'

He shot at me.

'Zohreya! He's up here!' Back to Lal. 'Lal! Put the weapon down! Step out with your hands in the air!' I needed to delay him, that was all. Get Zohreya up here with her Reeper so she could take him down without killing him. Needlers weren't kind that way. Patterson's pocket particle beam was even worse.

'Svernoi?' shouted Lal. 'I knew you were close! You think getting rid of me is going to be as easy as Anja?'

Not what I was expecting. I was certain too that I'd heard his voice somewhere before. 'Anja Gersh, Lal?' I shouted back. 'What do you know about her?'

'I know she wasn't as stupid as you think, Nikita! I suppose you're still in orbit, but I know you're listening, so hear this: you're committed whether you like it or not. I let the gens loose the moment these cavemen of yours showed up. If anything happens to me then it all comes out, straight to every news channel on this Neanderthal world just when ten thousand people have dropped dead and everyone's wondering why. You got that? You listening, Nikita? You can't stop it and you can't be free of it. So call your fucking foot soldiers off or I tell the world everything right now! We'll go down together and all of it will be for nothing!'

I crouched behind the stairs. Playing along bought more time for Zohreya. Lal telling the world about whatever it was that he and Svernoi were doing didn't sound too bad either. 'You'll have to do better than that, Lal. Convince me!'

His voice. Where had I heard it ...?

'Don't fuck with me! I know you've had your squad of Earth soldiers camped out a couple of miles away these last few days keeping an eye on me. What, you think I'm an idiot? You think I wouldn't notice? I suppose you're cushy and safe with Fleet. What will they do once they find out you're behind this. You think they'll shelter you? *I* think they'll push you out of an airlock faster than you can fart. They certainly won't let you come planetside to squeal. So call off your dogs.'

Gersh. I'd heard the voice beside Anja Gersh. In the interview tape ... Vismans! Gersh's assistant, Vismans. He'd had his face changed, but the voice, that nasal voice ...

I didn't much like what he'd said about Svernoi having a squad of his own close by. If it was true then our surveillance hadn't picked them up.

'Vismans! We're not with Svernoi!' I said. 'We're Magentan government agents. We know you're the one who reworked Gersh's formula. Give yourself up. It's over! We know pretty much everything. There's just one thing I don't get. What were KRAB for?'

Lal took half a step out of cover. 'Don't fuck with me through your pissant foot soldier, Nikita! If you think you can stall the transformation by withholding the trigger, that just shows you know jack shit.'

'Vismans! We're not—'

'Anja left records. Everything. All hidden away right under your n—' Vismans let out a strangled gasp. I couldn't see anything in the shadows past his doorway but I heard the buzz of a stunner and then someone fall.

A moment later I heard Zohreya: 'Friendly coming out. Don't shoot!'

She emerged, dragging Vismans by his feet, and dumped him in the middle of the floor.

'Air vents,' she said as if that was supposed to explain everything. 'I only stunned him.'

Off in her corner, Patterson groaned.

'What do we do with him, sir?'

'Tie him up for a start.' I got to work on that. 'What happened to the other two?'

'Nothing they won't recover from.'

'Did you hear what he said?'

'Some of it.'

'He can give us Svernoi! He can give us everything.'

Patterson twitched and flopped an arm. I rolled Vismans onto his back and took an image of his face.

'What did he mean about ten thousand dead?' asked Zohreya.

'I don't know. We'll have to ask him.'

'Turn off ...' Patterson was trying to get up. She almost managed all fours and then collapsed back again. 'Turn off his Servant, you idiots!'

'Shit! He's broadcasting something. Turn it off!'

Zohreya disconnected him while I finished tying Vismans' hands behind his back.

Patterson struggled to her feet. 'We have to get him out of here right now,' she croaked. 'Somewhere I can break his fucking head. And we all need to turn off our Servants. We have to assume Svernoi knows what just happened. That means the mole knows. That means whoever killed Horace Winston. We're not safe here. The bureau, the Tesseract—'

'And go where?' Zohreya heaved Vismans over her shoulder.

'He's got the whole story,' I said. 'Svernoi. Everything. We make a deal. Protection. Immunity.'

'Let him go? Sir, people died.'

'Rause is right.' Patterson finally lurched to her feet and

staggered upright. 'We've got five corpses dead from cerebral haemorrhaging. We've got a factory for a tailored gen that kills anyone with a certain genetic code. We've got two dozen illegal Earth paramilitaries ...' She stared at me, sizing me up. 'Rojash Vismans? You sure?'

'I'm sure.' I looked at his face. Close up I could see the discreet white scar lines of surgery.

'Then he can tie the whole lot together and wrap it in a fucking bow. Earth, Kaltech, Settlement 64, Svernoi, Fleet, all of them, whoever's involved! So yes, we ...' She stumbled and fell into a wall, nerves still misfiring from the stunner shot. 'Fuck!'

'I'll make the call.' I let her lean on me as we went up the stairs. Zohreya followed with Vismans.

'No! We don't talk to fucking anyone until we're secure. Then we get legal and Flemich and no one else, and we still don't tell them where we are. You got that, Rause? We cut a deal, we get a deposition, we get him on record, clean and legal and beyond reproach, and we do all of that tonight! Agreed?'

I paused. There was something I'd forgotten. Something to do with Rangesh and what Vismans had said.

'What's up, Rause? Now's not the time to fucking dither!'

'He said it was too late to stop it. What's "it"?'

'Look at this!' Zohreya stumbled as she climbed the steps. A video file popped into my Servant. 'This is what he was broadcasting!'

My name is Anja Gersh. I let it play. *I am a scientist working for Kaltech in Settlement 64 on Magenta and they're trying to kill me because of what I know. In the event I don't survive, this is my sworn dying declaration ...* I couldn't make out what I was looking at at first, or what the howling moaning noise was that rushed between her words, but then it came to me. She was in the mangled cabin of a Cheetah, tipped up at an odd angle and bent out of shape. I was seeing through her eyes.

'Jesus Christ! Turn your *fucking* Servants off!'

I ignored Patterson. 'You need to see this,' I said.

My research has been into possible treatments for Mohinder-Kali syndrome, a genetic condition from which I suffer ... The picture was shaking. The roaring noise was a Magentan storm. When Gersh turned her head I saw two bodies, limbs splayed, lying in a corner. They were in MSDF black jumpsuits.

The others with whom I have spoken here came with similar goals, each with a different neurological condition they had hoped to treat with a modified variant of xenoflora ...

I could hear movement. Something that wasn't the Cheetah shaking in the wind. I wanted to see what it was but Gersh kept staring at the dead soldiers. *We believed the purpose of our work was the assessment, test and trial of xenosubstances on animals with the long-term aim of developing curative medical treatments, but that's not the case. They're not looking for a cure for anything. They're looking for something else ... something that does ... I don't know. I don't think even they know. They're trying to change us. They're looking for a way to make us like the Masters ...* The picture suddenly shifted wildly. I heard someone swear and shout, *Brace!* and then the video cut and the next moment Gersh was at another angle and her breathing was all wrong, raspy and ragged, and the bodies had been flung across the floor, only it wasn't the floor, it was the ceiling. The Cheetah was on its back now.

Another voice: *You need to let the trauma drone do its work, Doctor Gersh.*

Gersh went on: *The primary reason for the existence of Settlement 64 is now Xenosubstance 1227, a tailored variant of a Magentan native xenoflora that has profound neurological effects on exposed humans. I discovered it. I engineered it and I know it works. It connects with the Mohinder-Kali gene, but it's not a cure, it's ...* She was almost out of breath. It hit me

278

then. She was dying. I caught a glimpse of a trauma drone as she looked down. Or up, whichever it was. Then the shape of another MSDF soldier, cradling his arm and limping but still alive.

It's ... something else. In the animals I've tested ... those with similar neurological conditions ... it largely causes rapid ... and catastrophic haemorrhaging ... triggered by ... acute audiovisual stimulation. But in rare cases ... it does something else ... It ... Her breathing changed again. *It wakes something up ... something we've never seen ... Cages crack ... metal bends ...*

...

Doctor Gersh? Doctor Gersh!

The video stopped.

'Will you *please* turn off your fucking Servants!' Patterson pulled away as we reached the top of the stairs. She meandered across the control room like a drunk and staggered outside. 'Fuck! Fucking stunner! I'd forgotten what it's like!'

Zohreya followed us out, Vismans over her shoulder. Our pod sat in the moonlight a hundred feet away. Rangesh stood beside it. The smoke had blown clear. The stars shone bright overhead, the half-moons giving as much light as an Earth twilight across a landscape of flat rock and wind turbines.

BLAM!

One shot. Zohreya went down. Patterson threw herself towards the control-room door.

'Fuck! Sniper!'

I scrambled to Zohreya and threw myself over her. I should have gone for Vismans, but that's not how these things work, not when you're in the field and your partner's just been shot in front of you. I dragged Zohreya into the control room. Patterson was backed against the wall, particle beam clutched in both shaking hands, quivering.

A second pod raced up outside. This one was armoured. I didn't see what had happened to Rangesh, but there wasn't much he could do, not when I had his needler.

'Fuck, Rause! Fucking move!' Patterson bolted for the stairs and vanished down them. I ignored her, ignored the pod too. Zohreya was alive. I felt her jumpsuit, looking for the wound. Like the rest of us she was wearing armour underneath. I found the hole where the bullet had hit her, right over the sternum. The armour had saved her, but I knew how it hurt. I'd had the same in Gibraltar, just after the explosion, when someone shot me, someone I never even saw. Winded me so bad I couldn't breathe. And tonight from Vismans too, though that one hadn't been quite so as bad.

Zohreya took a sudden great whooping gasp of air, pushed me away, staggered half to her feet, dropped to all fours, threw up and then collapsed into a ball.

Men jumped out of the pod. Four of them. I snatched up the needler, turned on my Servant and screamed to the Tesseract for help, but I'd left it too late. They had a short-range jammer blocking me. As I picked up the gun, one of them tossed something through the door. I heard a shrill whining ...

Sonic grenade.

Everything went black.

When I came to, I was outside on my knees. My wrists and ankles were bound with spider ties.

Zohreya was to one side of me, trussed up the same. Rangesh was on the other. There was no sign of Patterson. Two Earthers stood over us, one with a needler, one with a particle rifle, the sort that can vaporise entire limbs. Between them, Nikita Svernoi was yelling at the sky.

'Do I care how difficult it is? *Find* her!' He looked at me as I lifted my head. 'You awake? Then you can help.'

Svernoi walked to where Zohreya had dropped Vismans. He

pulled out a pistol and fired twice. Vismans jerked as the back of his head exploded.

'Not so cushy and safe and far away as you thought, Rojash,' he snarled. 'Didn't have to go this way, you faithless fucker.' He pointed the pistol at me. I couldn't help cringing a little, hunching up into myself. No way he wasn't going to shoot us.

'Just get on with it,' I said.

'Not yet. Aren't I missing someone?'

I didn't answer. Svernoi sighed.

'The rather clever rather angry woman who came with you to visit me in orbit?'

I shrugged. 'You're in Magentan territory now,' I said. 'That means I get to arrest you.'

Svernoi rolled his eyes. 'When you neutralised KRAB, it was hardly difficult to move my satellite device to another location. One you can't reach. Agent Rause, I want you to order your subordinate to surrender. Then I'll tell you where it is.'

That made me laugh. 'How stupid do you think any of us are? You want her to surrender so you'll have an easier time of it shooting us all in the head, right? We called for backup ages ago. They'll be here any minute. Whatever you do here, you're done.'

'You're lying.' He nodded at Rangesh. 'Try this then. If you don't deliver, I'm going to burn his limbs off one by one. And I want Agent Patterson to understand, without any shadow of a doubt, that if she makes this difficult, I'll take the trouble to burn her son too.'

I nodded. No way Patterson would believe a word of it. Which was just as well because I had a feeling that if she did, she'd trade all of us for Jamie in a shot.

'Before you do,' I said. 'What was it all for?'

'Really, Agent Rause? You haven't worked it out?'

'You killed my wife.'

'Loki killed your wife.'

'But you set him up.'

Svernoi shrugged. '*Some*one set him up.'

'And Alysha was his target.'

'Does knowing mean you can die happy?'

'How did you know she was on that train?'

Svernoi tapped a finger to his nose. 'Get Agent Patterson up here and I'll tell you.' He glanced at Zohreya. 'Maybe her first. Left leg. She looks strong enough to take it.'

The goon with the particle rifle levelled it. I struggled against the spider ties. Futile. Should have known better, but that's animal instinct for you. 'OK! OK! I'll try. But Patterson's not stupid and she's not a hero, and frankly she's not all that noble either. She won't listen and she won't come out.'

'Try anyway, Agent Rause.'

I pinged Patterson. No response. No way to know whether that was because her Servant was turned off or whether she simply had it muted.

Svernoi looked over his shoulder to the soldier with the needler, who nodded.

'So let me see if I've got this right,' I said. I didn't have much hope that Patterson alone was going to take down Svernoi and his four henchmen, but she was armed and free and I could at least give her a chance. Earth special forces and the best transgravity treatment money could buy still wasn't the same as being born and bred in Magenta's gravity. 'Gersh thought she was working on a cure for Mohinder-Kali. She didn't find one but she found something else. A gene-targeted killer that causes anyone with the disease to haemorrhage. She wanted to shut it down. You wouldn't let her. She turned to the Tesseract for help and found Alysha. Alysha sent a snatch squad for her but you were on to them. Somehow you hacked their weather feed after they took her. The storm killed them. But Alysha knew. So you had her killed too.'

'Interesting story, Agent Rause. Try your colleague again and I might tell you which bits you got right.'

'Dude! Don't do it, man!' The goon with the particle rifle bashed Rangesh in the face.

'You had someone in the Tesseract,' I said. 'You had to. Someone who warned you. Someone who helped you spike the feed to the extraction team. Someone who gave you Alysha.'

'Who put her on that train?' Svernoi didn't bite. 'Agent Patterson, Rause. Or someone loses a leg.'

I pinged Patterson again, and again Svernoi checked with the needler goon. I figured I knew what they were doing. They were trying to track Patterson by the bounce of my signal. I crossed my fingers her Servant was turned off instead of muted.

'It took poor Rojash here years.' Svernoi poked Vismans' corpse with his foot. 'Gersh did a good job of destroying her work before she ran. But that video I showed you? That was it. That was his moment, recreating what poor Anja's discovery did to people. I'd have shut the place down years ago otherwise. Ping her again, Agent Rause.'

Before I could do what he wanted, needler goon clenched his fist. 'We got her, boss!'

Svernoi smiled. 'Have them bring her up. Agent Rause, your cooperation is no longer necessary.'

Shit.

I shuffled forward a few inches, holding his attention. 'One thing then, since you're about to murder us anyway. Why have you got it in for people with Mohinder-Kali? Why do you want to kill them?'

Svernoi crouched in front of me. 'I don't want to *kill* anyone, Agent Rause. I want to *change* them.' He leaned closer, close enough that I could smell his breath. 'They don't haemorrhage, not in a conventional way. They tear themselves apart with the uncontrolled potential that Xenosubstance 1227 unleashes.

283

What Anja found was not a new medicine, or a drug or some-thing so mundane. She found why the Masters brought us here in the first place. In the xenoflora she found the key to some-thing. A crack. A doorway, call it what you will, but a way for humanity to be something far more, the next step of mankind's evolution, able to control worlds with sheer thought. Yes, a lot of people will die, but some will survive. The ones who can *control* it. *They're* the ones I want. They will be our future. The rest, the ones who can't ...' He shook his head. 'Blind, deaf and dumb to the terror to come, Agent Rause. I don't want to anyone to die at all, but five billion lost their lives when the Masters came to Earth. Five. *Billion*. People. So what are a few thousands, tens of thousands, millions even, in exchange for being ready when they return? Because the Masters aren't done with us, Agent Rause. They *will* return, one day. In our hearts we all know this. Your wife certainly did.'

The two other Earthers marched out, dragging Patterson between them. She was conscious and I didn't see any blood. Mostly she looked frightened. They threw her down to the ground beside us.

'You want to question her, boss?'

Svernoi made a face. 'Why? Just shoot them and let's get out of here.'

'Wait!' I scrabbled forward, struggling again against the spider ties.

'What now, Agent Rause?'

'Going to tell me who you've got working for you in the Tesseract before you kill me? You know, like a good villain?'

'No.' He raised his pistol to kill me. 'But your wife was—'

BLAM!

A muzzle flash right beside him. No gun. No finger on a trigger, no hand on a grip. No shooter. Nothing except a flash amid the moon shadow, point blank, like someone invisible was standing right there next to him with a gun. Svernoi's head burst like a ripe melon.

BLAM! BLAM! Two more flashes, two more head shots. The man with the particle rifle and the one pointing a gun at Patterson.

'Fucking hell!' Patterson rolled out of the way as the needler goon sprayed the air. I threw myself flat.

BLAM! Point blank in the face and down he went. Patterson was looking wildly about, looking for a sniper. But it wasn't that. I knew because I'd seen this before in Gibraltar.

The last man standing tried to run. He took a bullet in the back that knocked him down. Before he could get to his feet, some invisible force grabbed him by the jacket, picked him up and shot him in the back of his head.

GIBRALTAR

7.7.2214 ESDS   Restricted   FHQE3/IEC/0001174/Rause

[Transcript begins]

Inquiry Officer G. Beckett: State your name and number.

Rause: Agent Keon Rause, 44721.

Beckett: Agent Rause, please state in your own words the events leading to the incident on the morning of the sixth of June.

Rause: My team arrived at the Gibraltar Institute at 3.17 in the morning—

Beckett [interrupting]: Your team? Could you elaborate for the record, please.

Rause: Agents Jones, Tingle, Gale, Felton, Beadle, Beadle, Carter and Resnov. [Pause] We arrived at 3.17 a.m. We came in two vehicles. I was lead agent for the first, Agent Resnov led the second. My team entered through the front entrance, Agent Resnov through the rear.

Beckett: Your purpose?

Rause: We were to provide security for a demonstration later that morning as part of the Exhibition of Advanced Technology—

7.7.2214 ESDS   Restricted   FHQE3/IEC/0001174/Rause

Beckett [interrupting]: Security for? Again for the record please, Agent Rause.

Rause: The briefing we were given referred to a device developed from technology created by Dr Jandral Mongramyr in the Gibraltar Institute's advanced photonics laboratories, retro-engineering a piece of Masters tech. My understanding was that the device was some manner of personal stealth technology – a military-grade invisibility skin-suit. Informally we called it the ghost suit. I learned later that the Gibraltar Institute hadn't developed the suit at all. It was more archaeology than technology, retrieved in full working order from an exposed Masters spiral on [redacted].

Beckett: The location is classified and to be stricken from the record. Agent Rause, please confine your answers to the questions asked. Did you see the device?

Rause: Only in its inactive state. The institute had mounted the suit on a shell. The shell was powered down. We never saw it operational.

Beckett: Please summarise what happened after you arrived.

Rause: Following a handover brief, my team took charge of exhibition security. I deployed six of my agents on pre-planned patrols and two on random roving watch. We remained in constant communication with IC12. At approximately 4.15 Agent de Korte's team completed their shift and left. We continued our surveillance and observed nothing out of the ordinary.

Beckett: Conjecture, Agent Rause. Other agents will give their own testimony.

Rause: Correction. *I* did not observe, nor did anyone report to me, anything to incite suspicion.

Beckett: Until the explosion at 5.17?

Rause: That is correct.

Beckett: Please describe events to the best of your recollection.

Rause: I saw a flash. Something struck me and lifted me off my feet. I remember a roaring noise. At that point I lost a few seconds. The next thing I remember I was lying flat on my back. There was a lot of smoke and dust. I saw movement, a blurred shape. I believe I lost consciousness again for a short time.

Beckett: No one else saw any of this, is that correct?

Rause: As far as I know, yes. I was out for maybe ten seconds, but in that time the ghost suit was gone, the shell too. [Pause] I think I went back to the foyer then, but I'm afraid the only recollections I have are flashes. I returned to the exhibition hall, at which point someone shot me.

Beckett: And you didn't see who did this?

Rause: No. I saw the flash. There was no one there, but it was right in front of me. The bullet struck me in the chest. It didn't penetrate my body armour, but I didn't know that at the time. I couldn't breathe. I thought I was dying. Someone dragged me out, someone strong. The next recollection I have with any clarity I was in the waste collection pen at the back of the institute with Agent Felton. He kept asking me my name. A medical drone arrived a few moments later.

Beckett: And to be clear for the record, Agent Rause, you claim no memory of what happened between the moment you were shot and Agent Felton finding you?

Rause: None.

Beckett: Agent Rause, there were over two hundred lenses in situ, including surveillance drones, fixed cameras and more than fifty additional mobile aerial units. On that particular day, at that particular time, you were in perhaps one of the most watched locations on Earth, yet there's not a single frame of imagery recorded that shows the perpetrators of this attack. How is that possible?

Rause: I don't have the expertise to speculate, sir, but if I did, I'd say perhaps it was because they were wearing your damned suit.

Beckett: But there is no record of them entering to take it, Agent Rause. Nor, despite the level of surveillance, is there any record of *you* between the explosion and Agent Felton finding you. Would you care to speculate about *that*?

Rause: No.

Beckett: No further questions.

[Transcript ends]

Presiding Adjudicator: Director G. Smith (IEC001)
Inquiry Officer: G. Beckett (IEC047)
Present: SSR4C, DG005, Dale Cooper (independent witness)

SIX

THE INVISIBLE MAN

19

THE MOLE

'Where's Lal?' asked Zohreya between gasps as Patterson untied her.

'We need to get the fuck into cover! There's another sniper!'

'Two in the face,' I told Zohreya. 'And what we do, Patterson, is call for backup. Vismans is gone. Svernoi too. We've got nothing to hide any more; whatever they started, it's still happening, and whoever took Svernoi out could have killed us as easily as breathing if that's what they'd wanted.'

'There's no sniper,' said Zohreya. She hauled herself up and then crumpled with a hand to her chest.

'Then what the fuck killed Svernoi? The tooth fairy?'

'I saw a muzzle flash,' Zohreya said.

'So did I.' I checked with my Servant. 'We've got a tac-team from Disappointment on their way. Be about ten minutes.'

Zohreya struggled upright. She stood for a moment, scanning the landscape, then crouched beside Svernoi and started sweeping her fingers over the ground around him.

'What the fuck are are you doing?' snarled Patterson.

'It wasn't a sniper. Some sort of micro-drone with a chameleon skin perhaps? Here. This is what my eyes saw.'

She pinged us a snip of video. The same muzzle flash, as though someone had been standing right beside Svernoi pointing a gun at his head, only no gun, no one there to hold one, just the flash.

'I've never seen anything like it,' she said.

I had.

'I might use a kinetic-energy weapon from a drone overhead, a sniper rifle from one of the wind turbines maybe, but up close like this? This is work for a particle beam. Quieter and more sure. Fits better on a drone too. Less recoil … Here we go.' She rose triumphantly, holding a shell case between her fingers. 'Agent Rause is right. If whoever did this wanted us dead too, we'd be dead. Look. Pistol shell.' She passed it to Patterson.

'Doesn't anything fucking faze you?'

Liss? My head was spinning. Patterson and Zohreya were talking something through, something about Horace Winston, arguing whether or not they should go straight to the bureau with everything we'd found or try to trace Vismans' movements ourselves. The last thing I wanted right now was to answer lots of difficult questions about what three suspended agents were doing in the middle of nowhere getting themselves into a fire-fight with a chemist, but there was no walking away from this, not after what Vismans had said. Liss?

I'm here, Keys.

Where's here? I set up a trace on the link between Liss and my Servant. She was in the apartment in Firstfall.

Are you OK? I was worried. You've been away a while.

She was pulling data from my Servant, the medical alerts. Someone would see this later. An exchange of messages from one Servant to another right after the shooting. I was going to get grilled over that, but I didn't think I cared any more.

You were lucky, she said. I'm glad you're not hurt.

Liss, who hit the Gibraltar Institute?

I don't know.

Yes, you do! They were right in front of me. Just now. Someone in the suit from Gibraltar.

That's not really possible, Keys.

Liss, what have you done?

Come home. Come home and tell me everything. I worry about you.

I put an end to Patterson and Zohreya arguing by calling Flemich even though it was the middle of the night, putting it through the Tesseract so that what I had to say would be on record, and then telling him everything. I sent him my Servant's recording of what Vismans had said, Gersh's video clip and then Svernoi too. Best I could make of it, Vismans had put a whole stack of bad gens on the street somehow. I didn't know what trigger he'd been talking about when he thought I was Svernoi's assassin come to kill him, but it didn't sound good. I thought about passing on Patterson's theory that we had a mole in case it made any difference, but decided not. Just told him to be careful instead.

'Tac-team is a minute away,' said Zohreya. 'What do you want us to do?'

'We wait,' I said. 'We hold and hand it over. Everything.'

'No, we don't.' Patterson shook her head. 'We're the only people who know there's a mole in the Tesseract. We have to find out who it is and we have to do it now!'

'Patterson, whatever Vismans started, it's happening!' I said. 'Someone has to stay. We have to do whatever—'

'I'll stay,' said Zohreya. 'You go, sir.'

'I'll stay too,' said Rangesh. 'Got your back, Esh.'

Patterson hesitated, clearly not much liking this, but we were out of time. I could see flashing lights in the distance, a Cheetah racing in from Disappointment.

'We've completely fucked this up!' She was shaking as we got into the pod and started moving.

'We need to trace Vismans' movements.' I replayed the conversation we'd had. 'Can you hack his Servant?' We started moving.

'Not on my own. We need to—' The tac-team Cheetah flew overhead, all noise and a rush of wind, just high enough to clear the tops of the wind turbines. I watched through the rear windows as it landed beside Rangesh and Zohreya.

'You think they can spin a story between them?' I asked.

'Rangesh can spin anything, and if they're MSDF then half of them probably know Zohreya. They'll be OK.'

I dimmed the pod's interior lights and let us run on in the dark, ghosts skimming through drab grey moonlight. For a while neither of us spoke. Both waiting, I suppose, for a call from Zohreya, or from the Tesseract, ordering us to stop and turn ourselves in.

'What happened to Horace Winston?' I asked.

'The official story is that he hanged himself.'

'And the real story?'

'He was unconscious,' said Patterson. 'Doped to the eyeballs. Someone walked into his room during a shift change, straight past the guard on his door, spoofed the cameras, strung him up, broke his neck and then walked right out again past about twenty people with alarms going off left, right and centre. And no one saw them.' She shrugged. 'There might be a lot more, but if there is I don't know it. It went straight to Internal Investigations. I don't have access.' She gave me a hard look. There was a lot she wasn't saying. I wondered if she'd realised the same thing I'd figured out back at the wind farm. Our invisible friend. 'We should get you to a hospital, Rause.'

'No need.'

'Vismans shot you.'

'He shot you too.'

'Yeah, but with a stunner. It's not the same.'

'I'm armoured. I'm OK.' The adrenaline and the painkillers were wearing off. My Servant reckoned there was a good chance I had a cracked collarbone. Patterson was right, but I just wanted to go home. I wanted Liss. I wanted her to look me in the eye and tell me about Gibraltar. To tell me it wasn't her.

'If you say so. Looks like we're going to squeak in for the overnight train back to Firstfall.'

'You're tense,' I said.

'Really, Rause? You think so? Three of us were shot. We're all getting crucified tomorrow. So yeah, you're right, I am a bit fucking tense. You want to tell me about Gibraltar now?'

'No.' OK, so she'd figured the connection. Didn't surprise me.

'You know the next person to ask you isn't going to give you a choice, right?'

I tuned her out, had my Servant play some music. Patterson would tell the others, if she hadn't told them already. Couldn't blame her. In their shoes I could see how it looked.

We reached the mag-lev terminus. Patterson caught my arm as we boarded.

'I'm here, Rause, if you need me.'

I went straight to my cabin.

Liss?

She didn't answer. I tried over and over and got nothing. It wasn't like her. She was always there. That was what made her special.

Liss, what did you do?

It didn't make sense, but I stared at nothing trying to work it out anyway. I felt the train pull away. Another ride through the tunnel deep beneath Magenta. Somewhere along here was where Alysha had died. My Servant could tell me, if I wanted to know. A blip. A single spot, a flash of a second as we roared past at a thousand miles an hour. The place where I'd lost her.

Ten minutes out Patterson came back, knocking on my door. Didn't surprise me. If anything the surprise was that she'd let it go this far. Just me and her on a train with nowhere else to go, nowhere to run.

'Keon, we need to talk.'

'Do we?'

She closed the door behind her. 'I've given this some more thought and I'm not letting you do this.'

'Do what?'

She bared her teeth. Suddenly she was pointing her Reeper at my face. 'The needler Rangesh gave you. Where I can see it, please.'

I took it out of my jacket, slow and careful, and tossed it to the floor.

'Carrying anything else?' She was all over my Servant, poking and prying with a Tesseract code I didn't recognise, pulling out everything.

I shook my head.

'I've got a theory for you, Rause. You want to hear it?'

'Go on.'

'After Alysha set up the extraction for Gersh, Svernoi found her and bought her. She couldn't stop the extraction team so she sent them into the storm to get rid of them. Or maybe Svernoi did the actual killings and Alysha just gave him the codes – amounts to the same if you ask me. Then she ran. Svernoi set up her escape and then used Loki to kill her. Loose end, you see.' She shrugged. 'Or maybe he just didn't want to pay. Can't imagine she came cheap.'

I lurched forward and then stopped, brought up short by the barrel of Patterson's Reeper. 'Bullshit!'

'Why, Keon? Why is it bullshit?'

298

'Why would she do something like that?'

'Why do people ever betray their friends? Money, I suppose.'

'No.' I'd have jumped out of bed and rammed the words down Patterson's throat if she hadn't been pointing a gun at me. 'She wouldn't have done that!'

'I wish I didn't think so.'

'Where's your evidence?' I wanted to spit in her face. My Alysha a traitor? I would have known. She couldn't be!

'Fuck, Rause. I don't know why she did it, but she was the only one who knew about Gersh. She was the only one who knew what the extraction team were doing up there, and she was the one who directed them into the storm. I've seen the fucking records, you know? She sent them right into it, and then the next day she ran. So don't give me shit about how wonderful she was. Six people died. Seven if you throw in Gersh.' She leaned closer. 'Is there anything you know, Rause? Anything you haven't told me?'

I went cold. 'What do you mean?'

'Keon, no games. Not now. We have a xenosubstance with a catastrophic effect on anyone with Mohinder-Kali. Fuck knows why, but it is what it is. Vismans and Svernoi are dead, the gens are out there, we don't know where and we don't know how. You think Svernoi was working on his own? Kaltech are an interstellar corporation with an internal economy several times larger than Magenta. By their own admission they're using Settlement 64 to manufacture designer hallucinogens, ostensibly for medical purposes but apparently not. They're spreading a killer, Keon. A gene-targeted biological weapon. Horace Winston—'

'It's not a weapon,' I said.

'What?'

'That's what I didn't get. Why would anyone make a gen that kills people with Mohinder-Kali? But it wasn't meant as a weapon. They were making—'

'I don't fucking care, Rause! You're missing the point.'

'Then get to it!'

'Horace Winston could have put Svernoi and Vismans together. He was murdered in his hospital bed. We got to Vismans and Svernoi anyway, and now they're dead too. You buy Zohreya's chameleon-skin drone theory?'

I shook my head.

'An invisible hit man, Keon! One who knows our every fucking move. Or should I say hit woman? Do you really think I wouldn't put two and two together after that show back there? She's alive, isn't she? Alysha. She never died at all.'

I almost forgot she had a gun on me. 'What?'

'The mystery woman. Archana. We can't find her because she doesn't exist. Alysha made a shell of herself. She put the shell on the train and then she slipped away. Alysha and Archana are the same person, and that's why we can't find her. She left Magenta with you. Now she's back. Why? Fuck knows. Loose ends, maybe? You tell me. She hit the Gibraltar Tech-Fair, and you helped her. She took the suit. She's the one who killed Horace Winston, and she's the one who killed Svernoi. Where is she, Keon?'

'Alysha is dead!' I started sobbing. I don't think Patterson expected that.

'I hope not. Because if she is, Rause, then you're the mole. You have to be. Five years ago it was Alysha, and now it's you.'

'I was right there when Zohreya was shot!' I yelled. 'You saw me! Right there!'

'Shot by someone wearing the suit from Gibraltar! You going to pretend that was a coincidence?'

'Wha—'

'Shut up, Rause! Vismans said ten thousand dead. I need to know who and what and why and how. You need to tell me about Alysha. Right now! You need to tell me everything!'

I lay back, beaten.

'Where's your money, Rause? You lived like a pauper on Earth – I checked – but Fleet pays well, so where is it if it isn't with Alysha? I can make you the same deal we were going to give Vismans. Tell me what you know about her and Svernoi and you can walk away from this. Once people start dying, that's it. You go down for ever. You understand me?'

'I don't know anything.' I could barely speak. She was so close to the truth, and I'd missed it completely until I saw Svernoi die. 'I had no idea about Svernoi, or Vismans or Anja Gersh before I came back. I didn't help anyone steal the chameleon suit, and Alysha died five years ago.'

'I always liked you, Keon. It would be such a fucking waste, you taking the fall for this. You realise, right, that I'm about the only thing between you and a one-way trip to Colony 478? So fucking well tell me the truth right now!'

'Alysha's dead,' I whispered. Liss. Liss had done this. It was the only thing that made sense; but what didn't make sense was why. Why? Why would she ...?

I jumped up, never mind the Reeper in Patterson's hand. I wanted her to go away. I wanted it all to go away. I needed to find Liss. I needed her to tell me why she'd done it.

'Keon!'

'Alysha's dead, Laura! It wasn't her. I *know* it wasn't her. She wouldn't!'

'Sometimes we don't know the people we love nearly as well as we think.' Patterson sighed. I recognised the flatness in her tone. I remembered it from when she'd been Laura Murgrah. She'd made up her mind. I was guilty. And she was right, I was.

I ducked sideways and lunged, going for the Reeper. I wasn't quick enough.

20

ALYSHA 2.0

Alysha Rause stands on the other side of the door, ear pressed to plastic. No one sees her. She is invisible.

'Sometimes we don't know the people we love nearly as well as we think.'

Alysha knows the tone too. She knows Laura Patterson, knows her speech patterns. There is a finality to them. She doesn't hear Keon's reply as she kicks in the door. It shouldn't be possible, but she does it anyway. It is the strength of love, she tells herself.

Keon screams. He lies on his bed, spasming. His face is twisted and distorted, the look of a man who's taken a stunner to the head. The sight fills her with rage.

'You could have killed him,' she says.

Laura lifts the Reeper as she turns. Her Servant cries for help but too slow. Alysha smashes the pistol out of Laura's hand. She feels finger bones crack. She shuts down Laura's Servant. Laura scrabbles away, cradling her hand, backs into a corner, white-faced with shock. She stares at where Alysha stands.

There is nothing to see, but she knows Alysha is there. Laura was always the clever one.

'Alysha!'

Alysha doesn't answer.

Patterson closes her eyes.

'I have a kid,' she says.

'I know.' Alysha tries to sound regretful. She raises the pistol she stole back in Firstfall on the night Zohreya and Rangesh unravelled Vismans' factory. She takes her time, considering all possible outcomes, searching for variables not yet accounted for in her equations of what will happen after this moment.

'Liss ...' Keon twitches on the bed, trying to speak. His bowels and bladder have emptied. A stunner to the face offers only humiliation.

'I'm sorry, Keys,' she says. 'I didn't want it to come to this. All I ever wanted was to keep you safe.'

'Don't ... hurt ...' The words are so slurred and broken they are barely intelligible. It is only because she knows him so well that she understands.

'I'm sorry I was too slow,' she says.

She lowers the pistol. Not because Keon has asked her to, but because shooting Laura doesn't change anything. Others will draw the same conclusions. The evidence is there. Laura is simply the first to see it for what it is. She must find another way. Perhaps Laura herself, in her own calculated version of the truth, has offered an answer.

Alysha lifts the cloak-suit's hood from her face and lets them see her.

'You're a shell!' Laura's eyes are wide. Fear and pain and bewilderment.

She pins Laura to the floor. Laura struggles and screams but is no match for a shell. Alysha holds her still and injects her with a sedative stolen from Mercy on the night she killed Horace

Winston. She closes the ruined door and waits for Keon's face to change, for the effect of the stunner to wear off. Eventually he manages to sit upright.

'Hey, Keys,' she says.

He looks at her with a horror that might break her heart if she had one. But she doesn't. She understands. It's natural he should respond this way. He's only human.

'She's Internal Investigations,' Alysha says. She pulls a file from Laura's Servant, the transcript of Keon's interviews after Gibraltar. She sends it to him, not sure if it matters whether he believes her or not. 'I'm going to have to leave you now,' she says. 'I'll make it look as though Patterson got it right, as though Alysha built me before she died, a shell to watch over you and keep you safe. That'll stop the questions.' Perhaps. Perhaps not. She can only do so much.

'Liss! What have you done?'

It will be better for him, she thinks, to keep it short and honest. 'I was in your Servant in Gibraltar, Keys. It was easy to slip into the shell they were using to mount the suit. I did it because I love you. Because you had to come back and face the truth that I was gone. I did it to make you come home.' He will neither understand nor accept this truth, not now, not for many years, perhaps never. It will hurt him, but it is better than not knowing. She has already seen where that leads.

'You shot me!'

'Otherwise you would have seemed guilty.' He will blame himself. Nothing she can say will change that.

'Everyone thought that anyway! And you killed Svernoi!'

'He was going to execute you. I think … perhaps … there may have been some revenge there too. It's hard, sometimes, to be sure. Who I am. What I am. He did kill me, Keys.'

'And Horace Winston? Did *he* kill you too?'

'That was the Alysha in me.' It seems strange talking about

herself this way, but she has often felt it to be so, that she is two people rolled into one, one impulsive and human and full of fire, the other a machine of rational calm. 'I did that for Zohreya,' she says. The murder of a family sounds a fierce chord in the part of her that feels human, but there is more to it than that. 'And for you. To keep you away from what killed me. To keep you safe.' And how has that worked out? Badly. The algorithms that whirr in her superconducting heart have failed her.

Keon's stare offers only hatred and betrayal. 'Alysha would never do those things! Any of them!' The pain in his face is at last what it should be. Loss. Grief for a dead lover. Far too long in coming. 'Why, Liss?' There are tears. Rage and anguish at last.

'Because I love you.'

She knows that her words are a knife, even if they are true. Keon snarls and throws himself at her, hands reaching for her throat as though he might somehow choke her. As if she was human. He is still weak and clumsy from Laura's stunner. She lets him batter her and spend his energy. While he does she palms another sedative and slips the needle into his skin.

'Goodbye, Keon.' She wonders if he will ever believe that she loved him. Will it matter? She doesn't know. 'I'm not your wife. I never was. I'm only a simulation.'

His eyes roll back. 'Liss …?' The taut cords of muscle gripping her neck soften and turn slack. The sedative has its way. She catches him as he falls.

'I will always want what's best for you,' she says. Keon will never hear these words. They are for her, for the human part that yearns not to let go and yet knows it must. 'And I do love you. But now it's time we both moved on.'

Alysha 2.0 lowers the hood across her face and vanishes once more. She takes Laura's Reeper. She disables Keon's Servant, takes him in her arms and wraps her cloak around him and vanishes them both. She carries him as she carried him in Gibraltar after she shot him in the chest and left him dazed and stunned. She finds a quiet place and stands, ever patient as the train bullets to Firstfall. While she waits, she constructs a story. Laura's story. The story of Alysha's guardian shell, Keon's watcher from the shadows, the story that will save him.

The smashed door is found. Then Patterson. There is a commotion. Alysha hides, still and unseen. It passes her by. In Firstfall she carries Keon to a place where he will be safe. She cleans him with gentle care and changes his clothes and puts him to bed. No one sees.

She writes a note, two words only, into his Servant, then leaves and walks through the Firstfall tunnels to the steps of the Tesseract. The story she has made is burned into this shell's memories as deep as it can go. Relics to be found when the forensic q-code comes. On the steps of the Tesseract she removes the cloak-suit from Gibraltar and places it carefully beside her. She hopes one last time that she has done enough to keep the man she loves safe from the secret that killed her, then lifts Laura's Reeper to her head, erases her code and pulls the trigger.

And before she does, she thinks, *This is what love is*. And it doesn't matter that no one will ever know or understand.

21

MOHINDER-KALI

I woke in a strange bed, in a cheap by-the-hour hotel. No Liss, no access to the Tesseract, no access to anything. My Servant was disconnected. I thought for a bit about turning it on and then changed my mind. The moment I did, the Tesseract would pick it up. The bureau would know where I was. I probably didn't want that.

There were two dog tags on the table by the bed. Alysha's tags. The room Servant was off. Everything was dormant. Empty. Another thing I couldn't turn on without letting the Tesseract know where I was. Cameras were everywhere. The bureau would have search worms crawling through the city surveillance net.

On the other hand, what else was I going to do?

I couldn't believe Alysha was a traitor. I never would, no matter what evidence Patterson thought she had. I thought over what it would take for me to slip away unseen, and as I did I knew that I couldn't even leave this room. No one could live for a day on Magenta without being seen, without some camera or drone spotting them, without some interaction with the system. I guess if you were desperate you could go out into the wilderness away from the cities, out to the barren wild lands that were most of Magenta. One person on their own would be too small, too dim for the satellites to see. But you'd have to walk. No taking a pod. You'd have to face Magenta's weather. And even if you could do all that, how long before you starved? There was nothing out there except rock and wind and rain and the xenoflora, implacable in its enigma.

I couldn't run. I couldn't disappear. No one could.

I turned the room Servant on and waited to see what would happen. Maybe some alert went to the Tesseract, but the doors didn't lock. I turned on my own Servant. There was the message from Liss: *Amal Patel*. A stack of urgent calls from Laura, from the Tesseract, from Flemich, but the world didn't end and there were no pings as though someone or something had been just waiting for me to appear again. I slipped out of the hotel and summoned a pod. When it came I told it to take me to Patterson's apartment. I guess I owed her that – that she could be the one to bring me in.

The sky was dark when we emerged from the tunnels of the undercity. I felt groggy, dizzy and weak from whatever Liss had stabbed into me. The feeling didn't pass. When I checked the time, I saw how late it was. I'd lost the best part of a day.

I curled up in the back of the pod and closed my eyes. I dozed or else drifted in thoughts of longing. I lost track of time. I didn't want to know what else Liss had done after she put me under.

I'd made her to preserve something beautiful. How could that be wrong?

The pod stopped outside Patterson's place. I'd never been to this part of Firstfall, a district where the wealthy lived. Zohreya had her government apartment, probably much like mine.

Probably as sterile too. Rangesh? I suppose I thought of him as living in some hole in the Squats.

I stood outside Patterson's door, put my hands over my head and pinged her.

'Rause?' I imagined her flitting among the cameras, piping them to her lenses, checking to see if it was really me and then pinging the Tesseract for backup. I didn't move.

There was a long pause before the door opened. Patterson stood on the other side, dressed in a silk robe. One hand was wrapped in bandages. The other was holding a half-empty bottle of imported whiskey.

'Didn't think I'd ever see you again.'

I shook my head. 'She was never going to hurt me.'

'Alysha's shell?' Patterson blew a puff of derision and waved vaguely with her bandaged hand. 'Yes, I think I got that. Wish I could say the same. No, I thought you were going to vanish like your wife did.' She looked me up and down. 'You look like someone died, Rause.'

I swallowed the lump in my throat. 'This is where you take me in, Laura.'

'Take you in for what?'

'You're Internal Investigations, aren't you?' I said.

She looked away and spat out a laugh. 'How long have you known?'

'Liss told me.'

'Liss?'

'Alysha's shell.'

'And how long have you known about the shell, Rause?'

I shrugged. A part of me wanted to tell her I'd never seen it before, that last night on the train had been every bit as much of a surprise to me as it had been to her; to put on an act – bewildered, confused, angry. Another part wanted to tell her the truth. I settled for saying nothing.

'The shell sent me some data after it stabbed a needle into my neck.' Patterson's lip curled. 'I've checked as much as I can. Data forensics will do better but it looks like I was right – Alysha did make a shell the day before she died – but I was wrong too. It didn't go on the train instead of her; it was supposed to be a decoy while she vanished. You were away that day, weren't you? When she left?'

I nodded. I'd gone that morning. To Disappointment.

'So now we know.' She raised an eyebrow. Again I wanted to tell her that no, it was a lie, the shell was mine, Liss was mine. *I* made her, no one else.

I didn't say a word.

'There's forensic q-code looking for traces of tampering in the log histories. I'm going to take a bet it won't find any. The fabricator records back at the factory that made it are the clincher. Don't see how they could be forged. So I suppose Alysha was the mole all along, even after she was dead. But the shell ...? You going to tell me it followed you to Earth and watched you for five whole years and you never knew? A bit fucking implausible, isn't it?'

'She took the suit in Gibraltar,' I said. 'She told me that after she put you out. She did it to force me back to Magenta.'

'Maybe it spent most of its time as data.' Patterson gave me a long hard look and then waved the bottle at me. 'Come on in.'

I followed her down some stairs into a lounge. Plush, expensive, Earth-import furniture, all of it old and stained and worn. A clutter of shelves and antique books. A marble-topped table with a few chips in it and an empty shot glass on a coaster. Scattered around were paper-print photographs. Patterson cleared them away, but not before I saw what they were: pictures of a younger her, smiling, pressed close to her ex-husband Jamal. They looked happy. Just the two of them.

Beside them, propped up in a gold frame on the corner of

the marble, was a picture of a boy dressed in iceball armour, grinning.

'Jamie?' Patterson nodded. She poured me a shot and sat down and then told me about Liss self-destructing on the steps of the Tesseract.

'Forensics are going over what's left,' she said. 'The only piece of active memory from the shell reads like a confession. Alysha took a pay-off from Svernoi and burned the extraction team. Svernoi set her up with a way out, but she didn't trust him, so she cashed in your savings and built a shell, one that looked enough like her to act as a decoy. She didn't trust him not to go after you, too, so she programmed the shell to watch your back. It was supposed to protect you, but you were never supposed to know because you'd see it straight away for what it was. It was to terminate itself if you ever found out, all except that one piece of memory. I think she meant you to find it. It's addressed to you. It says at the end, "I love you, but some things just have to be."' She shook her head. 'Don't they just. Same shit as it spouted in the train and then some. If you buy that story, that shell was probably only meant to linger for a few weeks, but then Alysha died and there was no one to switch it off. So far the q-code reconstruction reckons that whatever program she had running in there stayed to the bitter end like it was supposed to, but I don't really see why I should believe a word of it. Forensics will find out. Or maybe they won't. I don't know that I care any more, but there are always traces, Keon. Nothing's ever clean.' She poured herself another shot and knocked it back. 'You want to add anything to that?'

I shook my head.

'Didn't think so.'

'You were investigating me from the start,' I said. 'From the moment I came down.'

'You asked for me. I knew what you were going to do. So

311

I asked to reopen Alysha's case. There was always something rotten about it.'

'Flemich put you up to it?'

She laughed. 'Flemich? Fuck no. I was investigating Flemich too. He always thought Alysha was as pure as the driven snow.'

'She was,' I said without thinking.

Patterson shrugged. 'She's dead, so I guess you can think whatever you want.' She sank another shot and filled my glass again. 'But they never are. Not really.'

We stared at nothing.

'What now?' I said when my glass was empty.

'What do you mean?'

'Is there a tac-team on their way to pick me up?'

'Why would there be? Did you do something wrong?'

'Don't play with me, Laura.' I helped myself to the whiskey bottle.

'There's no tac-team, Keon.'

I waited for the catch. Patterson yawned. She took the bottle back and went and got two big glasses and split what was left between us, half and half.

'Rangesh and Zohreya are still in Disappointment. Having a grand old time, I think. They managed to back-trace Vismans' movements. He put the gens into the city's water. So that's great, except half of Disappointment has his stuff inside them now, whatever it was he and Gersh were making for Svernoi. They're trying to work out how far it's spread.' She let out a long sigh. 'Me? I got to spend the day in the Tesseract going through endless debriefs. I only got let off on account of Jamie and my hand. How about you? Have any fun?'

'What did you tell them?' I couldn't resist, even if asking made me sound somehow guilty.

Patterson rolled her eyes. 'Zohreya and Rangesh? That space imps sung me to sleep with sprinkles of fairy dust while the

312

Masters kidnapped you? What do you think? I told them the truth, of course.'

'So they know about the shell?'

'The whole of fucking Firstfall knows about the shell!' She switched on the wall-screen and flicked through the news channels: immigrant murders in Disappointment, rumblings and speculation about an object under the ice in the planet's southern hemisphere. She stopped at footage of Liss on the steps of the Tesseract, appearing out of nowhere and blowing her head off. There wasn't much to see. It was a shell. The gesture with the gun was more symbolic than practical.

It. I shuddered. *Liss* ...

I watched it again. And again. And again.

'You should probably stop that,' Laura said.

I went back to the first story. The murders in Disappointment. Four Indian immigrants over the last day. No connection between them but all messy and bloody. Two dead from massive strokes. Two as though they'd simply exploded.

Like Shyla Thiekis.

Vismans' engineered xenoflora.

I connected to the Tesseract. I expected to be immediately shut down, or to find I had no access to anything any more, but I got in without a hitch.

'Laura!' I prodded her. 'You need to look at this.'

The Tesseract had two of the deaths recorded. Two men in a club together. Loud music. Flashing lights. Then screaming. The music stops, the lights come up, blood everywhere ...

I replayed Svernoi's video. The flashing lights in the laboratory before Ali Surash exploded. Then I asked for medical records. The bureau in Disappointment had started autopsies on the bodies but genetic tests weren't standard procedure. I tried to get into their general medical records instead but there wasn't anything. No genetic screening. The immigrants coming in from

Earth had their transgravity treatment before they arrived.

Laura was inside my Servant with me now, peering over my shoulder the way Liss used to, but different. Prodding and poking, directing my questions with an unfamiliar vitality.

'Can't be more than a few dozen people across Magenta who suffer from Mohinder-Kali. We've put out a warning, as widespread as we can. The Tesseract is trying to contact people known to have the condition. Transgravity treatment means genetic testing means we largely know who has it and who doesn't. So that's something, at least. We can contain the damage ... Who's Amal Patel?'

'A last message from Alysha's shell,' I explained as I looked him up. 'Disappointment mag-lev. The beggar, remember?' I'd pushed him into the system for transgravity treatment. Gene therapy. The good stuff. He'd been through pre-screening so they'd already done the genetic tests ...

It was just a hunch, but why else Liss would have ...

Positive for Mohinder-Kali.

I tried a general search for MK syndrome then. Anywhere it came up. I got hits. Not many, but more than I should.

The scene on the wall-screen suddenly changed as Laura switched to Channel Sixteen.

'You want to watch this,' she said.

'Disappointment,' I said.

'What?'

'The whole immigration thing. It's being sponsored by the Indian government. And Kaltech are Indian, right? And Vismans wasn't talking about a few people dying, he said ten thousand! They're shipping people in from Earth, Laura, people with Mohinder-Kali, only we don't know they've got it because we don't screen them because they have their transgravity before they arrive. They've set up a pool of test subjects!'

Something Vismans had said when I'd asked him about

KRAB. *If you think you can stall the transformation by with-holding the trigger ...*

The ones who'd already died. Loud music. Flashing lights. Strobes ...

The same as Ali Surash.

'The trigger was KRAB! Svernoi's satellite hijacker. Their backup was installed on the roof of the Magenta Institute but someone moved it. Svernoi as good as told me!'

Laura and I looked at each other. I started trying to explain, but I didn't need to. She was already howling across the data-sphere at Flemich, the Tesseract, anyone she could think of. As she did, she rested a hand on my shoulder.

The screen shifted. More rumblings about the bureau raid on Pit 779. The news channels didn't know about Horace Winston's murder yet. As soon as that happened they were going to put it together with Liss on the steps of the Tesseract ...

Laura pinged Rangesh in Disappointment. Rangesh! The trigger for the gens! It's the KRAB hijacker! You need to find it!

'No.' I called a pod. 'We need Eddie Thiekis.'

'What?'

I was pinging him already, throwing all the priority weight of the Tesseract behind the call. 'Eddie Thiekis. Rangesh said he controlled the satellite networks. Mister MagentaNet. That he could shut them down.' Urgent. It's about Shyla.

Would he believe me? Maybe. Would he believe me enough to listen?

We'd have a pod in about a minute but I had no idea where it should take us. For all I knew Eddie was off-world. I pinged him again, over and over.

They were playing Vismans' recording on the news now: 'My name is Anja Gersh ...' I swore. Svernoi was crazy but he wasn't stupid. He'd have had someone ready to take over. As soon as Gersh's confession was out they wouldn't have a choice but to ...

The wall-screen changed. A searing blaze and dazzle of flashing lights and images, too violent and fast to watch. I reeled from it.

You have reached the message service for Edward Thiekis. They were doing it. They, Kaltech, some part Svernoi had subverted, whoever *they* were. The trigger!

Eddie. I threw my Tesseract codes at the answering machine, hoping to crash through, but the machine wasn't having it. Shut the networks down! All of them! Shyla was an accident, but the people who killed her are about to kill thousands more. The flashing screaming screen raged on, a thought-killer. I couldn't focus. It was all over my lenses. I couldn't turn it off. They've taken over the networks! Kill them! Shut it down! For Shyla! Shut it—

The flashes stopped. My lenses went back to normal. The screens went blank. Something I'd never seen before. Words came up.

this channel is experiencing technical difficulties. service will be restored as soon as possible.

Laura flicked through the channels. Every one of them was the same.

'He did it,' she said. She sounded surprised. 'He actually did it. Fucking hell, Keon. Fucking. Hell.'

I stared at the screen. I didn't know whether she was talking about Eddie shutting down the networks or whether she meant Svernoi activating his trigger from beyond the grave.

'Everything's down. Planet-wide.'

There was a message in my Servant. The last thing to arrive before the networks died: You have thirty minutes, Agent Rause, to come to my offices and explain.

I tried to ping Rangesh but now I couldn't get through. Dead connection. Patterson looked at me with a face I hadn't seen before, like she was struggling not to cry. 'I can't call a pod!'

'I already did. Before Eddie.'

'Shit! I'd better get dressed then.'

The pod was at the door thirty seconds later. By the time we reached Channel Nine, Eddie Thiekis was waiting for us in the lobby. It poured out of me: the whole story of Svernoi and his mad experiment.

Eddie just sat and listened until we were done. 'How long do they need to be down?' was all he asked.

'Right now?' Patterson let out a cracked laugh. 'Fuck knows. Until everyone affected is clean. Weeks, probably.' Other people would answer that, once they knew. Come morning all of this would be out of our hands.

Eddie Thiekis nodded. I could see what he was thinking. It wouldn't bring his daughter back, but it was as big a fuck you as he could manage to the people who'd killed her. I knew exactly how that felt.

We took the pod back to Laura's apartment. I couldn't face going home. Couldn't face being on my own. Not without Liss.

'Spare a bit of floor?' I asked.

Laura snorted. 'Shit!' She shook herself. 'I'm still a bit drunk. Are you the mole, Keon?'

I shook my head. 'Amal Patel. Liss – the shell – was telling us where to look.'

'She might have been a bit more fucking clear about it.'

It was a fair point. But Alysha had always liked her cryptic clues.

'You can have the sofa if you like.'

We stumbled into Laura's lounge and stared in silence at the screen, waiting for something to happen. After a while, when nothing did, Laura picked up her pile of photographs. She

317

turned them face up and spread them across the table. 'You have any pictures of Alysha?'

I shook my head.

'I do.' She left and came back a minute later with a printed photograph of me and Alysha together, smiling into the camera and looking impossibly young.

'Where'd you get this?' I tried to work out where and when it had come from.

'Third year of the academy, when Alysha and I were friends. I took it then. You don't remember?'

'No.'

'She knew about us. I told her because I always got this sense of guilt from you when I was around, like we'd gone behind her back even though you two weren't together when you and I ... Well, you know. I took the picture because I wanted to see if I could pin it down.'

'And?'

'It worked.' She put the photograph of me and Alysha on the table among the pictures of her and Jamal. 'I pinned it down. The guilt was me, not you.'

'Gibraltar,' I said. 'It wasn't about Svernoi or Kaltech or any of that. She just wanted me to come home. That was all.'

'You said. Told you that, did it?'

I nodded.

'Tell you anything else?'

'Nothing that makes a difference.'

Laura knocked back another glass. 'I don't know what to think. I don't want to believe it, but she still looks guilty to me. Tell me something about her, Keon. Something wonderful.'

We swapped stories of Alysha and Jamal. The good stories that made us smile and miss them. Laura got out another bottle and we talked on, huddled together, sometimes laughing, sometimes with tears. She rested her head on my shoulder.

'I should never have tried to bring her back,' I said. The words slipped out on fumes of whiskey. I shivered.

'I should have let Jamie go.' Laura got up. 'But don't you dare ever tell him I said that. I love him more than life itself, despite everything, even if he's an absolute shit sometimes.' She walked out, lurching a little. When she came back she was carrying a glass bowl. She gathered the photographs, put them inside the bowl and then set them on fire. She settled on the sofa beside me to watch them burn and chinked her glass to mine.

'To ghosts,' she slurred, and shifted closer and pulled at me until I lay with my head on her lap.

'To moving on.'

'I'm sorry for you, Keon. I truly am. The ones we love are always the ones who fuck us.' She stroked my hair for a few minutes and then I felt the strength fall from her fingers, the strokes turn erratic and then stop. 'Really so very sorry ...'

She slumped. Her hand fell still.

'Did Alysha really make that shell?' she murmured. 'Or was it you?'

I pretended to be asleep.

'I'd understand if it was you. I think I'd give anything to go back. To find the moment when everything was just perfect and freeze it that way for ever.'

I drifted away and dreamed of the memories we'd burned, of Alysha, the real Alysha, smiling a sad smile and a wave of goodbye.

SEVEN

EPILOGUE

22

XENOSUBSTANCE 1227

'You mean you just, like, ran out of the house?' Rangesh was in full flow, arms waving, eyes wide, strapped into his seat in the Cheetah. We were on our way to Settlement 64 again. 'You didn't say, like, "Mummy might be late home today because she totally has to save the world again and stuff"? Dude! What were you thinking? That was so an opportunity you will not get again!'

At 10.56 yesterday evening something had launched a sweeping attack on the Magenta satellite network, overriding the signal of every public broadcast with one of its own. In the handful of minutes before Eddie shut the networks down, fourteen people had died, all in Disappointment, all new Earth immigrants, all with Mohinder-Kali. Fourteen too many but at least it wasn't ten thousand. The MSDF were still trying to pinpoint the source of the hijack; the working theory was that Svernoi had moved it back to Settlement 64, so that was where we were going.

'It was mostly Rause.' Laura actually smiled.

'Still, we could totally, like, head back and land outside your front door and—'

'He's in school.'

'Then we go there! Think about it, Laws, how totally awesome that would be. You'd be, like, the coolest mum, ever!'

'He wouldn't believe me, Rangesh.'

Rangesh beamed. 'I'll tell him then. "Hey there, Jamie, it's your uncle Rangesh here. Going to have to make your own way home after school today because your totally awesome mum has to save the world from bad guys and, like, thousands of people from death and stuff, just like she did yesterday."'

Laura shook her head. 'It's not funny, Rangesh.'

'Too late, man. I already hit send.' He grinned at Zohreya. 'Hey! Esh! Shouldn't we intern you or something. I mean, because aren't we, like, at war with Earth or something now?'

Zohreya flipped him a finger.

I closed my eyes and let the banter wash between them. We were going back to work.

We found the hijacker and shut it down. Took a few more days to screen everyone in Disappointment for Mohinder-Kali. The ones who tested positive were told to stay at home and avoid loud noises and flashing lights for a couple of weeks until the gens flushed through their system. Dull, but better than having your head explode. Within a week we had the networks back up and running. Magenta breathed a collective sigh and went on about its business, vigorously trying to make like none of this had ever happened. Just a crazy man with a crazy idea, working on his own, and the gens that Anja Gersh had built were merely a terrible mistake that made you bleed and die in a perfectly ordinary if tragic way, and the video Svernoi had given to me and to Laura was of a man with a bomb hidden inside him.

I knew better of course, but I wasn't going to say. For now

the lid was back on Pandora's box. I doubted it would stay there for long. These things never did.

I quietly opened a new case. I called it *Archana* and wrote a few words: 'What if Alysha really did make a shell?'

But she hadn't. That was just something Liss had made up to explain her existence for Laura and the Tesseract. Alysha was dead. It was time to let her go. I scrubbed out the words and wrote some new ones: 'What if Alysha was innocent?'

For now I left it at that.

A few weeks later I went to the memorial to the May Day dead. Laura came with me. It wasn't much more than four names scratched into a piece of stone. There was no one else there. Probably no one had come to visit it for years. I left Alysha's dog tags beside it.

'You sure you don't want to keep them?' asked Laura.

'I'm not really a memento sort of person these days.'

'Remember her as you want her to be, Rause.' She touched a hand to my shoulder. 'Never mind the rest. Just the good bits.'

'Easier said than done.'

Laura made a face. 'I know.'

Odd how Liss had been right in the end. Kaltech and Nikita Svernoi had guided the hand of the Loki bomber, but I was never going to know the whole truth, whether Alysha had been a traitor or whether she'd been running from one. And maybe that was for the best. I knew what she'd found in Settlement 64, and how what she'd discovered there had put her on that train. I painted my own picture of the rest and filled in the blanks with whatever colour I liked best, and that was how I was going to keep her.

'You want a beer later?' I asked.

Laura shook her head. 'Jamie's got iceball.'

'Is there a night when he hasn't?'

She looked at me sourly. 'You want to come and watch, you're more than welcome.'

'Sounds like it might be fun.'

'Then I haven't said it right.'

'Do they have beer?'

'No.'

'Can I bring one?'

She laughed and wrapped an arm around my shoulder. 'Bring two and I might get to like you, Rause.'

The ghost of Liss echoes through Firstfall's bitsphere. She pauses at a place that makes shells, a brisk business on a world like Magenta. The place is Archana Robotics. The records show that five years ago Archana Robotics made a shell for Alysha Rause. The name was a clue left for Keon; the records he now believes are forged are a truth that has awaited for him all this time, but no one ever told him, and five years is too long. Alysha isn't coming back.

She will watch over him. The part of her that is Alysha still loves him. But it's probably best he doesn't know that Laura got it right, that Alysha really did build a shell and gave it her dog tags and her Servant and vanished under a veil. She'd known the fate awaiting her and sidestepped it. She was never on that train at all.

Keon has enough now to let her go. But Liss still wonders who she is.

Alysha Rause, this woman in whose image she has been made.

ACKNOWLEDGEMENTS

A long time ago in a flat far, far away, eight men and women got together to play a game. In matters of plot and character, maybe no more than a few names and and character traits remain, but the world we built together – Magenta – has largely survived. So thank you to Sam and Alex and Pete and Nigel and Ali and John and Tony for giving me a world that was basically purple and where everyone is miserable because of the high gravity and the shitty weather. Thank you (Alex, I think, but it was a long time ago and I could be wrong) for the "areas of snail devastation" that appear in Magenta's entry in the Colonial Encyclopedia. Thank you Nigel for the special sauce and attempting law-enforcement while wearing a kaftan. I don't remember which one of you invented the Wavedome, but I do remember that the world had to be pretty much on the point of utter destruction before you'd all actually get out of there. Thank you Sam and Ali (and Emily) for feeding us endless pizza. Spinach and egg? Who knew?

Thanks to my agent Robert Dinsdale, my editor Marcus Gipps and the rest of the editorial team at Gollancz who have the patience to tease out the best from the story they were offered. I should probably thank Marcus for not letting me name any characters after 80s arcade games, no matter how much we all liked Ready Player One. Thanks to Richard Morgan for the excellent Altered Carbon, which I read after I'd written the first draft of this and which raised the bar I was trying to reach. I still haven't reached it. Thanks to Craig and Hugh and Sophie and Stevie and all the other people whose names I don't yet know as I write this but without whom this wouldn't exist.